COVER SHOT

A NICHELLE CLARKE CRIME THRILLER

LYNDEE WALKER

SEVERN RIVER PUBLISHING

Severn River Publishing
www.SevernRiverBooks.com

This is a work of fiction. Names, characters, businesses, places, events and incidents are either the products of the author's imagination or used in a fictitious manner. Any resemblance to actual persons, living or dead, or actual events is purely coincidental.

ISBN: 978-1-64875-515-6 (Paperback)

ALSO BY LYNDEE WALKER

The Nichelle Clarke Series

Front Page Fatality

Buried Leads

Small Town Spin

Devil in the Deadline

Cover Shot

Lethal Lifestyles

Deadly Politics

Hidden Victims

Dangerous Intent

The Faith McClellan Series

Fear No Truth

Leave No Stone

No Sin Unpunished

Nowhere to Hide

No Love Lost

Tell No Lies

To find out more about LynDee Walker and her books, visit

severnriverbooks.com/authors/lyndee-walker

For Gabriel, who can always make me laugh. Never stop smiling. I love you.

1

Number one rule of local news: if it bleeds, it leads.

Rule number two? Timing is everything. When nothing is bleeding, reporters pay attention to things they might ordinarily ignore.

Like, for instance, the Twitter message flashing in the corner of my screen late on a quiet October afternoon.

TIME GROWS SHORT. THEY WILL PAY.

I slumped back in the chair in my little ivory cubicle at the *Richmond Telegraph*, my eyes scanning the words again.

Sure, every crime reporter in America has picked up a few nutjobs—the internet just makes it easier for them to find us. My habit of sticking my nose into some of my more tangled stories makes me a bit of a troll magnet, too. But three messages in two weeks, all in the same harsh all-caps characters, all just ominous enough to be interesting—my eyebrows jumped to my hairline as I scrolled back to reread the first two.

Thirteen days before, at three-forty-seven in the afternoon: SECRETS=DEATH. THEY WILL TALK.

Five days later, at four-nineteen: LOVE>MONEY. THEY WILL HELP.

They who? Pay for what? Help with what? Asking questions is my job, which works out nicely for my borderline-nosy nature. My fingers inched toward the keyboard, and I jerked them away.

Journalism in the age of the Internet 101: never engage with a creeper. Whoever LCX12 was, he had the upper hand, because he knew exactly who I was. And where I worked.

Two good reasons to stuff my fingers in my pockets and go back to blowing off the messages.

But the lack of anything better to do combined with a surge of what-if-itis (What if someone gets hurt? What if I can help?) kept my attention on the screen.

I clicked to the profile.

No name, no tweets to show, no followers or following.

Strike one.

I studied the handle: LCX12.

Initials? Couldn't be but so many last names beginning with X. I clicked over to the DMV site (my paid subscription to their records service often comes in handy), and logged in. Search parameter: twenty miles around Richmond, last name, first letter. Find.

Thirty-nine matches. More than I hoped for, especially since I had no clue if this goose trail went anywhere.

Surely no one would be so stupid as to send stuff like that from an account with their initials on it. Then again, criminals usually aren't the smartest people drawing breath.

I copied the names into a file and checked birthdates: nine in December and three on the twelfth of another month.

I made another list for those, clicking back to the messages.

A few minutes of staring at them later, I reached for the phone, my fingers clumsy as I tried to dial a once-familiar number.

Kyle Miller.

A ring trilled in my ear. Deep breath. My long-ago ex had grown up to be a Bureau of Alcohol, Tobacco, Firearms, and Explosives SuperCop. The kind who'd saved my life more than once. And he no longer wanted to be my ex. Which would be great, absent one super-sexy boyfriend-type guy.

Kyle had kept his distance for weeks—nursing some emotional wounds after his physical ones healed, I figured—but he'd help. I hoped.

Fifth ring.

Voicemail.

Dammit.

"Kyle, it's Nichelle." I forced brightness into my voice. "I have a...situation here I could use your help with. Can you give me a call back when you have a second?" I tapped my pen on the desk. "Business. That's all. This is weird."

I hung up, unsure what was stranger—the vaguely threatening DMs or me being nervous about talking to Kyle. Kyle, who'd taught me to drive a stick, taken me to prom, and taken my virginity two months later.

Lacking help from my favorite ATF agent, I dialed my favorite police detective.

"I thought you'd forgotten about me," Aaron White said when he picked up his cell.

"Slow news week." I leaned back in my chair. "A nice seat in a courtroom, going home at dark—it's been lovely. What've you been doing with yourself?"

"Working. I'm still buried in cases you're not writing about anymore, when I'm not fielding reporters' phone calls. The joy of budget cuts."

"Preaching to the choir, detective," I said. Days at the courthouse covering trials are easier than ones spent poring over fresh crime scenes, but work is work. "I have something that might be interesting enough to talk about here, though. Wondering if I can pick your brain when you have a few minutes."

"I'm tired of looking at this file." Aaron's voice held thinly disguised curiosity. "Want to grab a drink?"

"Perfect. Meet you at Capital Ale in twenty?"

My scanner bleeped just as an ear-splitting pop of static issued from something in Aaron's office. I set the phone down and turned the scanner up.

"Remains discovered." Shit.

I picked up the phone.

"Rain check?"

"Slow news week. You jinxed us," Aaron growled. "That's a condo complex on the river. See you there."

"Sorry. I'll buy you a beer after."

"Two."

"Deal."

I clicked off the call and slung my bag over my shoulder, the messages taking a backseat to the first possibly newsworthy corpse we'd had in almost two weeks.

So much for quiet.

2

Every car in the parking lot without a Richmond Police Department insignia sported a European one, the October splendor of the James River's tree line stretching beneath the high-rise's walls of windows.

Views (and cars) like that come with hefty price tags.

I pulled out my cell phone and texted my editor: *Save me a few inches. Got a corpse in the condos at Rockett's Landing.* Dead rich people get news space even when nothing sinister is afoot.

Almost instant reply: *Will do, but I can't hold the front. It's expensive. Tick tock, kid.*

I checked the clock. Forty-five minutes until they'd shoot page one.

Plenty of time. I hoped. I kicked open the door of my little red SUV and put one scarlet Louboutin on the concrete, nodding to Dan Kessler from WRVA. He didn't respond, but since he didn't have eyes for much of anything but his makeup mirror, I wasn't offended.

I strolled toward the uniformed sentry at the head of the round driveway.

"No ma'am, I cannot tell you when we'll have our mess picked up," the officer, who couldn't have been more than a week out of the academy with his fresh face and starched shirt, explained to a tall, thin woman with gorgeous blonde hair that could've been dyed to match the dog tucked under her left arm.

"I have guests coming at seven." She waved a hand toward the coroner's van. "This will make them uncomfortable, to say the least."

I hung two steps behind her and clicked out a pen. The sunlight glinted off her Chanel sunglasses, making me reach for my Kate Spade ones.

The cop shot me a pleading look over her shoulder and I shrugged. Then his eyes skipped over the press credentials hanging from my neck and rolled skyward. I could almost hear the "frying pan, fire" in his head.

Turns out, a pissed-off socialite is even less appealing to your average cop than a reporter. After twelve more seconds of grilling from her, he straightened his shoulders and cleared his throat, trying for an air of authority his round, friendly face wasn't suited to.

"We can't rush a murder investigation for a dinner party," he said. "We apologize for any inconvenience our presence may cause. You may go up to your apartment anytime."

Murder investigation? Hot damn. I clicked out my pen and pretended to doodle.

Ms. Social Network opened her mouth to reply and he stepped past her, giving me a guarded look and a grudging "Can I help you?"

"Nichelle Clarke, *Richmond Telegraph*." I stuck my hand out and opened my mouth to ask if Aaron had arrived yet when Ms. Social Network stepped in front of me, her eyes still on the cop.

"I understand wanting to be thorough, but surely you can keep this out of the newspaper."

I raised an eyebrow. "Last time I checked, what goes in the paper and what doesn't is my boss's decision."

The cop smiled, his wall dropping a bit. Good. I nodded and noticed the dog, who was wriggling like mad.

"Be still, Percival," she snapped, cinching her arm tighter. He yelped, and I shook my head.

"I think he needs to—" I began.

Too late.

She screamed as pale yellow liquid spread from her cashmere-covered ribcage to the pocket of her cream linen trousers. Her arm flailed and the dog whined as he tumbled toward the concrete. I dropped my pen and dove, my arms sliding between little Percy and a nasty impact.

He licked my hand and I scratched his ears as I stood and set him on the grass.

"He must be ninety percent fur," I said, brushing dust off the knees of my navy pants and watching him hike his leg on a marble planter full of mums. "He weighs nothing at all."

His owner was too busy bemoaning the state of her outfit and cursing the dog to notice, so I turned back to the cop, noting the silver nameplate that identified him as Officer Palmer. "Anyway."

"No press allowed in the building," he said with an apologetic smile. Better than surly. Maybe he was a dog person, too.

"I was actually on the phone with Aaron White when the dispatch went out," I said, holding up my cell phone. "I was hoping to get a statement before our Metro deadline."

"If you know Detective White, you know how much trouble I could get into for giving you an unauthorized comment," Palmer said. "He'll be down shortly to brief you."

I stepped back and nearly tripped over Ms. Social Network, who was busy swatting Percival with the *Vogue* Fall fashion issue.

"That's three times as big as he is," I said. "How would you like it if someone smacked you with a BMW?"

"I beg your pardon." Her mouth fell open, revealing a collection of perfectly-bonded teeth. "How I care for my dog is none of your business." She bent toward him again, magazine raised.

I pulled out my cell phone and cued up the camera. "Maybe not. But something tells me the folks who write our society column will recognize you. There are a few people on the SPCA charity board who make frequent appearances on those pages. People you might not like to have annoyed with you." I smiled.

Her hand drifted back to her side. "He. Ruined. My. Outfit." The bonded teeth stayed clenched.

"I hardly think it was his fault. My Pomeranian doesn't have fantastic bladder control even when I'm not pressing her midsection into a Louis Vuitton clutch."

"No comment." She sneered and flounced toward the door. I snapped a photo when she stopped to growl at the doorman.

"What're we shooting? Anything interesting?" A familiar purr came from behind me.

"Hey Charlie." I spun and flashed a smile. "Nothing you want to know about."

"My mission in life is to know everything you know, isn't it?" Charlie was the on-air investigative and crime reporter at Channel Four, and my biggest competition in Richmond. Ruthless, but sharp—if we weren't both so competitive, she'd have made a good friend.

I laughed. "I don't know much except there's a woman on her way upstairs who's pretty ticked about this murder interfering with her evening."

Charlie pulled out a notebook and waved to her cameraman. "White gave a statement already?"

"Haven't seen him," I said.

"What makes you so quick to cry murder, then? Bored?"

"Call it a hunch." And the uniform playing sentry was green and let it slip, but Charlie didn't need to know that.

"I can't put your hunch on the air."

I shrugged. "Suit yourself. You said you wanted to know what I know. There's what I know."

She rolled her eyes. "I'm sure your readers will be very interested in your intuition. I'll wait for the real story. Who could get murdered in this building?"

"You know as well as I do how these things go. My money's on a jealous spouse. Or a fed-up paramour."

She turned for the door, but was promptly stonewalled by Officer P.

I watched her bat her three-foot eyelashes at him for a full minute before he smiled and pointed to the lawn. Stifling a laugh, I turned my attention to the doorman. Could I catch his eye without Officer Palmer seeing me?

I stowed my notebook and press credentials in my bag and scanned the parking lot. Two radio reporters and the Channel Ten truck had just pulled in. Palmer was busy sweating the idea of fending off three reporters at once, but I had faith. If Charlie and I couldn't get past him, he made a good gate-keeper. I'd drop that to Aaron later and get him an attaboy. He hadn't let me in, but he wasn't a jerk about it.

I waited for my colleagues to pounce before I strolled an arc around the taped-off walkway, looking for Charlie. She was back in her van, staring at her iPhone.

The doorman wore a sapphire and silver uniform, his legs shoulder width apart, hands clasped behind his back, and eyes scanning the parking lot on repeat. When they landed on me for the second time I offered a purposely shy half-smile. He nodded, but didn't move other-wise. Damn. I stared at the yellow tape flapping gently in the October breeze. It's not illegal to go under it, but the doorman might not know that.

I waited for him to look my way again and waved. He tipped his head to one side, his flat-topped hat sliding two centimeters as his eyes ran from my hair to my scarlet slingbacks and back to my face. He shot a glance at Officer P (still fighting off the media) and stepped away from the door.

"Are you visiting someone?" he asked, his voice deep and smooth as dark chocolate.

Sort of. I smiled. "There are police cars in the parking lot. Everything okay?"

He shook his head. "Since cops crawling all over the place is a pretty clear sign, I'll say no, it's not. You didn't answer my question."

"What question?"

"Visiting?"

Oh, right. "Percival," I said.

One eyebrow went up.

"He's a dog." And the only creature in the building I could name. "Little gold long-haired Chihuahua?"

"Is that what she named him? Cute little fella. Wish I had his touch with the ladies."

"Something tells me you do just fine." I cast a glance at my shoes. I hate playing games to get information, but it's occasionally a necessary evil.

Especially when it works.

He grinned. "Can't complain." His posture relaxed, and he leaned a shoulder against the wall. "You can understand, I'm sure." His eyes lingered on my left hand and its bare ring finger.

"I work too much to have time for anything else."

"You some kind of dog whisperer?"

My temperamental toy Pomeranian flashed through my thoughts, and I nodded. "You could say that."

"Poor dog. I can't decide if I feel worse for him when she leaves him up there alone to whine at the door or when she dresses him up and carries him around like a trophy."

"How long has she had him?" I asked.

"Three months, give or take."

Ten more questions, and I knew all about Percival and his owner (Clarice. And the cute, cut doorman was Jeff. Aries, thirty-one, and single. He told me the last thing four times.)

By then, Officer Palmer had dispatched the rest of the local press corps to the lawn. I rested one finger on Jeff's arm. "I'm late for my appointment." True. Technically. I was a week late for a dental appointment I kept forgetting to call and reschedule.

"They said residents only." He waved one arm toward Palmer, a heavy steel watch with intricate swords flanking the face rattling on his wrist.

"He's not looking." Yet. Batting lashes. Good Lord.

I followed Jeff's glance at Palmer, who was eyeing the knot of reporters and talking into his radio. To Aaron, no doubt.

"What harm could I possibly do?" I asked. (Answer: none. I don't snoop in crime scenes to cause trouble. I do it to get leads, and I've done it enough to know how to be careful.)

"Come on." He lifted the tape and smiled, hustling to open the door for me.

I ducked inside and half-ran for the elevator before he could get the last of "Do you want to get coffee sometime?" out of his mouth. The last thing I needed was a new guy in my life. And he could probably do with less workaholic and neurotic than I had to offer.

The elevator binged and the doors whispered open to reveal Aaron—standing beside Chris Landers from the homicide division.

"Nichelle," Aaron drawled, the clear lack of surprise in his voice making me smile with self-satisfaction.

"Detectives."

"Residents. Only. How hard is that?" Landers barked. "Damn rookie."

"To be fair..." I began, and he raised a palm.

"Save it. I know exactly how persuasive you can be when you put your mind to something. I also know I gave a direct order and it wasn't followed."

I raised an eyebrow. "You done? Because before you go jumping poor Officer Palmer, you should consider that the doorman let me in. And that this building has more entrances than the one Palmer is guarding. Charlie will figure that out before long."

"There's an officer on every door, and the damned doorman—" He bit off the last word and shook his head. "So hard to find competent help these days."

My eyes skipped back and forth between the two of them, but all I got were tight smiles. Which could mean ten thousand things, since there was a corpse upstairs.

"You headed out to brief the press?" I asked, pulling my notebook and pen out.

"Briefly." Aaron winked.

"Ha ha. What's going on? Landers looks harried, so this isn't rich Uncle William who died in his sleep."

"No one ever said you were slow," Aaron said.

"Name?" I poised my pen.

"Not available pending notification of next of kin," Aaron said.

"Fine. Can I have the basics?"

"Caucasian male, sixty-four, open homicide investigation," Landers said.

"Cause of death?"

"Don't know."

"Signs of trauma?"

"Yes." Aaron smiled when I looked up.

"Care to elaborate?" I asked.

"Sorry," he said.

Hmmm. It wasn't like I'd asked to sit in on the autopsy. I glanced at

Landers, who was scowling at the world in general and me in particular, and wondered if he was the reason for Aaron's attack of tight lips.

"Okay. For now," I said.

"Anything else?" Aaron asked.

Sixty-something white guy with money who didn't die of a heart attack. "Was he married?" Because the wife could be a good source.

"No." Aaron's half-smile said he knew what I was thinking. "He lived alone."

Damn.

I jotted that down and let them turn me back toward the door. The elegant clock set into the marble wall by the elevator said it was coming up on six-thirty. If I could get an email off to Bob, we'd have the story on the web well before the eleven o'clock news.

Jeff furrowed his brow as Landers shot him a go-to-hell look when they walked me back outside, and I smiled and shrugged. He shook his head and resumed his post.

"I'm going to write this up," I told Aaron. "Holler when you're ready to go?"

He nodded. Landers stared at his phone.

I thanked them and strode to the parking lot before Charlie could see me talking to Aaron.

Sliding into my car, I opened an email to Bob on my cell phone.

Richmond Police suspect foul play in the death of a man discovered Tuesday in a condominium overlooking the James River. The victim, 64, was Caucasian and lived alone, Department Spokesman Aaron White said.

Detectives declined to comment on cause of death, and are awaiting notification of family before releasing a name, but said a homicide investigation has been opened.

I added the remaining few details I had, threw in a description of the building, and emailed it to Bob. Clicking to my messages, I texted him: *Check your email, they think he was murdered.*

He replied with confirmation twenty-one seconds later. Even threw in a "thank you" and a smiley face.

"The end is nigh," I muttered, looking at the little yellow emoji with my gruff-but-lovable editor's name at the top of the screen.

"Seems like some crackpot is always saying that," Aaron said, leaning on the closed door of my car. "What's doing us in this time? Plague? Zombies? Nuclear fallout?"

"Emojis. Bob's use of them throws the universe off-kilter. It's going to rip up the whole space-time continuum."

"That's actually the most plausible end times theory I've heard in a while." Aaron laughed. "Bob Jeffers did not put a smiley in a text message."

I flipped my screen around. "He's arrived in the twenty-first century."

"Lord save us." Aaron shook his head.

"You wrapping up?"

He nodded. "Your story done?"

"For now. Unless you have new information to share."

"Not just yet. Give me some time."

"Why?" I paused, possibilities ticking through my head. "Who was this guy?"

His microscopic flinch told me I was on the right trail. "It's complicated."

Cop-speak for, *The victim wasn't your ordinary sixty-something white guy.*

I studied Aaron's friendly face. He was the king of getting information without giving up much—except with me and Charlie. But he wasn't budging on this. Today, anyway. And I'd already turned in my story, so it wasn't worth pushing when I needed his help with something else.

"Keep your secrets," I said, gesturing to the passenger seat. "I have other sources I can pester."

He walked around the car and opened the door. "I'm aware. And I feel a little bad for unleashing you on them."

"They don't deserve your pity, Detective."

He buckled his seatbelt and closed the door. "So what's this you need to pick my brain about?"

"Messages. I've gotten a few odd ones from the same account the past few weeks."

"What kind of account?"

"Twitter." I turned off Main toward Shockoe Slip and cut my eyes to him. "Why?"

"I can't get a warrant for social media unless the person is making actual threats," he said. "There's no harassment statute."

"Law hasn't caught up with technology?"

"It's a little more basic than that, even," he said. "When someone calls or texts or pages you and you don't want them to, they're using a service you're paying for to contact you. So it's essentially theft of service. Which means that even if what they're saying isn't threatening, there's a legal basis for making them stop it. But you don't pay for your social media accounts."

"I pay for the services I use to access them, though."

"Which is the sticking point for the House of Delegates every time this comes up. But so far, they haven't managed to convince enough people that it would stand up in federal court to get the law passed."

Huh. "I don't think this person is out to get me. But I'm beginning to think they might be more than just talk. Wondering if you'll see something I haven't."

"Happy to give it a look."

I parked the car and climbed out, chatting about the brilliant foliage and the mild October breeze as we walked the two blocks to the restaurant.

Settled in a booth across from the bar with a glass of Moscato to Aaron's Sam Adams Octoberfest a few minutes later, I dug out my phone. "Is there a way to find out who owns this Twitter account? The profile is blank, but if there's some magical police thing you can do, maybe you could send a car by to check on them?"

"You can register for an account with any name you like, so the profile might not help us if it was even filled out," he said. "They might have opened it just to get in touch with you. I can trace an IP address, but that'll take a couple of days."

"I'll send you a link." I pulled the messages up on my screen and handed him my phone.

His baby blues scanned the screen at least four times before he spoke.

"I feel reasonably safe that this person isn't threatening you. But these sure border on threatening someone."

"I know. But who? Why? When? There are so many variables. I started a list of possibilities. I'm kind of hoping the handle is initials."

He snorted. "Surely not. But if you'll email me the list I'll run them."

I smiled at the waitress as she set platters of cheese fries and soft pretzels in the center of the table. "Thanks, Aaron."

"No promises, but maybe we'll get lucky. Someone PMing a reporter isn't trying to keep but so much of a secret."

"I'd just like to stay ahead of him if I can. Figure out what he's up to before someone gets hurt."

"Yes, please. I've enjoyed the quiet lately." The looked that flitted across his face told me his quiet was over the second he stepped into that condo.

I changed the subject to personal stuff as he finished his first beer and let him get a third of the way into his second before I asked about the victim again.

"Did the coroner give you a window on time of death?" I toyed with the straw in my ice water.

"Nichelle." Aaron's tone held a warning edge. "I swear I'll give you what I can when I can, but lay off."

"Lay off what?" I feigned innocence.

He plunked his mug down on the table. "You know what. Even if they had offered a guess—which they have not—I couldn't give it to you. Not today."

Why the hell not? I bit my tongue to keep the words from tumbling out, shaking my head. "You know you're just making me more curious."

"I'm aware of the dangers of that. Frankly, I'm hoping your internet friend will keep you busy for a few days."

"Possibly."

"I'll remember to thank him if we have to arrest him."

I handed the server my MasterCard, then took Aaron back to the highrise to get his car. Watching his broad shoulders disappear across the parking lot, my brain flipped into hyperdrive. No time of death. No cause of death. No name.

Whatever was going on up there, it wasn't your run-of-the-mill murder.

I stepped out of the car and surveyed the building in the deepening twilight. The front right corner of the next-to-top floor blazed with ten times more light than any other unit, beams streaming out the windows like used car lot beacons.

A glance at the door told me Jeff had been replaced by an older man with stooped shoulders and a rumpled uniform. Flirting likely wouldn't get me anywhere. I climbed back behind the wheel and jotted down the floor and location of the investigation scene.

First up: find the condo's owner. All I needed was a place to begin.

3

My headlights bounced off a silver Lincoln logo when I turned into my driveway, and my heart flipped clean over before it began hammering.

I dabbed on some lip gloss and ran a hand through my hair before I hustled to the door, pushing it open to find the sexiest man I'd ever personally touched sitting at my little bistro table. One candle, two glasses of wine, and a vase holding a long-stemmed rose dotted the tabletop.

My face split into a grin. "I could get used to coming home to this on random Tuesday nights."

Joey stood and pulled me into his arms. "And I could get used to doing this whenever I feel like it." His dark eyes glittered in the candlelight as he lowered his lips to mine.

Butter-soft cotton slid under my fingertips as I ran my hands up his chest and over his broad shoulders, muscle hard under the fabric. His lips were gentle over mine, moving slowly as one hand crept up to cup the side of my face. He pulled back a millimeter, his fingertips skating sparks across my cheekbone. "How was your day? You said it's been slow, so I thought it was a good time for a surprise."

I stretched up on tiptoe and kissed him again, flicking the tip of my tongue at the crease of his lips and smiling when his arm tightened around my waist. "Anytime is a good time for this sort of surprise," I breathed when I pulled away.

"Noted." He flashed a smile and turned, handing me a glass of wine. "I'm still learning the rules. I haven't done anything like this in a pretty long time."

"That's nice to know." I moved to take the chair across from his, but he sat down and pulled me into his lap before I got it away from the table.

"What's nice to know?"

"That you're not..." I sipped my wine, fumbling for words that wouldn't sound insulting.

"Not some sort of man-whore?" He chuckled and I felt my cheeks heat.

"I didn't mean it that way!"

"You did a little bit."

I sipped more wine and studied him over the rim of my glass. Thick, jet black hair, olive skin, a strong jaw and straight nose—he was a beautiful man. No way there was a shortage of women throwing themselves at his... pick an appendage. He was sweet, sexy, and still more than a little mysterious—hence my uncertainty. We'd been seeing each other pretty often (and sharing a bed on a regular basis) for months. But I knew next to nothing about his life. And for all that my livelihood was questions, I was terrified to ask him the simplest ones.

He bounced a knee under me. "You okay?"

"Just thinking."

"Care to share?"

I put my empty glass on the table, feeling a bit tipsy with that on top of the Moscato I'd had with Aaron. Turns out, they call it liquid courage for a reason. "What are we doing?"

"Having a perfectly wonderful Tuesday night," he murmured, nuzzling my neck.

I sighed and tipped my head back as his lips explored my collarbone. "Is that all?"

He paused at the hollow of my throat and raised his head. "That's not enough?"

I sat up straight and pushed his shoulders gently. "Not what I meant. I'm just wondering how this is supposed to go. I mean, what are we? Can you call someone a boyfriend when you're almost thirty? And does that apply? Are we not seeing other people? Can this ever go anywhere, really?"

The questions tripped out of my mouth so fast he furrowed his brow trying to keep up.

"Sorry," I said, grabbing the wineglasses and moving toward the fridge. "Maybe we should have another drink."

"No apology necessary." He leaned back in the chair and loosened his tie. "I knew this was coming. I thought about broaching it last weekend, but my nerves got the better of me."

My hand froze in mid-pour. "What do you have to be nervous about?"

"Are you seeing him? Miller?" His voice was so soft, I would've missed that if there'd been a car speeding down the next block over.

"He won't even return my calls when I have a stalker." I laughed. "So I'm going with no."

"You have a what?" Joey's expression flipped from tentative to annoyed in the space of a blink.

I waved a hand. "That's a dramatization. Somebody who wants an audience for their crazy, probably, but my lack of anything better to poke around in got me curious. I tried to call Kyle to ask his opinion. He didn't answer, or call back." I heard a tinge of sorrow in the last words. Part of me would always love Kyle. But he wanted me to be in love with him, and I just wasn't. Not now. Didn't mean I wouldn't miss having him around.

Joey sat back in his chair. "What brand of crazy are they selling?"

"Not sure. Someone has to pay for something, they say. Aaron's working on it." I pulled the other chair out and sat, crossing my legs at the knee and putting the glasses on the table.

He nodded. "Nothing else interesting going on?"

"Murder in some ritzy condos down on the river."

He smiled. "I guess that's what you get for saying it's been slow?"

"Karma." I paused, letting myself wonder for two seconds why Joey was in my kitchen when there was a wealthy, older man on the way to the local morgue.

No. He wouldn't. I didn't even need to ask.

While I knew just enough about Joey's involvement with organized crime to know I didn't want to know more, I also knew he wasn't a bad guy.

I have an infallible creep detector—close to a decade covering crime will do that to a person. Fifteen months after he'd shown up in my living room with a story tip and a sexy smile, I could safely say he might be a lot of things (good cook and better kisser among them) but he wasn't a murderer.

"Stay out of the middle of this one?" He pushed his chair back and stood, locking the door and pulling me to my feet. "Though if you must snoop, I make a decent bodyguard."

"I'm doing my best to stay in the safely-nosy zone. But maybe my body could use some guarding, anyway."

I spent the next hour completely unconcerned about mysterious victims or internet creeps.

My only regret as I kissed him goodbye in the pink-purple predawn shadows the next morning was that I still didn't know what was really going on between us.

Save for the amazing sex—that one I was clear on.

"Call me later?" I asked as he backed toward the front steps.

"Count on it." He turned for the car and I smiled as I watched him walk. Damn, he was gorgeous. And from the way he'd sounded the night before, there was a decent chance he was mine. I shushed the whisper that this was a rainbow-colored fantasy road to nowhere and shut the door, considering a plan for the day.

Shower, gym, dead guy.

My cell phone binged from its spot on my nightstand as I twisted the hot water handle. I frowned and scooted around the corner to the bedroom. Who was texting me at six-thirty?

Kyle.

Sorry, been crazy here. Just got your message. Coffee this morning?

Complicated. Why did everything have to be so damn complicated?

I bit my lip, the uncertainty in Joey's strong voice when he'd asked about Kyle the night before running around my thoughts. But Kyle was my friend—just my friend—and I wanted his help.

Sure, I tapped back. *Thompson's at nine-thirty?*

Bing. *See you then.*

Sigh. *Thanks.*

Bing. *No problem.*

Somehow, I had a feeling coffee with Kyle could lead to a big problem for my new...whatever Joey and I were doing. But as much as I knew Aaron cared, he had a murder, which meant my creeper messages would get attention when he had some to spare. Kyle was more friend than colleague, therefore more likely to make my issue a priority. Surely, if Joey needed to know we'd seen each other, he'd understand that.

Wouldn't he?

4

I took extra care with my outfit, the sundress, sweater and four-inch peep-toe Louboutins a look I knew Kyle would appreciate. I just didn't admit it to myself until I was running out of the gym for the morning news budget meeting.

Tapping my foot through the sports rundown, I tried to pay attention when my boss moved on to Metro. Bob had inherited the section after the editor quit, and his "temporary" fill-in was going on two years. Not that anyone minded. Bob's place among journalism's elite was secure—and he had the Pulitzer on his wall to prove it.

"Anything new on your dead guy this morning?" he asked, raising one bushy white eyebrow in my direction.

"Not yet, but I'll find something." Even if I had to go back and bat my lashes at Jeff the doorman to do it.

He nodded. "Of course you will. I'll save a hole—just try to let me know if you think it's page one or metro front, and how much space you need."

"I'll call you by three."

My friend and favorite southern cook, Eunice Blakely, had a Sunday feature coming on a breast cancer survivor for awareness month. I smiled as she went over the story, my mom's battle with the disease fresh in my thoughts even six years into remission.

"Everyone said she was going to die," Eunice finished. "And Kim talked to three doctors who said flat-out that she should have." She held up a photo of a striking redhead with gorgeous skin and a smile to match. She didn't look much older than me. "Her husband calls it a miracle. She credits willpower and a determination to see her kids grow up. Divine intervention or no, she's been cancer-free for two years."

"TV doesn't have this?" Bob tapped a pen on his desk. "She's pretty. They should eat it up."

"She told Kimberley she'd never talked to a reporter. Their husbands work together. When I told them last month I wanted the breast cancer story to beat all breast cancer stories for October, she went to these folks. Took her weeks of begging to get them to sit for an interview, from what I understand."

Team coverage of the early flu epidemic was leading Metro, with a rural school district that had closed for two days to disinfect buildings and over-crowding at the local hospitals. "Do I need to ask again if everyone's had their flu shot?" Bob's dad-knows-best voice made me smile as I nodded.

Half-listening to the business rundown, I scrolled through the emails in my cell phone with one eye on the clock. Three lawyers who wanted to plead their cases in the paper instead of a courtroom, and a patrolman who'd worked a DUI I'd written up the week before (I said it was slow). With the dead guy, the drunk driver would move to the back burner, and the attorneys could wait 'til I'd talked to Kyle and done some digging on the body in the condo.

"Nice, y'all. Perfect weekend ahead—murder on one, feel-good angels and miracles inside." Bob leaned back in his chair and laced his hands behind his head, every ear in the room waiting for the dismissal he'd used each day of my eight-plus years at the *Telegraph*. "My office is not newswor-thy, so get out and go find me something to print."

I hopped to my feet and whirled for the door, just enough time left to make my coffee date.

"Nichelle?" Bob's deep voice carried over the chatter of our section editors.

"Yeah, Chief?" I paused in the doorway and looked over my shoulder.

"Stay ahead of Charlie. It'll keep Andrews in his cave."

I nodded, the reminder of our publisher's push for Bob's retirement unnecessary. It had kept me running on coffee and Pop-Tarts until I'd beaten every reporter in town on the daily for five months. Bob had never let me down, and I wasn't about to sit by and watch Rick Andrews take away his only reason for getting up in the morning.

Maybe finding my creeper would lead to an exclusive that could be good for both of us.

* * *

Kyle was already there, head bent over his iPhone, a latte cooling on the table in front of him.

"You let your hair grow back out," I said as I walked up behind him. "I thought the buzzcut was part of the hotshot federal agent uniform."

"I'm a rebel." He grinned, tucking the phone in his back pocket as he stood and reached to hug me.

"I like it," I said, squeezing his shoulders briefly before I stepped toward the counter to order my caramel white mocha.

The cryptic DMs pinged through my head again as the barista put the finishing touches on my latte. Dropping a dollar in the tip jar, I spun back for the table and pulled out my phone, still not sure how concerned I should be.

"I don't think this person's pissed at me, but I'm worried that someone might end up getting hurt," I said, opening the thread and handing Kyle my cell phone.

He bent over the screen, his mouth twisting to one side as he read.

"This is all you've gotten?"

I nodded. "Bizarre choice for a creeper. He can't write a manifesto in 140 characters."

"True. But he's also harder to trace." His fingers moved absently over the bristles of his auburn goatee. "They have so many users, who are all online at different times, that the site is damned near impossible to police."

I sat back. "Fantastic."

"Why you, though? And why haven't you blocked this," he looked back at my phone., "LCX12?"

"I don't have the first damned clue why me. And because I want to see what they're going to say next. Duh. If I block it, how am I going to figure out what it means in time to help?"

"Help who?"

"Whoever 'they' are."

"That's a mighty big umbrella you have there, Nichelle."

"I'm hoping you can help me shrink it."

He twisted in the chair and rested his elbows on his knees, his left hand still worrying the goatee. "I think you're right that you're not in immediate danger. But if you insist on getting into this, you could piss them off. Which is never wise with someone who's unstable."

"Of course," I said.

"White know about this?"

"I showed him last night. He said he could try to trace an IP address. But he has a dead rich guy giving his homicide unit heartburn."

"I saw your story this morning. What's up with that?"

"Nothing you've heard about?"

"Subtle."

"Just checking."

"I haven't heard a word."

"So it's probably not a dead shady rich guy. That puts my money back on a bad business deal or a pissed-off girlfriend. Aaron did say he wasn't married, so it wasn't a wife."

"Not his wife, anyway." Kyle arched one eyebrow.

"Ooooh, I hadn't thought of that." I pulled out a notepad and pen and jotted it down. "I like the way your brain works."

He grinned. "Cause of death?"

"They haven't released it yet."

"Huh. Obvious trauma?"

"Yes, but they won't say what kind."

He tipped his head to one side, picking up his cup. "I wonder why not? Historically, you can manage to wheedle almost anything out of the PD."

"This is what I get for saying 'it's been slow' out loud. Dead people shrouded in too much mystery, surly detectives, and a crazy person who likes my Twitter photo."

"Maybe you should change it." Kyle pulled out his phone. "Do I even follow you? What's your handle?"

I rolled my eyes. "RT underscore crime NC."

He poked at his screen. "There you are." He shrugged. "Just a publicity shot. Nice one, but nothing come-hither-y about it."

"Because I'm the come-hither-random-Twitter-guy type. They have another app for that."

His blue eyes widened. "You have an account there?"

"Do you?"

"I asked you first."

"As if." I snorted. "Speed dating via surface judgement. Not my thing, but thanks for asking."

"Your surface judges just fine from where I sit," he said.

"I appreciate your opinion, though I think it's clouded by your knowledge of my brilliant personality and sharp wit."

Kyle laughed. "Not clouded. Enhanced. But we should probably stick to business. Your new guy might not like you coming to see me otherwise."

I dropped my eyes to the table, biting down on the "he's not the boss of me" because it was childish, and also because Kyle was right. And were the stiletto on the other foot, I couldn't blame Joey, because I'd feel the exact same way.

Nodding slowly, I raised my head. "We okay?"

"Fine." The word was clipped, and he ran a hand through his hair, mussing the curls attractively.

Handing back my cell phone, he sighed. "Send me what you have. I'll see what I can turn up."

"Thank you." I tucked the phone away and smiled. "Anything interesting going on in your world these days?"

"Nothing I want to talk to the media about."

"Off the record."

"Still tracking down the rest of that gun ring. Monitoring Caccione activity."

I swallowed hard, keeping my face carefully blank. But how much longer until Kyle figured out Joey had ties to the crime family he was investigating? His refusal to talk to me for the past few months either meant he was on the trail, or he was too pissed to worry about it.

The look on his face said it could be either, or something else entirely.

"How's that coming?" I kept my tone light.

"They haven't chosen a new leader," he said. "However that goes down these days. It's less *The Godfather* and more a business—but we're having a hard time getting any dirt on who might be in line for a promotion."

"You've been watching for three months and have nothing?" I couldn't decide if that was shocking or relieving—or both.

"It's one of the biggest, best-connected syndicates in the country. Maybe in the world. You don't build that kind of empire without a talent for keeping secrets."

Joey's stoic, drive-Nichelle-batshit-crazy expression flashed through my thoughts. Ain't that the truth?

"How about you?" Kyle asked.

"The publisher wants Bob to retire. I'm determined to stay ahead of everyone else in town, because as long as we're winning the news wars, they can't force him out."

Kyle nodded. "Anything for a noble cause. Totally you." He paused, his eyes softening. "Since you're clearly not going to offer, I have to ask: whatever happened with your grandparents?"

Ah, my crazy family: my grandfather was kind of a medium Hollywood bigshot, and my mom got pregnant at sixteen and refused to get married. Plus, she insisted on keeping her baby. This was a point of so much contention, they disowned her. Seventeen years later, they sent me a big fat check and an I'm-sorry letter, but it took eleven more years for me to pick up a phone and call them. Kyle had witnessed much of the angst involved.

I smiled. "My grandmother's nice. We talk on the phone a couple times a month. She's been following my work online since college, and she likes to hear about the behind-the-scenes parts."

"Have you met them?"

"Even if I could take the time off, I'm not sure how I want to handle that. But all in all, it's certainly better than I thought it would be. I was so afraid and resentful for so long."

"I'm glad."

"And?" I prompted.

"And what?"

"You have something-I'm-not-saying face. What're you thinking?"

"That I want to know if she told you anything about your father."

The hundred-thousand-dollar question.

That I was still a little chicken to ask. Even when my mom poured out the whole story, I didn't get a name—she didn't offer, and I didn't pry. I called my grandmother for the first time fully intending to find out, but it's a funny thing: when your throat closes around a question every time you start it, it never quite gets out there.

"I haven't gotten around to that."

"Afraid of the answer?"

"It seems."

His lips tipped up in a sad smile. "I know the feeling."

I put one hand over his. "I'm sorry." It was just above a whisper.

He nodded, patting my hand before he ran one of his through his hair again and stood. "I'll work on this and let you know what I find. You watch yourself. And call me if you need me."

"Thank you." I stood, hefting my bag onto my shoulder. "I appreciate that. And I'm glad you're doing well."

I waved as he pulled out of the parking lot. I hated that Kyle was sad because of me. Surely I was smart enough to figure a way to help him—as soon as I dug up a little more on Aaron's mystery murder victim.

* * *

Journalism in the age of the Internet 102: part of the reason newsrooms have smaller staffs is because computers make it possible for me to accomplish in a half-hour what would've taken my 1979 counterparts three days of hunting through files.

Back at my office, I flipped my laptop open and pulled up the website for the condo complex. I copied the architectural firm's name into my Google bar, and in ten minutes, I had a set of blueprints for the building on my screen.

The bright as noon unit from last night? Number seventeen-oh-four.

Clicking open another window, I pulled up the city's property tax record database. A few keystrokes and three clicks later, I had a name.

David Maynard. I jotted it in my notes and tapped the pen on my blotter.

Journalism in the age of the Internet 103: the computer can only get you so far.

While the odds were overwhelmingly in favor of Maynard being the victim, I couldn't print it. Could be him. Could also be the landlord (Maynard was the seven-year-old condo's original owner). Or maybe the victim didn't live there at all. What if it was a guest, a friend, a relative? The information was handy, but without confirmation, its usefulness was limited to one sentence that would mostly fill space and show Andrews I'd done my homework.

I also knew Charlie well enough to know if she hadn't finished this particular task, she would before the end of the day. So I needed something she couldn't get before six. Where could I find it?

The cute, flirty doorman.

Let Aaron keep his secrets. A way around the answer was there for the taking—I just needed the right source.

5

Jeff the doorman was standing at his post when I pulled up, but the RPD uniform between the parking lot and the front door was twice as broad—and ten times as prickly—as Officer Palmer from yesterday. I tucked my notebook into my bag and touched up my lip gloss before putting on my best haughty expression, channeling Percival's owner as I strode purposefully toward the door.

"Miss?" The barrel-chested police officer took two steps toward me as I crossed the opposite end of the driveway, but was waylaid by an agitated man in a four-thousand-dollar suit who gestured toward the door and then the top of the building as he talked.

I didn't stop walking until Jeff moved to open the door.

"Percival in that much of a state, or did you miss me?" he asked as he pulled on the heavy steel handle, and I returned his smile. He was cute, and probably not too used to being turned down.

"I'll never tell." I stopped just inside the door, shooting a glance at the elevator. Hopefully Landers was occupied, if he was around.

"Then I choose to believe the latter," he said. "Nothing wrong with a Wednesday morning ego boost."

My smile widened into a grin. "I am here on business." Every word true. I leaned on the wall and feigned innocence. "There are still police cars all over the place. What's that about?"

He raised his eyebrows and lowered his voice. "Someone died."

I popped my mouth into an O and widened my eyes. "How awful! Who was it?"

"Dr. Maynard. Great man. Nice. Really smart. I can't imagine why anyone would want to hurt him."

"Hurt him? Surely they don't suspect..." I let it trail off and he nodded. Bingo. I arranged my face into an appropriately sorrowful expression.

My brain flashed through what I could safely ask without looking too interested. It's a tricky line, getting someone to talk about something sensitive. "What kind of doctor was he? Did he work at one of the hospitals?"

"A long time ago, I think," he said. "But he had his own office for the whole time I've known him. Retired to pursue his passions, he said."

Kyle's jealous wife theory flashed through my head, but I couldn't start picking at the good doctor's personal life without making Jeff wonder why I wanted to know.

"That's so sad."

"It is. I heard building management last night, trying to convince the cops he'd had a heart attack. Don't want to upset the other residents. Might affect their income, or something. But the detective said there were marks on the doc's neck."

Jackpot. No one else would have that yet as long as the coroner's office didn't put out a press release before the end of the day.

"How wretched." I shook my head. "On both counts. A man is dead, and people who knew him are worried about money."

"They liked the doc fine, but the dollar is king, for sure."

"The police going to be around much longer?"

"I hope not. People get stopped out there and then bitch to me for twenty minutes about freedom and why the cops have a right to stop them from entering the building. I like this job because folks are mostly pleasant. I get to chit chat with them about their lives as they come and go."

I nodded, looking him over again. "What did you do before this? Or have you always dreamed of being a doorman?"

"I have not." He chuckled, turning to push the door open for a petite woman with silver hair and a fox stole. At eleven in the morning on a warm

October day. "Mrs. Eason, you look lovely, as always." Jeff smiled. "Anything exciting happening today?"

She shook her head, a disapproving eye on the RPD officer twenty or so feet away. "I'm afraid not, Jeffrey." Her voice quavered as she pulled the stole a millimeter tighter. "I'm on my way to Blythe and Rogers to start arrangements for David's services."

I shrank back into the ficus decorating the corner, mouth shut and ears open, eyes on Mrs. Eason. Chanel blouse, Stuart Weitzman shoes, Louis Vuitton bag—she was a walking Saks billboard.

"I just don't understand why this whole business has to be so unpleasant," she said, shooting another something-I-stepped-in look at Officer Surly. "Why can't they go away and let him rest in peace? Do you know, they won't even let me set a date for his funeral until they're through with this nonsense?"

"I'm pretty sure they think someone killed him, ma'am." Jeff's eyes flicked to me as he spoke, and I cast mine down and tried to blend in with the papered wall behind me.

Mrs. Eason waved her hand. "Preposterous. Who would want to hurt my David?" She shut her heavily made-up eyes just too long for a blink, sniffling as she reopened them. "I can't believe he's gone. He had such a gentle soul. Brilliant mind. Kind heart."

Her David? My fingers itched for a pad and pen. On so little sleep and so much caffeine, I hoped I could trust my brain to keep it all straight until I could write it down.

Jeff patted her thin shoulder. "I'm so sorry for your loss."

She blotted the corner of one eye with a lace handkerchief, squaring her shoulders and squeezing Jeff's hand. "You're a good boy, Jeffrey. Thank you."

"Drive carefully, ma'am."

She strode to the parking lot, folding herself behind the wheel of a Jaguar parked in the first space. Brow furrowed, Jeff watched until her tail-lights disappeared.

I stepped forward, another glance at the elevators telling me I was safe to chat a bit more.

"Wow. What an awful way to have to spend your day," I said.

"She's a tough old bird." Jeff smiled. "Lived through more than most people I know, and that's saying something."

"Sounded like she was close to the doctor." I held his gaze with one of friendly concern, nothing more. I practiced that look in the mirror at least a couple of times a month.

"They were friends. Getting to be closer, maybe. Her husband passed on last Christmas. She took up going to the opera with the doc. And now he's gone too."

That piqued my news radar, though I couldn't see that frail woman strangling any sort of grown man. But if the husband was dead, too...

"How heartbreaking. How did her husband die?" I was so curious, I forgot to be indirect.

"Heart stopped."

"Was he ill?"

Jeff eyed me a little warily. Oops.

"Just curious," I said hastily. Still true. "You might call it a bad habit." I widened my eyes and flashed a grin for effect.

He smiled. "No worries. There was a tangle of reporters out front all afternoon and evening. I imagine they'll be here again today. Too damned nosy for their own good."

I held the smile and nodded. Oh, boy.

"It was a sudden thing," Jeff said. "Mister Eason. He was pretty fit, for an old guy. Vietnam veteran, retired CEO—he ran every morning along the river. Early."

My brain ticked back ten months and change.

"They found him down there. Just off the jogging path," I mumbled, more to myself than to him.

His eyebrows went up. "That's some memory you have there."

"I must've read it somewhere," I said dismissively. "Things I read get stuck in my head." Things I hear, too, but not as readily. I needed to go make some notes.

I took a step backward. "I just remembered something I have to do." Lame.

He pursed his lips, his eyes flicking from his watch to the elevators. "What about Percival?"

Think fast, Nichelle.

"It's for him," I said. "I forgot to bring his favorite treat with me. He does better when he gets rewarded." Two steps back. I needed a notepad, and I needed to not get any further into this hole with Jeff. He looked suspicious enough already.

A shrill "You have GOT to be kidding" came from the far end of the drive, and we both turned toward it. Ms. Social Network, Percival being dragged behind her on a rhinestone-studded leash, screeched a full-throated "go away" at the police officer, trying to shove past him to get to the door.

Captain Surly spun her around and folded one arm behind her back, saying something I couldn't hear. Jeff took a step toward the scene, then turned to look back at me. "You said—"

"So nice chatting with you, Jeff," I blurted, spinning on one Louboutin and sprinting for my car.

So. Close.

I didn't even check the rearview to see if snotty Clarice was headed to jail.

* * *

A block up, I squealed the tires pulling into the Virginia War Memorial parking lot. Throwing the car into park, I snatched a pen and pad out of the console.

David Maynard. Doctor. Single. Possible girlfriend with a dead husband. A funky, suspicious dead husband if I remembered right.

My hand flew across the page, my brain replaying the conversations of the past half-hour and hoping like hell there were no details left out.

Private practice. Maybe the office website had a photo of the doctor. I made a note.

Pulling my cell phone from my bag, I texted Bob an *I have something*. Maybe a big something, if Charlie didn't get it before eleven.

I opened a new message, my fingers still hesitant to type the name "Shelby" into my phone.

Our copy chief and I had the longest-running feud in *Telegraph* history, fueled mainly by the fact that she'd always wanted my job (still did), and wasn't above any means of getting it (until recently). We were at a peace accord of sorts these days. Maybe.

I stared at the screen. How to ask without tipping my hand? Shelby and I might not be out for each other's blood anymore, but the quickest way to lose an exclusive is to blab it all over, even in your own newsroom.

When you have a sec, I need a file from you. Filling in holes. Good. Vague. Send.

I tapped a pen on the notepad in my lap, my thoughts racing. Sex and money are both great motives for murder, but little Mrs. Eason as the Black Widow? Not a lock, but I'd seen stranger.

Bing. *Which one?*

The philanthropist CEO guy they found down by the river last Christmas. I'd read the story on my laptop while munching cookies at my mom's kitchen counter, and the memory of being annoyed at Shelby filling in for me on a body discovery was pretty fresh ten months later.

Bing. *Old guy. He had a heart attack. That's what the ME said.*

That's what I thought I read. I chose careful words. *Updating my files. Do you still have the ME's report, by chance?*

Tap tap tap.

Bing. *Yep. Want me to put it on your desk?*

I shook my head at the screen, hearing a helpful tone in her high voice as I read the words. So. Weird.

That'd be fabulous. Thanks!

I clicked the phone off and dropped it back into my bag, staring out the window at the white marble walls of the memorial. Bruises on the neck were certainly a pointer to strangulation, but it wasn't definitive. So the best I could do was suspected cause of death.

And I was on the fence about printing the name. Did anyone else have it? Probably not. So why not sit on it for a day or two? Keeping it quiet would score big brownie points with Aaron, and it might keep the family, if there was one, from hearing it on the news before the cops could track them down. Andrews wouldn't know—or care, as long as I had it first when it did go out. Plus, it kept my research under wraps if I didn't put the victim's name in the paper when the PD wasn't releasing it. I could maybe stay one up on everyone else by digging up everything I could on Maynard before they even knew who he was.

Solid plan.

I started the engine and checked the clock: eleven-thirty. Four hours until Bob would want to know how much space I needed.

Thank God for the internet.

6

Journalism in the age of the Internet 104: the World Wide Web knows all. The trick is where to look. I found a photo of Dr. David Maynard in thirteen seconds.

Then hit a cinderblock wall trying to find out anything else about him.

My puzzle-loving side found that fascinating. The rest of me found it damned frustrating.

I tapped my fingers on the edge of the keyboard. No yellow pages listing for a practice. No whitepages listing for a home or a business. No results in the galleries of physicians on the local hospital pages.

After an hour of spelling his name nineteen different ways (yes, the image result came up on the first try, but there are at least nine ways to spell Smith), I was no closer to anything resembling a bio.

No Facebook.

No Twitter.

I clicked back to the photo. Maybe this wasn't the same guy Mrs. Eason was mourning. Twisting a lock of hair around my index finger, I stared at the screen.

An attractive, if a little plain, gentleman stared back, his round face comfortable in its smile. It was a headshot, so I had no point of reference for height or size except average shoulders and full cheeks. The age was maybe a little off too. My chin dropped to my chest.

"So who are you? Where did it pull this from?" I muttered, clicking to the source page.

Holy Manolos.

From us. The photo was in the *Telegraph* database, on the local server. I logged in and searched the offline archives.

Fifty-nine hits. I clicked into the most recent article, which turned out to be no kind of recent at all.

Nine years ago, Maynard retired from the RAU medical school. And from the hospital, where he was the chief of oncology. His career change had warranted a feature on the society page because of the gala the hospital's board threw for him. No one could say enough good things about him. Brilliant, caring, patient. A true loss to the local medical community.

The man himself was quoted as saying he'd miss the bustle of the hospital, but looked forward to pursuing his true passion.

"Which is?" I scrolled down, but that was it. Either the reporter didn't ask, or they didn't print it.

So I still had a big fat question mark over where he'd disappeared to. Almost a decade later, his doorman said he'd been in private practice, but not for how long or where. And the internet, usually my best friend when researching a story, had nothing for me. Why?

I tapped more. The furrow in Jeff's brow when I bolted told me asking him more questions about the doc would blow my dog trainer cover wide open. But someone had to know.

I scrolled back to the top of the article and checked the byline.

Elizabeth Herrington.

Didn't ring a bell, and the story ran nine months before my first day at work. I clicked through a few more articles, but the dates were positively ancient, the reporters' names unfamiliar. Not much in the way of content, either—mostly side mentions in pieces on the medical school, though there was one headline about a drug breakthrough a dozen years ago. Maynard's name popped up in that one thirteen times. Brilliant doctor. But I already knew that.

Strike one.

Damn, damn, damn.

I hopped to my feet and strolled to Bob's office, tapping on the open door.

"Hey, Chief?" I poked my head around the corner. He waved me in, keeping his eyes fixed on his screen. I plopped into the Virginia Tech orange armchair in the corner near his desk. A glance at his borderline-obnoxious Hokies wall clock, hanging just above and to the left of his Pulitzer on the opposite wall, told me I was running out of time.

"What's up, kiddo?" His chair squealed as he turned toward me, and I smiled at the affection in his voice. Bob was doubtless the closest thing I'd ever had to a father, and as such, I didn't smack him for calling me kiddo.

"Elizabeth Herrington." I paused when his face took on the distinct expression of a man who had, in fact, been smacked.

He closed his eyes for a long blink and tried for a smile. "There's a name I haven't heard in a long while," he said. "What brings her up?"

Yeah, no story there. Curiosity bubbled in my throat, but I swallowed hard and breezed into my next question. No time for reminiscing today.

"She did a feature story a while back—"

"Have to be a long while back," he interrupted.

"It was." Focus, Nichelle.

He nodded, raising his bushy white brows expectantly.

"About my murder vic. Turns out he was a doctor. Bigshot over at the RAU Medical campus."

Bob sat straight up, the color vanishing from his face in a blink.

"Not David Maynard." The words sounded choked, and I flinched. It had never once occurred to me I'd be the bearer of bad news when pitching Bob a story.

I scrunched my face and leaned forward, softening my tone. "I'm afraid it sounds that way," I said. "Aaron hasn't released anything yet, but I went back to the building this morning and had a chat with the doorman. Did a little eavesdropping. That's the name I got."

He slumped into his chair. "Damn."

I pinched my lips together and looked out the window. I hated the thought of upsetting Bob, but I needed to stay on top of the story to keep Charlie at bay and make sure his job was safe. Some days, ambition sucks.

"I'm so sorry to have to tell you like this, Chief," I said softly. "The thing is, I was wondering if you knew how to get ahold of Ms. Herrington, because I'm hoping she remembers the story. I've looked and looked for some background on the victim—" Bob's head snapped up and I stammered, "On, um, Dr. Maynard—and I can't find anything." Something clicked in my head. "Even her story."

He braced his elbows on his knees and dropped his head into his hands. "Huh?"

"Nothing came up in the search results. Nothing. Not even the story I read about his retirement."

"Then how did you read it?" Bob raised his head slowly, a divot between his eyebrows.

"Rabbit trails. I found a photo." I bounced my foot, puzzle pieces taking shape in my brain. "There was an image result for a picture of him from the article. But the article itself never came up. Nothing did. No matter how I tried spelling his name."

"Maynard. M-A-Y-N-A-R-D." Bob shook his head. "How is that possible? He was brilliant. Surely there's stuff about his research all over the web."

"Not a single hit." I bit my lip.

"That's odd."

"No, it's so far past odd, it can't see odd in the rearview." I jumped up. "Hold me a spot on one for an exclusive on possible cause of death. The coroner hasn't released anything, but I have a solid 'unnamed source close to the investigation' that cited marks on the victim's neck. Charlie's head is going to burst into flames just at that. And I'll see what else I can find. Andrews won't know what hit him."

"I appreciate the effort, Nicey," Bob said. "But handle this with care for me? David was beloved—it's going to hit a lot of important people pretty hard that he's gone. Especially if the PD suspects foul play."

"You got it." I paused in the door and turned back. On one hand, I wanted to ask Bob how he knew the doctor, and how well. Maybe he had information that could help me. On the other, I didn't want to make him sadder if I could talk to other people first. "I'm not using his name yet, but maybe I can get the inside scoop from our old society editor. Can you send me Miss Herrington's contact info, if you have it?"

"I don't know—or give the slightest shit—how to get in touch with that..." Bob's eyes fell shut and he took a slow, deep breath, "...woman. Nor do I have any interest in you pulling her into anything to do with this newspaper. Find another source."

I sighed.

Nothing's ever easy.

* * *

Thirty minutes of cursing at my laptop later, I stirred my third latte of the day and smiled across the table at my best friend's husband. Chad was a computer geek through and through, head of network security at one of the banks that occupied a tower a few blocks from my office.

"Thanks for coming to meet me," I said.

He raised his cup. "Thanks for the coffee."

"Kids doing okay?"

"They're great. But you could ask Jenna that." The hazel eyes behind his square glasses were curious. "What's up?"

"Ever direct." I smiled. "That's okay. I like direct. I have a computer problem."

"You have to update your antivirus stuff, Nichelle," Chad groaned. "How many times have we been through this? Do. Not. Dismiss. The little box. That's going to cost you more than a cup of coffee."

"I didn't," I protested. "Well, I did, but I swear I'll stop, and that's not why I'm here."

He tipped his head to one side.

"How could someone get erased off the internet?" I asked. "Like, no results. Nothing, not one. And on a guy who should have plenty of hits."

"You spelled it right?"

"Double and triple checked. There's nothing there."

He pulled out his laptop. "Spell the name for me."

I obliged. "Doctor. Shining star of the RAU medical faculty and Richmond's best oncologist."

Oncologist.

Bob's wife died of cancer. Shit.

"Spell it again," Chad said.

I did. "Nothing there, right? Except one photo in the image results."

"That's not possible." He tugged at his left earlobe. I knew him well enough to know that meant he was annoyed. "My grandmother has five hits, for Christ's sake. Everyone has a search history."

"Everyone but this dude," I said. "What I need to know is how."

"Not a clue," Chad said, typing furiously. "But I'll find out. If someone wiped him off the web, it's the greatest hack in history. I want to know how they did it."

Me too. But more than that, I wanted to know why.

* * *

Besides Bob, who had been at the *Telegraph* longer than me?

Eunice and Larry topped the list. And while Eunice was the current queen of Features, nine years ago she would've had more chance of knowing a Saudi insurgent leader than the society editor. Her days as a war correspondent were cut short by a helicopter crash in Iraq that earned her a dozen pins in her hip and parked her at a desk.

Larry wasn't in the photo cave, but his monitor was on, so he hadn't gone far. When I didn't find him in the break room, I went to the elevators to wait. He was likely outside smoking.

The smell that preceded him off the car three minutes later confirmed it.

"Those things will kill you," I said, falling into step beside him.

"I'm too stubborn—" Pause. Cough cough cough. "—to die."

I snorted. "I'm glad you think so."

"What's up? Need another photo enhancement for one of your crazy stories?" Larry raised his eyebrows, a hopeful gleam in his eye.

"Careful, I'll stop buying you beer if I get the notion you like helping me," I said.

He scowled. "Hate it. You're a pain in the ass, you know it?"

I grinned. "You love me anyway."

"What do you need this time?"

"To know if you remember a society editor named Elizabeth—"

"Herrington," he said flatly. "No one who's been around for long enough could forget her."

"Why not?"

He waved me into the photo cave, dropping into his chair and glancing around the empty room before he whispered so low I had to lean in to hear. "Why are you asking about her?"

"She wrote a story I'm having an issue with, and I'm hoping to find..."

I broke off. What was I looking for? No one she'd told about Maynard's sendoff would remember anything a decade later, right?

Right.

There had to be something, even if I wasn't sure what the something was.

Larry shook his head, his mouth popping open like he was going to speak, then snapping shut again.

"What is the story with this woman?" I threw up my hands. "Bob won't sa—"

"You asked Bob? Don't ask Bob!" Larry barked.

Good Lord. "Why?"

"Nothing good will come of it." Larry sat up, his eyes solemn. "Leave him out of it, you understand?"

"What the hell did she do?" I had to start the sentence twice to keep my volume down.

"She destroyed his hero. Bob was so idealistic back then, it damn near killed him."

7

"I. Am. So. Lost." I stared at Larry.

He nodded. "Of course. The *Telegraph* has always been your happy place, right?"

"Except for Shelby. Well. Old Shelby. I'm reserving judgement on New Shelby."

He chuckled, then stood when Lindsay strolled in with a memory stick in her hand and took a seat at the next table. "You feel like coffee?"

"If I have any more caffeine today I'm going to see noises." And I was no coffee lightweight. "How about a walk?"

He waved a hand. "After you."

Larry didn't say another word until we were outside and halfway down the block. I just knew I was about to hear the secret of life by the time he finally opened his mouth.

"The paper was Bob's whole life. Always was. Still is. Always will be."

Um. "I hate to break it to you, Larry, but me and Lindsay and the guy who puts postage on out of town subs—we all know that."

He rolled his eyes, pulling his faded Richmond Generals cap down over his forehead and leaning into the brisk wind that reminded me winter was on its way. "Don't get ahead of the story."

I slowed my gait and watched his profile expectantly.

"Back when Bob was the city editor, the guy who ran the *Telegraph* was a bit of a legend in the business."

"Herman Kochanski. He covered the Kennedy assassination for the *Morning Telegram* in Dallas."

"And the March on Washington for the *Post*." Larry nodded. "You know how you feel about Bob? That was how Bob felt about Herman."

I nodded. "That guy was a whole week of one of my college classes. Witnessing History, it was called."

"He did a fair amount of that." Larry turned onto Grace Street and I followed. "He knew Bob was special five minutes after he walked into the newsroom looking for a job. Not unlike you." Larry winked.

"Thanks. Keep going."

"Herman wasn't that much older than Bob. He was just so damn good, and always in the right place at the right time. They were a lot alike, those two. They were friends, but Bob looked up to Herman. Hero worship situation. Their wives got to be fast friends. Sophia sat with Bob's wife through every miscarriage, and stayed with her sometimes if Bob was working late."

I nodded slowly, my brain running ahead to Elizabeth Herrington, a slow ache starting in the pit of my stomach.

"Oh, no." I didn't mean to say it out loud.

Larry shot me a sideways glance. "You're smart, too. So Elizabeth started working for us about three years after Bob did. She was young. Not pretty when you looked hard, but no one could tell her that, so people didn't notice."

"You mean men didn't notice."

"Some men. I like my faces pretty. Symmetrical. Maybe it's a photog thing. The nose on that woman—looked like the Good Lord flipped a light bulb over and plopped it in the middle of her face."

I snorted. "If she wasn't pretty, why would Herman sleep with her? That's where you're going, right?"

"There you go, jumping ahead again."

"Sue me."

"Herman and Sophia were a great couple. Everybody loved them. They loved each other. But marriage is hard work." He cut his eyes sideways and laid a finger over his lips. "Shhh. That's a thing they don't tell you until after you're hooked. Hell, nobody tells most people. Why do you think so many folks get divorced?"

I nodded, waving for him to go on with the story.

"Sophia had three kids in five years. Little munchkins are cute, Nicey, but don't let them fool you. Being a parent is as frustrating and demanding as it is wonderful. Being a working mom who wants to have it all is pretty near impossible. Sophia was the kind of woman who wanted to be everything for everyone. She nursed Grace through depression. She ran a successful CPA firm. She hovered over her babies. All of which left her exhausted."

"Too exhausted to be everything for her husband?" I was surer where the story was going with every word.

"I'm spilling all the old people secrets today, so listen up: men aren't really big babies in every sense, but we do get a little childish about feeling ignored by the women we love. Just keep that on file in case you need it someday. Because when men who make their living communicating don't talk to their wives, bad shit happens."

"Like Elizabeth?"

He nodded.

"Something I didn't notice about her until my own wife pointed it out to me was that she never had many girlfriends. But she was first to volunteer to go play racquetball, or grab a beer after work—with the guys. She was cool. Easy. She liked writing whatever pieces anyone offered, so she said, but what she really wanted was the society page. She started staying late when Herman did. He was moping and didn't want to go home to a house full of kids and chaos and a beautiful wife he thought was ignoring him on purpose. Elizabeth was right there with a beer and a sympathetic ear. She listened to him. Laughed at his jokes. She was a beacon of no responsibility. And then the Berlin Wall came down, and Herman wanted to go handle it himself instead of letting the wire feed it to us." Larry laughed at my furrowed brow.

"Ah, the heydays. Fat newspapers and not a block in town that didn't have a three-quarters or better sub rate. He barely had to wheedle the publisher. They put him on the next plane. Didn't even blink when he asked if Elizabeth could go with him. He lied to Sophia and told her he was taking me. I've always resented him a little for that. She was a fine lady."

"Elizabeth wasn't a photographer."

"I wasn't going to sleep with him."

"Touché."

"They got drunk in the hotel bar and she asked him into her room. I'll give you three guesses where they ended up, and the first two don't count." Larry shook his head. "But—so the story goes—the next morning Herman jumped up in a full-on, I'm-so-stupid-what-the-fuck-have-I-done-here panic. Elizabeth told him she'd forget all about it if he gave her the society page. So he did."

I shoved my hands into my pockets, leaning into the wind. "Burying that sort of secret is never as easy as people think."

Larry nodded. "Herman wasn't an asshole. He was a good guy who did a stupid thing. The guilt put a canyon between him and Sophia. Both of them were miserable. She was scared out of her mind, just knew he was having an affair, and he was killing himself with scotch because he couldn't stand lying to her. That's where I came in."

"Uh-oh."

He sighed. "We were drunk. It was Christmas, and we still had parties where the paper paid for bartenders and the whole nine. It got late. Bob, Herman, their wives, me, and a couple other guys who are long gone now, were sitting around telling war stories. Bob made a crack about Herman always snapping up the plum assignments for himself, especially when they involved foreign travel. And Sophia turned to me and said, 'How did you like Germany, Larry?'"

Ah.

"And I said, 'I'll tell you if I ever get to go.'"

Ha.

"You could've heard a flea fart."

I laughed in spite of the heavy feeling in my stomach. I knew how much Bob adored his wife. Still, so many years after her death.

"Everything went to Hell?" I asked.

"It took Bob and Grace fourteen seconds to read what was going on. Herman just started bawling and saying he was lonely and he was so miserable and angry and it didn't mean anything. Sophia stared at him for a minute before she threw her drink in his face. Italian, if you couldn't tell by her name."

I nodded, and Larry kept talking. "Bob jumped up and called his hero a miserable bastard and took the women home. I was so sloshed, it was over by the time I figured out what had happened."

"But she still worked here?"

"Herman left that spring. Sophia said she could forgive him, but she couldn't stand him being in the same room with Elizabeth. So they moved. To San Francisco."

"And Bob got promoted."

"A no-brainer, after his piece on the Klan won the Pulitzer. He hated Elizabeth, though. Tried everything he could to get her out of the newsroom. Begged friends to offer her jobs in other cities. Right, wrong, or indifferent, he believed she destroyed his friendship with Herman, and he resented her for it."

"I see." And I did. Larry's scornful tone notwithstanding, I flat lacked ability to identify with Ms. Herrington: I'd run the Boston Marathon in stilettos before I'd go out drinking with a married man—and forget letting one into a hotel room. I have plenty of guy friends, but there's a big, fat line between friendly and fire-playing, and hotel rooms sit on the warm side of it.

I understood why Bob disliked this woman. Then again, I also got his disappointment in Kochanski. No wonder it was still a sore spot.

One finger drummed against my thigh, my thoughts returning to Dr. Maynard. "I know she was here for a long time after that, though. Years later, she wrote a story I read this morning."

Larry nodded. "She knew how much Bob loathed her, and she kind of got off on it. Said she wouldn't give him the satisfaction of quitting."

Wow. "She could give Shelby a run for her money. And that takes a special kind of b—Um. Person." I stopped walking, leaning against the chilly blocks of a nineteenth-century art deco wall and sighing. "So there's no one in the newsroom who can tell me if she ever mentioned my guy."

Larry shrugged. "You could go ask her."

"Bob told me to find another source. After what you just said, I'm slightly afraid he might fire me for that."

He snorted. "I'd say never, but...He really did hate that woman. She finally managed to land a rich husband, which is why she wanted the society page in the first place."

I nodded, turning back toward the office. On one hand, I didn't want to meet this awful woman Larry had described. And I didn't want to even risk opening such a deep wound for Bob.

On the other, I needed some kind of lead—any kind of lead—on Dr. Maynard.

Couldn't hurt to know where to look if I ended up with no other choice.

"You don't happen to know her married name, do you?"

"Eason. He was a suit of some flavor."

Eason. As in, Mrs. Eason who was planning Maynard's funeral?

Jiminy. Choos.

8

Larry asked me thirty-seven times between the corner and the elevator what was the matter with me. I couldn't say. Not even really because I didn't want to share the lead, although that was part of it. Mostly, I couldn't make my mouth work with my brain running on fast forward.

What the hell kind of woman was this? Could our old society editor be Richmond's very own Black Widow? Maybe it was a good thing Bob's friend had moved three thousand miles away. Not just for his marriage, but for his ability to keep breathing.

I rushed to my desk and typed "Elizabeth Eason" into my search bar.

More than three hundred hits. Clicking to the photos, I studied her nose. Larry was right about the shape, but I pulled an old staff photo from Elizabeth Herrington's society column to compare, anyway. It was her.

I scrolled through images, mostly from our society pages. Fly on the wall to belle of the ball.

Mrs. Eason and her husband—tall, with thick white hair and the distinguished look handsome men get as they age that's so damned unfair—were in photos of every major gala given in Richmond in the nine-year period between when she married him and when he died. Another click took me to her name in Shelby's story about the circumstances surrounding his death. She found the body. Not damning by itself, but worth looking into.

Why the cops hadn't looked at her harder topped my list of questions, but I didn't dare call Aaron and ask about Maynard's maybe-girlfriend. He'd freeze me out of the whole investigation if I wasn't careful.

Who else might know?

I snatched up the phone and dialed my favorite prosecutor's cell number. My friend DonnaJo answered on the second ring.

"Tell me you're writing about something interesting. I'm so tired of looking at misdemeanor crap I'm going to claw my own eyes out," she said in place of hello.

Funny thing about working in law enforcement: while you dislike criminals, you kind of depend on them. Same goes for crime reporting. Murders are awful, but they're a lot more intriguing than a bunch of kids who got caught with some weed behind the 7-Eleven.

"I've got a homicide that's stranger than average, if the way Aaron and Landers are clamming up about the investigation is any clue," I said. "Vic used to be a bigshot doctor at RAU Medical Center. Taught oncology at the med school, too."

"Fantastic. Well, not for him. But you know what I mean."

"Indeed. I'm currently curious about his neighbors. He lived in that big steel and glass condo complex down at Rockett's Landing, and the lady down the hall is planning his funeral. Her husband died under mysterious circumstances last Christmas."

"Trying to run down a lead no one else has, huh?"

"Always. It keeps me employed. Which pays for my shoe habit. Leads equal shoes. Ones nobody else has are best, on both counts."

"I take it she wasn't arrested in the husband's death?"

"Nope. What I'd like to know is why."

"And you don't want to ask the people who, you know, make the arrests, because...?"

"Aaron's being weird about this one. I usually get decent access in a murder investigation, but this guy—nothing. Not even the basics that go in a press release."

"The police report is public information." A note of curiosity entered DonnaJo's perfect soprano.

"They claim it's not done. They have seven days to file it, but then everyone else will have whatever they don't redact, and I don't want to spend a week fighting with Aaron about it. I can find the information on my own. Staying ahead of Charlie has the bonus of keeping the publisher off Bob's ass these days, which makes me happy."

"Gotcha. What's the name?"

"The dead husband or the widow?"

"Either. Both. Whatever."

"Eason."

"Richard Eason, the coal tycoon?"

"Found on a bike trail down by the river."

"Yep. That's him." I heard computer keys clicking. "I was supposed to be at the funeral, but I had court that day. My folks were friends with him. A long time ago. My mother hated his new wife."

Oh really, now? "How come?" I didn't bother to try for casual. DonnaJo knew me too well.

She laughed. "Social climber. My mom said she was a real bitch, too. Fake, only interested in what people could do for her. But my mom and Mrs. Eason—the first one—were tight, so her opinion could be jaded."

Maybe, but it fit with Larry's story. I scrunched my nose. I hadn't set eyes on Elizabeth Eason for more than ten minutes, and I didn't like her.

"How'd she end up with this guy? Did they say?"

"His wife died, and he was torn up. Seriously devastated. They were that cute little couple who stays in love forever, you know?"

I nodded, thinking about how much Bob still missed Grace.

"He met this woman at some social event, had a couple of drinks, and was nice to her—says my mother—and she kind of attached herself to him and didn't let go. Six months later, she stepped right into Mrs. Eason's shoes."

"What did your dad say?"

"That Mr. Eason told him she was great in the sack. Something about extraordinary jaw muscles. He didn't tell me that, mind you. I heard him say it to my mom."

"I'm sure that was a fun conversation for her."

"She said she was going to vomit and told him to shut up."

I laughed. DonnaJo's mother was a card-carrying member of the DAR, a timeless beauty with the kind of genteel grace that seems bred into women from old-money southern families. I couldn't imagine her having a conversation about anything racier than the cover of the Junior League's Christmas cookbook.

DonnaJo kept clicking keys. I stayed quiet for a second.

"Nothing here. We never even got a file on his death," she said finally. "What did the ME say?"

"Heart attack."

"Huh." She paused.

"What?"

"He was in great shape. He was a basketball player in his UVA days, and an Army vet, and he worked out four times a week for, like, ever. He was my dad's running partner."

"Interesting." I managed to keep my voice even. Barely.

"I know stuff like that can happen to anyone, but that's...weird."

"It is indeed." I twisted the phone cord around my finger, thanking DonnaJo for her help.

She sighed. "It doesn't seem I had much to offer today, but you're certainly welcome. Go see what you can find out. And Nichelle?"

"Yes?"

"Keep me posted."

I hung up and dialed Aaron. While I wasn't letting any of my own leads slip, I needed to know what —if anything—he was saying about the investigation.

"You ready to talk yet?" I asked when he barked a hello.

"Talk in the general sense? Sure. I hear the new Denzel movie is fantastic." His smirk practically dripped out of the phone.

I rolled my eyes. "Noted. But I'm wondering if you're inclined to give me any more on this murder victim. Name?"

"No comment."

"Come on, Aaron."

Three beats of silence, followed by a sigh. "I really am sorry. I can't release it yet." Which meant asking him to confirm it was Maynard might just get me yelled at.

"But...why?" The words popped out on autoplay, my brain whirling ahead to my story. Charlie wouldn't run the name without confirmation. So I'd sit on it for another day or two.

"I'm still trying to figure that out myself," Aaron said. "Let me know if you dig up a reason, huh?"

* * *

I dropped the phone back to its cradle, leaning back in the chair. "What a mess."

"What's a mess?" The familiar tenor came from behind me, and I managed a half-smile for my favorite sports columnist.

"The Middle East," I said, sitting up and spinning the chair to face my friend Grant Parker.

"True. Though I'm pretty sure it's about seven-thousand miles outside our coverage area," Parker said, the arched brow over one bright emerald eye telling me I wasn't fooling him. "I assumed you were lamenting a local mess. Need a sounding board?"

Yes. But I didn't want this getting around until I had a better handle on it.

"I'll holler when I do," I promised. "I don't have enough pieces of this puzzle yet. But thanks."

He nodded, leaning against the doorway to my cube and folding his arms across his chest.

I blinked expectantly, but he stayed quiet.

"You waiting for Mel?" I asked finally. It was five-thirty, and Parker's girl-friend was our city hall reporter. Her cube was next to mine.

"Zoning meeting. Probably won't be over until late." A drop in his tone set off a warning bell in my head.

"What's up?"

"Maybe I could use a sounding board of my own today." Parker's voice quivered and he pulled in a deep breath, closing his eyes.

Something was shaking the unshakeable Grant Parker?

I nodded and offered an apologetic smile. "I have a couple of things to wrap up, but if you want to hang out for a bit, we could grab a drink?"

"I could use one." He took a step backward. "Text me when you're ready to go."

I back-burnered the nervous look in his normally supremely confident green eyes and opened a blank file, resting my fingers on the keys and debating how much I wanted to give away.

Richmond police are still searching for clues in the death of a man whose body was discovered in a condo overlooking the James River Tuesday afternoon.

Detectives haven't released the man's name pending notification of next of kin, but they suspect foul play. Wednesday, a source with knowledge of the investigation said there was bruising around the victim's neck.

I recapped the scant details of the day before and finished with a plea for anyone with information to call Crimestoppers.

Channel Four's website told me Charlie had less than nothing. Her latest story, posted after one, sent my eyes rolling heavenward as I scanned the copy. "Pissed-off residents? Really?" Blah. Score one for the newspaper.

Clicking open an email, I sent my story to Bob with a note that no one else had suspected cause of death.

I thumbed through my notes to make sure there wasn't a trial I'd forgotten, then scanned the day's new police reports. Two fender benders, a drunk driver, and a domestic violence call. Nothing worthy of space in the middle of a murder investigation.

I put my index finger on the top edge of the screen, pausing before I flipped it shut.

I shouldn't look.

But Andrews probably would, and I had less than no desire to be blindsided this week.

Tapping the monitor back to life, I punched in the address for River City 411, a blog written by wannabe reporter and former RPD dispatcher Alexa Reading, alias Girl Friday (or my personal pet name: Gigantic Pain in My Ass).

She'd posted about the body in the condos at noon, well after everyone else in town had reported on it. Good. I clicked the post and found paraphrasing of my story and Charlie's, plus a few thinly-veiled conspiracy hints, suggesting Charlie and I were in the PD's back pocket.

"Favoritism, my foot," I muttered, closing the browser. She'd been less of a problem since she got fired from the PD for leaking information about an open investigation, but she was still irritating as hell. I could never tell when she'd actually manage to stumble onto something.

Not today, from the looks of it. I'd take it.

My email bleated a message arrival from Bob, and I made a couple of minor corrections to my story and sent it back with a note that I didn't have anything else for the night and I was headed out.

Texting Parker a *ready to go*, I stood and stuffed my laptop into my bag. Richmond's favorite former almost-professional athlete appeared in my doorway and waved me out in front of him.

"You okay?" Parker asked as I unlocked my car doors.

"I was just going to ask you the same thing." I tossed my bag in the back and climbed behind the wheel, fixing him with a what's-up look when he settled into the passenger seat.

"I'm fine." He fiddled with the razor-sharp crease in his khakis. "I think. I am."

I started the car and pointed it toward Carytown, waiting for him to elaborate. No such luck.

"You want food with your drinks?" I asked finally, turning onto West Cary and looking for a parking spot.

"I could eat." He flashed a ghost of his trademark megawatt grin and I patted his arm.

"Have y'all been to the new soul food place? Great food, a good bar, and quiet booths."

He nodded, and I zipped the car into a street spot.

We walked the half-block to the restaurant in silence, evening's chill already hanging over the shaded sidewalk.

Settled in a booth with a Shock Top and a Midori sour on the way from the bar, I leaned forward and covered Parker's hand with mine. "Hey," I said softly. "It'll be okay."

He raised his tousled blond head and met my gaze with hazy green eyes. "Yeah. I know."

"Is it—" I paused and smiled a thank-you at the waiter as he put our drinks down. "Are you and Mel okay?"

Parker downed half his beer in one swallow and thumped the mug down on the tabletop. "Yep."

The waiter held up an order pad.

I asked for chicken-fried steak and mashed potatoes, suddenly glad I'd skipped lunch. Parker got pot roast with greens.

I glanced at his almost-empty mug and smiled at the waiter. "Bread. Lots of it, please."

"With butter." Parker's lips tipped up in a half-smile.

The server nodded, a basket piled high with wedges of perfect cast-iron cooked cornbread appearing moments later. Parker slathered butter on one and wolfed it down, his gulps of beer leveling off to normal swallows.

I opened my mouth to tell him to spit out what was bothering him just as my scanner blared an all-call. Snatching it from my bag, I turned the volume down and poised a pen over my napkin to jot notes.

It fell to the table when the dispatcher started talking.

"Lockdown situation, fifty-eight-hundred Monument Avenue," she said, the tightness in her voice only noticeable because I knew my cops so well. "All units in the vicinity requested for backup. Officers on scene. Proceed with caution—shooter on premises."

I shoved my things back into my bag, grateful I hadn't had more to drink, and raised my eyes to Parker's. "You're coming with, unless you want to walk back to the office."

He stood and threw a handful of twenties on the table, his beer buzz—and whatever invited it—vaporizing. "Fifty-eight-hundred Monument. That's..." He trailed off, his eyes widening when I nodded.

"The hospital." I scribbled a note for the server to give the food to someone who could use a hot meal and ran for the door, Parker on my heels.

9

Actual lead in my Louboutins wouldn't have gotten us near St. Vincent's any faster, though the tangle of emergency vehicles outside made parking and walking up take longer than I would've liked.

"No TV trucks yet," I noted, scanning the street as we stepped onto the hospital grounds.

Parker checked his watch. "They're finishing up the six o'clock now. They'll be here."

I scanned the crowd, my eyes lighting on a curly brown head bobbing along the top of it.

"Detective Landers!" I raised one arm when Chris Landers turned his lanky, rumpled-suit-clad frame toward us.

I grabbed Parker and dragged him behind me. "Landers hasn't had the benefit of your star power," I hissed when he protested. "Maybe meeting a celebrity will make him chatty."

Parker rolled his eyes. "At your service."

Landers met us under a hundred-year-old magnolia that shaded half the circular drive. He nodded absently to Parker and focused on me. "How do you get yourself into these things?"

My eyebrows lifted. "Excuse me?"

Landers shook his head, his eyes on my notebook and pen. "He wants to talk to you."

"Who?" That was Parker, because I was pretty sure I knew who, and was busy trying to avoid vomiting on my new heels.

Landers kept his eyes on me. "The shooter. White male, late thirties, average build. One rifle reported. He wants to talk to you. You and Charlie Lewis. That's all he's asked for."

Talk to me. I swallowed the nausea and tried to focus.

Hot damn—the headline fairy had a funny way of making up for Aaron's silence, but I'd take it.

Nodding to Landers, I pulled out a notebook. "Where's the phone? Is Charlie here yet?"

"Haven't seen her." Landers laid a light hand on my back and pointed me to the tricked-out RV the SWAT team used as a remote command center. I'd only seen the thing a handful of times, and I'd never been inside. Parker stayed close behind me.

"Don't promise him anything," Landers coached. "Do ask short questions that will help us find out what he wants." He opened the door to the RV, turning to look at me. "And whatever you do, don't piss him off."

My stomach tightened as the responsibility settled around me. I smiled, hoping the nerves didn't show, and put one foot on the bottom step. "I have a decent set of interview skills, Detective. And I want to help." I climbed into the RV, raising my voice over the beeps and chatter of various radios.

"Don't you ever go home?" Aaron's voice came from behind me and I grinned and spun on one heel.

"About as often as you do. Your wife remember what you look like?"

Aaron laughed. "She did get me mixed up with the cable guy last Thursday." He turned back to the console in front of him, lit with a glow from the flatscreens on the wall. SWAT gear-clad cops with long rifles filled five of the screens, the others occupied by the hospital's four entrances.

"Fast work," I said, nodding to the video feed. "You heard from anyone inside?"

"A nurse on the fifth floor called 911 with a report of a gun in the ICU. The facility has been locked down, but we're not sure how or who did it."

"Security?"

"Probably. But they're not armed with anything except pepper spray, and we haven't been able to get through to them. Or anyone else."

A thousand news clips played in my head on fast forward. "Dead?"

"Don't know. No reports of shots fired. But the phones just ring. Dispatch kept that nurse on for six and a half minutes, talked to the shooter for about thirty seconds, and he hung up."

"Cell phones?"

"Dead zone. They have signal blockers in the patient areas." Landers slumped into a small black chair that was bolted into the floor. "Something about making sure the heart monitors work properly. And the brass is going nuts because the place is standing-room only thanks to this damned flu thing. This guy has a packed house to bargain with."

"Don't they have a protocol for this? I mean, my friend's kids have 'lock-down drills' at school." I shook my head. "Whatever happened to a good old-fashioned tornado?"

"Everyone has protocol for it until it happens to them." Aaron leaned back in his chair and sighed. "You can run drills ten times a day, but when someone walks in with a gun, everything but basic survival instinct goes right out of your head."

I jotted that down. "So what do we know about this guy? He's a media junkie of some sort, it seems, but what else?"

"Not a damned thing," Aaron said, spinning his chair to another bank of monitors on the opposite wall. "We've tapped into the hospital security feeds, but the guy knows where the cameras are, because he's been careful to avoid them."

"So he's there a lot," I said, more to myself than to them. "An employee?"

Aaron shrugged. "Probably?"

"Landers said he wants to talk to me and Charlie."

Aaron sighed, running one hand over his face before he nodded. "He got on with dispatch to say he wouldn't talk to us. Only to you. Something about the public having a right to know."

"Guessing he didn't share what they have a right to know?"

Landers snorted. "Of course not. Where's the fun in that?"

I sucked in a deep breath and squared my shoulders. "You have a call-back number?"

Aaron picked up a phone. "I do. You ready for this?"

"Never know what the day will bring, right? That's why I love this job." I tried for another smile, but from the sympathy on Aaron's face, I wasn't fooling anyone.

He dialed, and I tried to keep my heart from exploding. Aaron's voice was far away: "I have Nichelle Clarke here from the *Telegraph*, just like you asked. Are you ready to talk to her?"

I shut my eyes for two beats and whispered a fast prayer, putting a hand out. I opened them when Aaron didn't give me the phone.

"I'm afraid I can't do that," he said. "She's standing right here—"

His eyes narrowed, his lips disappearing into a thin white line. "No, sir." He shot a sideways look at Landers, who could've been hiding psychic powers the way he rolled his eyes and muttered "Of course."

"Of course what?" I hissed, my eyes flicking back to Aaron as he spoke again.

"Impossible. We'll all be waiting for you to call us back. Just don't do anything rash in the meantime."

He cradled the phone and Parker, who'd been so quiet I'd forgotten he was there, boomed "What now?" from behind me.

Oh. Uh-oh.

"He doesn't want to talk to me on the phone." The words came out in a robotic monotone as my knees went to water, my eyes finding Aaron's.

Parker's long fingers closed around my elbow and I leaned on my friend as Aaron nodded. "Face to face, he says. Wants Charlie to bring a camera in. Seems our guy has a soapbox and he wants an audience." He turned to a young officer with serious brown eyes and a buzzcut who was working another phone. "You get anyone yet, Dawes?"

Dawes shook his head. "They just ring, sir."

I got my feet back under me and nodded an all's well to Parker as Landers slammed his hands down on the console in front of him. "There are almost three thousand people in there, dammit. Blow the delivery door and let's go in."

Aaron's left hand drifted to his temple, his foot bouncing hard enough to shake the chair. "Let's see if he calls back. At least give it a few minutes. Right now we have less chance of injuries if we wait."

Landers shot me a look, and I froze—his single raised brow said more than I needed to know.

Could I?

I coughed the fear out of my throat and turned to Aaron. "Let's talk about this."

He raised one hand. "Absolutely not. I can't send you into an active shooter situation. He was explicit—no cops, you and Charlie come alone."

I nodded. "I got all that."

"It's too dangerous, Nichelle. Too much for us to ask. This isn't what you signed up for when you decided to be Lois Lane."

"She is pretty tough," Landers said. Before Aaron got his mouth open to shush Landers, Parker rounded on him with a roar the shooter probably heard from inside the hospital.

"You are not sending her in there." His flat tone and lack of volume control left no room for a question mark.

Landers tipped his head to one side, unruffled. "Officially? Hell no, I'm not. But everyone in town knows Miss Clarke's reputation for tenacity. Could I really stop her if she was of a mind to get inside?"

Parker stood up straighter, his voice falling lower, and shouldered between me and Landers. "If you're any good at your job, of course you could. But if you were any good at your job, you wouldn't consider offering up my friend as a sacrifice to get some information, would you?"

Landers balked, his shoulders slumping a bit. I shoved Parker to one side and shot him a shut-the-hell-up look from the corner of my eye. "I'm standing right here. And you know damn good and well there's no keeping me out of a story I want into."

"Nichelle, you cannot be serious."

No, I could not. I could not walk into a building to interview a crazy man with a gun. God knew what he wanted with me. Maybe he had a crush on Charlie, but I hadn't been on TV in months, and last time I was, it was with a banged-up face.

Then there was the other hand. The one that made me run on caffeine and Pop-Tarts six days out of seven making sure my copy was the best in town.

"What if I can really help, Parker?" I asked, catching his gaze. "Instead of failing to make people feel better after someone dies, I could stop people from dying. How can I walk away from that?"

"How about because he just said the guy has a gun? He could just want to kill you. He could want high-profile hostages. Maybe he wants to …" He trailed off, a horrified look coming over his face. "I don't want to think about it. You cannot go in there."

Landers sighed. "He's right." He turned to Aaron. "You want to wait?"

"Just for a while."

I planted both feet and reached for a pen. "I'm going inside."

Parker opened his mouth and I raised one hand. "Possible psycho. I heard. I also heard the bit about there being thousands of people locked in that building. He asked to talk to me. I'm the only person who can help right now." I turned to Aaron, who sported wary eyes and a hard line to his mouth. "Put a vest on me and call him back."

"A vest doesn't protect your head, Clarke," Parker said, his tone a mishmash of tension and defeat. "You don't need the story that bad." He glared at everyone in the RV in turn, his eyes coming to rest on Landers. "And you don't need to go do this guy's job for him."

Landers came half out of the chair and I put a hand on his arm. "His heart is in the right place. Find me a vest." I turned back to Parker and tried for a reassuring smile. "I'm always careful. This is more about making a difference than the headline. That's just a nice bonus."

Landers turned back to Aaron. "What d'you say? Whole lot of people in there. You think he'll cave, or do we put kevlar on her and station SWAT at the doors?"

Aaron's foot-bouncing went from shaking the chair to shaking the floor under my feet as he locked his baby blue eyes with my violet ones. "This is a whole other level of dangerous. I might venture to call it stupid, even."

"I've seen stupid before. I prefer to think of this as brave." I didn't blink.

"That's a fine line, sometimes." He didn't either.

Three hours (minutes, in which my heart hammered enough for three hours) of staring later, he shut his eyes. "Find her a vest."

I opened my mouth to reassure everyone (mostly me) that I wouldn't get myself killed, and the door swung wide, a familiar purr coming from outside. "Which detective asked to see me, again?"

Charlie.

Damn.

"Impeccable timing, as always," I said a little too brightly, turning around. "Looks like our lucky day, Charlie. The shooter won't talk to our friends here, but he wants to talk to us."

"Us? As in, you and me?" Her eyes took on an ambitious sheen, and I could practically see thoughts of "Channel Four exclusive report" flashing across her head in neon. She could get it on the air six hours before I could have it on people's doorsteps. "Just point me to the phone."

"No phone. He wants to see you," Landers said. "Active shooter, one rifle, no known shots fired."

Charlie froze. "See me?"

"The two of you."

Ambition vanished, incredulity and fear taking its place. I turned back to Landers while Charlie gaped. "Three. Two..." I murmured.

He raised an eyebrow and I rolled my eyes back toward Charlie, trying and failing to avoid smiling when she found her voice and howled. "One," I whispered as she screeched, "What?"

Landers blinked, then put a finger in his ear and wriggled it around. "I'm standing right here. And I only have the two eardrums, like everyone else."

Charlie ignored him and whirled on me. "Have you lost your mind? How the hell could you be thinking of going in there?"

"I might be able to diffuse it before anyone gets hurt. He wants to talk to me. I talk to people for a living. Why not?"

"Because this dick just said the words 'active shooter,' that's why not."

"No need for name calling," Landers drawled.

"You're a detective, aren't you?" She tossed her hair.

I coughed over a laugh and shook my head. "Now, children." I raised a brow at Charlie. "I'll take that as a no?"

She narrowed her eyes and stomped out the door. Landers didn't look sorry to see her go. "She always so easy to get along with?"

"She has her moments." I turned back to Aaron.

"At least one of you has some sense of self-preservation." He shook his head.

"No takebacks," I said.

"You. Will. Be. Careful." He punctuated each word with a slam of his hand on the console. "I mean it, Nichelle. I've seen you do a lot of shit in the name of a headline, but this guy has to know the chances of him coming out of there alive are fairly low. Maybe Charlie's right."

"Charlie's almost never right." I tried for flip, but the tremor in my voice gave away my frazzled nerves. "At least not when I can help it."

He reached for the phone. I only half-heard the conversation as Landers hauled a kevlar vest out of a bin under the counter. Snatching the thing, I yanked it on and let Landers fasten it up as Aaron replaced the receiver.

Aaron rolled his eyes as Landers pulled the last strap tight.

"What am I looking for?" I squeaked, trying to wriggle a more comfortable posture in my twenty-pound corset.

Aaron handed me a two-way radio. "Keep this on, and scream if you need help. He's going to open the front door. Go up to the fifth floor, and announce yourself loudly. But don't go back into the ICU." The words were stern. "I want you near the windows. Let him come to you."

I glanced at the rooftops of neighboring buildings. There were snipers up there as sure I knew a Manolo from a Louboutin.

"Y'all aren't going to shoot him if he hasn't hurt anyone, are you?"

"We have no way of knowing that," Aaron said. "What we do know is that there are thousands of hostages in that building, and we have to neutralize this situation as quickly as we can."

Shit. I didn't want to get anyone shot, especially without a feel for what was going on.

"I'll be safe," I promised, my voice reflecting more conviction than I felt.

Landers flashed a thumbs-up, and Aaron shot me a dad-like look. "I'm allowing this against my better judgement. And only because you'd probably find a way to sneak in. This way, I get to put a vest on you."

In perfect fairness, I'd snuck into many a crime scene. But a face-off with a gunman and no cops present wasn't exactly on my bucket list, so I couldn't say for sure what I'd have done if the evening had gone differently. Did it matter? I was about to walk into the exclusive of a lifetime. I pulled in a steadying breath and followed Landers out of the trailer and up the sidewalk.

"Don't do anything stupid," he said.

I pulled my cell phone from my pocket and opened a new text message to my editor. *Stop the presses and clear the front. I'm going in to interview the shooter who shut down Saint Vincent's.*

"I generally pride myself on being smart," I said, tucking the phone away and looking up at Landers. "And I have no interest in coming out of here with any more holes than I'm going in with."

* * *

It was so...quiet.

I'm not sure what I expected, but dead, utter, you-could-hear-a-gnat-sneeze silence was pretty far down my list.

I'd been through the doors at St. Vincent's a million times. The hospital has noise. Muzak. Loudspeakers. Phones. People.

Bustle.

Not today.

The front desk was empty, and the lack of sweet old lady smiles from the candy stripers was more ominous than the stillness. Something was definitely wrong here.

I pulled in a deep breath and uprooted my feet from the tile just inside the door, turning to nod at the SWAT captain who'd walked me in and wondering if I was really brave or just really stupid. Some days, it's a toss-up.

Squaring my shoulders, I strode to the elevators and jabbed the "up" button. Of course I was scared. But I'd dump my shoe collection into a storm drain before I'd let on.

The elevator crept upward and I patted the vest, assuring myself every-thing would work out fine. I had a radio to Aaron in my bag, and a mission —get myself, and everyone else, out of the building safely. I was good with people. And Aaron had SWAT on point at every door, ready to blast in at my first gasp. It was fine.

The bell for the fifth floor binged and the doors whispered open, loud in the silence.

Still no people.

I walked past a nurses' station and peeked into a patient room. Rumpled bed, half-eaten dinner on the tray. No patient.

I kept walking, the *click-clack* of my stilettos on the tile echoing off the walls like firecrackers.

The squeak of a door froze my foot in mid-air.

I turned, a single eyeball peering at me through the barest of door openings. It widened, and the door slipped shut again. The sign marked it as the break room.

Hoping the staff had jammed everyone in there, I kept walking.

No blood was a good sign. No gunfire was a better one.

The ICU was at the end of the hallway, the sliding glass doors closed. It took eleven hundred years for me to walk close enough for them to open.

"Who's there?" A man's voice, high and stressed.

And a rifle cocking.

Shit.

I cleared my throat. "Nichelle Clarke, *Richmond Telegraph*."

"Miss Clarke?" He sounded unsure. "You're alone?"

"The police said you wanted to talk to me." I took a teensy step forward. I wanted to see the guy. I didn't want to get shot, though. "You ready to chat?"

Sneakers squeaked across the floor.

I closed my fingers around the mace canister Kyle had given me when I refused to take the handgun class.

Squeak. Squeak. Squeak.

Rifle lax in his hands, the man who'd caused all the uproar appeared in the doorway.

And I let out a huge *whoosh* of air and reached for a pen.

Three inches shorter than me, he was slight, but muscular. Thinning brown hair, glasses, and jeans and t-shirt that had been slept in more than once. And his eyes—round, hazel, and...sad. Not angry. Not crazy.

Anguished.

Desperate.

He wanted something, but it wasn't to shoot me.

"I'm Nichelle." I offered a smile. And a hand.

He nodded and let go of the stock of the gun, keeping his other hand closed around the barrel. "I didn't know what else to do."

"Taking a building full of sick people hostage is pretty far down my list of ways to spend Wednesday night," I said, keeping my tone light.

The ghost of a smile flashed on his unshaven face. "Mine too."

"All evidence to the contrary." My nose picked up a hit of B.O., my eyes skimmed the clothes again, and a puzzle piece clicked in place.

Aaron said he knew the hospital.

"You don't work here, do you?"

He shook his head, his face crumpling. "I can't lose her. They're going to let her die. Money is greater than love after all."

* * *

Oh. My.

LOVE>MONEY.

It took a second to find my voice.

"Are you LCX12?"

He nodded, tears slipping down his face.

I pulled out a notebook and a pen. Eight years of dealing with some of the worst society had to offer had honed my asshole radar to a fine point. This guy was desperate and depressed, but he was no murderer.

And he had a story to tell.

"Help me understand." I poised the pen.

"How?" He shook his head, slumping back against the wall and sliding to the floor, his hands still on the gun. I ran my eyes over the weapon.

The safety was on.

Any lingering doubt about his motive vanished. I studied him. Completely middle of the road, unremarkable thirtysomething dude. Except for the rifle—I'm no expert, but it looked pretty standard, too. Hunter?

Maybe. Still, though. How does Average Joe end up here?

"You've been sending me messages for weeks," I said. "Why?"

"I needed people to listen."

"I'm listening now." I reached into my bag and clicked off the radio. I knew as sure as I knew my shoe size that Charlie had weaseled her way back into the RV, and if I was going toe-to-toe with the gunman, she could find her own lead. Aaron would get over it. Surely he'd heard enough to stand down for the time being. My eyes stayed fixed on the top of the man's bowed head.

"Someone you love is sick." I glanced at his left hand. "Your wife?"

"She has cancer." His shoulders quaked with sobs.

"And she's in the ICU, so it's bad." I didn't bother with the question.

"Stage four ovarian cancer." His voice took on a bitter edge, his head thumping back against the wall. "We've tried everything. I'm drowning in medical bills. We had to sell our house. But she was in remission for ten months. It was worth every penny to give my babies their mother back."

Heat flushed my cheeks and the backs of my eyeballs pricked. I blinked hard, scribbling every word. He stopped talking, and I looked up. He shrank into the wall, clutching the gun like a life preserver and shaking his head as tears dripped from his chin and spattered his threadbare t-shirt.

A vise closed around my heart. I had been there. Vomiting into a plastic trashcan every time I ate because the fear of losing my mother was too much to stomach.

I half-wanted to hug him, but I wasn't suicidal. I nodded instead. "I'm so, so sorry."

"Everyone is sorry. The insurance company people, who won't pay for anything else because we've reached our lifetime maximum. The nurses, who come in and make small talk about the drawings the kids make for her and try to smile at me. And the fucking lying doctors, who tell me she's dying and there's nothing else they can do." His voice took on a hard edge, and he brushed at the tears. "They will stop lying. Or they will pay."

He flipped the safety off and looked over my shoulder. "I just have to find the chickenshit bastards first."

10

"Whoa there, cowboy," I said, raising both hands slowly. "Why would the doctors lie to you about being able to help your wife?"

"They can cure it." His fingers tightened on the gun. "I know they can. They can make her better. But they won't."

I studied his face, the five o'clock last Tuesday shadow and too-wide eyes making me want to run back outside. Or cry. I felt sorry for the guy, but he sounded a little looney.

Not murderer-looney. If he killed anyone it'd be plain old bad luck.

But my gut said I was about to get an earful of a cancer cure conspiracy. Since I'd done a mind-numbing amount of research on such things when my mom was in a cancer ward, I felt suddenly qualified to try to talk him down.

Probably not the smartest (or sanest) idea I've ever had.

"Far be it from me to disagree with the man with the big gun, but a cure for cancer would be the biggest news story in...pretty much ever. I would have heard about it. Trust me." I tried for a smile.

It only made him flip the gun to his shoulder and spin for the door. "No. This is why I need you in here. Because it's time people finally knew the truth."

"What truth is that?"

He did a slow one-eighty and lowered the rifle to his side and his chin to his chest.

"We love stand-up," he said, so softly I had to step forward to hear.

Okay. I waited. He missed five beats before he continued. "I heard a comic do a bit on cancer once. A long time ago, before Amy got sick. 'There's no money in the cure. The money's in the medicine.' That's what he said. And he's right. Think about how many drug companies will lose billions of dollars a year if they cure cancer. This isn't about people. It's about business and money."

His words flowed through my ear to my hand and onto the page. I didn't stop to consider them. Get the story now. Have an opinion later.

"And you think someone in this hospital has this miracle cure you're looking for?"

"If no one on the oncology staff has it, they can get it. The doctor who discovered it is here in Richmond. Half of these guys play golf with him. I hear he's got a killer putt, when he's not refusing to help young mothers see their children grow up."

No.

Way.

"Who's the doctor you're looking for?" I couldn't force my mouth around the words. Three attempts later, they tripped through my lips.

"David Maynard. He used to be the head of oncology at the university hospital. He went to private practice, but he refused to see us. Said he couldn't possibly take a non-trial case. I guess he'll see her now, won't he?"

I shook my head, my dry tongue rasping against the roof of my mouth. "He can't. He's dead."

* * *

My eyes followed his slow-motion crumple all the way to the floor.

I flinched when I heard the rifle hit the tile. It didn't fire, though. I stepped forward, the sight of his body curling into a ball as he repeated a drawn-out refrain of "no," making the tear-pricking return.

"I'm so sorry." Lame, but they were the only words I had.

"She'll die." He didn't look up. "Maynard. Getting Maynard's attention was our last hope. I can't live without her. What am I going to do? My babies—how am I going to tell them their mother's not coming home?"

Sweet cartwheeling Jesus. I didn't want his children to lose their mom any more than I'd wanted to lose my own.

I cleared my throat. "Why do you think Dr. Maynard had something as huge as a cure for cancer that he kept a lid on?" I'd been sure my Twitter stalker was delusional just moments ago, but...Well, Maynard was dead, and the cops did think someone killed him.

A cure for cancer?

Fame. Fortune. Instant spot in the history books for the genius who produces that string of chemicals.

People have killed for less.

"Money. Everything is always about money." He spit the words into the tile. "If I had enough of it, my Amy would be going home with me. We did all the DNA mapping. A whole summer in Houston. But it's not as effective for ovarian cancer as it is for some others. Seventy-five thousand dollars, no insurance accepted. No brainer. I cashed out my 401K and we got on a plane. They gave her some prescriptions and told her she'd be fine. No chemo, even. Just pills.

"But then she started having pain and bleeding again. By the time she told me and we got her in to see a specialist here, it had metastasized to her liver and lungs. Stage four, sorry folks, we can't help you." He sat up. "I spent hours in front of my computer. I applied for every clinical trial there was. Her cancer was too advanced for Maynard's peer group. He told me to try again next time. I don't have a next time. She's dying." His words faded into a wail. "Oh, God, she really is."

In a blink, the entire range of human emotion flashed across his haggard face. Anger was last, twisting his mouth and brow such that he didn't look like the same guy who'd been sobbing half a minute before. He snatched up the rifle and braced it against his shoulder, standing and turning in a slow arc.

"Come out, cowards! Do I have to actually kill someone to get your attention?"

Silence.

He slammed one heel back into the wall as he roared again, swinging the gun wide.

I dove for the tile, not really sure if the scream that sounded so far away came from me or someone else. Two shots split the silence.

Five beats. Ten. My heart slowed to slightly less than verge-of-bursting speed and I raised my head.

"That's not going to help her," I said softly.

"Nothing's going to help her." The words were hollow, his arms going slack as he dropped back to the floor.

I scanned the hallway for any sign of injury.

The room just behind my online friend looked vacant, the two-thirds of the bed I could see from my angle neatly made.

The open doorway across the hall was empty, silence settling back over the floor. I swung my gaze back to the grieving husband.

"I'm so sorry." Still too little. But I had nothing better.

He sobbed. Just once. "Yeah. Me too."

He dropped the rifle. I eyed it for a full two minutes, part of me thinking I should grab it before something stupid could happen, the other part whispering I might be the something stupid if he freaked when I moved for it.

He didn't seem to notice it wasn't in his hands, and he was still babbling.

Curiosity, shoes, and white chocolate are generally my biggest weaknesses—if you don't count my mother. The fleeting mention of a cure, even from a man who might well be a few sandals short of a spring collection, was enough to keep the questions tripping out of my face.

"How can you be sure Dr. Maynard had this magical key?"

He pulled in a hitching breath and dragged the back of one hand across his face. I inched closer, my pen biting into my clenched fingers.

"I saw some messages in a forum about cancer survivors," he said. "Probably five or six months ago? It was late, and I remember sitting up and shaking off half-sleep, thinking I was dreaming. They didn't say anything outright—the group was open to whoever found it. But I'm a communications guy. Pretty good at reading between the lines. I PM'd one of the people in the conversation, and at first she avoided my messages. But I kept trying, telling her about Amy. I finally sent a photo of her with the kids. The first Christmas she was sick, they spent the holiday with her in the hospital. That got me a reply."

"And this person told you to find Maynard?"

"She said he could help us. Really help us. Fix it."

I scribbled.

"How did she know?" I held my breath.

"Because he did it for her."

I jotted the words in my notes by force of habit, not likely to forget them. What the everloving hell was my dead doctor into?

Deep breaths. Someone could have sent this guy on the wildest goose chase in the history of medicine, but I knew down in my bones that it wasn't an impossible story. If Maynard was keeping his discovery a secret, it fit that his patients would guard it too. My mom, her hair coming out in clumps and her frail, chemo-weakened frame, flashed through my thoughts. If it had really come down to the wire for her, I'd have signed a confidentiality agreement in blood for a glimmer of a chance at a cure.

"So you reached out to Maynard."

"I emailed him in the middle of the night and then watched my inbox like a kid looking for Santa Claus."

Wait.

"Where'd you get his email address?"

"From his website." He gave me a look that said maybe I wasn't as smart as he'd thought.

A website that wasn't there anymore.

But it had been as recently as the spring.

"But he wouldn't see you?" That was a sticking point for me, with all the wonderful things so many people said at his retirement party, added to what Jeff the doorman told me. If he was such a compassionate guy, wouldn't he want to help a young mom who had everything in the world to live for? Wouldn't he want to help...everyone?

"I begged. I offered him everything but one of the children. He said he couldn't."

"Why?" It popped out before I could stop it. I wasn't even really asking him so much as asking the universe in general. The why in the story is the heart of what I do, and this one didn't make any sense.

"He sounded sorry. And he told me to try his next trial. But she's not going to make it to the next trial."

Especially not with Maynard on the coroner's table.

His hand ran absently over the stock of the gun, and I started to step backward. Was he a murderer? No. Not in his right mind. But grief-stricken people can do some crazy stuff.

He looked up. "I'm not going to shoot you. Whatever this has done to me, it hasn't made me a monster."

"I didn't really get the feeling you were going to shoot anyone," I said. "I have a pretty good eye for the type. You're not it."

"I wanted to." His voice dropped in tone and volume. "In my blackest, worst minutes, I wanted to think I could make someone else hurt as much as I am. Maybe that would make Maynard see Amy. But the truth is, I'm not that guy. I don't want to be the cause of anyone else feeling like this. I just don't want to feel it anymore. And now there's no way out of it."

He lifted the gun, flipping the barrel back toward his face.

I blinked, my brain refusing to process the scene for a split second. When the reality of it crashed in, thoughts of his children and dying wife followed in almost the same instant.

Oh, hell no.

Not today, dude.

He braced the barrel under his chin and stretched a shaking hand for the trigger, and my foot shot out in a perfect *ap'chagi*, my Louboutin flying off end-over-end toward the wall as the rifle slid across the floor. A four-inch difference in the length of my legs, and I still made it there first. I snatched the thing up and whirled, kicking off my other shoe, and he fell to his knees, spreading his hands in front of him on the floor. One gulped breath issued back as the deepest, most horrifying scream I'd ever heard.

"Why?" he sobbed. "Why us?"

Dear God.

There were, quite literally, no words.

"Let's get you back where you belong and get the cops out of here." I stepped toward him.

"There's nothing for me. Not without her." He was limp as an over-cooked noodle, but I managed to haul him to his feet and still keep my grip on the gun.

"There's your children. They need you." I steered him gently in the direction of the patient rooms. "And right now, your wife needs you."

He nodded, dragging one hand across his face. "My girls. Amy keeps saying I have to be strong for my girls. She's right. She likes to be right."

My eyes flicked to the closed door in front of us. "Your children aren't here?"

He shook his head. "My in-laws have them. Bring them to visit, take them to school. The doctor said we should keep their lives as normal as we can." He turned brim-full eyes on me. "Maynard was the key. I can't believe he's dead. What did we ever do to deserve such awful luck?"

I'd never said the doctor was murdered. The fact that this guy didn't know it was most of what I needed to assure myself he wasn't behind it.

"He didn't just die." I eased away from him, watching to make sure he could stand on his own, then studying his face for a reaction as I spoke. "Someone killed him."

His eyes popped wide. "I would never," he said.

"I believe you."

His eyes fell on the gun, clarity in them for the first time since I'd walked in. "The police...What the hell have I done?"

"Taken thousands of people hostage and discharged a firearm in a public building." Pity and resignation twisted around my words. Jail wouldn't be fun for him.

He nodded and opened Amy's door. "Thank you, Miss Clarke," he said. "I knew you could help us."

I turned toward the elevator, the rifle vibrating thanks to the adrenaline overload that had set my hands to trembling.

Before I could figure out how I was going to keep Landers from locking this guy up on an aggravated assault and weapons charge (I wasn't above begging), another scream almost made me drop the gun.

I turned and spied a nurse standing in the open doorway just across from where I'd talked to the wannabe gunman.

She shrieked once more before she dropped to the tile.

11

I sprinted in bare feet as a doctor and second nurse crept out from under the station desk and scrambled to the doorway.

Their murmurs told me the first nurse had fainted. I peeked into the room, which appeared to be a meds supply center, to see why.

And wished I hadn't. Blonde hair, matted with blood and bits of something I didn't care to identify, a black-red hole above the left eyebrow.

My eyes took in a sharp business suit and gorgeous Prada pumps on autopilot before I turned away, my stomach churning around the cornbread and cocktail that seemed hours upon hours ago.

Clumsy fingers fumbled in my bag for the radio. "Aaron." My voice came out as little more than a rasp. No reply. I shook it, then noticed the lack of the little red LED in the top corner. Could help to turn it on. I clicked the switch and tried again.

"Nichelle! What the hell is going on in there? I have SWAT ready to blow open a door, and a highly agitated federal agent at my elbow who wants to draw and quarter me for letting you go inside."

"Simmer down, Kyle," I said, my voice shaking. "Aaron, I have the gun."

"You what?"

"I have the gun. The guy turned it on himself and I kicked it free and grabbed it."

"Jesus, Nichelle—" That was Kyle.

"Everyone okay?" Aaron.

"I'm fine. But I have a woman up here who is decidedly not."

"And the shooter?"

I froze. That guy didn't do this. Did he? I looked at the rifle, still dangling from my free hand. Maybe it was a better thing than I knew, me having this gun.

"His wife is a patient. Terminal cancer. He's back in with her." I swallowed hard. "Long story. I'll fill you in."

"Coming in now."

"You come out this inst—" Kyle's most commanding ATF agent voice blared from the speaker. I pushed the talk button and cut him off.

"The situation up here has been diffused, Kyle." The adrenaline tremble extended to my voice. "And I'm perfectly capable of taking care of myself."

A tap on my shoulder nearly sent me right out of my skin. I whirled to find the nurse who hadn't fainted, her pink and purple scrubs creased from crouching under the desk.

"Excuse me, miss—are you a police officer?"

I chuckled, which seemed slightly ridiculous, what with the dead body and hostage situation. "I can't do the shoes." I smiled, trying to lighten the mood. "I'm a reporter at the *Telegraph*. But the police are on their way in."

"Poor Mister Ellinger." Her soft soprano broke, her dark blue eyes filling with enough compassion for two hundred Peace Corps volunteers. "He loves his wife so much. We see a lot of heartbreaking things up here, but that's made me cry more than once in the past few weeks."

I nodded, putting a hand on her arm as her eyes brimmed with tears.

She took a hitching breath and continued, "I suppose he finally just snapped. I thought I'd nodded off and was dreaming when he walked off the elevator waving a gun. It took me probably three minutes to hit the alarm and call 911."

"You're the one who made the call?" I asked.

She nodded, one tear slipping off her lashes and trailing mascara down her cheek. "He leveled the gun at me and told me to call the police. That he had something to say and needed them to be here so people would hear it."

I closed my eyes. He needed them to be here so I'd come. I flipped the safety on the gun and laid it down.

"Did he ask you to call anyone else?"

She shook her head, two more tears escaping. "No. He said no screaming, because he wanted Amy to sleep. And he told me to call the police. I pushed the silent alarm so security would lock the building down and did what he said."

My eyes slid toward the meds closet. "And then?"

"I closed the doors to the patient rooms and locked them, and got under the desk like we're supposed to. The only shots were just a few minutes ago."

I nodded, shaking off the adrenaline and rooting in my bag for a notebook and pen.

"Can I get your name?" I asked.

"Alisha. Alisha Royston." She sniffled, wiping at her face and smearing mascara all over half of it.

"Do you know this woman?"

"Her name is Stephanie. Stephanie Whitmire. She's a marketing rep at Evaris. I just can't believe…"

I nodded, turning when I heard the elevator bing. Kyle rushed off first, Aaron and Landers on his heels.

"Nichelle!" I wasn't even sure which of them was shouting. Or if it was more than one of them.

I raised the hand that held my pen and tried to smile. Kyle broke into a run, clearing the rest of the hallway before I could open my mouth to say, "I'm really fine."

His big hands closed over my head, his eyes scanning me from head to toe while he palpated methodically for signs of injury.

"I appreciate the concern, Kyle," I said, grabbing his wrist when his arms dropped below my waist. "But really. I'm fine."

He crooked one finger under my chin and tipped my face up to his. "You don't appear to be hurt. But you are cracked in the head somewhere. This place have a psych ward? Because I'm admitting you to it. Where the hell did you get the notion it was a good move to walk into an active shooter hostage situation?"

I stepped backward, feeling temper bubble under all the adrenaline rushing through my system. "Remember those messages I showed you the other day?" I tried to control my voice. He was worried, not being a jerk. "This is who was sending them. Landers said he asked to speak to me. Me and Charlie. And she wouldn't come in—"

"But of course, you would," he interrupted. "I'm on my way home after a long day. Thinking, 'I'll have a beer and see if I can find some football on TV.' Then I get a newsbreak on the radio—there's a shooter inside St. Vincent's. The hospital is on lockdown, the staff won't leave the patients and come out. Oh, and the cops reporter from the *Telegraph* just went inside. I thought I was going to have a stroke driving my car. I'm still not sure how the damned thing steered itself over here. Do I look like Knight Rider?"

He paused for a breath and I laid a hand on his arm. I didn't care for him bawling me out, especially in front of my detectives, but I couldn't fault him for caring about me. "Kyle. I'm fine."

He put his hand over mine and squeezed, then pulled me to him and cut off my air supply with a bear hug, dropping his chin to the top of my head. "But what if you weren't? Why is the story that important?"

I wriggled until he relaxed his hold enough to let me breathe, aware that Aaron and Landers were picking up every word. Every touch. They were talking to witnesses, sure, but they were good cops, and good cops are champion busybodies.

"Hey there, pot. I'm kettle," I said, stepping back so I could look at Kyle when he let go of me. "You chase cases into danger every week. I watched you get shot a few months ago going after the bad guys, remember?"

"I'm a cop. You're not. I'm trained to protect myself."

"Until your luck runs out." I wanted to stuff the words back into my throat as soon as they hit the air.

He froze for a split second before he forced a smile. "Let's hope it holds. Generally speaking, my life is pretty charmed."

"I pray for it every night. I didn't mean to be harsh."

"I hate to interrupt." Aaron's tone said he didn't mind one bit. "But I'm going to need a statement, Nichelle. The radio had a mysterious transmission failure."

I spun to face him, my lips already forming the first syllable of "I'm not sure what happened."

"When did he shoot the woman?" He got the question out before I could talk.

"He never went near that doorway," I said. "Not after I came in. He didn't even look that way that I can remember. I don't know for sure what happened to her."

Aaron's brows went up and he checked his watch. "I'm thinking the guy with the rifle had something to do with it." He turned toward Landers, who was bagging the gun as nurse Alisha pointed toward Amy's hospital room.

I grabbed Aaron's arm. "Wait." My mouth filled with cotton, a bunch of it leaking up to my brain. What to say? There was a dead woman ten feet away, and it sure looked like a bullet had done her in. But I felt so sorry for the guy. And I sympathized with him, to an extent. Not his methods, maybe, but his desperation and intent. Fear and grief can make people do some screwy stuff.

Did he kill someone? Maybe. Could Aaron and a jail cell wait 'til his wife was gone? Very possibly, though I hadn't the first clue how. But there was justice, and then there was cruelty. Why take this dying woman's husband from her in her last days? And what about his kids?

So many questions. A few answers this week would be really freaking nice.

"Aaron, please. Hear me out." I gestured toward Landers. "Stop him."

Aaron locked his eyes with mine. "Why?"

"Trust me."

More staring. "I suppose I have good reason to." He heaved a sigh. "Chris!"

Landers' head appeared in my peripheral vision in a flash. Did he run?

"What's up?" he huffed.

Yep, he did.

"I don't know. But Nichelle seems to not want you to go talk to the shooter. So I thought we'd see why. Nobody's going anywhere."

Landers nodded and they both turned to me.

No pressure. "I know you've had a rough evening. And I know your suspect is in that room. I saw him go in there. But...do you have to take him out of there right now?"

"Why would I have the slightest intention of doing anything else?" Landers sounded impatient. And annoyed.

Because the thought of it broke my heart. But Landers wouldn't care unless I could convince him I had a point. "This man is half out of his mind because his wife is lying in that room dying, and if you haul him to jail, you're taking away the person who loves her most when she needs him the most. She didn't do anything. How is that fair?"

Aaron listened without comment, twisting his mouth to one side when I paused to breathe.

Landers tapped a foot and opened his mouth, then snapped it shut again. He and Aaron exchanged a long look.

"If the suspect was sick, we'd put a guard outside his door and leave him here." Aaron's words were quiet. Kyle's eyebrows shot up and Landers rolled his eyes.

My face split into a grin. "Like a modified house arrest? Y'all are over-crowded anyway, with all the drug arrests the last few weeks."

Kyle vanished, reappearing a minute later with my shoes. I took them and smiled a thank you, my eyes staying on Aaron and Landers, who looked for all the world to be having some sort of silent battle of wills.

"Come on, Landers." I slid my feet into my Louboutins. "They have young kids, and she's dying." I paused, fixing him with an I-know-you're-not-an-asshole stare. "Don't do this."

He sighed. "Do you know what happens to us if we walk out of this building without a collar?"

"The press will have a field day," Kyle said.

I tipped my head to one side. "Are you kidding? Who are you talking to?"

They exchanged a look. "Girl Friday," they said in unison.

Ah, Alexa. Yeah, she'd bitch.

"No one reads her blog anyway," I said. "She's still got the same two hundred conspiracy nuts she had in June. She even lost a few followers after she got such a huge piece wrong. I can handle that. And you can, too."

"Never mind the press," Aaron said. "I have pretty thick skin and I'm used to being raked over the media's brand of coals. The problem will come from the brass."

Landers nodded, stepping toward Amy's room.

"Wait!" I grabbed his arm. "They won't be mad."

Two skeptical faces.

"They won't. This is how you're going to pitch it to them. The PD has had more than its share of bad press the past...say...eighteen months."

Kyle snorted and I shushed him.

"I'm offering you the best PR ever on a silver platter. Work the case, get some leads, and leave this guy where he is. Let Charlie harpoon you at eleven, and at eleven-oh-three, the *Telegraph's* website will go live with an exclusive report from inside the hospital that includes several inches on how wonderful you two are. How Richmond cops take that whole 'to protect and serve' thing seriously. I know it's true. Let me splash it across the front page tomorrow."

Kyle's head bobbed an approving nod.

"Trust me, guys." I smiled. "They can't slam you when you look like heroes in the paper."

I held my breath.

Landers didn't move, and Aaron nodded. "Here's what I can do. I can put a uniform outside the door tonight and I can argue for it. But if they say no, we have to come pick him up tomorrow."

"What about her family?" Landers jerked his head toward the storage room door. "There are people somewhere who are going to miss her, too. What are we supposed to tell them?"

"That you're investigating her death and are confident you'll have the culprit in custody soon." A twinge accompanied the words, because he had a point. But it's not like the family wouldn't see justice served. And something was up, even if I couldn't put a finger on exactly what through all the adrenaline haze.

"Look, you don't have him on murder." I raised one hand when Landers made a face. "You don't. Not without the ballistics. You have him on discharging a weapon in public. I'm not asking you to let a criminal walk. Just to be sensitive to a unique situation."

Landers shot a glare at Aaron, then turned to face Kyle. "Is she always this big a pain in the ass?"

"I'd say it's sixty-forty." Kyle grinned and winked at me over Aaron's head. "But she's so darned plucky, it makes it less annoying."

I rolled my eyes, then raised one brow at Aaron. "So? What do you say?"

He tapped his fingers together, staring at Landers, who was still looking in the general direction of the body.

"We don't have proof. We have conjecture," he began.

"Pretty goddamn logical conjecture," Landers snapped.

"Didn't say it wasn't. But here's what I know for sure: Nichelle isn't crazy. And she is fair. She also knows something she's not sharing."

Landers's eyes flashed my way. "Have to get the story first. Just like my dad."

"Same song, different day," I said. "I think I've proven the people are more important to me than the headline, but thanks for that vote of confidence."

"Hell, Chris, who's to say one of us wouldn't do the same in his shoes? I can't imagine, if I'd lost Barbara when my girls were little. I might have gone more than a little crazy, too. We'll put a uniform outside her door to watch him, and keep this floor secured. It can't hurt anything. And the Chief will like the good press."

"How long are you going to keep that up?" Landers didn't look happy, but he wasn't arguing.

Aaron looked at me. "As long as I can. But I'm not sure what that looks like. If they order him picked up, my hands are tied."

Loud and clear.

I smiled. "Thanks, Aaron. I owe you one."

"Eh. We're even. Go on home. And make this worth the ass-chewing I'm about to take, huh?"

"You got it, Detective."

I hoped to hell I could make good on that promise.

12

Charlie's blue eyes narrowed when I stepped outside the police tape, but my gaze skated right past her and her cameraman to Parker, who looked more pissed off than he had when I went inside.

And then past him to Joey, who was leaning against the back of my SUV, tapping his iPhone screen furiously.

Oh. Shit.

My thoughts spun through several scenarios in about three seconds, and none of them ended well for me. What if Kyle got bored talking shop with Aaron and Landers and came downstairs before I could get Joey out of the parking lot? Every time their paths crossed, it intensified the possibility that Kyle would recognize Joey—his files on the Caccione syndicate were extensive, and included a boatload of photos.

And what about Parker? He wasn't a cop, but he was a hell of a good reporter. The less everyone in my life knew about my boyfriend, the better. Which my psychiatrist friend Emily had all sorts of opinions on. Opinions I didn't care to consider.

Parker stepped toward me, already shaking his perfectly tousled blond head. "Glad you're still alive. Do you know how pissed Bob is? He saw us leave together and started ringing my phone about twelve seconds after you went in there."

I winced. "I texted him. I needed him to revise the front and hold space." My editor loved my exclusives, but often hated the ways I went about getting them.

"He even yelled at me."

Damn. I was in for an ass-chewing of my own, killer story or no.

"I'm fine. No one has any call to get bent out of shape. In fact, I'm better than fine. I saved the day and got the exclusive. Not a bad night."

"I think the call to get upset comes from your blatant disregard for your personal safety," Parker said.

"I second that." Joey appeared behind Parker's shoulder. Take your eyes off him for three seconds, and look what happens.

"I did not—" I began.

"Let's not," Joey interrupted. "Every news outlet in town has a report of a gunman in the hospital and one foolish reporter who chased the story into the line of fire."

"I was careful." I patted the vest, keeping my tone soft. He was worried, not looking to pick a fight.

"You could have been more careful," Parker said, curious emerald eyes on Joey.

I ignored the pointed introduce-me glance and kept my attention on my new beau. Who looked downright furious to anyone who knew him well. Parker probably thought he was mildly annoyed.

"The story is believable to anyone who's met you, even without the corroboration." Joey kept his eyes locked on mine, his voice tighter than his tailored vest.

"Am I hurt?" I kept my face and tone bright, unstrapping the vest and reaching for his hand.

Returning the pressure on my fingers, he sighed. "Don't appear to be. But one of these days that luck will run out."

"I've learned my way around a dangerous situation." I pulled the vest off, handing it to a patrolman who rushed by on his way to help keep a mob of shouting family members from charging the doors.

"It's the habit of jumping into the deep end that bothers me." He smiled with that one and I returned it, squeezing his hand again. "You could stop that anytime."

"Hear, hear." Parker ran a hand through his hair. "The ATF guy was furious. Tried for a half-hour to get in there after you. The cops got all out the ass about him bigfooting their territory. They argued jurisdiction until you called the all-clear, and White told them to shut up and took him inside."

Joey flinched on "ATF guy" and looked more than a little hurt by the time Parker stopped talking.

Oy.

"He heard it on the radio on his way home," I said.

"And he's still stuck on you." The tightness was back, Joey's eyes roaming the crowd. "Enough to come running."

I linked my fingers with his and tried to pull his eyes back to mine. "I have no idea what Kyle is stuck on. He's an old friend. But he is just my friend."

Parker coughed out a nervous laugh and leaned close to me. "Why do I have a feeling I'm chewing on my toes, here?"

I smiled. "Because you're smart. I hope they're not too sweaty. Kyle is a sore subject right now." Which I didn't completely follow. I chose Joey. I wasn't sure of much else about our relationship, but I didn't want to be without him, and I didn't want to be with anyone else.

Parker nodded a we're-not-through-with-this and smiled, pulling me into a hug. "I'm glad you're okay, Clarke," he said, the unease I'd been worried over as we left the office nowhere to be found. "I'm going to catch a ride back to the office."

"We'll talk tomorrow?" I asked. "Sorry we never got around to it."

He nodded. "Whenever you have time."

"Sure. Sorry if I worried you."

He glanced between me and Joey. "I'm suddenly glad Mel covers the council. No guns."

I nodded. He waved and moved to the knot of reporters, catching Dan Kessler from WRVA, who was headed back to his van.

"Why must you continue to take these chances?" Joey put his hands on my shoulders.

I settled mine on his waist, a soft smile playing around my lips. "Stubborn. It's a genetic flaw. Ask my mother."

"I'd love to." His voice dropped and turned serious. My heart stuttered. Something told me there was a double meaning in those words, but I couldn't stop focusing on the story (stories? There were at least three intersecting at the moment, if my math wasn't off. And it could very possibly be. Numbers aren't my strong suit.) for long enough to consider the implications.

Dead people and research now. Romance later.

Story of my life.

I glanced around and locked eyes with Charlie. My gaze meeting hers was all it took to bring her running in my direction. I started to make a break for the car, then felt guilty and paused. Before she could cross the lawn to the driveway, though, the doors behind me opened and Aaron and Landers walked out. Followed by Kyle. I met his eyes and saw a flash of something I couldn't identify when they landed on Joey. He made it two steps toward us before the press corps surrounded them, everyone screaming questions over each other. I grabbed Joey's hand and strode to my car before Aaron could get "one at a time, folks" out of his mouth.

"You want me to follow you?" Joey asked as he opened the driver's door for me and gestured to his sleek black Lincoln, parked across the street.

I brushed my lips across his. "I'd love it. I have to file some copy with Bob, but I can do that from the car. I want food, and to hear your thoughts on this. But then I probably should work."

He pinched his lips together. "Story of our life."

Our. My stomach jumped at the tiny word, and I shook it off.

Focus, Nichelle.

I smiled. "Burgers okay with you?"

"Following you, baby."

I pulled my brain back from the "relationship term overload" cliff and climbed into the car. "Great."

I parked at the restaurant before I stopped grinning.

Pulling out my laptop, I turned on my cell phone hotspot and opened an email to Bob. I laid my notes on the console, but I only glanced at them a couple of times—not the sort of experience one is likely to forget, really.

. . .

Richmond Police diffused a hostage situation at St. Vincent's Medical Center Wednesday evening, clearing the scene and returning the hospital to order while protecting thousands of patients and staff members.

One woman was killed during the incident, though it wasn't immediately clear to witnesses exactly how that happened.

I clicked over to Facebook and searched for Stephanie Whitmire. She was twenty-seven. Single, no kids, GMU grad working in marketing. Good enough. I clicked back to the story and added a few lines, plus a bit about the body discovery. Heaping more praise on the PD, I threw in a note about disarming the gunman before I read back through it and clicked "send."

Anyone who wanted details would have to quote my story, which always burned Charlie right the hell up. And should make Andrews leave Bob alone for at least a couple of days.

That put an extra bounce in my step as I shut off the computer and stepped out of the car to go inside. Joey leaning against the front doorframe and the smell from the grill held promises of a fantastic evening.

* * *

Joey settled into the age-marked walnut booth across from me, his tailored Armani as out of place as Birkenstocks at a runway show.

"I take it this place doesn't have an extensive wine list?" He winked.

"If there's ever been a bottle of wine in this building, it found its way here on accident." I laughed. "But they have great iced tea, and the best burgers and fries in town."

"You do know good food," he said.

I smiled at the waitress, her cropped red curls bouncing as she listed the specials.

"A taco burger?" I interrupted.

"Taco seasoning, hot sauce, tomatoes, cheddar, lettuce, and spicy mayo," she said.

"I think I have to try this. A burger that tastes like Mexican food can't be bad."

I went for the spicy fries, too, and a sweet iced tea. She turned to Joey, her eyes widening a little when she looked at him closely. Tell me about it, sister. Three months of something resembling a real relationship, and I still paused to admire his perfection every five minutes.

"And what can I do for you?" Her voice dropped a full octave when her eyes zeroed in on the third finger of his left hand. I cleared my throat. She didn't appear to notice. To his credit, neither did Joey.

"I'll have what she's having," he said.

"Brave," I said.

"There are scarier things in life than food," he said.

She jotted it down and walked away, a sashay in her step that wasn't there before.

"Do you ever go anywhere without getting hit on?" I asked.

"What, her? She was nice, but I wouldn't call that flirting."

"She stared at you like a ten-ounce sirloin she'd like to smear some butter on." I laughed.

"Nice of you to notice."

"I don't really care." I laced my fingers with his, electricity skating up my arms when our hands touched. "But you'd have to be blind or slow to not see it. I notice."

"So do I," he said. "Miller isn't going away, is he?"

"He's been my friend for almost fifteen years. So I'm going with no."

"He wants more than friendship."

"Lucky for you, I do not."

Joey rolled his eyes and I sighed. "Let's talk about something more fun, shall we? Like whatever it is you're trying to get yourself killed over this week?"

"Come on. It's been at least a couple months since the last time I tried to get myself killed."

"Keep the streak going past this week." His eyes sparkled, softening the flat tone.

"You got it. This is weird, but not run-for-your-life-Nichelle weird."

"You never see the run for your life part 'til it's too late."

"Do you want to hear this, or not?"

"Fire away."

"Pun intended?"

"Absolutely."

I told him the whole story, glossing over the more heart-pounding bits, finishing with my Twitter DMs and the cancer cure theory.

He shook his head. "No wonder you're so amped up. The more tangled a story gets, the more determined you always are to unravel it."

"It's an illness," I said. "This whole thing is like a maze of rabbit holes. But I'll find the pot of gold at the end."

"You're mixing metaphors."

"I'm exhausted and still riding the adrenaline high. I trust you to keep up."

"Doing my best." He smiled.

"I have a friend checking on the computer stuff."

"What else do you know about the victim?"

"Not much. He might have been seeing our old society editor, Mary Social Climber. Married a corporate bigshot who died last year."

Joey shook his head. "Is this Richmond, or Mayberry?"

"Small world, right? I'm trying to figure out how to dig up more about her without tipping my hand."

He sighed, and the whole story flew slap out of my head when he met my gaze and traced a light finger over my knuckles. "Be. Careful."

I nodded, my lips refusing to work.

Our food appeared in front of us, and I heard the waitress say "let me know if I can get you anything else" from ten miles away. I couldn't tear my eyes from Joey's until he let go of my hand, growling stomach be damned.

He smiled and picked up a fry, nodding approval when he popped it into his mouth. I hefted my burger, my thoughts returning to Amy the dying cancer patient, and pinging from there to my mom. The clinical trial that saved her was the worst four months of my life. And try as I might, I couldn't shake the idea that Maynard was onto something that might give Tom Ellinger the same miracle. Might save my mom if she got sick again. If the past couple days was any indication, following this hunch wouldn't be easy—but I could safely say I'd never wanted an answer more.

I bit into the burger, every bit as tasty as it sounded. My mom had been so sick. She couldn't eat, needing to be fed through tubes and needles.

Couldn't eat.

Because of the trial drugs.

Clinical trial. That I'd found on the NIH website.

Because they catalog drug trials.

I sat up straight and almost dropped my burger to the sawdust-covered floor.

"What?" Joey paused mid-chew and covered his mouth with one hand.

"I know where to look. The guy said he was trying to get his wife into a trial with Maynard. I know I can find information on the trial and its success rate online."

Joey's lips tipped up in a resigned smile. "Do I get to finish my burger?"

"Don't dawdle. We'll come back when you can fully appreciate the food and there are no dead people. Promise."

"The day we get to have a date with no dead people, I'll wear a Carmen Miranda costume in a parade down Main Street."

I snorted iced tea at the mental picture, motioning for him to eat.

Fingers itching for a keyboard, I wolfed down three-quarters of my food in five minutes. Finally. A lead. What was Maynard up to? And did it get him killed?

13

Joey followed me home and walked me to the door, peeking inside uncertainly when I opened it and watched Darcy dart for the lawn to pee.

"Should I stay?"

"You're always welcome. I'm going to be buried in research for a while, but you can hang out if you want."

"How long?"

"Until I find what I'm looking for. Fifteen minutes? An hour? Three hours?" I shrugged. "Some days, I wish I had a job that shut off at five."

"I wouldn't know you if you did." He brushed his fingertips over my cheekbone and chills rippled across my skin. "And you wouldn't be happy. Or nearly as interesting."

"But it would be less dangerous."

"And less fun. Less you."

I nodded. I'd considered PR or advertising at intervals for five years. No dead people, no grieving family members. More money. Fewer hours.

Less ability to do good in the world. Less exciting.

I couldn't do it. I loved not knowing what the day would bring when I walked into the newsroom.

I smiled up at Joey, glad at least one thing was sailing smoothly in my typhoon of a week. "Stay," I whispered. "I have to turn off the computer at some point."

"You're sexy when you're chasing a story, you know that? Just stop trying to get yourself killed, and we're all set."

"You, too." I grabbed his tie and pulled him inside, kissing him quiet.

His arms went around me and he swept his tongue between my lips, then softened the kiss and lifted his head. "Even with all the complications, you are the best thing that's happened to me in a long time." It was barely above a rough whisper, but I heard every word. My heart stuttered, then melted.

I laid my head on his shoulder. "You. Too."

He squeezed, then let go and swatted my backside playfully. "Go on. I know your mind is half on your murder victims."

"Not half. Maybe a quarter." I smiled an apology. "But that doesn't mean I'm not enjoying every second of this."

"Crack the case. Then I'll have your full attention. I promise I'll need it tonight."

Damn.

I closed my eyes and shook my head. "Mean. You are a mean man."

"Let's see if you're still singing that tune in the morning." He flashed a wicked grin and my insides liquefied.

I kicked my Louboutins into a corner and ran for the kitchen table, opening my laptop before I sat down. Internet, don't fail me now.

I heard Joey talking to Darcy in the living room, and my pulse sped. I clicked the browser open and tried to focus. Maynard. Desperate grieving husband.

Answers.

I typed the web address for the National Institutes of Health and tapped a finger on the edge of the keyboard as the page loaded.

The whole thing looked different than when I'd stared bleary-eyed at a screen, looking for hope for my mom almost seven years before. I clicked through nine pages before I found where to search the clinical trials.

I typed Maynard's name into the box and held my breath.

Three hundred seventy-nine results.

Holy Manolos.

While I wasn't prepared to believe my depressed shooter just yet, I was more than thrilled to have found something—anything—on Maynard.

Until I started scrolling.

All the trials were dated from more than nine years ago.

Every. Single. One.

I clicked back to the search bar. Could he have listed it under another name? His clinic, maybe?

Not sure I'd say likely. But thanks to the magical disappearance of everything else about the guy, I couldn't search for the clinic name. Because I didn't know it.

Dammit.

How else would they sort the results? I clicked a random trial profile.

Drug, developer, doctors, protocol, timeframe, city, hospital.

Bingo.

I typed "Richmond" into the search field and narrowed the results to the current calendar year.

Thirty trials. Thank God. I wasn't losing it.

I thought. Until I scrolled down.

Maynard's name wasn't there.

I tried the University hospital. Same result.

"For the love of God!" I shoved the computer away, stomping my foot and turning for the wine rack.

"Trouble, baby?" Joey was leaning against the doorjamb when I turned back with a bottle, a corkscrew, and a glass.

"It's not there. Who the hell was this guy and what was he into? He's done a bazillion clinical trials in the past two decades, but not one in the past year, no matter how I search."

"Why are you so convinced he did?" Joey took the glass I handed him and sipped the summer red.

"Because the guy said. Ellinger, the husband. He said he tried to get his wife in and Maynard said she didn't fit the peer group."

"And you trust him because?" Joey's eyebrows went up.

"Why would he lie? He's likely going to prison for what he did today, even if he didn't kill that woman, and leaving his daughters with no parents at all. If he didn't truly believe Maynard could help him, why the hell would he do that?"

Joey nodded slowly. "Good point."

"But I know my way around drug trials. The one I found on this very website," I sat down and gulped my wine, waving toward my laptop screen, "saved my mom. If he was running a trial, it should be here."

Joey tapped a finger on the stem of his glass. "Should it?"

"Huh?"

"It seems the first question is just that: should it be there? Is it required that they report them, or do they just do it so they can have the findings published and maybe find participants?"

Another gulp. "Excellent question. I don't know, really. I assumed."

He walked toward me and laid both hands on my shoulders, massaging gently. "Tense much?"

I nodded and let my chin drop to my chest. "That feels..."

His hands shifted slightly and I felt his breath, and then his lips, on my neck. "Not nearly as good as you will in a little while."

I shivered, then smiled. "You don't say."

He dropped a kiss on the nape of my neck and patted my shoulder. "Get your work done."

"Nothing like an extra dollop of motivation." I picked up my cell phone and smiled at him. "Let me make a couple of calls."

He retreated to the living room and I stared at my phone. I didn't want to ask. I didn't want to get yelled at. But I also couldn't continue to ignore a source that was literally at my fingertips with so much hanging in the balance.

I clicked the speed dial and steeled myself.

"Just exactly what part of 'don't get yourself killed' is unclear to you?" Bob barked in place of hello.

"But I didn't, Chief," I chirped. "Right as rain, and I got the exclusive to boot." I couldn't have him mad at me and depressed. The guilt would last for days.

"You went into a building with a shooter who had taken people hostage. I'm not sure who's crazier: the gunman or my favorite reporter. Dammit, Nichelle."

Yep. Still mad. I softened my voice. "You know what this is like, Bob. I had a chance to help. To get in there before it turned into a massacre. How could I say no to that?"

He sighed. "I know." The edge faded. "But it doesn't make me worry any less."

"I appreciate it. Truly. But I'm good."

"Your piece was outstanding." There was more than a tinge of pride in the words.

"Thank you." I paused. "Hey, listen, I need to ask you something. I'm kind of afraid to ask, and I'm so sorry to bring it up, but what can you tell me about David Maynard and his research?"

Silence, followed by a shaky breath. "Why do you need to know?"

"Something the shooter said." I tapped a finger on the table. "I'm not going with it until I have it dead to rights, but the guy was in there—all this happened because he wanted Maynard to treat his wife. He's convinced the doc had discovered a cure, Bob."

I could practically see the hand go to his temple. "Jesus."

"I know how crazy it sounds. But I'm going to chase it down, because..." I swallowed hard, fear sticking the words in my throat. Because of my mom. What if she needed it?

"I know," he said softly.

I coughed. "So what was special about Maynard when he treated Grace?"

Heavy sigh. "He was brilliant. And he was a good man. Everyone we knew said if anyone could save her, David could. By the time she was diagnosed, it had spread to four different places." He paused, and my eyes filled. Sorrow dripped from the speaker. "Never did like going to the doctor, my Grace. She blew it off until she started having fainting spells."

Oh, hell. It was in her brain? I didn't want to say it out loud, but damn.

"David said it would be risky, but he'd do his best to put it into remission. And for a while, he did. The day he told us her tumor was shrinking was one of the happiest of my life."

I felt a but coming. Of the worst variety.

"But then it came back, and it was just everywhere. It spread faster than they could find it. Two months, and she was just..." He took a hitching breath. "She was just gone."

"I'm so sorry." My brain clicked through what he'd said.

Fact: Maynard couldn't cure Grace Jeffers.

Also a fact: it was years ago, and he managed to beat back a brain tumor other doctors said would be fatal and give Bob and Grace extra time. Was he on the verge of discovering something Earth-shaking that long ago?

It certainly sounded that way.

"Do you remember anything about the treatment protocol he used?" I asked gently.

"Not really. Highly experimental, he said. Something about a virus." He sounded drained.

I scribbled *VIRUS?* in my notes. It was a starting point, anyway.

"Thanks, Chief. I'm so sorry." He couldn't tell me anything else, and no matter how much I want the story, people always come first.

He cleared his throat. "It's okay. Did I help?"

"Always." I wished him a good night and clicked off the call, tapping my computer screen back to life. All those trials.

Wait.

The NIH would definitely show up in search results, and Maynard's name was all over this stuff.

I snatched the phone up again and opened a text to Chad.

This just keeps getting stranger. There are trials with his name on them all over the NIH site. But a search returns nothing. How is that possible?

I put the phone down and opened the RAU Med School page. A search of their site returned three hits on professor emeritus Dr. David Maynard. One story on a plaque unveiling in the medical school lobby, one bio page, and one farewell letter written by the dean. Since I couldn't interview people who knew him on account of no one knowing he was dead yet, I bookmarked the bio. Having his backstory ready to go when Aaron released his name would be handy.

My phone bleeped a text arrival. Chad. *This is pissing me off, Nichelle.*

Join the club. Any ideas?

Bing. *There are about a half-dozen ways I can think of to pull something like this off, and I'm sure I'm not thinking of all of them. I asked a couple of friends for help. The only thing I can tell you right now is whoever did this is a smart SOB. Search engines are supremely difficult to hack. The nerdiest of computer nerds run the damned things.*

I stared at the words. *So how many people can do something like that?*

Bing. *In the U.S.? A small handful, and most of them are in one of the big political dissension groups. I have to figure out what was done before I can get who did it. But I will.*

Thanks, Chad. I owe you. Hug Jenna for me.

Bing. *You bet. She says to tell you don't get shot.*

Deal.

I dropped the phone back to the table and scribbled a three-mile list of questions for the morning. First up: a call to the NIH offices to get the hows and whos of drug trial registration. I shut the computer and stood, wandering to the living room. Joey leaned over the coffee table, looking for a place to fit a puzzle piece. I cleared my throat from the doorway and he smiled.

"All done?"

"No. But I hit a stopping place for this evening."

He crossed the room and pulled me to him, his kiss chasing the story from my thoughts as my hands wandered up over his shoulders, pushing his jacket back.

"Have I said how glad I am that you didn't get shot?" He turned and walked backwards down the hall, pulling me along as he kissed my neck.

"I thought it was implied," I whispered as we crossed the bedroom threshold.

"I suppose it's more show than tell." He eased me back onto the pillows.

"Show me."

He did.

* * *

Daylight slanted through the windows way too early and way too late at the same time. I blinked, stretching my legs and smiling when Joey stirred next to me.

"Good morning, beautiful." He cleared his throat. "Sleep well?"

"Like a baby."

"Me too."

I trailed my fingers across his chest, looking at the ruby red of the Japanese maple in my flower bed through the roman shades.

In the sun.

In October.

"Shit!" I bolted up and grabbed for my cell phone, but it wasn't on the night table. Bedtime had been disorganized the night before—enough that I worried Darcy might have eaten my gorgeous new Louboutins.

"What?" Joey folded one arm behind his head, looking mildly amused as I leapt from the bed and ran for my closet.

"The sun is up. The sun doesn't come up until ridiculously late this time of year. What time is it? I have work to do." I pulled on cream linen pants and buttoned them, then grabbed a silk tank and a grey sweater. "Bob's going to kill me."

"In general, I think he'd have to get in line."

"Doesn't mean he wouldn't push his way to the front. He's used to being first. He's been the boss since forever." I crammed my feet into a pair of charcoal and cream leather Kate Spade ankle boots, then paused.

Wait.

Since his old boss left.

What did Larry say? San Francisco.

I'd bet that guy's wife knew a fair bit about Mrs. Eason. A smart woman with an internet connection can dig up enough to write a biography on a husband's paramour, and I wanted intel on our former society maven.

I dropped a kiss on Joey's head and told him to make himself at home, then ran to scrub my face, grab a coffee, and fly out the door. My eyes lit on the clock when I started the car. Seven forty-five. Dammit.

I kept a heavy foot on the gas the whole way to the office, thankful the Fan (the historic part of Richmond named for the way it spreads from the city center like the lace and silk confections that served as the old south equivalent of Louis Vuitton handbags) isn't far from downtown.

My backside touched my customary orange velour-covered armchair just as Bob nodded to Spence to close the door.

"Hell of a story this morning, Nichelle," Eunice said. I beamed. Eunice was a fantastic writer. And a former hot zone war correspondent. Any praise was high praise from her.

Bob nodded. "You kicked the crap out of everyone else in town. Not that I approve of your method," he shot me a warning glare, "but the story had a great human aspect nobody else even touched on. I didn't sleep five minutes last night, thinking on this. I want a series. What are the chances you'll be able to get White to let you talk to this guy again?"

What? I was so ready for Bob to be depressed after my call the night before, his obvious excitement was downright unsettling.

I furrowed my brow and shook my head.

"I'm afraid I haven't had enough caffeine to follow that yet," I said. "I'm sure Aaron won't care how much I talk to the guy, if the guy will talk to me."

"Didn't he ask to talk to you yesterday?"

"Yeah, how'd that all come about?" That was Eunice, who leaned forward, laser-focused on my reply. All she needed was popcorn.

"He wanted to tell me something." I chose words carefully. "But I'm not sure that's still the case today."

"You saved him from suicide and kept him out of jail," Bob said, waving a dismissive hand when I opened my mouth to object. "Don't think I don't know you traded the cops that advertorial chunk about how wonderful they are for leaving that guy with his wife. I've been around this track a few times, and I know you, kiddo. He'll talk to you."

"What am I talking to him about?" I blinked. "You skipped that part."

"Right. I want a series. Inside the health care crisis. What people will do for those they love. This is great human interest stuff, wrapped up in a crime story."

"You know this guy might be a murderer." I flinched at the memory of the woman lying in the pool of blood and gore on the floor of the closet. "You sure you want to use him for a story like that?"

"That is exactly why it'll sell papers. What's more gripping than a murderer your average Joe reader can identify with? What if he did kill that woman? Was it an accident, or something more calculated? Who was she? The quotes you got from the nurse are fantastic. Nice guy. Devoted family man. Who snapped. This is it, Nichelle. Your chance to do something bigger. Something transformative. To really get inside this huge issue." His eyes drifted to the Pulitzer on his wall, the coveted community service medal for a series he did on racism in the mid-eighties. My mouth suddenly rivaled the Sahara for lack of humidity. I grabbed my coffee and gulped.

"You're ready." Bob leveled a serious gaze at me, his bushy white brows drawing down over his eyes. Everyone else in the room disappeared.

"Am I?" My stomach hung somewhere around my knees. He was talking about the kind of story I'd always dreamed of.

"You'll kill it. No pun intended. Everyone in Richmond will be asking their best friend, their neighbors, their kid's teachers: how far would you go for love? What would it take to push any of us to that breaking point?" He sat back in the chair and steepled his fingers under his chin, a confident grin spreading across his face. "This is going to be great."

"I'll call Aaron as soon as I walk out of here." I met Bob's eyes and tried to match his smile, because I knew what he wasn't saying.

If I could hit this, it'd keep Andrews off Bob's case for good.

No pressure.

14

Aaron didn't answer his desk phone. Or his cell.

I left messages on both, then looked up a number for the NIH and dialed. For a day that started with oversleeping, it was shaping up. And there was the whole sexy boyfriend bonus.

I gave the receptionist my name and told her I needed to talk to someone about registration of clinical trials.

"Are you a doctor?" she asked.

No. But I didn't want the media relations people. The communications industry is a very six degrees of Kevin Bacon world, and I wanted this trail hidden from everyone else. Especially with the unsearchable online thing making Maynard hard to research.

That whole situation was plain old creepy. Like Marty McFly's vanishing family photo for the twenty-first century. Shudder. I jotted a note to call Chad after lunch.

"I don't need to register a new trial. I just have some questions about the requirements." Every word true.

And it worked. "Sure thing. Hold please."

Next up was a woman who didn't sound old enough to be answering anyone's phone, let alone a government health organization's, but her answer spiel said she worked in the clinical research division and her name was Emma.

"Good morning, Emma. I'm hoping you can clarify a few things for me." I left my name and occupation off.

"I'll sure give it my best shot." Her voice was high and sweet. Seriously, was she twelve?

"I'm wondering about the requirements for registration of drug trials," I said brightly, adding an edge of authority to my tone. "Specifically, if a private practice is running one, does it have to be registered?"

"Any trial of medicine or equipment used on human subjects must be registered within twenty-one days of the first administration of treatment. The only exceptions are phase one drug trials or studies designed to discover something other than a medical outcome." She'd obviously quoted that line more than a few times.

I tapped my pen on my notebook. And Maynard had registered hundreds of the damned things. So where was the new one?

Curiouser, indeed.

I looked over the words I'd just scribbled. "What if you're not testing it for approval?" I asked, trying for nonchalant.

I'm a lousy actress.

"Why would you test a drug on people if you're not trying to prove it works?" The suspicious tone aged her voice considerably.

"Just hypothetically," I said.

"We don't get much in the way of hypotheticals, missy," she said, and my mental picture morphed from middle schooler to feisty grandma. "Testing and approving new medications is serious business, and we treat it accordingly."

"Of course you do," I said hastily, wondering if Maynard was keeping secrets, or if their computers had been hacked. "As well you should. I'm just trying to make sure I understand fully. I'm pretty new to this."

She chuckled. "I remember when I was new. It's been a while."

"Not from the sound of your voice."

"You should've heard me when I was twenty," she said. "My first year here, people thought there was a child playing with the phones. It was a bear getting to know everyone who calls regularly."

I smiled. Three and a half minutes on the phone, and I liked her. Her tone warmed and I decided the feeling was mutual when she said, "Tell me what you want to know."

"Is there ever any reason for a doctor to fail to register a trial?" I asked.

"Not in my time here. Which has covered everything from swine flu to the chickenpox vaccine. To say nothing of Viagra. Good Lord, what a year that was. They had a hundred times more applicants than any reasonable trial would hold."

I giggled, jotting that down just because, and considered her words. Maynard had driven this block a few times. Two possibilities, then: someone had erased just his recent work from the NIH database, or he wanted to keep his secret more than he wanted to obey the law.

"Your computers haven't been hacked recently, have they?" I asked in my best innocently-wondering voice.

I could almost hear her brow furrow. "Not that I'm aware. Why do you want to know? And who did you say you were with?"

"Just trying to learn as much as I can," I said breezily.

"You still didn't say who you're with," she said.

Damn. "Thanks so much for your help, Miss Emma. Have a lovely day." I laid the phone in its cradle and tapped a fingernail on the handset, turning toward my computer. This internet thing was becoming a stickier wicket with every new clue.

The greatest hack in history, Chad said. Time to brush up on my information technology skills.

* * *

I read for an hour about how impossible it is to remove anything from search results. Celebrities and public figures can plead a case to have good results show up ahead of bad ones, and in other parts of the world, the government can dictate what's there and what's not (searching Tiananmen Square Massacre in China, for instance, returns zero results). But things don't work that way in the land of the free. Or they're not supposed to, anyway. Which is likely why Chad was so frustrated.

Resisting the urge to call him just yet, I pocketed my cell phone and strode to Parker's office. His door was open, his chair facing the computer screen on the opposite wall. I tapped lightly, reluctant to break his concentration if he was in a groove.

He spun the chair to face me and smiled. "Morning. Glad you're still breathing."

I rolled my eyes. "Back at you." I stepped inside and leaned on the wall. "Thanks again for letting me drag you along yesterday. Sorry we didn't get to talk."

He waved a dismissive hand. "Hostages take priority."

"So what's up? You seem less bothered this morning."

He grinned. "I'm not bothered at all. I—"

"You'll never guess which Councilman voted against the school funding tax hike!" Mel barreled around the corner, her breathless tone telling me she'd sprinted from the elevators. Maybe from City Hall.

"Morning," I said.

"Hey, Nicey." She stopped short and smiled. "Glad you didn't get shot last night."

"Me, too."

"Am I interrupting?" She shot a glance from me to Parker and he shook his head.

"Just shooting the breeze. I missed you last night." He waved to the chair across from his desk. "Come tell me about the meeting."

She crossed to the desk and sat, and I raised my eyebrows at him. "Rain check?" I mouthed.

He nodded slightly and I turned for the door. "See y'all later."

"Really glad you're okay," Mel called before she launched into the details of last night's council blowup.

Coffee in hand, I wandered back to my desk. Too much of this was related for it to be coincidence.

I picked up a pen and clicked it in and out, staring at a silver-framed photo of Jenna's kids. The whole freaking thing was crazy. Maynard couldn't have found a cure for cancer. People would know. Who can keep that quiet?

I nodded. Someone would find out.

And if it was the wrong someone, the discovery may have gotten Maynard killed.

Wriggling my computer awake, I noticed the name of the *Telegraph's* old editor in a whitepages search bar. I clicked to page two of the results and there they were: Herman and Sophia Kochanski, an address in San Jose.

I wanted to know more about little Mrs. Eason and her growing collection of dead men.

Clock check: too early to call West Coast retirees and not risk pissing them off. I copied the number into my cell phone.

Opening a file on my laptop, I started typing out what I knew. Just so I didn't forget anything.

Three pages of suspicions later, Aaron had texted twice to apologize for being unavailable and say thanks for the PR bump my story had given the department.

Glad to help. Need a favor. Call when you can. I tapped back.

Will do.

Still on his good side meant he'd tell me whatever he could get away with. And Charlie had blasted him for not making an arrest, so I'd get a jump on her because she was in the doghouse.

I checked the day's court docket (nothing that required my butt in a seat) and the other police reports (feather light. Still quiet, except for the oh-so-mysterious dead doctor), before I grabbed my bag. The hospital was open for visitors, and I needed to interview Tom Ellinger.

I made it three steps before my cell phone rang. DonnaJo.

"What's up, sweetie?" I said in place of hello. "You bored with the criminals you have today?"

"I found something on the one you're looking for, I think. Can we get coffee?"

Of course we could.

15

DonnaJo walked into Thompson's twenty minutes later, not a blonde hair uncoiffed despite the gusting wind that said fall had arrived and winter wouldn't be far behind.

I smoothed my mahogany waves out of my face and smiled as she stepped into line behind me at the counter. "Still bored?"

"It's working in my favor, finally. I couldn't shake the stuff you were asking me about the other day, so I did a little digging."

"Where? You said y'all didn't have a file."

"I had dinner with my parents last night."

Oh? I raised an eyebrow at DonnaJo as I ordered a skinny white mocha and a turkey bacon English muffin. She nodded, asking the cashier for a caramel latte and following me to the other side of the counter to wait for our drinks.

"So what did you find out?"

"My dad plays golf with Mr. Eason's attorney."

Oooh. I liked the sound of that. I grabbed my coffee and found a table. DonnaJo followed, folding her willowy frame into the wooden ladderback chair across from mine and sipping her drink.

She put the cup on the table and leveled her I-know-something-you-don't-know look at me. The one that made her a favorite of unsuspecting jurors everywhere. She should hold a patent, hand to God.

"Just tell me! You're not trying to convince me, remember?" I sipped my latte, holding her gaze over the rim of the cup.

"So, I told you how much my mom hated the new wife?"

I nodded.

"Well, so did everyone else Mr. Eason ever met, from what the lawyer said. Especially his daughter."

"He had kids?"

"Just one. And she got most of the money. Wife number two got the condo and an annuity that earns interest and provides her a modest monthly income."

Three hundred and ninety-six society photos—with Elizabeth Eason in a different gown in each one—flashed through my head on fast forward. She wouldn't care for a modest monthly income. Not even a little.

I chewed a bite of bacon. "Who oversees the trust?"

"Eason's daughter, Sarah Jane. She was a classmate of mine at Saint Catherine's."

"What does she do now?"

"Anything she damn well pleases if she's got all her dad's money. She was a housewife for the past several years anyway. She has two little ones." The edge in DonnaJo's voice told me she hadn't changed her mind about her own biological clock, which she'd long wished would run out of batteries. She neither knew how to take care of nor understood children, so the reason any human would want to reproduce escaped her.

"And is there friction there? Between her and Elizabeth? Over the money?"

"I have it third hand that the wife erupted into a screaming rant that would've made Alexis Colby proud when the will was read. She swore he told her he'd changed it and left the bulk of everything to her, and given Sarah Jane a trust."

"But the lawyer knew nothing about this?"

"Mr. Eason never said anything to him."

"So if the wife found out he hadn't changed the will..." I let the words trail off.

"Could it have made her mad enough to kill him? Maybe. But with what? What could she have done that would convince the ME he had a heart attack?"

I tapped a finger on my chin and picked up my cup, shaking my head before I took a sip of my latte.

"And that's a stupid motive for a murder that wasn't in the heat of the moment. Because when she'd had time to think about it, she'd have realized killing him when he hadn't written her into his will would leave her in a tough spot. The comfortable life was what she was after all along, from what I hear."

DonnaJo nodded. "True."

"Did your folks seem surprised you were asking about her?"

"I didn't really tell them why." She grinned. "And I'm decent at manipulating a conversation. But my mother really hates her. She gets this look on her face when she has to talk about something she finds unpleasant—like she's internalizing a scream because she just stepped in dog poop. It's kind of funny when you know what it means."

"And you get a look when you know something you're not saying. It's how you keep juries on the edge of their seats. So let's have it."

She dropped her head back and laughed. "My mom heard some of her friends at the club talking a few weeks back. Seems this woman had moved on to someone else who would be able to keep her in the lifestyle Mr. Eason got her accustomed to."

I put down my cup and forgot to breathe. She was planning his funeral. But to have it confirmed? Jackpot.

"A doctor." DonnaJo continued. "My dad sort of knows him, but not well. Daniel someone?"

"David Maynard?" I managed to force it out in a whisper instead of an excited shout.

Her perfectly arched brows disappeared under her bangs. "Yeah, that's it." She paused, her pink lips popping into an O. "Holy Shit."

I nodded. "He's the victim Aaron and Landers are being so quiet about. I'd say it'd be nice to have a copy of his will, but I think you're already there."

"Any idea who his attorney was?" she asked.

"Nope. But this story gets more tangled every day."

"Let me make some calls. Before I get buried in the gunman from the hospital. Notice I haven't asked you why the hell you gave White such a glowing write-up for not arresting a clear murder suspect."

"I did, as a matter of fact." I winked.

"I respect you. And I get that you don't want to share when you've got something in the works. But I'm going to hear that story at some point."

I flashed a smile. "Call me if you find Maynard's attorney?"

"Of course. I'll keep my ears open, too. Cops talk to lawyers."

"I really appreciate it, DonnaJo."

"Just remember it the next time someone screws up and a criminal walks?"

"Deal."

I turned for the door and her voice stopped me. "Hey, Nichelle?"

I spun back, my smile fading when I spotted the official-looking envelope in her hand. I'd been around the courthouse enough to know a subpoena when I saw one.

I met her eyes and she twisted her mouth to one side. "Nichelle Clarke, you've been served with this summons on behalf of the Commonwealth of Virginia."

"Dammit, DonnaJo." I eyed the paper like normal people would look at a rattlesnake. "I'm supposed to cover the news, not be the news. I can't report on the trial if I have to testify."

"Sorry, friend. You're my only eyewitness. I need you in front of the jury." She tucked the envelope into my bag. "November twelfth, nine a.m. Do not make me send the sheriff after you."

I stuck my tongue out at her and turned back for the door.

"You mad?" she asked.

"No. You're just doing your job. I get it."

"Thanks. Enjoy your weekend."

I wished her the same and tossed my bag into the passenger seat.

A subpoena.

Because I didn't have enough to worry about.

* * *

I did a double-take when I walked through the revolving door at St. Vincent's. The smiling candy stripers at the front desk had been replaced by two guys who had to moonlight as bouncers. In a rough part of town.

I smiled. "Good morning. Heading up to visit a friend."

"Which floor?" The gruff baritone came from the one on the left. His cohort gave me a once over and returned his attention to the door.

"Five."

"Patient name?" The narrowing of his eyes told me dropping Amy Ellinger's name would get me shuttled right back out the door.

"My friend is a nurse, actually." I kept my tone even and bright. "Alisha Royston."

He checked a clipboard and nodded, waving me toward the elevator and wishing me a good day.

I punched the up button, wondering if this place would ever get back to normal. And how long it would take. The talking heads on the national cable channels were having a field day with yet another gunman—in a hospital, no less. Every TV station had a shrink talking about Post Traumatic Stress Disorder and how it could affect medical staff at inopportune times. Probably a sad commentary on the world when only one victim meant it wasn't big enough news for the networks to send reporters to Richmond, but I was glad they hadn't. My story had been picked up by the wires, which meant notoriety for the *Telegraph* and fewer phone calls for me. They didn't have to call me, they could just use my copy. Bonus: it also meant Andrews would stay in his office.

I stepped off the elevator on five, turning toward the nurse's station. A dozen steps down the hall, and I could see Alisha's golden-brown bun glinting under the fluorescents.

I stopped at the counter, scanning the hallway as I waited for her to finish making notes. Remnants of crime scene tape clung to the doorways, but the cops and forensics folks had cleared out. Probably worked all night.

"Hi there." Alisha's voice quavered slightly and I pasted on my brightest everything-is-going-to-be-okay smile and turned to her. She laid her clipboard on the counter and offered me a quizzical look. "Can I help you with something?"

"I was just hoping I could talk to you a little more. About yesterday. And maybe a few other things, too." It was the oncology ward, after all. She had to know who Maynard was.

She pulled in a deep breath and managed a smile. "All's well that ends okay, right?" She stepped behind the desk and waved for me to follow her. Closing the door to a cluttered little office a few feet away, she gestured to a chair and waited for me to sit before she took the other one.

"You had the gun last night," she said. "You got it away from him?"

"He wasn't going to hurt anyone. He had turned it on himself. He just doesn't want to lose his wife."

She nodded, her eyes shiny with tears. "He stays right by her side all day every day. Reads to her. Talks to her. The pain meds keep her pretty out of it, but he doesn't waver."

"There's no chance?"

"The federal government says I can't answer that."

The tear that slipped down her cheek was all the answer I needed. Damn.

"He's desperate. Maybe even a little crazy because of it. But no one's going to turn up a manifesto in his home or anything. This isn't your typical I'm-going-to-kill-them-all scenario. No matter what CNN is saying."

"I heard that on the radio this morning." She shook her head, another tear escaping. "It's been so hard for him to face the fact that no one can help them. The chaplain's been in there every day for two weeks, and he says he's never seen someone cling so stubbornly to hope." She sniffled. "He loves her so much. Every woman wants to be loved like that. I know I sure as heck do."

Amen, sister. "He's convinced there's someone who can help. Or there was, anyway."

Her brows shot up in such a look of pure surprise, I couldn't believe she knew anything about what Maynard might have been into.

"Maybe he is crazy. There's no...Well. I think he's wrong about that."

Strike one.

"Do you know a Dr. David Maynard? I know he worked at the university hospital, but it can't be such a big circle of people."

"Everyone knows Dr. Maynard. He's kind of a legend around here. But he left the hospital and went into private practice. Really private. I'm not sure I've heard much about him for the last couple of years."

Huh. Now what? Truth or consequences. Maybe both. But if I wanted an answer, I had to ask the question. "Mr. Ellinger down the hall there, he met someone online who told him Maynard could cure his wife."

Her jaw landed next to her sensible white shoe on the yellowed tile. "What?"

If she was pretending, her acting chops were going to waste. I nodded. "That's what he wanted to tell me yesterday. He wanted Charlie to bring a camera in here so he could go on TV and demand that Maynard come treat his wife."

"But he can't—no one could—that's insane," she stammered.

Strike two.

"I'm having trouble finding much information on Dr. Maynard's work. Do you happen to know where he went or what he was doing after he left the university? Or maybe know anyone who does?"

She tipped her head to one side, biting her lip. "Not personally, but one of our physicians might..." She trailed off, then snapped her fingers. "Oh! You need to talk to Wesley!"

Her face brightened as she nodded. "Dr. Maynard's research assistant—a few years ago, anyway. He was in the medical program when I was in nursing school. Brilliant guy. If anyone could help you, Wesley could."

Jiminy Choos. "You don't happen to have a phone number for him?"

"Sure." She pulled out her iPhone and jotted it down for me.

This day was looking up again.

I smiled a thank you and tucked the Post-it into my pocket.

"I don't suppose I could talk to Mr. Ellinger? I don't want to bother him, but I have a few more questions."

"You're welcome to give it a shot. He hasn't done anything but stare at his wife since last night. They have police officers outside her door, but I don't think he even realizes they're there."

She led me to Amy Ellinger's room, and I nodded at the two uniforms Aaron had parked outside the door. I recognized one of them as a patrolman who'd worked a bad accident about a month back.

"How are you this morning, Miss Clarke?" He didn't look happy to see me.

"Doing well, Officer. Yourself?"

"Wondering why we have to babysit this looney tune instead of locking him up. Rumor is, it has something to do with you."

Alisha pursed her lips, her flashing eyes already telling him which bridge his lack of compassion could take a flying leap from. I put up a hand and smiled my best southern belle smile. "I'm sure I haven't the faintest idea what you're talking about."

I turned from them without another word, and Alisha patted my shoulder as she turned back to the desk. "Good luck," she whispered.

The flood of memories that smacked me in the face with the smell when I opened Amy's door almost knocked me to the ground. The sharp bite of industrial-grade cleaners covering the sour-sweetness of illness, the air heavy and poorly circulated—I could practically hear my mom's wispy voice. I paused to let my knees find their strength, surveying the space.

Typical ICU chamber. The bed sat opposite the door, the slip of a woman in it tethered to six different machines by various tubes and wires. The blue plaid armchair looked comfortable, but wasn't if you actually sat in it.

Tom Ellinger half-laid in the chair, his face another day shaggier, his eyes a millimeter more sunken. He clung to his wife's small, pale hand while she slept.

I cleared my throat.

He didn't look up.

The scene was one I remembered so well I hated myself a tiny bit for interrupting it. I wanted to help him. But I also wanted the story. And that made my skin feel a size too tight when I tried for a smile.

"Tom? Can we talk for a few minutes?"

He just stared.

I took two steps forward. "Please? I need you to help me understand what happened yesterday."

He blinked twice and looked around. "Yesterday?" His lips moved like they had to remember how to work.

"With the gun? You asked the police to let you talk to me?"

His eyes narrowed before a look of horrified realization broke over his thin face.

"A gun. I was going to scare them. Make him come see her. I wanted to talk to the press, but the girl from the TV station didn't come in. Was that yesterday?" He blinked at me. "You came. You were here."

I nodded. "You sent me messages."

"I wanted Maynard to help her."

I smiled. "What does 'LCX' stand for?"

"My lacrosse number."

I wouldn't have gotten that in ten million years. Somehow, that made me feel better about failing to stop this before it started.

I nodded, changing my focus to the bed. "This is Amy." I didn't bother with a question. "May I say hello?"

He nodded, a sad smile showing his teeth, which could stand a sand-blasting. Alisha wasn't kidding when she said he hadn't left this bedside. "She's so beautiful," he said. "Isn't she? Always so beautiful."

I nodded, stepping closer.

"Amy, baby, this is Nichelle. The lady from the newspaper. Remember, I told you about her? She came to help us. Dr. Maynard can't help, but we'll find someone. I promise." His chin trembled on the last word and a tear slipped off his lashes, following the path of hundreds of others before it.

I smiled, a swallow sticking around the lump in my own throat. "It's so nice to meet you, Amy. I hope you're resting comfortably."

"She seems to be. Not as much noise today." Tom shrank into the chair. "I don't want her to hurt. But I don't want her to leave me. What am I going to do?"

Go to prison, especially if he really killed that woman. I pulled a note-book and pen from my bag, writing his comment down.

"How did you get here, Tom?"

He shook his head. "We were so happy. Always. So happy. She's been my whole life since I was nineteen. How do I just let her go? There has to be a way to fix this. I fix everything—it's what I do. Making her happy makes me happy. Without her..." His shoulders started to shake and I laid a gentle hand on one of them as the flat unfairness of life socked me in the gut.

Isn't this what most people are looking for? That kind of forever love I'd always thought lived only in romance novels and fairy tales? These two had managed to find it, and here the proverbial rug was being snatched from under them in the cruelest way possible.

Not. Fair.

It broke my heart.

And the fact that there was less than nothing I could do about it pissed me right the hell off. I like to help people. It's one of the reasons I almost get myself killed poking around sticky stories on a pretty regular basis.

So how could I help these folks?

By finding the truth. Twelve hours of over-analyzing every word of my last conversation with Tom had left me with a list of questions—most of them about David Maynard.

I tapped the pen on my notebook. "Tom, can you tell me a little about Dr. Maynard? You said last night you found his name in an online forum. Do you remember the address? Or even the name?"

He shook his head, his eyes still on the floor. "I searched. I searched and searched so many different things. Something clicked and there was this chatroom. They didn't say things outright, but there was this undercurrent of something. Like a code."

I scribbled. "You don't remember anything about how you found it?"

He scrubbed at his eyes with both fists. "Survivors. They were all survivors, and one post was from a woman who'd had the same thing Amy does, and she got better. I sent her a private message."

"Do you remember her name?"

"I didn't get it. Just her handle. DaisyMae."

I jotted that down. Needle, meet ginormous global information haystack.

"And she told you to call Maynard? Eventually?"

"It took a while, but yeah."

"How many conversations did you have with her? Do you think some of them might still be on your computer?"

"Just three or four over about a month. And no." He shook his head. "My Janie spilled juice on my laptop and fried it. I had to get a new one, and none of the web history is there."

Damn damn damn.

He raised his head, his eyes dark with remorse.

"I saw the news," he said. "The woman who died..." He glanced at Amy. "Is her family okay?"

I sucked in a deep breath. "The PD is waiting for ballistics. While I can't think of an entirely logical alternative, I'm hoping one of your shots didn't hit her."

His brow furrowed. "Shot."

"I'm sorry?"

"One shot. I fired one."

No. "I heard two."

He shook his head. "I had two shells. I never really wanted to hurt anyone. I figured two was enough to scare them. I only fired one."

I arranged my face into a neutral expression and nodded. "All that adrenaline. Maybe I heard an echo." So not likely.

A soft moan came from the bed, and Amy wriggled, then quieted when Tom squeezed her hand.

I took a deep breath and leveled my voice. "My mom had breast cancer."

He sniffled, sitting up a little. "Is she alive? Who treated her?"

"The staff oncologists at Parkland. I was lucky to get her into a gene therapy trial there. It's been gone six years now, but the fear of a recurrence lives in the back of my mind every minute," I said. "I know how you feel."

He nodded. "Cancer fucking sucks."

"You can say that again. And again."

He met my gaze and held it for a second, then dropped his head back and laughed. It rolled from deep in his chest in waves, filling the small, sticky room. Amy's eyelids fluttered. "Tom?"

He hit his knees next to the bed, squeezing her hand. "I'm here, baby. Right here."

"You laughed. In my dream. I miss you laughing." Her voice was heavy, thick with the narcotics.

"I did laugh. I can't remember the last time I did that."

"Do it again." She licked at her lips to no avail. The painkillers gave my mom cottonmouth, too.

His eyes promptly filled and spilled over. "I can't."

She opened her eyes—a brilliant blue—and pulled her torso off the bed. "You must. My babies...you must laugh with them. Please."

He nodded, his tears still pattering onto the bleached sheets.

Jesus.

"Fuck you, cancer." The words tumbled out before I could stop them, the scene in front of me wrenching my heart such that I couldn't keep my mouth shut. My hand flew up to cover it.

Amy started, then fell back to her pillows with a pained sigh. She stared at me for ten seconds before she started to giggle. Her face betrayed the fact that it hurt, but she kept on. I grinned.

"Blunt, but no less true," I said. "I'd beg your pardon, but I don't think it's necessary in this case."

Amy giggled harder.

Tom met my eyes and smiled, still more tears welling up in his as he mouthed "thank you" and laughed with her.

I nodded, backing toward the door. Adding in what I hadn't used the day before, I could write the story Bob wanted.

Their happiness, however fleeting, followed me all the way to the elevator.

Tom's assertion about the rifle shells followed me out of the building.

One shot.

But he'd been half out of his mind—still was, really. Could he accurately recall such detail?

One more piece for the puzzle. Now to fit a few of them together.

I climbed into my car and pointed it toward the university hospital. I didn't have time to call Wesley for an appointment. If Maynard had a research assistant who knew why Tom Ellinger thought my murder victim could cure cancer, by God I was going to know it too.

16

The atmosphere in the lobby was subdued here too, the people milling about clearly shaken by what had happened across town not twenty-four hours earlier.

I stopped at the front desk (still staffed by bright-smiling baby boomer candy stripers) and touched the screen to pull up the automated physician's directory. Digging out my notebook, I found Dr. Wesley's last name (Goetze) and punched the keys. A photo and directory information appeared on the screen.

Young. Handsome. I scrutinized his perfectly styled bronze-gold hair and too-white smile. He looked smarmy. Maybe this photo wasn't a great one.

"Suite twelve-twenty-one?" I asked, meeting the smiles of the women behind the desk. They nodded in unison, the taller one's fire-engine colored hair so teased and shellacked it didn't stir. The soft gray of the shorter woman's hair brushed her shoulders as she turned toward the bank of elevators and pointed.

"Go to the lift there," (she had the cutest lilting British accent) "and ride up to twelve, then turn left when you come off."

I smiled. "Thank you, ma'am." Spinning for the elevator, my foot froze in midair when she called "I hope you beat it."

I turned back. "Excuse me?"

"Twelve-twenty-one is the oncology suite. You're so young. But they're doing great things."

I smiled. "I sure hope so."

She nodded, and I turned her words over in my head all the way upstairs. Something worried around the back of my thoughts, but I couldn't pin it down, and the harder I tried, the vaguer it got.

I pulled the office door open, and Tom Ellinger's words came back: "The money's in the medicine."

All evidence to support. The waiting room could have been lifted from a spread in *House Beautiful*, with soft cerulean walls and shining cherry floors, right down to the works of art that doubled as tissue boxes.

I stepped to the desk and smiled my sweetest smile at the pretty young receptionist. She smiled back, but the inviting look faded when I asked to see Dr. Goetze without an appointment.

"He's extraordinarily busy." She shook her head, dark curls bobbing attractively around her heart-shaped face.

"I understand that." I pulled out my press credentials and handed them to her. "But I really need to talk to him. The day is winding down, and I'm hoping he can squeeze me in."

Generally, any business owner who's not afraid of an indictment is eager to talk to the media. Mentions in the editorial section are better than free advertising.

Her brows went up and she offered a stiff smile. "I'm afraid Dr. Goetze is a busy man."

I blinked. So not the reply I expected, it left me speechless (not an easy task) for a full thirty seconds.

"I'm hoping he can help me with my current story," I said. "And maybe I can help him out too, mentioning his work in my piece."

"I don't think so. But feel free to call for an appointment. We're booking non-emergent cases into January."

I turned back for the door, dumbfounded. Of all the places I'd ever been asked to leave because I was a reporter, a doctor's office wasn't on the list.

Why would the guy turn down free publicity?

Probably because he had something to hide.

*   *   *

I plopped into my desk chair just as my phone rang.

"Crime Desk, this is Clarke. Can I help you?" I tilted my head and pinned the handset to my shoulder, reaching for a pen and still fuming over the dismissal from Goetze's assistant.

"Miss Clarke, this is Emma DeBell." The high, reedy voice made my pulse gallop. How the hell did she figure out who I was? "I can't quite believe I'm calling you, but there's something about you I like. You have a few minutes to chat?"

Closed door, opened window.

"I always have time for a smart lady who can do her detective work, Miss Emma. What's on your mind?" I fought to keep my voice even. If she'd gone to all the trouble to find me, surely she had something interesting to share.

"I hung up yesterday not terribly sure why anyone would ask such a thing. Who would do a clinical trial and not register it? Then I looked up the number you called from and got curious. What does a newspaper reporter want with that information?"

I jotted notes on the back of an old press release I pulled from the recycle bin, staying quiet. Best to let her say her piece before I started asking questions.

"The law changed to require registration with us almost a decade ago. Without it, the results wouldn't be verifiable, the drug wouldn't get approved. Not to mention, the new laws say whoever was the principal interest in the trial could be fined or lose their federal funding. It makes no sense," she continued, almost as if she were talking to herself.

I scribbled faster, pinching my lips together to keep questions in.

"Unless someone was testing a drug they didn't want people to know about." She paused, and I caught a sharp breath. Bingo.

Play dumb, Nichelle. "Why would anyone do that?" I asked.

Miss Emma was too smart. "I have a feeling you know more about that than you're letting on. Isn't that why you called?"

I drummed my fingers on the desk, running my tongue across my front teeth. If I didn't trust her enough to ask the questions, how could I expect her to trust me enough to answer them?

But trust is a difficult thing to come by in the news business.

"You still there, Miss Clarke?"

I needed the lead. She was currently my best shot at it. "Have you ever heard of an oncologist named David Maynard?"

"There aren't many people in this building who haven't. Brilliant man. It was a shame to see him retire so early."

"But he didn't really retire. He went into private practice."

Her tongue clicked, and then I heard computer keys clicking in the background. "I think you must be mistaken."

"Pretty sure I'm not."

"Dr. Maynard was as devoted to his research as any decent man is to his wife," Emma said. "For years, he ran multiple trials at a time, and made great strides in treating patients who were once considered terminal. But his last study was recorded nine and half years ago."

"And that's exactly why I'm asking these questions."

A small, gulpy grunt issued through the handset. "No."

I could practically picture her sitting at her desk shaking her head.

"But, Miss Emma—" I began.

"Dr. Maynard was committed to finding a cure for cancer. It was his mission for over twenty years. He wouldn't run an unregulated medical study. Do you know how dangerous that is?"

"I can't say I know for sure, but my mom is a survivor, so I have a pretty good idea. But like you said, it was his mission. If he thought he was doing it for the greater good, wouldn't he do whatever he had to? It's not like he had forever to crack it." I paused. Aaron's silence on the name was a huge bonus in some ways and damned frustrating in others. "Do you think you know anyone who might be able to tell you what Dr. Maynard has been working on?"

She was quiet for a minute, her computer keys clicking again. "Maybe. John Phelps is a good friend of his. He works in our infectious disease lab. I can ask. Discreetly, of course."

"Perfect." Bob's words floated through my head. "Where would I look for information on an experimental treatment Dr. Maynard used several years ago?"

More clicking.

"What kind?"

"Something to do with a virus?"

"Let me see what I can find out."

I thanked her and started to hang up before something else occurred to me.

"Miss Emma?"

"Yes?"

"I wonder if you might be able to get me a list of trials or studies a Dr. Wesley Goetze is currently working on? I know only those open for patients or completed are searchable online, but I'm curious about what might not show up there. He's affiliated with the RAU hospital and med school."

"Finding both could take a bit of time, but I can poke around. You think he's running undercover studies, too?"

Probably not. But he was hiding something more valuable to him than free publicity.

Out loud, I said, "He was once Dr. Maynard's RA. And he seems a little camera shy. I'd just like to know what he's up to."

"Well then, so would I." She giggled. "This is fun. Should we have code names?"

I grinned. "I'll be Lois."

"And I'll be Nancy. The Eagle flies at night when the watchtower is dark. Or something." More giggling.

"Have fun snooping, Nancy. And thank you."

"Absolutely."

* * *

A teensy bit of research on the latest treatments later, I was ready to set Maynard aside for a bit.

Nervous as a june bug at a toad convention. But ready.

"Your chance at something bigger," Bob had said.

Something bigger.

Something better? Something helpful?

I hauled in a deep breath, opened a fresh document, and hoped I could do the story justice.

Tom Ellinger is a communications specialist for Virginia Telcom. His wife, Amy, is a stay-at-home mom who used to teach preschool.

They were married seventeen years ago next month, after meeting on a blind date only three months prior.

"I've always loved her," he said Friday, sitting next to her bed in the Oncology ICU at St. Vincent's, cradling her frail hand between both of his. "Since the first time I laid eyes on her. She's my everything."

The Ellingers bought a house, built careers, had three little girls, and lived their every day happily ever after. Until Amy's doctor told her she had cancer.

"We did all the gene mapping—a whole summer in Houston. Seventy-five thousand dollars," Tom said Wednesday evening. "No insurance accepted. No brainer. I cashed out my 401k, and we got on a plane...It was worth every penny to give my babies their mother back."

When Amy's cancer returned several months later, Tom sat in front of his computer for months, searching for hope.

Every time he thought he'd found some, it was dashed as quickly as it flared. He's spent the past few weeks keeping vigil at the hospital, watching his beloved slip away courtesy of stage IV ovarian cancer.

Wednesday evening, he walked into the hospital with a rifle, intending to publicly demand treatment for Amy from one of the nation's top oncologists.

I leaned back in the chair and stretched, reading over the words in front of me five times before I started typing again. Nobody needed to know the name of that particular oncologist yet. I added more from Tom, as well as a comment from Aaron about the quasi house-arrest and the case being under investigation.

I mentioned the sentry outside Amy's door twice to pull some of the heat off Aaron for not hauling Tom in immediately, and quoted Tom's inquiry about the victim and his claim that his only intent was to frighten people.

Checking the Virginia code for possible penalties for what I'd seen Tom do, I listed them in order of severity. The hostages topped the likelihood list from where I sat, as a class three felony. That's five to twenty, plus a fine of up to a hundred grand. Simple discharge of a firearm is a class one misdemeanor, but if anyone is hurt unintentionally, that's upped to a class six felony, which carries one to five years in prison and a twenty-five hundred dollar fine. Stacked on top of each other, those two would guarantee he missed his daughters' childhoods. And murder? Depending on how hard-assed the prosecution wanted to get, Tom Ellinger could go to prison for a long time. Or worse.

I finished up with Tom and Amy laughing together as I left the room that afternoon.

Though the painkillers keep Amy sedated most of the time these days, Tom woke her Thursday afternoon. By laughing.

"You laughed, in my dream," Amy said, her blue eyes struggling to open through the narcotic fog. "I miss you laughing."

Tom obliged with more laughter, and Amy joined in.

"She's been my whole life since I was nineteen," Tom said. "Making her happy makes me happy."

I read the piece again, goosebumps popping up on my arms in all the right places, then attached it to an email to Bob.

I stared at the screen for a few beats before I stood, wondering if my boss was really as okay as he'd seemed at the morning meeting.

Peeking around the corner, I found Bob hunched over his keyboard, grumbling about lack of talent.

"Present company excluded, right, Chief?" I asked, putting one foot across the threshold.

"Always. What's going on with you?"

"I got an interview with the gunman—and his wife—today." I plopped into my usual orange-velour covered chair. "You want inside the healthcare crisis? There won't be a dry eye in the city by breakfast tomorrow."

"Did he do it?" Bob swiveled his chair toward me and leaned back.

The question of the day. Tom's insistence that he'd only fired once was interesting, but certainly not concrete. Once was all it took, after all.

"I don't know. Hell, today I couldn't even tell if he knows. He's half out of his mind with grief."

Bob's face fell a touch, his eyes taking on a faraway look. "That bad, huh?"

I leaned forward and patted his hand. "I know you get it."

"He really thinks David had found it? A cure?" Bob's eyes were misty when he raised them to mine. I could practically see the what-ifs running through his head.

"I'm sorry."

"Stay on it, kiddo." He nodded, clearing his throat and turning back to the screen.

"No reminders necessary. I have a Saint-Bernard-size dog in this one, Chief." I stood and turned for the door, the phone call I'd been dreading all day not put-offable much longer. I needed a next of kin for Stephanie Whitmire, and an update on that investigation, if Aaron would give me anything.

I called his cell first, and he clicked it on after the fourth ring. "If you say anything about 'slow news,' I'll arrest you."

I laughed. "Never again, I swear on my favorite Manolos."

"What do you need from me today? Sorry I've been out of pocket."

"No worries. I got most of my stuff without you. But I need a follow on Stephanie Whitmire. Contact information for next of kin?"

"That would be her parents." I heard papers rustling. "Ron and Candy." He reeled off a phone number.

I scribbled it down. "Thanks."

"They were pretty torn up," he said. "She was an only child. Not sure they'll be up to talking to you."

I sighed. "This is the sucky part of this job. Why should they talk to me? I wouldn't talk to me, in their shoes. But they pay me to ask."

"I know the feeling." Aaron's tone went from resigned to faux-nonchalant in the space of a breath. "Your day going okay?"

"Just fine," I said breezily. "Yours?"

"About the same."

"You have anything new on David Maynard's death today?" I tapped the pen on my notepad.

"Not that I can—" Aaron bit off the word in mid-sentence and fell quiet, then sighed. "Damn. Did you know that already, or am I going to get in trouble again for being overtired and having a big mouth?"

"I knew it," I said. "Tax records plus a little snooping equals a name. I haven't run it because the longer Charlie's chasing an ID, the more of a lead I have on her when you release it. And because I don't want to get you in trouble, of course."

"Of course." He chuckled. "My hands are tied, Nichelle. I can't comment on the record."

"Off the record?"

"Where else would you get specifics? Nowhere anyone above me would buy, at any rate. Girl Friday would blast the PD playing favorites and trading favors with the *Telegraph* all over the internet."

"What you get in this business is at least a third who you know and how much they like you, and your bosses know that as well as mine do. It's part of what makes me good at what I do."

"I don't want the extra attention in the middle of this investigation." A frustrated note left me wondering what the heck was going on, but I left it. I was more interested in what he wasn't telling me than why, for the moment.

"Fine. I can find it on my own."

"No doubt," he said. "Just do me a favor and cite your sources in your copy?"

"If you'll do me one and give me a twelve-hour heads up when you're going to release Maynard's name."

"Deal."

"Any idea when that's coming?"

"My gut says whenever drop-dead on the report is."

A whole week? "Who the hell is sitting on this lid, Aaron?"

"No comment."

I rolled my eyes and hung up, dialing the Whitmires. Answering machine. I left a message, half-hoping they wouldn't even listen to it. I hate bothering grieving family members, and I didn't think these folks could shed any light on anything. Wrong place, wrong time, sad story, but no mystery about it.

My cell phone buzzed a text arrival.

Aaron's private cell number. I clicked the message up on my screen.

Who's sitting on the lid might help you figure out what's under it.

Aaron didn't want to stonewall me. And if he was feeding me tips, it was because he thought whoever was giving his marching orders was wrong.

I clicked open a glowing story approval from Bob and wrote the follow on the Whitmire case, then closed my computer and packed up for the night.

As I turned for the door, I ran through my leads on fast-forward. Which puzzle piece could I turn to make the picture clearer?

Maynard's right hand.

I'd struck out with Goetze's receptionist, but he couldn't hide behind her forever.

I checked the clock. Six-forty. Probably too late to catch up with him tonight.

I strolled to the elevator, liking the idea more as I thought it over. Could I eyeball Goetze from his staff directory photo?

If it wasn't too old or too retouched, that was an excellent possibility. And who eats lunch in the office on Friday?

17

Journalism in the age of the Internet 105: standing unobtrusively in odd places isn't as hard today as it was in 1954.

Why?

The smartphone.

Without my cell phone to feign interest in as I pretended to check email and football scores, I would have looked pretty silly leaning up against the side of the hospital, wedged between the wall and a crepe myrtle.

With it, I looked like I had some kind of Facebook emergency I couldn't put off for less prickly surroundings.

Bonus: I had a perfect vantage point for who was coming and going from the building. And the likelihood that most of them would even notice me was next to none.

Tapping my thumbs on the keys, I typed gibberish into a notes file as I people-watched. I scrutinized every guy in a suit worth more than my first car, figuring Doctor Decorator Office probably looked pretty GQ.

I was so preoccupied with men's fashion, I didn't see her until it was too late.

"Why are you hiding in the bushes?" The words dripped from a sneer, and I felt my eyes narrow behind my sunglasses. Really, universe?

"Alexa," I said, the frost in my voice hard to miss. "I'm standing on a public sidewalk, sending an email. Not that it's any of your business."

"An email. That had to be sent from inside a tree."

"I'm under the tree."

"You're not fooling me. You're chasing a story. What is it? No, never-mind, I'll find it for myself."

Deep breaths. Don't draw attention.

Throttling her would draw attention, wouldn't it?

Damn.

I pasted on a smile instead. "Take your best shot." She wouldn't dig up any of this in a million years. I hoped.

"I intend to. Should be easier with my new job in the hospital cafeteria. Thanks for that, by the way—I went from a polyester uniform to polyester with a hair net. And I owe it all to you."

"You owe it all to yourself, blasting confidential information all over the internet. All we did was unmask you. Which says something about detective skills all by itself, doesn't it?"

"You tattled."

"Because all the cops around here are so stupid they wouldn't have gotten to you." Sarcasm and annoyance sharpened the words. I looked over her shoulder at the sidewalk. Her prattling was distracting, and I didn't have time to be distracted.

"I bet I'd still be there today," she said. "You don't know how that department works."

"Because working there for what—forty-five days? You know more than I do?" I pinched my lips together. "Whatever gets you through the day, doll."

"You like them. Your piece yesterday was nothing short of PR for the damned detective squad that walked out of St. Vincent's and left a murder suspect unsupervised."

"First, they didn't leave him unsupervised. Second, he's a person of interest, but they don't have proof yet."

"Whatever gets you through the day, doll." She rolled her eyes as she sing-songed my words back at me.

I opened my mouth to reply just as I caught a glimpse of curly bronze hair and an Armani suit (I knew because Joey had one just like it) on the sidewalk at my eleven o'clock. I leaned forward and pushed a branch down. Dr. Goetze. I was as sure as my twenty-twenty eyes could be from forty yards out.

Alexa narrowed her eyes and turned, and I shifted my gaze to a leggy redhead in scrubs that could've been painted onto her body-by-Les-Mills figure.

"Gosh, would you look at the time? I have an appointment to get to, and I think we're done here," I said. "Just as nice chatting with you today as always."

I brushed past Alexa, trailing the redhead (and Goetze) into the parking garage and hoping Alexa wasn't trailing all three of us.

Why did I let her aggravate me into an argument? I needed to be following this guy alone. Dammit, Nichelle.

No time for self-flagellation. I kept the corner of my eye on the good doctor as I tromped up the garage ramp behind the nurse. She turned down an aisle and I paused, stuck for what to do. I dropped my car keys, then spun a three-sixty to look for them on the floor.

No Alexa in sight.

Huh. Maybe her break was over.

I turned toward my own car, still watching Goetze's curls bob over hoods one row below where I'd parked. The lights flashed on a chocolate-colored BMW convertible, and he slid into the driver's seat as I flung my door open and dove behind the wheel.

I let the redhead and her green Honda get between us as we pulled out of the garage, then followed him left when she turned right onto East Broad. Hanging back far enough to be unobtrusive, I rehearsed an introduction in my head.

Surely he wouldn't really object to free publicity. The receptionist had probably been told to keep everyone who wasn't a patient from sucking up his time. Right?

I stayed behind him through nine lights, the buildings lining the street growing more aged with each one. Just when I began to wonder if his lunch date was in Charlottesville, he cut across three lanes and hung an abrupt left, then wound his way through a maze of side streets that held a mix of industrial buildings and postwar tract houses before he lapped back around to Broad and pulled into the parking lot at a greasy spoon that had obviously occupied the same real estate since 1950. Without a facelift.

I parked in front of the shiny new French bakery next door and scanned the cars in the diner's lot. Every one manufactured before I graduated college, save the Beemer and a Mercedes E250 coupe.

I arched a brow. A pair of seventy-thousand-dollar cars fit in this part of town about as well as hiking boots at the beach.

I grabbed my bag, plus a copy of *Cosmo* from the backseat for camouflage, and strolled inside.

The sign on the menu rack invited me to seat myself. I kept my sunglasses on and scanned the tables, spotting Goetze in the far corner. Ensconced in a booth with Maynard's protégé was a wiry man with horn-rimmed glasses, a graying combover, and a Rolex that cost more than I made in three months weighing down his wrist.

A fat manila envelope lay on the table between them.

I checked corners for Rod Serling. Had I walked into a gangster movie?

I took the table caddy-cornered from them and opened the magazine. Sixteen articles on pleasing your man and four on fashion. I flipped to a random page, not processing a single word for flicking my eyes to the back of Goetze's head every twelve seconds.

He turned to the waitress and barked an order for ketchup I had no trouble hearing from where I sat.

I ducked behind the magazine and rolled my eyes. I've always thought you could tell a lot about a person by the way they treat servers, dogs, and kids. Dr. Goetze was joining Percival's owner on my list of Least Favorite People I've Encountered This Month. And I deal with murderers and politicians on a fairly regular basis.

"What can I get you, doll?" The waitress (the blue name tag pinned to her pink uniform read Kari) stopped at my table, popping gum and poising her pen over her ordering pad.

I smiled. "Can I have a BLT with fries and a coffee, please?"

"Sure thing." She jotted it down and smiled, nodding to a fashion spread on the hottest fall boots. "I like the tall ones."

I smiled. "They're great, aren't they?" I stuck a foot out from under the table, my Kate Spade suede boots with button-up sides poking out of the hem of my pants. "I have a thing for shoes."

She sighed. "I wish I could. I'd never make it through a shift in those."

"They're not easy on the arches." I checked Goetze. He was shaking his head, and his friend sported a brow so furrowed you could hide trinkets in the folds.

She turned for the counter. "I'll go put this in. It'll just be a sec."

"Thanks, Kari."

"No problem."

I returned to *Cosmo*, but kept my ears on the argument at the other table. Goetze snapped at Kari three times (once for forgetting the ketchup, twice for failing to read his mind) before I finished my sandwich.

Pulling out my cell phone, I clicked it to silent before I snapped a couple of photos of the doctor and his friend. Just in case.

Dawdling over my food, I skipped my eyes over the doctor's lunch meeting as often as I dared. Goetze kept his voice low, but the discussion was obviously heated. I counted three times someone put a hand on the envelope in the center of the table.

Captain Rolex finally grabbed it and strode for the door, leaving Goetze to fume, toss one last sharp retort at poor Kari, and slam some cash on the table before he stalked out.

I stared openly after him.

Of all the things I'd expected, this hovered near Goetze riding a unicorn to lunch with Tinkerbell on my list. Any doubt I had about why the receptionist had shooed me out of his office vanished like thirty-dollar Louboutins on the Saks clearance rack.

"I really wish that guy would find another place to argue with people. He's an ass, and he never leaves a decent tip." Kari's voice came from my left as she refilled my coffee.

I whipped around to face her, then took a sip—the place had good coffee and better fries—trying to downplay my interest.

"He comes here a lot?"

"Couple of times a month. Always with that dude."

"Any idea why? The car, the clothes..." I shrugged and looked around. "He seems like he'd be a better fit somewhere downtown."

She laughed. "I can't tell if they like our food or if they're trying to hide something. They sit back there and whisper like they're plotting to take over the world, then they leave. Then they come back and do it again."

I'd watched for long enough to know Goetze and his friend paid her less than no mind.

"Do you know what they're talking about?" I asked, going for casual.

Either it worked or she was bored enough to share anyway.

"Money. Numbers. Mostly a lot of stuff that makes no sense. Sometimes I catch big words that sound like they made them up. There's usually one of those envelopes, but the other guy always leaves with it."

The hairs on my arm pricked up. Try as my saner half might, I couldn't shake the feeling that Tom Ellinger was right about David Maynard. At least partly.

My gut said Goetze knew something. But who was Captain Rolex and why were they arguing?

I sighed. All roads led to new questions.

One answer. That's all I wanted.

I thanked Kari, tipped her more than my check total, and headed for the car.

"Come back anytime," she called, grinning as she pocketed the twenty I'd left on the table.

"I had fun chatting with you," I said.

I started the car and pointed it in the direction of police headquarters. Aaron couldn't "no comment" his way out of this.

18

"What do you mean, he's not giving interviews? That's his job, Sam." I stared openmouthed at the desk sergeant, still trying to process his words. "He's the Public Information Officer."

"He said no reporters." Sam smiled apologetically.

"But he is here?"

"In his office all day."

"And I can't see him. What the hell is going on?"

Sam shrugged. "Rough week. Two murders in three days—that hasn't happened in a while. Even if one of them is pretty cut and dried, everyone seems all hot and bothered over the whole mess. They don't give me the details, though."

"Me either," I grumbled, backing away from the desk.

I made a show of shuffling back out the door, my brain clicking through how I could get to Aaron. Sam was a decent roadblock for most reporters, sure, but I'm not most reporters. Or I don't like to think I am, anyway.

I turned left out of the front door and ducked into the parking garage. I'd never intentionally memorized Aaron's plate number, but knew by heart all the same, thanks to my brain's weird total recall for things I'd read.

I searched all five rows twice.

His car wasn't there.

That was actually a good thing, provided he was where I thought he was. Getting past security and into the PD when you don't have permission to be there isn't easy.

Aaron and Landers had been incognito since the shooting at the hospital.

Maybe they were overwhelmed, like Sam said.

And maybe I'd take up big game hunting in my spare time.

I started my car and whipped a u-turn on Grace Street, heading for Rockett's Landing.

Whatever was going on here was all tied up in Maynard's research—and in his murder.

Aaron could run, but he couldn't hide.

* * *

Between a Tesla and a Mercedes SUV, I found Aaron's car. Directly across from Landers'. In his office all day, my ass.

Faltering when I saw Jeff, I bent to remove an imaginary pebble from my boot. Pretty sure he knew I wasn't a dog trainer after my display with Mrs. Eason. Could I convince him he was wrong without outright fibbing to him? Probably not.

Did I care about lying to him in the grand scheme of things?

Probably not. I just didn't want to if I could help it.

If he found out I was a reporter, though, my chances of getting into the building would tank faster than a line of Christian Louboutin baseball cleats.

Straightening, I pasted on my most confident smile and strode to the door.

"What can I do for you today?" The friendly tone covered suspicion well, but the undercurrent was still there.

"I—" I paused, everything I planned to say running clean out of my head. "Percival!" My eyes fixed on the makeshift pen behind the column to the right of the front doors, and the chihuahua curled on a blanket in one corner of it.

"You still supposed to be training him?" Jeff looked doubtful.

Think fast, Nichelle.

I scooped the dog out of the pen and put my bacon-scented fingers under his nose. He began licking them happily, and I scratched behind his ears. "We have a date today, don't we, boy?"

"He's never that affectionate with anyone," Jeff said, his eyes wide as he watched the dog.

Sure. Anyone who doesn't smell like food.

I just smiled and continued petting Percy.

"I'm not sure she's going to pay you," Jeff said. "She dumped him on me this morning with an order to get rid of him. I guess pet relocation has been added to my job duties. I didn't have any place to put him, and the building director wants her happy, so he had maintenance rig that up. He's just been chewing his toys and sleeping."

"Probably enjoying the vacation," I said.

"You here to take him off my hands?" He looked hopeful, his earlier doubts seemingly forgotten.

"For a bit." Every word true. "Can I take him inside and work with him for a while?"

"Please." He pulled the door open and flashed a grin, patting the dog. "Good boy, Perce."

I swear I heard him say "lucky dog" as we passed, but I pretended I didn't. I barely kept myself from breaking into a run on my way to the elevator. Percy worked better than a clipboard. Anyone who wrinkled a brow my way smoothed it right back out when they saw him flopped over my right arm, one paw tucked under his chin, his eyes closed blissfully as I petted him. If he were a cat, he'd be purring.

I took the elevator to the next-to-top floor and peeked around both corners before I got off.

No cops.

Deep breath.

The doors started to close and I poked the "open" button. I wouldn't get a chance like this again. I might piss my detectives off, sure, but they wouldn't arrest me. And I was pretty pissed myself. Everything I'd done to help Aaron, and he wasn't giving interviews?

Um. No.

I called up the tax records in my crazy photographic memory and strode off the elevator looking for Maynard's condo.

Rapping on the door, I took a step backward, just in case Aaron decided to shout.

My jaw dropped when Kyle pulled the door open.

* * *

"What the hell are you doing here?" tumbled off my tongue as Kyle barked, "How did you get up here? Secured building my foot. White, what kind of show are you running here, man?"

Kyle moved to shut the door and I stuck a foot in it. "No way, Kyle. I'm not going anywhere."

"You will if I have someone come up to escort you out."

"What was that, Miller?" Chris Landers appeared in the hallway across from the door with a furrowed brow, then rolled his eyes when he saw me.

"Goddammit, Clarke, we said no comment. Active investigation."

"I went into the hospital for you the other night. You don't get to blow me off this week."

"I didn't take that crazy asshole to jail because you asked me not to. We're even."

I opened my mouth to snap back and Kyle stepped between us. "Now children, let's not squabble."

"I'm not squabbling," I huffed. "And I'm not leaving here until you two tell me what the hell is going on."

"I'm not telling you a damned thing about an active investigation." Landers's volume dropped, but his voice took on a sharp edge.

"Funny how you don't have that reservation when I'm risking my neck helping you out." I pulled myself up to my full height, hugging Percival so tightly he wriggled. I stroked the dog's fur, trying to keep hold of my temper.

"Cheap shot," Landers said, stepping toward the door. "No one asked you to go in there."

"What would have happened if I hadn't?" I shouldered past Kyle into the condo, taking in the tasteful postmodern lines of the black, white, and gray color scheme.

Kyle knew me well enough to hear the danger in my tone, and took a step backward.

Aaron chose that moment to step out of the bathroom at the end of the hall, still drying his hands on a paper towel.

"Hey, Nichelle." His eyes were unsurprised, his lips turning up at the corners.

"Did you tip her off?" Landers rounded on him, and Aaron shook his head.

"No," I said, before Landers could lose what he still had left of his temper.

"I know her." Aaron tried to swallow a laugh. It didn't work. "I told you telling Sam I wasn't giving interviews wouldn't do anything but piss her off. Didn't I?"

"You told the desk sergeant to stonewall Nichelle?" Kyle laughed too.

I tried unsuccessfully to keep a straight face. Percival yipped, and I scratched his ears, everyone laughing harder the more Landers sputtered.

"You're a good detective, Chris, but you do have a few things left to learn from us old timers," Aaron said, catching his breath.

Landers sighed and threw up his hands. "Like what? That you just let the press run all over a crime scene because they're stubborn?"

"I don't see gloves or booties on any of you," I said coolly, setting Percy on the brushed silk sofa, then thinking better of it and moving him to the rug. Which probably cost more than the sofa. Whatever. "So forensics isn't coming back. Which means you're looking for something fingerprints aren't going to compromise." Like research notes?

I bit down on the words that might have tipped my hand. Until Landers stopped being so stubborn, I wasn't sharing anything. Let him run his own investigation, if he thought he was so much smarter than me. We were probably following the same trail, but maybe not.

"What do you know?" Kyle studied my face carefully, and I tried to let it go blank.

"I have no idea what you're talking about, Agent Miller."

He folded his arms across his chest. "You're here for a reason, and it's not because you want to know who the vic was, because White says you already have the name."

"I want to know what's going on with the case."

"I call bullshit," Aaron said. "There's dogged, and then there's snooping. You only snoop when you think you have a moral reason to. What's up?"

My mom's bright blue eyes flashed through my thoughts, and my stomach wrung. I knew maybe better than anyone how crazy the whole thing sounded: a cure for cancer? No way. But what if? What if my mom got sick again and the key to keeping her alive was in this building and I walked out and left it because Landers didn't like me?

Nope. He was just going to have to deal. I scooted toward the marble-topped desk in the corner, wondering if I had a chance at getting a look inside it.

"Unless you're going to read me some Miranda rights, I don't think you get to question me," I said, resting one hip on the edge of the desk and adding an aloof edge to the words.

"You want us to tell you things we don't want to share," Aaron said.

"But you're not doing it," I countered.

"Touché," Kyle said.

Landers still loitered in the doorway to what I assumed was the bedroom, pouting.

"I'll answer one for you if you'll answer one for me," Aaron said.

"White." Landers's head snapped up, a warning edge in the word that would've sliced through a tin can.

I tipped my head to one side, my eyes on Aaron. If he wasn't going to pay Landers any mind, neither would I.

"On the record?"

"I can't do that right now and you know it."

I nodded. One question. Better make it a good one, because Aaron wouldn't have offered without an ace up his sleeve.

A hundred queries spun through my head, all of them clamoring to be first. Who was their prime suspect? Was Maynard running a drug trial off the books? Was he seeing Mrs. Eason?

I considered each in turn for a full three minutes. I could still possibly find the answers to most of it on my own, and there were a couple of questions in there I wasn't sure these guys could answer, anyway. But there was one thing I couldn't get anywhere else. And it would save me a lot of work to have Aaron answer it. "Unnamed PD source?"

"Depends on what you want to know."

"White." Landers was quieter, but no less pissed.

Aaron kept right on ignoring him.

"The standard background on these people." I waved at the building in general. "Did it turn up anything that set off alarm bells for you?" I crossed my fingers behind my back, not breaking my lock on Aaron's gaze even when Percy scratched at my ankle. Hopefully his bladder wasn't full.

"Unnamed official source." Aaron stressed the second word.

I nodded, reaching for a pen and notebook. Andrews would have to shut up for at least a couple more days.

"We're still sorting through some things," he said. "You know the woman down the hall had a husband die last Christmas."

I nodded. "But she wasn't arrested."

"Not enough evidence isn't the same as nothing wrong," Aaron said. "Just so I'm telling the whole truth."

I scribbled that down. Not that I could name her—or anyone else—as a suspect, but maybe something they'd found would click into my puzzle.

"Any other doctors in the building?"

"One, but she has an alibi and swears she didn't know Maynard. Two white collar convicts who run different companies."

I raised an eyebrow. "Really, now?"

Aaron nodded. "We're holding one for questioning."

That I could print. Score.

"What does he do?"

"Divisional VP at Evaris." Aaron nodded when my eyebrows shot up. Evaris was a drug company. A large one.

"Can I get a name?"

"Alan Shannon."

I scribbled, and Aaron kept talking. "The daytime doorman is retired military, and he swears this guy isn't the type. But the woman—the one down the hall who used to work for you guys—she says the doc seemed afraid of something. We're trying to find out what."

I got every word before I looked up. "Thanks, Aaron."

"Don't make me regret it."

I nodded.

"How's the rest of the investigation coming?"

"Slow," Kyle said, before Landers cut him off with a razor-sharp "Aaron said one question."

I rolled my eyes and Kyle shrugged. "It's true. I talked to Bonnie this morning. She says people are dragging their feet on purpose, but she doesn't know why."

Huh. I scribbled, biting down on a smile. Bonnie was the forensic biologist at the coroner's office who thought Kyle was so cute. Good for him.

"Why would they do that? Shouldn't it be just the opposite? This guy was a genius, and a big shot in the community. I can't even find anyone in my own newsroom who didn't think he was some sort of god. Or just shy of it."

"We are painfully aware of that, I assure you." Landers sighed and folded his long frame onto the sofa. Percival trotted over and nudged his outstretched hand. I softened a millimeter. Dogs are good judges of character. Though to be fair, Percy's frame of reference was pretty skewed to the asshat side of things.

"Everyone from the Chief to the goddamned Governor is on our asses wanting this wrapped up." Aaron tossed me a pointed glance. "Quietly. I get more pressed every hour to bring in your grieving gunman and call it a day. He was there with a gun when Miss Whitmire was shot. Hell, he'd even been here, asking to see the doc. Might as well put a Christmas bow on his head."

"Isn't that just a smidgen too easy?"

"Why do you think we're here? No stone unturned." Aaron picked up a magazine and shook it, then flipped through the pages.

"I think the Governor might have called in a favor," Kyle said, spreading his hands in a why-am-I-here gesture.

"Someone actually assigned you to this?" Kyle was a hotshot SuperCop.

A federal one. Why would the federal government give a rat's ass about a dead doctor? "Random murder cases aren't ATF jurisdiction."

"Care to tell us something we don't know?" Landers was still snippy, but at least he was talking. And that snippiness was probably directed at whichever ATF commander had decided the local cops needed Kyle on this case. I shot him a sympathetic nod. I know how it feels when the national news folks descend on one of my bigger stories.

"Hey, man, I didn't ask for this." The tension in Kyle's voice told me I was on the money.

"We know that," Aaron said, the congenial manner that made him the RPD's king of confessions (and usually kept him locked behind a desk) sending Kyle and Landers back to a simmer.

I nodded to Aaron. "So what are you doing here? They usually keep you pretty close to the office."

"This damned flu epidemic has a third of our detective squad out." He shrugged.

And if they had him in the field, the PIO was unavailable for comment. Two birds, one convenient, logical stone.

"Give me a break, Aaron."

"We are. You wouldn't still be here otherwise." Landers.

"Please. The only reason I'm still standing here is because you guys want to know if I know something you don't."

Aaron grinned. That ace he had lurking was about to fly. "Speaking of: what's the number one thing you don't want Charlie to know?"

"Nicely played, sir. No one else gets any of this until we've run it?"

Aaron exchanged glances with Landers and Kyle and they nodded agreement.

"Ellinger wanted Maynard to see his wife."

I scanned their faces, quickly, and found myself delighted we weren't playing poker.

I couldn't read a thing, except the curiosity in the lines around Kyle's eyes. It was the same look he got when I let him get to second base in the back of my old Mustang a million years ago—his eyes crinkled like that, he tried for third, and I sat up and took him home.

I kept my gaze on him, wondering if he was going to try another fast one here.

"We figured that, from your article and what we've heard about Ellinger," Aaron said. "There are twenty places that could go, which is why we're still looking."

I nodded.

Kyle cleared his throat. "But Ellinger is still on the hook for the dead woman at the hospital."

I tried to mimic the poker faces.

Mine sucks.

"What are you not saying?" Kyle kept his voice neutral, but I heard the effort it took under the simple words.

"I said one question, agent."

Aaron chuckled, and Landers muttered a word that would get my mouth washed out with soap to this day. Kyle didn't even blink.

I waited a beat. "Ellinger swears he only fired one shot. I heard two."

Kyle just nodded. "That's a little out there, even for you."

"I'm not saying he's right. I kind of think he's not, which is why I haven't paid it much mind. But you guys are making me wonder."

I glanced around the tastefully modern condo, the open floor plan and breathtaking views lovely, but nothing in sight that revealed one clue about the man who'd lived in the space.

What were they looking for?

My eyes fell on the desk, and a bottom drawer that was still slightly open.

From the size and the tabs I could see through the crack, it was a file drawer.

I turned back to the guys, usually among my favorite people to work with. The look they exchanged screamed that I couldn't trust any one of them.

I collected Percival from the rug and smiled. "Do me a favor and have a look at Ellinger's rifle? I'd like to know if it was loaded when they processed it into the evidence locker."

Aaron nodded, his face curious and apologetic at the same time. "I'll see what I can do. This is complicated, Nichelle."

"The good ones always are." That came from Kyle, with a weird look I didn't want to try to read.

"Let me know if Bonnie comes up with anything. Off the record," I said.

He walked me to the door, then stepped into the hallway and pulled it shut behind him. "We need to talk. Not here, though." He jerked his head backward.

"Name a time and place."

"Can I come by your house tonight? As soon as I wrap up here, though I have no idea when that might be."

I didn't hesitate. "Of course."

I patted his shoulder and carried Percy to the elevator, wondering what kind of penalty dognapping carries in Virginia.

"You learning how to talk yet, bud?" Jeff scratched the dog's ears when I stopped at the door and I laughed.

"If I could manage that, I could quit my job. The TV shooting schedule would preclude working." I winked.

"You seem like the kind of lady who can make the impossible possible," he said. "Just wondering."

I shook my head and patted the dog. "So are you keeping him?" he asked. "She said she just couldn't handle him anymore. I'd take the little guy, but I don't need the responsibility right now."

I froze, Percy's slight weight warm on my arm. Visions of shelter pens danced through my head. I couldn't give him back to Jeff if he had nowhere to go.

But where did I have for him to go? Darcy was a princess—she wouldn't take kindly to competition in our house.

"She just left him here?" I scratched Percy's ears.

Jeff nodded, scooping up the dog's toys and blanket and handing them over.

I turned for the car, my brain racing through everyone I knew. Bob wasn't home enough to have a dog. Parker? Mel was allergic. Jenna would kill me—she liked having Darcy over for playdates, but didn't need anything else to feed and care for.

I settled Percy in the back with his stuff. "We'll find someone who will love you, bud," I said.

He chewed his designer bone, unconcerned.

Turning into the *Telegraph's* garage, I spotted Eunice's forest green Subaru station wagon.

Eunice, who'd lost her beloved Terrier, Combat, over Labor Day.

I love it when the universe gift wraps answers.

19

Eunice's eyes popped wider than a Texas summer sky when I poked Percy's face around the edge of her office door. He yipped and immediately started wriggling.

Not fond of the notion of dog pee all over my favorite new pants, I set him down and prepared to run for paper towels. But instead of lifting his leg, Percival darted for Eunice, bouncing at her feet and whining.

She scooped him up, and he set about licking her face. Jeff's words floated through my head.

"I hear he's never that affectionate with anyone," I echoed, smiling when my friend squeezed the dog to her ample chest and grinned at me.

"He's too cute for color TV, Nicey," she said, her voice warmer than I'd ever heard it.

"He needs a good home."

She froze, tightening her arms around the dog and staring, slack-jawed, at me. "Really?"

"His former owner needs a new fashion accessory, and I thought you might be ready for some company."

She nodded, closing her eyes and bending her head to Percival's. "Would you like to come home with me?"

He licked her nose.

"I'd say that's a yes. It's even Friday, so you can get him situated over the weekend." I grinned. I'd never seen Eunice look sadder than the day Combat died. I'd rarely seen her look this happy, either.

"I just sent the Sunday front to production." Eunice tucked Percy under one arm and closed her laptop. "Let's go home, little guy." She stood and turned to me. "What's his name?"

"She called him Percival."

Eunice wrinkled her nose. "Stuffy. But whatever." She scratched his chest and picked up her coral Land's End tote. "He'll be spoiled enough for it to suit him, anyhow. I cooked for Combat every night."

Eunice was a champion southern chef. "Really? Can I come home with you too?" I asked.

"Darlin', I'll cook you whatever you want for a month. I wonder how many recipes I can find calling for white chocolate."

"I'll take some white chocolate chip banana bread and a batch of armadillo eggs, and we'll call it even." I stepped back to let them out and scratched Percy's ears, handing Eunice his paraphernalia. "You two take care of each other."

She shuffled toward the elevator, talking to the dog and humming, and I turned for my desk, ridiculously pleased with myself.

Now if I could just figure out this story. What had Aaron said? Mrs. Eason. He was looking at her, too.

Time to call Mrs. Kochanski.

* * *

I dialed the San Francisco number I'd found for the Kochanskis that morning, and tapped a finger on the desk as it rang. Had I lost my mind, calling Bob's old friends to ask about a once-upon-a-time mistress? Those kinds of wounds don't always heal completely with time.

But what if Elizabeth Eason really had killed Maynard? And maybe her husband, too? These folks would know her and how she operated.

Just when I was about to give up, a breathless "Hello?"

"Mrs. Kochanski?" I asked.

"Yes, can I help you?" Her voice was warm, with a note of polite removal.

"My name is Nichelle Clarke. I'm the crime reporter at the *Richmond Telegraph*," I said.

Silence.

I waited, knowing full well she might hang up.

"There's something I haven't heard in a while." I heard a deep breath go in. "What's going on at the *Telegraph* these days?"

"Same thing that goes on at every other paper in the country. Trying to keep our heads above water." I kept my tone light.

"How's Bob?" she asked softly.

"He's good."

"I was so sorry to hear about Grace." Her voice dropped to just above a whisper. "She was the sister I never had, but I was afraid having us show up at the service...Well. Bob had a falling out with my husband. I'm not sure how much he talks about it."

"He doesn't. I heard a version of events from Larry," I said.

"Larry is a good man." Her voice brightened. "And a damned fine photographer."

"He spoke highly of you."

"I'm glad to hear that. I've often wondered if they all hated me for making Herman leave the paper." Her voice caught—only a small hitch, but I didn't miss it. I felt like a jackass for bopping her with painful memories out of nowhere on a random Friday.

Asking uncomfortable questions (of people lacking a badge or an indictment, anyway) has never been my favorite part of my job, but it's often necessary. I find it best to just blurt them out when the opportunity presents itself. There's no such thing as tact when you're asking about something that might make the person on the other side of the conversation cry.

"If anyone hates anybody, it's not you, ma'am. That's why I called. I'm wondering if you can tell me anything about Elizabeth Herrington?"

A sharp breath in, followed by a gurgle that sounded halfway between a cough and a hard laugh.

"There's a name I could go forever without hearing again." Every degree of warmth vacated her tone.

"I'm sorry to bring this up, truly, but I need to know what kind of person she is. Can you help me?"

She was quiet for so long I thought she'd hung up.

"Mrs. Kochanski?"

A deep breath, followed by a sigh. "I read the papers. I keep up with industry gossip. Bob loves you. He trusts you. But this is a very personal thing you're asking me about. I'm not comfortable talking about it on the record. I'm not sure I'm comfortable talking about it at all."

"I would never quote you," I said, the words running together they popped out so fast. "I'm stuck. Grasping at anything I think might turn up a lead. I'm working on a story about an unsolved murder. Maybe two."

She barked a short laugh. "No, really."

"That's the truth."

"She's a murder suspect?" The flat tone gave way to glee. "Do they still fry people in Virginia?" She caught a sharp breath. "Heavens. Don't answer that. I'm sorry."

I bit down on a laugh. So much for time healing all wounds.

"I think I can safely say I get it, ma'am."

"Don't call me ma'am. I probably am that old, but I don't like to think about it. I'm Sophia. Tell me what kind of background you need on...that woman. I can safely say I've never thought she had any morals. Or conscience."

"And I guess you don't live with Herman Kochanski for decades without picking up a feel for reading personalities."

"You do not. My Herman is...special. We're happy. But I still think about her. She's a good reminder to pay attention to our marriage. We've never slipped again, since that almost destroyed our family. And my kids were too young to remember most of the bad years, thank God."

"How was she with other people?"

"She was excellent at seducing my husband."

I snorted. Touché. "She married a local businessman several years ago and left the paper. Larry said it was one of the happiest day of Bob's career."

"Bob is loyal to a fault. He never forgave Herman, but still."

"Her husband was pretty wealthy," I said.

"Was? Is it him you think she killed? The more you talk the better I like this. I mean, except for the poor schmuck she married."

"His death was ruled an accident," I said. "But the murder of another man she knew—a doctor—makes me wonder. I just want to get a feel for what you remember."

"She was a scheming, devious little trollop."

"Interested in helping other people?"

"Not a whit. She didn't care about anyone but herself. We had four children—little children—and she took my husband up to a hotel room without a thought for anything but what she wanted." She spat the words, then cleared her throat and offered a shaky laugh. "Listen to me. So emotional after all this time."

"That's exactly what I needed to know."

"Cold. Calculating. Self-serving. Grace told me she heard her comment at a party once about how she just wanted to marry some rich old bastard and inherit all his money, and the society beat was the fastest way to that. Better than politics, she said, because those guys never leave their wives and run background checks on their mistresses."

I jotted her comments down, starring "inherit all his money." It seemed from what DonnaJo said, this plan backfired. Maybe Maynard was insurance?

"Thank you for talking to me."

"I hope I helped. With your story."

"And maybe the PD's investigation?"

"Maybe."

I smiled, wondering if this would've been what it was like to talk to Bob's wife. I'd always been sorry I hadn't gotten to know her.

"Looking forward to reading it," Sophia said.

I thanked her, wished her a nice day, and hung up.

Checking the clock, I flipped my laptop open.

After three. I owed Bob a story, and Charlie's early report would be on TV in about half an hour. I sent him a message that I'd have his copy ready by five and got up to hunt for caffeine, wondering what Charlie knew. And, as much as I hated to admit it, what Alexa thought she knew. Her blog had been a pain in my ass for months, and with a big story in the works, I should probably keep an eye on it.

* * *

What Alexa actually had? Not much.

But you couldn't tell it from her homepage.

I managed to refrain from spitting soda all over my computer by nearly choking myself, scrolling and reading as I coughed.

Girl Friday had been a busy little bee, her new career slinging hospital food notwithstanding. She had two posts already on the conspiracy between the *Telegraph* and the RPD to keep a murderer out of jail.

"I try to be a good person. But I really hate you," I said, my eyes on her little notebook and pen avatar.

"It appears the feeling is mutual. And Andrews is pissed," Shelby's voice came from behind me, and I turned in my chair.

"Andrews saw this?"

My former nemesis just nodded, not a trace of the old animosity on her face. "Fair warning: he's yelling about the paper being used to barter with the cops and how it hurts credibility."

"Yelling. At who?"

"Bob."

"Damn him. Thanks, Shelby." I bolted out of my chair and charged for Bob's office, Andrews' nasally twang reaching my ears from several feet away.

"Dammit, Jeffers, this blogger is making us look like amateurs. What do you have to say for yourself?" he bellowed as I shoved the door open and stepped into the room.

They both whirled on me. "That was closed for a reason," Andrews snapped.

"Nichelle, it's a bad time." Bob's face looked a little haggard and a lot resigned, and the combination pissed me right the hell off. I ignored him and turned to Andrews with a tight smile.

"I gather you're chewing Bob's ass for a decision I made." I maintained control of my temper only because the little ferret in front of me was Bob's boss—and mine, technically—though I didn't like to think about that. "I thought maybe I should be present for this conversation."

"You have final approval over what goes on our front page now? I must've missed an email."

Deep breath. Count to five. "I made a decision, in the middle of a crime scene, and made a deal with Aaron White. And I stand by that decision."

"This Alexis whoever, this blogger, is using a poor decision on your part to call this newspaper's credibility into question. I'm disappointed, Miss Clarke. You usually show better judgement."

I flicked a glance at Bob, whose face portrayed a conflict that made my heart twist. He wanted to defend me, but didn't really want to step into the line of fire again.

I'd been working my ass off for months to keep Andrews at bay, and now here sat my boss, in trouble with a jerk whose entire knowledge of the news business would fit in Bob's pinky fingernail. Because of me.

Dammit, Nichelle.

Bob opened his mouth and I shook my head slightly.

I got this one, Chief.

"Then we're even, Mr. Andrews." The words held a layer of frost even Andrews couldn't miss—and his head is generally so far up his own ass, that's saying something. His eyes widened and I waited a few beats before I continued. "I'm disappointed that my publisher is leaping to judgement, siding with an actual amateur, when I've proven myself more than capable of doing my job well and landing this newspaper exclusives that increase revenue. Why do you have that little confidence in your staff?"

Bob leaned back in his chair, throwing me a quick wink before he turned an interested gaze on a sputtering Andrews.

"Of course I have confidence in our staff." Andrews waved a hand at the Pulitzer on Bob's office wall. "Your portfolio certainly speaks for itself, but..." He paused, looking around for an answer to pop out of the air and rescue him. His face lit with a smug smile and he focused on me again. "I'm concerned that you've gotten too close to your sources."

Alexa's words, lifted straight from her blog. At least our publisher was reading something.

"The story is always first for Nichelle," Bob said. "I've never been surer of that."

I smiled. Thanks, boss.

But hush up.

"Actually, if you want to know the truth, the people edge the story by a hair, sir." The word tasted funny as it slipped out directed at someone I had so little respect for, but I needed Andrews to calm down and leave Bob alone. "I think that's what makes me good at what I do. And no one is sure exactly what happened at St. Vincent's."

"I understand from Charlie Lewis, Alexis what's-her-name, and your own report that there was a woman with a bullet in her head and a guy with a rifle. Is two and two seventeen now?"

I kept my face arranged in a carefully neutral expression—not easy when the top of my head was ready to blow off. Andrews had about seven years and a million-fold brown-nosing chops on me, making him the youngest publisher in the paper's history. He'd come from the advertising side of the great journalism divide, which meant the bottom line was his only real concern. Everyone in the room was well aware of that. While I was thankful to still have a newspaper to write for in an age where they were shuttering all across the country, Andrews putting on like he cared about integrity would've been laughable—if it hadn't been so infuriating.

"I appreciate you keeping up with my competition, but I feel it necessary to point out that I was the only reporter inside the hospital," I said. "That was a huge exclusive for this newspaper, and I'm interested to see what it meant for our rack sales yesterday. And our advertising sales today."

He didn't miss the disdain in the words, blinking for a second before he replied. "I'm sure sales are up all around."

Like he doesn't check them more often than Perez Hilton checks his Twitter.

"Then why are you so upset?"

More blinking. For so long I had to join in before my eyes shriveled into raisins.

"I—well, I saw that article and I was concerned," he said. "The newspaper isn't supposed to be a PR sheet for the police. Everyone knows that."

"I think I've proven that I'm willing and able to call the PD on the carpet when it's necessary, have I not?" I raised a brow and Bob erupted into a coughing fit that poorly disguised his laughter.

Andrews dropped his eyes to his shiny brown wingtips, folding his hands behind his back. "I suppose that's true."

"I'd like to think I've earned some credibility and respect. I've been at this for a long time to have my bosses doubt my abilities."

"Also...true," Andrews grunted.

"So there's no reason for you to be concerned," I said, touching his elbow with one finger and steering him toward the door.

He looked like he wanted to stay but didn't really have a viable reason to when I walked him across the threshold and closed the door behind me.

"You're sure you know what you're doing?" he asked, his eyes not meeting mine.

"I do. And I know what you're doing, too. Leave Bob alone. If you have a problem with the way I'm handling a story, come talk to me."

He stiffened. "The editorial content of the newspaper is Bob's responsibility. Beyond that, I have no idea what you're talking about."

I bent my knees and caught his eye. "I believe you do. And there are enough people here who won't stand for you forcing him out the door to make your life downright hellish. Try explaining the loss of every one of your top reporters and columnists to the board."

He took a step backward. "I don't care for ultimatums."

"I'm not giving you one. Just helping you see the situation more clearly." I smiled. "The news staff is a family. We squabble, we eat, we gossip—and we stick together. I haven't figured out why you're so hot to get rid of Bob, but do everyone a favor and lay off."

He gave me a measured once over and turned on his heel, striding to the elevator without another word.

His abrupt exit made me uneasy, and I walked back to my chair mulling over the last thing I'd said to him.

It was true: I didn't know why he had it out for Bob. I assumed it was simply that my editor was getting older, but people work into their seventies all the time.

Maybe I assumed wrong.

20

Orange tinged the crimson leaves on the sprawling maple in my front yard, the backlight from the sinking sun giving the illusion the branches were on fire. Gorgeous. And somehow soothing.

I sat in my car in the driveway and stared at it, my week running through my head on fast forward.

Two hours of computer research had gotten me basics on Goetze and Andrews both, but there were still roughly a thousand places to look for details—and a million things I didn't know. Probably two million things I didn't know I didn't know.

I was no closer to any meaningful history on Elizabeth Eason-née-Herrington, and beginning to think I'd just have to suck it up and go talk to her. Telling someone she wanted to marry rich and inherit a fortune was interesting, yes. But proof of anything? No.

Then there was Kyle. Him helping the PD with the Maynard case was the weirdest thing I'd seen in months—and in my line of work, that's pretty out there.

I searched what I knew about ATF jurisdiction for a reason they'd be interested in the random murder of a brilliant oncologist and came up with jack squat. The FDA, the NIH, even the DEA—sure. But Maynard didn't have anything to do with guns or tobacco. Or booze. Did he?

"Hell if I know." I shoved the kitchen door open and bent to scratch Darcy's ears. "From what little I've been able to turn up, the doc might have been into any number of things."

"Any idea what sort of things?" Kyle's voice came from the foot of the steps, nearly sending me out of my skin.

I shook my head as I filled Darcy's bowl. "I didn't get to spend the day searching the man's home and his private files. Unlike some people I know."

"Lord knows what you'd come away with if we let you loose in there." Kyle took a seat at my little bistro table, watching me rinse the dog food can and toss it in the recycle bin. When I turned to face him, he smiled. "Maybe we should give it a shot."

"Name the time, Agent."

"This is a weird case," he said, nodding when I opened the fridge and waved a Dr Pepper can at him.

I poured two over ice, taking the seat across from Kyle and tapping a finger on the tile of the tabletop. Did he know about the Google thing? I'd give it even odds. So either I could ask and see if one of the government's computer geniuses had figured it out, or I could trust the private sector skills of my BFF's professional hacker husband and keep my hand to myself for a while.

"More twists than a water spigot at a bath house," I said, raising my eyes to meet his blue lasers.

"You're not going to tell me what you know."

"Not unless you're going to tell me what you do."

"The hush order on this came from higher up than I can see." He spread his hands in an I-can't-help-it gesture. "They'll have my ass. And my badge."

I clicked my tongue against my teeth. "Last time I checked, no one had me under surveillance."

"Funny thing about that: you don't know when someone does. That's sort of the point."

I blanched. "You need to tell me something, Agent Miller?"

He raised his hands in mock surrender. "I'm not saying I do. Or anyone I know does. Just that I can't talk to you about this case."

Except to tell me why he couldn't talk to me about it. Which I would pick apart later, no doubt as I stared at the fan when I was supposed to be sleeping.

But for now...focus, Nichelle.

"If you didn't come here to tell me anything, you couldn't possibly have thought I was going to tell you something. So that leaves me wondering what's up. I mean, you're good company and all, but I have Charlie breathing down my neck, a blogger who's after my head on a platter, and the publisher gunning for Bob—and possibly me, since I told him off this afternoon."

"Oh yeah?"

"He's trying to push Bob out. Today he used my stuff as ammo. Pissed me off."

Kyle nodded. "That's my girl. All work and no time for play." His eyes softened.

Uh-oh. Not that kind. "How's it going with Bonnie? I've heard you mention her a couple of times this week. Any sparks?"

He rolled his eyes so fast I couldn't swear it wasn't my imagination. "She's okay. Really smart, which I like, and pretty. We're going rock climbing this weekend."

"That sounds fun." And normal. It occurred to me that Joey and I didn't do much but eat and have sex. No complaints, but variety could be good.

"She's a little brainy to be into stuff like that—you're more the adventurous type, really—but she seemed game when I asked, so we'll give it a shot."

"I'm glad. I want you to be happy."

"Are you happy?" The half-octave drop in his tone told me the three words were loaded.

"I am." I looked straight into his eyes and spoke with no reservation. "I don't want you to be hurt by that, but I need you to know where things stand. I am happy. I am in a relationship. I am your friend. I don't want to lose you as a friend, but I don't want our friendship to jeopardize what I've found, either."

He scanned my face for a good minute after I stopped talking, then slumped back in his chair. "I do have to tell you something."

I felt my brow furrow and leaned forward. "What's wrong?"

He heaved a sigh big enough to put the big bad wolf to shame. "It's about your boyfriend."

Oh.

Shit.

* * *

I closed my eyes, trying to keep my face blank. No showing fear until I knew what he'd found.

"Why would you need to talk to me about that, exactly?" I put on my best offended tone. "Running a background on your competition seems low, Kyle. I thought better of you than that."

He bristled. "For your information, I wasn't doing any such thing. I knew last time I saw him here that I'd seen him before. I just couldn't remember where."

Double shit.

I held his gaze, but didn't say a word.

He shrugged. "I tried to blow it off—not like there aren't a hundred guys who look like him, right?"

I happened to think Joey was pretty extraordinary in the looks department, but perhaps this wasn't the best time to share that. I nodded.

"But then I ran across this surveillance photo. I'm as sure as I can be that your guy is in it."

Damn. I managed to avoid flinching by focusing on "sure as I can be." That wasn't proof.

"Why on Earth would the ATF have a surveillance photo of him?" I asked. The words sounded cold and distant, even to me.

"You tell me."

"I'm thinking that's not the way this conversation is going to go."

He slammed one hand down on the table and leaned forward. "This guy isn't who you think he is."

"Says who? You have a grainy photo as evidence."

"As one piece of evidence."

Shit, shit, shit. "Along with what? Google Earth images of a car that might be his?"

"Nothing."

I raised an eyebrow. "I'm not in the mood for games tonight."

"Not trying to play one. I mean, I couldn't find anything else. Not even a speeding ticket. It makes no sense."

"I call bullshit, Kyle. How would you even know what to search for?"

"I had fingerprints." The words dropped like rocks.

"Kyle. Tell me you didn't."

He shrugged. "I want you safe more than I want you happy with me. I pulled the files from the shooting in June," he said. "Ran the prints. There were some in the living room that didn't turn up as yours, your mom's or mine. The RPD guys all wore gloves—but I don't even have to ask if he'd been at your house earlier in the week. In the living room. The far corner of the couch, near the lamp table. Right?"

I had nothing for that. I blinked slowly. I'd had actual nightmares about learning something about Joey I didn't want to know. Kyle as special guest host for this horror show come to life was just a bonus that showed God's sense of humor.

I nodded. "So?"

"So like I said, I ran the prints and he's a ghost in the system. Nobody is that clean."

"You came here to tell me he doesn't have a criminal record?" I wasn't sure what the hell to make of that, but Kyle was the wrong person to discuss my confusion with.

"How much do you know about him?"

"As much as I should." It occurred to me that if Kyle's search had turned up a last name, he knew something I didn't, but I couldn't think of a tactful way to ask, so I filed that away for later.

"What does he do for a living?"

"Transportation," I blurted the first thing that came to mind, knowing an "I don't know" would just make Kyle more curious. Joey mentioned friends in the transportation industry the first time I'd met him. It fit. Kind of.

"Never met a trucker who wears Armani on his days off. And he doesn't have a Class C license. "

"He's not a driver, you dork," I said. "There are other jobs in transportation besides that."

"Like what?"

"Like, I'm not helping you with this, because I'm more than slightly offended that you're looking."

"Nichelle, the guy could be dangerous. Why does he keep turning up at crime scenes? I know you'll never tell me, but I'm pretty goddamned sure he's responsible for the other body they hauled off from Fauquier in June. Do you have any idea what you're getting yourself into?"

"Choose words carefully" flashed in sapphire neon behind my eyelids with every blink. Don't raise suspicion, but don't tell him anything he doesn't know. Simple.

Not.

Convince him I'd be safe. That was the exit ramp.

I smiled. "I'm well aware of what I'm getting into." Okay, no. I was as aware as I wanted to be. "He's not a bad guy, Kyle. Truly." Not to me.

Kyle searched my face for five heartbeats before he dropped his chin onto his hand and sighed.

"The photo..." He stopped, drumming his fingers on the tabletop. "It was from the file I'm working on the Caccione family. He is not a good guy, Nicey."

I folded my hands in my lap. "I like him, Kyle. More than I've liked anyone since..." I threw my hands up. "In a long time. I work around criminals ninety hours a week—my asshole radar is pretty good. I just don't get that vibe from him."

"Promise me you'll watch yourself. Call me if you need me."

"Always."

The conversation faded to wallflower-awkward silence.

I cleared my throat. "So...how 'bout them Cowboys?"

He laughed. "Having a good year, aren't they? I miss watching football with you."

"Your eardrums don't."

"True. You know the players can't actually hear you through the television."

"That's your opinion."

His eyes turned sober. "You'll be careful? I can think of all kinds of reasons the mob would be interested in you, and most of them aren't any kind of romantic."

"He is not the mob." Not when he was with me.

"Who gets to be our age and hasn't ever had a ticket?" he asked.

"What if the computer ran the prints wrong?"

"Not terribly likely."

"Yes, Kyle, computers are fail-proof." I rolled my eyes.

Computers. Tipping my hand on one little thing was a small price to pay to change this particular subject.

"Speaking of computers and records," I drained the rest of my soda and put the glass on the table, "have you guys noticed that Maynard is conspicuously unsearchable online?"

Kyle's eyes crinkled at the corners with a grin. "We're trying to figure out how. And why. You have a theory?"

"You going to share yours?"

"Come on, Nichelle. We're not your competition."

"Sharing information about a big story I have in the works almost always comes back to bite me in the ass, no matter whether it's the cops or people in my own newsroom," I said. "I've been burned enough to be pretty shy."

"What if you could help the investigation? Your job is to report on it, not do it yourself, right?"

True. And doing it myself generally gets me in trouble. His face held up under careful scrutiny for ulterior motive.

"Not a word to anyone," I said. "Anyone. Not Aaron, not Landers, not your boss, not your priest. Certainly not Charlie." I cut him a warning look. "Or Bonnie."

"In the vault." He raised his right hand. "On my grandmother's grave."

Wow. Kyle's grandmother's funeral was one of a handful of times I'd seen him cry, and we'd been through a lot together, once upon a time.

I nodded. "Jenna's husband is a professional hacker, and he's on it. But it's bizarre. He's been cleared from every major search engine, but not from individual sites. A search of the NIH turns up a ton of hits. A search of our servers brought up several articles and the big society piece on his retirement."

Kyle's fingers moved to stroke the bristles of his auburn goatee. "Huh."

"It's all got something to do with whatever he was researching."

Kyle nodded. "We figure the same thing. We just don't know what. There are no records. Most of the folders in his file drawers were empty."

"Stolen?"

He shrugged. "Who knows? Maybe he really didn't want anyone to know what he was doing."

"I take it you've been to his office?"

"Yep. Stem to stern, we searched. The girl who works at the desk had a fit, hollering about HIPPA and how we couldn't touch patient files without a warrant. But there wasn't anything in them, anyway."

"How many files we talking about?" My fingers worked at my hair, twisting it into knots.

"A hundred? Not too many."

So small trials.

"What do you mean there was nothing in the files?" I asked.

"I mean nothing. File folders. No papers inside."

"Who was the receptionist?"

"I think she's the nurse, too. It's a small office for a guy who was supposed to be such a big shot."

That fit. If I was following the right trail, the doc had wanted to keep what he was doing quiet. The big question was still why. And what. Oy.

Kyle watched my fingers loop my hair faster and faster. He poked my shoulder. "Something is rattling around in your head making you worry your hair like that."

I nodded. "Tom Ellinger wanted Maynard to treat his wife. Because he thought Maynard could cure her."

Kyle closed his eyes. "You are not about to tell me this dead doctor might have discovered a cure for cancer. Are you on something?"

I spread my hands. "You have better theory? Because I know exactly how crazy this sounds, but everything anyone has found so far sure in hell seems to point that way."

Kyle closed his eyes, lacing his fingers behind his head. "Holy. Shit."

"Indeed."

"You can't print this."

"I'd get myself laughed right out of the business for printing it now," I said. "Which is why I don't want anyone else knowing about it until I can dig up some more information. I mean, if it's true, it's not just the story of the year. It's the story of the...century. The millenium. Can you imagine?"

He shook his head. "But why keep it a secret?"

"Um. I'd say his murder shows he had a good reason."

Kyle took a long swallow of soda and nodded. "Indeed."

21

I sent Kyle off with a heartfelt well-wish for his date with Bonnie that made him smile, then reached for a bottle of wine and a corkscrew on my way to a hot bath and possibly bed shortly thereafter. If there's been a longer week in the history of the world, I wasn't there for it.

My cell phone started twittering the theme from *Peter Pan* before I got the foil off the bottle and I contemplated ignoring it for a full ten seconds.

My scanner was relatively silent, so it would be more in-depth than normal Friday night work. Not interested. But I reached for the phone anyway.

There's an inherent wiring short in my brain that would make it explode if I ignored a ringing phone. Not an altogether bad quality for a reporter, I suppose.

Joey.

I grinned. Him, I found positively enchanting.

"Hey there." I put the phone to my ear and opened the bottle.

"Hey yourself," he said. "Busy day?"

"You could say that." I pulled a glass from the rack and poured it half full of Moscato, padding toward the couch. "How about you?"

"Same. But I was thinking about you and I wanted to say hi."

Butterflies took off low in my stomach. I swallowed a sip of the wine. "Hi."

"I take it from the level of vague in your copy today that you're working this weekend?"

"Probably. Though I'm really trying to not work tonight."

"I wish I could join you."

Kyle's words floated through my head and my gut twisted. "Lots going on?"

"Boring stuff." Joey's tone was dismissive, but there was an undercurrent of our unspoken don't-ask-don't-tell in it, too.

"Mine, too."

"I doubt that. Anything new?"

"Eh. Same old, same old. Trying to save the world. Got my first subpoena."

"Witnessing things can lead to that." I could hear the laugh in his voice.

"Yeah, yeah, they tried to kill me, nobody else was there. Blah blah." I laughed. "Like I don't have enough to do. This story has more twists than a party size bag of pretzels. And Kyle is dating a forensic scientist who says someone's dragging their feet on the autopsies. Which also doesn't fit. The whole thing stinks."

"Really now?" He didn't even try to keep the interest out of his tone. "When did that happen?"

He wasn't talking about the murders. I laid it on thicker. "Sometime between Labor Day and this week. We haven't talked much. He seems to really like her, and I know she's had her eye on him for a while."

"Well. Good for him."

I listened hard. Reservation, yes. But was that excitement I heard? I could hope.

"I'm happy for him." I let the words fall slowly.

"I'm glad to hear that." The warmth in his voice could've melted Antarctica. Score.

I smiled. "I'll see you soon?"

"Next week? I'll make time to get down there," he said. "Right now I should go back in."

I didn't want to know in where. "There's a hot tub calling my name."

"Damn, now I really wish I was there," he said.

"Me too."

I clicked off the call and stared at the almost-finished Norman Rockwell on my coffee table, snapping a few of the five thousand tiny pieces into place and wishing the puzzles in my head would come together. But maybe Kyle dating would resolve the corner of the Joey puzzle that was wrapped up in jealousy. And maybe clearing my head would help me see a few pieces of the Maynard mess differently. I fit the last bit of the bottom corner in and took the wine to the bathtub.

By the time the water chilled a second time, I'd managed to turn the shouting questions in my head down to a dull roar. They were almost quiet as I fell asleep, Eunice floating through my thoughts for some reason I wasn't awake enough to place.

* * *

Shoving a mug under the coffeemaker, I yanked my hair back into a ponytail before dawn Saturday, as grateful for my first good night's sleep in a week as I was annoyed at having it pre-empted by a locker room drug bust at a sprawling suburban high school.

I parked near the field house a half-hour later, joining a small knot of reporters on the track as the first rays of dawn painted the bleachers on the far side of the field pink-orange.

"What? No special pass inside today?" Charlie rolled her eyes as her cameraman waved at me, flipping her perfect blonde bob and tapping a foot as she pointed out shots she wanted for her piece.

"He asked for you, too," I said when he stepped away to get the footage. "Not my fault you chose to stay outside."

"Losing the story is my fault for being sane? I know no one who would have gone into that building, except you."

"People might have died."

"Someone did. And whatever you're up to with keeping the gunman out of jail, you should know that when I figure it out, you'll be lucky if you don't get lynched. I know you traded White a sickeningly sweet PR piece for that. The woman's family knows it, too. You're too goody-goody for any motive short of some misguided bleeding heart crap, but I'm warning you: you won't look good when I get through with this."

My stomach lurched. Charlie and I had always been rivals, but neither of us had ever gone after the other in so blatant a fashion.

"Out for some blood, Charlie?" I kept my voice from trembling—barely. "I'm O-negative if you have to call for a transfusion."

"Nothing personal. My producer is tired of losing to you. You've kicked everyone's ass for months, like you think you're some sort of journalistic superwoman. Hell, I heard people in our break room talking about your piece on this murderer yesterday. Asking each other what they'd do in his shoes. Sweeps week means payback. I thought you'd appreciate the warning."

I closed my eyes, hatred of Rick Andrews burning in the pit of my stomach. Charlie wouldn't stop 'til she got something. And there were six hundred and seventy-eight ways to spin that story that would make me and Aaron look like lying idiots and Tom Ellinger look like a murderer. And people would believe it. Journalism even before the age of the Internet 101: perception is nine-tenths of the truth, and everyone loves a good scandal.

Hell.

"Charlie—" I didn't quite get the word out before Aaron stepped to the tape line at the edge of the grass and started his rundown.

By the time I finished talking to the coach and a pair of bawling mothers, Charlie was gone.

I sped to the office and filed the story, then spent my "day off" poring over notes and reading old studies Maynard was linked to. The research was all over the map. Chemo drugs, some I'd never heard of and others that had revolutionized treatment. Gene therapy. Non-invasive homeopathic approaches.

I clicked another link and found an article about treating brain tumors with live Polio virus. I blinked at the screen. The research in front of me was new—and working. On more than half the patients in the trials.

But Maynard had done it almost a decade ago, with at least some success, according to Bob. Hoping Miss Emma could find details on that, I saved the article on my screen. If Maynard had been that many years ahead of the research curve, maybe Ellinger wasn't nuts.

Not sure which of these roads might lead to his murderer, if any of them did, I closed the computer at four-thirty, ready for a long walk and a game of fetch with Darcy. Charlie's voice on the TV followed me into the elevator, and I wondered how much she knew. The only safe way out of this was to find the truth—assuming I was right and it wasn't the obvious choice—before she got her hack job ready for air.

Tick.

Tock.

22

"I love you, Mom. Send pictures of that bouquet, and I'll call you in a couple days."

I smiled at her "I love you more" and said it back twice before I hung up the phone and stretched. Being woken on a Sunday by a call from my mom was significantly more fun than waking up to Aaron's grouching about bored over-privileged kids the day before.

Hearing her voice had been more welcome than usual after a week peppered with painful reminders of almost losing her.

It also redoubled my determination to find the why in Maynard's murder. Aaron and Kyle wanted the who, and the how. The why was always a nice bonus for them, but would they dig for it with so much pressure coming for an arrest? Nope. Which left that stone to me. And if there was a sliver of a chance what was under it could save my mom if she ever again needed saving, I would find the right rock or die trying.

But first, coffee. I was always more productive with caffeine on board. I shuffled to the kitchen and brewed a cup of vanilla caramel creme before I let Darcy outside and went to the front door to grab the newspaper.

"Coffee and comics. Now this is Sunday morning." I put a bowl of Pro Plan in front of the dog and settled myself at the table, hunting for the Lifestyles section.

I pulled it free, my eyes lighting on a half-page photo of a gorgeous redhead hugging a preteen with each tanned arm.

"Miracle Mom," the headline screamed in ninety-two point Chancery.

The gibberish I'd been trying to recognize at bedtime Friday settled into actual words in my head: "Doctors said she should have died," in Eunice's Virginia drawl. I popped the section front straight and read every word of Kim's article four times.

"Jiminy. Freaking. Choos, Darce."

The dog ignored my jaw hitting the floor, licking her bowl clean and trotting off in search of a toy.

I stared into the bright blue two-dimensional eyes of Felicia Lang, who'd been dragged from the jaws of death two years before, lying in an ICU bed with a cancer-ravaged body and an utter lack of hope.

And our best feature reporter had artfully written around the cause of this miracle.

I'd bet my last cup of coffee that was because the woman wouldn't say how she got well.

And I'd wear Uggs all winter long if it didn't turn out to be Maynard who pulled off the last-minute rescue.

I groped back through my memory for the Tuesday staff meeting that seemed an age ago. Kim had to beg for the interview, Eunice said. And only got it because her husband knew these folks.

I scrambled to my feet and ran for my phone. So much for a lazy Sunday morning.

* * *

Kim knew jack squat. Four hours talking to the Langs, and no matter how she phrased her questions, they wouldn't spill.

Yes, it was odd. No, she didn't see the need to push. It was a feel-good feature. She saw the medical records and photos—the woman really had been hanging across the threshold of death's door.

I thanked her and hung up, underlining the phone number she'd offered for Felicia Lang. Dialing it wouldn't get me anywhere but hung up on. But three minutes with WhitePages got me an address.

Hot damn. Seven blocks from me. And the story said Felicia Lang worked with the local animal rescue center.

A quick shower and a little makeup, and I clipped Darcy's leash to her collar before we strolled out into the autumn sunshine.

Nineteen hours (or a good twenty minutes of Darcy investigating every weed and pebble in the Fan) later, I tried to be unobtrusive, staring at the Langs' antebellum brick-front home.

I knew the block. Senators and CEOs were counted among its residents. "These folks can be good at keeping secrets, girl," I murmured to the dog.

Darcy nosed at a dandelion, unconcerned. Until a squirrel darted out of a bed of ivy.

Darcy is not a fan of squirrels.

I grabbed for her, but it was too late. She slipped her collar faster than Joey can unhook a bra and charged the rodent, who had enough of a sense of self-preservation to turn and run back into the yard.

"Darcy!" I hissed, jangling her collar.

Completely. Ignored.

Yipping like a bloodhound, she tore through the ivy bed, the squirrel's tail waving in her face like a racetrack flag.

For the love of God.

I stared, not wanting to put a toe on the perfectly manicured blanket of rye in front of me. The squirrel leapt onto a tree trunk and scurried up, turning to look back at Darcy from a high branch. I could almost hear the "nyah nyah nah nah nah," and binoculars might have shown me a little pink tongue poking out at the dog.

Darcy clawed at the bark, her whole body on alert, baying like she'd chased Charles Manson up there. I jogged up the driveway and down the sidewalk and scooped her up, clipping her collar back in place and pulling it a centimeter tighter. "No running off," I said, bumping her nose with mine. I turned back for the street as the front door opened to reveal our Sunday Life section cover boy.

He paused, raising an eyebrow at me, before he turned his head and bellowed. "Mom! Someone's here to see you!"

I flinched. I wanted an introduction, sure, but I was fresh out of icebreaker ideas. And pretty certain I'd come across as a stalker, likely as not.

I pasted a smile in place as the kid grabbed a skateboard from under the porch and disappeared up the street. Felicia Lang appeared in the doorway thirty seconds later, wiping her hands on a blue dishtowel. "Can I help you?"

I held Darcy up. "The dog saw a squirrel. Sorry to bother you."

"She's adorable!" She laid the towel on a table and bounced down the front steps, scratching behind Darcy's ears.

All right then. Point for Darcy. I smiled. "Thank you. She's my princess. But she's a handful—she slipped her head out of her collar and took off though your flower bed before I could grab her."

Felicia frowned and put two fingers under Darcy's collar. "It's too loose."

"I worry about tightening it because she's so tiny," I said. "Most of the time she's just in our yard, and there's a fence, so I don't worry."

She nodded. "It's hard when they're so fluffy. What you think looks too tight isn't. But you could always get her a harness."

"Do they make those this small?" I knew good and well they did, but wanted to keep the conversation going.

"Sure they do. Any pet store should be able to help you." She stroked Darcy's fur. "You want to be able to take her on walks without worrying about her getting hurt."

"I'll look into that, thanks." I tipped my head to one side, studying her face, and snapped my fingers. "I know where I recognize you from! You were in the newspaper this morning. What a great story."

She smiled, dropping her gaze to the aggregate sidewalk. "Thank you. I'm a girl blessed."

"My mom is a cancer survivor too," I blurted. "Six years in remission."

"That's wonderful," she said. "What kind of cancer did she have?"

"Breast cancer. I managed to get her into a clinical trial for a new drug several years back." I kept my tone light, conversational.

She nodded. "Sometimes getting in on the floor of a new treatment saves your life." The words were so soft, I almost didn't hear them over Darcy's breathing.

"Were you in a trial, too?" I asked. "For which drug?"

"It was—" she paused. "That's not exactly how it worked."

I fiddled with the dog's leash. She didn't want to talk about this, if Kim couldn't get it out of her. But talking to a survivor's daughter and talking to a reporter are two different things. Usually. And I wasn't looking to quote her.

"I still find myself looking all the time for successful treatments. My mom is great, but I worry. What if it comes back? How would we fight it?"

She nodded, turning to sit on the steps and gesturing for me to join her. "I can certainly understand that." She bit her lower lip.

I perched next to her, petting Darcy. "Who treated you? Someone local?" I held my breath.

She nodded. "He's a brilliant man. We're just lucky he happens to be in Richmond. I wouldn't be here if it weren't for him."

"My mom is in Texas, so I don't know many of the doctors here, but I'm always happy to add new ones to my list."

"Dr. Maynard keeps his patient group small," she said. "But he really cares about everyone he treats. No one is just a number or just a paycheck to him."

Bingo. I swallowed hard and tried not to croak out the next question. "I read in the paper that you were nearly end stage. Do you know how he saved you?"

She shrugged. "Not specifically. Other than he said he was working to perfect the treatment so it could be made available to everyone."

I nodded. "Were there other people in the trial with you?"

"Not many. A handful of us, and a control group."

"Do you still talk to the others?"

"One or two of them. Almost all of us lived."

"Almost?"

"Dr. Maynard was different. He treated the control group, too, after he'd had time to gather data. But before he got to that point, we lost one person. It really shook the doc up for weeks. I remember going in one evening and he was shouting at another man, who was yelling right back at him."

Interesting.

"You didn't happen to notice what they were fighting about?" The words popped out before I could stop them, and she gave me a raised brow.

"Not that it really matters," I said. "Just curious. I always wondered what went on behind the scenes when we'd sit in the doctors' offices and people watch."

She nodded. "I don't remember. Something about test results and registration. It didn't make sense to me."

Ah, but it did to me. I squeezed Darcy a little tighter, Goetze and his lunch companion floating through my thoughts.

"Do you still see this Dr. Maynard for check-ups?" I asked. "I mean, if I wanted to get him to take a look at my mom's charts, do you think I could?"

"Only once a year," she said. "Other than that, I see my regular OB/GYN. But there's no harm in asking him to look, right? He's brilliant. Truly in his own class." She reeled off the office address and I recited it over a dozen times in my head.

I smiled. "You look fantastic. Feeling good?"

"Fabulous. As dark as those days were, I hope I never stop seeing every new one as a gift. And I hope your mom's health remains good."

A child bellowed from inside the house, and I stood. "I think that's your cue."

She laughed. "I love it. It was nice to meet you..." The eyebrow went back up.

"Nichelle," I said. "And this is Darcy."

She scratched the dog's head again before she turned to go inside. "Good luck."

"You too."

I trotted back down the drive toward my house, turning her words over in my head.

Un-freaking-believable. If David Maynard hadn't found the golden grail, he was two breaths from it. So someone made sure he stopped breathing.

23

Stepping out of Amy's room the next day, I closed the door softly and sucked in a deep breath before I turned for the nurse's station.

In my hand was a notebook full of heart-wrenching love story, with a healthy dose of everything that made the U.S. healthcare system unfair. In my head was a brain just as full of questions.

If I could get Alisha talking about Goetze again, maybe she'd share something I could use. Or maybe she'd remember something about Maynard.

Anything was better than the big fat black hole currently in the middle of this puzzle.

I waited at the end of the counter for her to turn around, my eyes roaming the hallway. People moved quietly in and out of the rooms, the doctors and nurses bending their heads and talking in hushed tones. I spotted a slight, rumpled man staring at me as he shuffled down the hallway. I waved. He ducked his head, his thick black hair shining under the fluorescents, and scurried into a room three down from Amy's.

Huh.

I took a step toward the door, then paused. He was keeping watch over someone he loved, who had to be pretty sick to be in this ward.

But why run from a simple wave?

Before I could follow that rabbit trail too far, a doctor stepped out of the room next to Amy's, making notes on a tablet touchscreen. He tapped with the stylus twice and stuck it back in his pocket before striding into the room across the hall.

My scarlet Manolos grew roots into the linoleum, my eyes still fixed on the space the doctor had vacated.

All this time, we'd been looking for Maynard's files.

And it wasn't that he was crazy and didn't keep them, or that they'd been stolen.

They were electronic.

I reached into my shoulder bag and tapped a finger on my cell phone. I loathe feeling stupid.

There was a good chance Kyle would feel just as dumb. So would Aaron. They spent days tearing apart the doc's home, after all. By time comparison, they should've had this way before now.

I had Kyle's number half-dialed and stopped.

What if they did?

To hear them tell it, the President himself wanted them to keep quiet. If they'd found Maynard's iPad, would they tell me?

Nope.

Was there a way for Charlie to land here? Or Alexa?

If I could, so could they.

Damn.

I was still debating calling Kyle when Alisha turned to me.

"Good morning!" she chirped. "Good to see you again. Mrs. Ellinger has been doing so much better since you were here the other day."

"She didn't look better this morning."

"She has more lucid moments. At this stage of her illness, that's pretty remarkable all by itself. She seems to be in less pain."

"I'm glad to hear that." I smiled, swallowing the lump in my throat and thinking of Felicia Lang. Had she been as sick as Amy?

"What brings you back here this morning?" Alisha widened her eyes expectantly.

"I'm doing a series on the Ellingers. What happened here last week. Why it happened. How. What are the underlying issues that drive people to act out violently? No one's ever really gotten to interview a guy who walked into an occupied building and started shooting. They usually don't make it out."

She shook her head. "I saw it with my own eyes, and I still can't believe it. They're such a nice family. He's such a nice man. How on Earth did he end up there?"

I nodded. "That's actually part of what I wanted to ask you about, if you have a second."

"Of course." She stepped to the counter and leaned on her palms. "I'm happy to help however I can."

"How well did you know Dr. Goetze?"

"What does that have to do with the Ellingers?"

"I can't explain in detail right now, but can you humor me?"

She tipped her head to one side, then nodded. "We dated. Briefly."

Better than I'd hoped for. "Did he ever talk about Dr. Maynard and his research?"

"Wesley talked about work all the time. He was obsessed with Maynard. Called him a genius."

"What were they working on?"

"Didn't Wesley tell you?"

"It seems he's too busy to talk to me."

"Why wouldn't he talk to a reporter? That's like free advertising for his practice."

"He could just be busy. But I admit curiosity. And when one source stonewalls me, I find another." I winked.

"Maynard is the kind of doctor you expect to find living in a tent in Africa, vaccinating children. The only reason he isn't is because he's convinced he can help more people working in oncology."

"Lots of research, right?"

"Yeah. For the university, and for the pharma companies, too."

"What's the difference?"

"Depends on the studies. The drug companies fund more and more of them these days. They have deep pockets, and they want a doctor to sign off on the results."

"Who owns the results if they pay for the study?" I don't get paid to assume.

"They do."

And they make billions of dollars every year off the medicine to treat a disease Maynard was trying to cure.

So he went off the grid to try to save the world.

And got himself killed.

Puzzle pieces arranged themselves in my head, and I couldn't say the picture didn't make a hell of a lot of sense.

I looked around, thinking about Tom, and the poor dead woman. Stephanie.

Something tickled the back of my brain. Alisha's soft voice, chaos, too many people talking.

Oh, man.

A drug company.

Suppressing the urge to overshare by asking one question, I pulled in a slow breath and chose another. "Alisha, how many shots did you hear that day?"

"Two. He only fired two."

Two. Yep.

Except...what if?

I thanked Alisha for her help and sprinted back to my car.

* * *

Digging through my notes for the comments from the day of the shooting, I finally found what I was looking for. Alisha had said it: Stephanie was a marketing rep at Evaris.

Evaris, the third-largest drug company in North America.

Evaris, where there was a VP who lived in Maynard's building and had rankled Aaron enough to get hauled in for questioning.

So the first victim was (maybe) trying to keep something from a drug company. And the second was an employee at one.

Less than zero chance that was coincidence. I snatched up the phone.

"Miss Emma? Can you tell me which pharma company Dr. Maynard worked with? Or if there was more than one, which one he worked with the most?"

"Hello to you too, missy." Emma's wispy voice brightened. "I was going to call you this morning and I got busy. Your Dr. Goetze doesn't do much in the way of research, which is odd for someone with his background."

Huh. Somehow, I was going to have to get in to see that dude.

"I found the report you asked for, too," she continued. "It's a field of research that's exploding right now, using live viruses to make the immune system attack cancer. But Dr. Maynard pioneered it almost ten years ago. Brilliant, brilliant man."

I scribbled, nodding. "Thank you so much for your help."

"And what kind of clue did you turn up, Lois Lane?"

"I'm not sure yet. But I have a hunch. And my gut rarely fails me."

"Drug companies, huh? I thought you were going to ask for something hard." She clicked computer keys in the background. "Here we go." She fell quiet for a minute, probably reading. "Not companies. Company. Doc Maynard worked exclusively with Evaris, according to the data I have."

Evaris. Hot damn.

No freaking way two people connected with that place turn up dead in a week and it's unrelated.

All of a sudden, Tom Ellinger's insistence that he only fired one shot seemed like the detail we should've paid more mind. What if he wasn't guilty of killing anyone?

Someone sure wanted Aaron and Kyle to think he was.

Hoping I wasn't crazy for chasing this rabbit, I thanked Miss Emma and hung up, staring at my computer for a full minute.

What did I know?

More than this morning. Both victims had a strong tether to Evaris.

Stephanie Whitmire wasn't just an unlucky bystander. That was huge.

What did I need to know?

Still the top of the list: exactly what Maynard was working on. The more I learned, the surer I was that the key to the whole damned thing was rooted in that. Kyle and Aaron likely thought the same thing, but whoever had told them to hush had enough power to keep them from talking. I liked my tablet theory, but couldn't think of a place to take it right then.

I clicked to Channel Four's website. I know from having my ass kicked a few too many times: if I can think of it, so can Charlie. And she was plenty steamed at me.

I scrolled through the political stuff that goes with election season, looking for Charlie's byline. Her only story of the day was an armed robbery at the RAU Starbucks (two thousand bucks and the clerk's cell phone). A robbery I still needed to write up. Damn.

Sometimes the best way to untangle a sticky story is to work on a straightforward one. I tabled my new lead and clicked to the PD's reports database. Finding the one I wanted, I called the head of campus security and got the specifics.

I hung up the phone with a giggle, opening a blank document.

Richmond Police are asking for help identifying two suspects in the late-night robbery of the Starbucks in the student center on the Richmond American University campus.

"Witnesses interviewed at the scene reported two Caucasian females in masks and bikinis," Al Gableman, Chief of the campus police department, said. "A review of the security tape appears to show two young women in swimsuits, but no masks are present."

Gableman said the clerks on duty at the time of the robbery were all male.

I kept the language as plain as possible, but there was no candy-coating it: the guys got distracted by boobs, and the bikini bandits got away with the loot. Gableman at the campus PD said they didn't have a clear shot of the women's faces, but he'd send Larry stills to run with the story. Facebook would eat it up, and Andrews would be pacified for another day. I hoped.

I finished with numbers for the RPD and the campus police, then read back through and checked Bob's budget email. Fourteen inches. That would fit just about right with a small header. Perfect. One easy thing a day was better than none. I proofed it one last time and sent it to Bob.

Clock check: four thirty-five.

I flipped back to my what-do-I-need to know list.

Item two: Stephanie Whitmire.

What did a drug marketing rep know that could have gotten her killed?

24

I went back over Stephanie's social media profiles, checking photo tags and noting names for her boyfriend and closest friends. Clicking through their profiles, I found my in—one of the women in most of the victim's photos was a coworker. I needed intel on Evaris, and young single woman plus dead BFF equals someone who almost certainly will want to talk. I pulled up a private message window.

Hi Casey,

I'm a reporter at the Richmond Telegraph *working on a story about Stephanie's murder. Can I buy you a glass of wine after work?*

Send.

A green light told me she was online. Message read. Reply bubble.

Steph's mother tells me the guy who killed her is not in jail because of you. Bite me.

Ouch. Trying again.

I was there, and there's more to this story. I know you don't know me, but you can believe I want to find who killed your friend every bit as much as you do. What harm could one drink be?

Message read. Crickets.

I watched the window for a full minute before I clicked back to

Stephanie's profile. Maybe there was someone else. Clearly someone not the woman's parents, from Casey's reply.

I was just about to call the boyfriend's cell (I'll never understand why people put their phone numbers on public profiles, but it doesn't stop me from being grateful for it) when my messages binged.

From Casey:

Meet me at Sine at six-thirty.

Perfect. I copied the boyfriend's number to keep him in reserve and clicked to the drug company's website. I had just enough time for a little reading before happy hour.

* * *

My cell phone binged a text arrival as I stepped out of my SUV in Shockoe Slip at twenty after. I nearly dropped it thanks to spontaneous applause when I saw it was Chad: *Call me when you have time to talk.* Maybe he'd found something. And I wanted to know if there was any way cyberspace could locate Maynard's iPad.

Heading into an interview, give me a half hour?

Bing. *Sure.*

Swinging the heavy door open, I waved to the hostess as I strode to the bar. I recognized Casey from her Facebook photos and perched on the stool next to her, nodding to the bartender when he turned to look at me.

"I'll have a glass of the Williamsburg Governor's Reserve, please," I said, turning to Casey.

"I'll take a double scotch, neat," she said.

The bartender smiled and turned to get the drinks.

"Thanks for coming to meet me," I said.

"I'm not here for you. I'm here for Steph. And her family. Do you know how much it hurts them that their daughter is gone, and the man responsible is still sitting next to his wife? And they have to see it in the newspaper every day, this story of how a 'nice guy' was driven to the brink." The words flew from her lips like daggers, each cutting deep.

I deserved it: Would I be angry in her shoes, with the information she had? Damn straight. "If I'm wrong about this, I will issue a public apology to the family." I kept my eyes and tone kind.

The stiff line of her mouth softened slightly, and I held her gaze for another ten seconds before I spoke again. "But I don't think I am, Casey. I get more convinced every day that someone set this man up. And I don't think Stephanie's death was bad luck. Is it possible that she knew anything about a drug trial? Maybe a trial Evaris didn't want anyone else to know about?"

Her eyes popped so wide a passerby would've thought I'd slapped her.

The bartender put napkins and drinks in front of us, and I thanked him without taking my eyes off still-silent Casey.

"You're going to need to say something."

She blinked. "We didn't work on trials. We sell meds, we don't create them." The words were stiff.

My internal lie detector bleeped.

"You don't have to work on trials to know things," I prodded gently.

"Steph didn't tell me what she knew." Her eyes dropped and so did her tone.

Uh-huh. I just bet she hadn't.

"Come on, Casey. What's going on? You're here for Stephanie, remember?"

She grabbed the scotch and downed it in two swallows. My turn for the wide eyes.

The ones Casey turned back on me were scared. "She didn't tell me what. Only that she was afraid."

I pulled a notebook and pen slowly from my bag. "Do you mind if I write some of this down?"

She waved a hand. "No names."

"Of course."

I jotted what she'd said so far and looked up.

"Did you tell the police this?"

"What?"

"That she was scared."

"I haven't talked to the police. Steph's parents said they didn't ask too many questions. They say they know what happened. The funeral is tomorrow."

I nodded. "Can you remember anything else? Did she tell you how she found out about what made her afraid? Or exactly what she was afraid of?"

"Getting in trouble. She got an email. Someone copied her on it by mistake, she said. But whatever was in it, she kept saying she wished she could unsee it, and she was afraid they'd notice she'd gotten it. I thought she was being dramatic."

And you didn't think this worth mentioning when she turned up dead? I bit down on the words before they could tumble out. I wasn't there to point fingers.

"Do you know if she saved the email that upset her? And where?"

Casey nodded. "She said she backed it up to her cloud."

"Any idea how to open her backup?"

"She gave me the password." A tear slipped down one perfectly spray-tanned cheek. "I swear I thought she was being paranoid."

I patted her hand. "Anyone else probably would, too. Any chance you have that password on you?"

Casey shook her head. "It was weeks ago. I didn't think she was serious. Something about her birthday."

My heart dropped into my stomach. Damn.

She dissolved into tears. "I'm so sorry, Steph."

I bit my lip, my eyes lighting on the plastic badge dangling from her neck. Maybe not the best idea ever, but I was running out of time.

I patted Casey's shoulder until her sobs quieted, then handed her a napkin for her nose.

"I wish I could be more help to you." She blew her nose, then sniffled as she wiped at her eyes.

I smiled. "You actually could."

"How? I told you everything I know."

I nodded to the badge. "I'd like to have a look around Stephanie's desk. Surely they haven't cleaned it out yet."

She shook her head. "They asked me to, but I couldn't bring myself to touch her things. You think you might find something?"

What I thought was that a trip to Evaris could be the fastest way to an answer. And Casey could get me inside. I glanced out the window at the low-hanging harvest moon and stood, dropping some cash on the bar for the drinks and waving for Casey to follow me.

"Only one way to find out."

* * *

I scanned the ceiling for camera bubbles, but didn't see any as Casey pulled off her badge and swiped it through the electronic lock on the door leading in from the garage.

"We're on the sixth floor," she said, punching the elevator call button.

I glanced around. "Is anyone usually here this late?"

"Not that I know of," she said. "Most people knock off by about six."

I stepped into the elevator and tried to settle my jangled nerves. It wasn't like I was breaking in. I was with an employee.

Funny how looking for something nobody wants found can make a girl edgy.

The doors whispered open to a dark, quiet maze of cube walls and gray carpet. Casey eyed me as she stepped off the elevator. "You okay?"

I nodded. "Just hoping this isn't a wasted trip." I tried my best for an easy smile.

"You really think there's more to this than the police are telling her parents, don't you?" She gestured to a hallway and I followed her, nodding.

"I promise I wouldn't be here if I didn't. Sneaking around dark office buildings isn't exactly my idea of a stellar evening."

"I hope there's something here that will tell you for sure. Her mom is so heartbroken. Some closure for them would be nice."

We walked silently past a row of doors with platinum nameplates, and I almost tripped over my own feet when I saw Alan Shannon's name on one of them. The same Alan Shannon who lived in Maynard's building worked in spitting distance of the other murder victim?

Aaron told me his alibi checked out and they'd let him go, but roughly a million crime stories have taught me that true coincidences are rarer than magical glass slippers.

Casey turned and stopped, pointing me into a cube not twenty-five feet from Shannon's office.

I swallowed hard, a bulletin board with photos of Stephanie and Casey and other folks I assumed were coworkers catching my eye. Playing softball, having drinks, dressed up for Halloween. No way this woman was a bystander. She'd stumbled across a secret. A secret so big someone was willing to kill or pay big bucks—or both—to keep it quiet.

I lifted stacks of folders and paper on the desktop, no keyboard in sight.

"Computer?" I asked.

Casey shrugged. "We all have company-issued laptops. She probably took it with her."

Strike one.

Thirty-five minutes of flipping through folders and rifling through drawers later, I was more than a little ready to tear out half my hair. Nothing. Or, nothing that looked like anything, anyway. Since I couldn't walk out with the contents of Stephanie's desk and I wasn't sure I wanted to bring Shannon up with Casey, I was at a loss.

I looked up. "I don't even know what I'm looking for. You don't remember anything else?"

She shut her eyes. "I wish I'd paid better attention. I can't even tell you what I'd give to go back and listen to her." She twisted her lips to one side. "I also have to pee."

I picked up another folder and nodded. "Can I stay here?" Holding my voice steady wasn't easy, what with the slightly underhanded plan forming in my frontal cortex.

She nodded, adding that the bathrooms were on the other side of the floor and promising to be back shortly.

I held my breath until she was out of sight, then dropped the folder I was holding onto the desk and slipped off my shoes, picking them up and padding quickly to Shannon's door.

I tried the knob, whispering a prayer under my breath.

Locked.

Of course.

Glancing around, I reached up and pulled a pin out of my hair, working it slowly into the lock the way Joey had taught me. Prodding gently, I felt a lever give. A push lock.

My face broke into a grin. That, I could handle. Find the right one, pop it, and it's all good.

Twenty-eight seconds later, I swung the door wide.

Three maple filing cabinets lined the cream-colored back wall, which was dotted with mounted animal heads that seemed to follow my every move. Shudder.

Could I find something? No idea. Casey would be back in a few minutes.

I crossed quickly to the desk and surveyed the drawers. If I were hiding something, I wouldn't put it in the big file drawer. Or the side one.

The top? I slid it open and shoved my hand inside, feeling for paper.

Nothing but a pack of Winstons. Yuck.

I turned for the file cabinets, flipping through neatly alphabetized folders and catching a breath when I saw Maynard's name. I wriggled that one free.

Empty.

Forgetting my bare feet at the wrong moment, I kicked the cabinet, then bit blood out of my lip trying not to howl. Eyes smarting, I hobbled to the credenza next to the desk and opened it.

A cell phone dock, an electric razor, and a stack of plain white printer paper. I sighed. I suppose if I was trying to cover up something that would cause thousands of people to die, plus murdering a couple here and there, I wouldn't leave a confession laying around my office either.

I leaned forward to flip the door closed and a glint in the cabinet caught my eye. Pushing the speaker dock aside, I reached behind it.

And found a thumb drive taped to the back wall of the cabinet.

Could be nothing. Could be perfectly legit work documents. Could be love letters—or porn.

But maybe not.

I shut the cabinet and stood, dropping the drive into my pocket.

Just in time to hear voices in the hallway.

25

I froze, my eyes on the door. Casey was coming this way, and she wasn't alone.

Her companion was definitely male.

Damn.

No one could see me leaving this room, especially not given that Shannon might notice his drive was missing.

I flattened myself against the wall behind the door and closed my eyes, trying not to breathe too loudly.

"Really, such a tragedy about poor Stephanie," Mr. Mystery said. "I know you two were close."

"I miss her," Casey said softly.

They passed the door, and I strained to listen.

"It's horrible when an accident like this takes someone we love," he said. "Makes no sense. Why was she even there that day?"

It took everything in me to stay against the wall. The guy was fishing. Hopefully Casey was too smart to bite.

"Sales call," Casey said. "We had lunch that day and she told me she had to run by St. Vince's on the way home and check the fifth floor ICU supply of Zanthrin."

My fingers folded into a fist at my side.

Someone sent her there. Not just to the hospital. Not just to that floor. To that room.

When they were out of earshot, I slid my shoes back on (ouch) and slipped out, pushing the door lock—and wiping the knob—as I went.

I hovered at the end of the next cube row and watched until Casey's companion walked away, ducking when he got close to me.

He kept moving, giving no indication he'd spotted me.

I swallowed a wave of nausea and counted to fifteen before I stood.

Captain Tell Me About Your Friend knew something about Stephanie's unwanted email—I'd bet my new Prada boots on it, watching him disappear around a corner.

Just like I'd watched him disappear out the door when he finished arguing with Goetze over the big envelope at the diner.

* * *

Casey had no trouble buying that I'd gotten lost on the way to the restroom, smiling apologetically when I told her I didn't think there was anything useful in Stephanie's desk. I thanked her and left it at that, unable to come up with a single reason why I should know she'd been talking to anyone.

We were halfway back to the restaurant before she mentioned him.

"Even Mr. Crenshaw asked me about her tonight," she said, staring out the window and fiddling with her hair. "It's like no one can believe she's gone."

"Who's that?"

"The head of our accounting department," she said. "I ran into him when I went to the restroom. It's funny how the company is so big, but everyone knows everyone, kind of. He seemed really sad."

Sure he was.

I dropped her at her car and thanked her again, scribbling the guy's name on a napkin I pulled from the console before I pointed the car toward Jenna's.

If I couldn't run down Stephanie's ominous email, maybe I knew someone who could.

* * *

Chad listened to the short version of why I thought there was a killer on the loose without comment, throwing in a couple of nods I suspected were for effect. I finished talking and he stared at me, flipping a paperclip through his fingers, for a solid two minutes before he sighed.

"Jenna's told me about your crazy investigations before, but to be honest, I kinda thought she was exaggerating." He dropped the paperclip to the wooden tabletop in their dining room. "She wasn't, was she? You have one hell of a mess on your hands here, and my considered advice would be to give it to the cops and let them handle it."

"Which would be great if one of them wasn't already convinced they have their murderer locked down, or if I knew who was giving their marching orders."

The second Evaris became a large piece of my puzzle, I started questioning the motives of the hush-hush stuff my cops were dishing out. Not that I thought the guys were in league with big pharma. But who might be keeping them quiet and why—I couldn't say for sure.

Add all that to my everyday drive to beat Charlie, my obsession with protecting Bob, and this idea that there might be a freaking cure for cancer lurking somewhere in this mess, and I couldn't make myself back off if I'd wanted to. Which I didn't.

"But your job is to tell the story. Not to create it. Right? I get the rushing to beat all the other reporters, but there have to be limits. And whatever you're into, people who go to this much trouble to hide something don't play around."

I saw the worried lines around his eyes and smiled. Chad was a good guy. "Getting the story first is the big thing. I work for that every day. The 'crazy investigations' you're talking about only happen when I think the story I'm being given might not be right. My job is to give my readers the truth, or as close to it as I can find. When I think there's something missing from a story, I hunt for it. That's what makes me good."

Chad nodded slowly. "I understand and respect that. But what if you're in over your head?"

I opened my mouth to reply and stopped, tapping a finger on the table as I studied his face. "Why? What did you find?"

"This is upper level stuff, Nichelle. It's not a glitch. It's not a high school kid playing around with his laptop. Someone who knows what the hell they're doing did this."

"How?"

"Best I can tell, the easiest way is with a virus. But to write a virus that would find and erase just his name, then manage to successfully upload it to one of the most secure servers in the world? That's not just for fun. That's...that's a lot of fucking money is what that is, Nichelle."

The kind of money Evaris would have sitting around?

"How much?"

"I couldn't begin to guess. Hundreds of thousands, at a minimum. Guys who can do this kind of stuff don't work cheap."

I nodded. "And they don't leave tracks?"

He chuckled. "Not that I could find. I've run through hundreds of lines of source code for the search engine, but I'm not really sure what kind of variation I'm hunting. I have a buddy who used to work for the government. He's nosing around. He's good. But even he was impressed by this."

"Thanks, Chad."

"It was the most interesting thing I did this week."

"Speaking of the doc and computers: I wonder if he might have kept his patient files in a tablet. And if there's a way to find it if he did." I offered a hopeful half-smile.

"There's no locating it remotely if it's turned off, even if you have his password. You'd have to search the old-fashioned way."

"That's what I was afraid of."

"Sorry."

"S'okay." I grinned. "Want another assignment?"

Jenna's head popped around the edge of the doorway. "How come everyone but me gets to help you play Lois Lane?"

I stood up and hugged her. "You're the moral support section. Your job is the most important."

She turned for the wine rack and laughed. "In that case, let me get to work."

"A big bottle," I said.

"You staying for dinner?"

"If I'm invited," I said. "Hey—speaking of, are we doing girls' night Friday?"

Jenna glanced at Chad, who shrugged. She nodded. "Chinese?"

I made a face. "Only if we can go to Fat Dragon."

"Deal. And don't get my husband shot at, okay?"

"Never."

Jenna disappeared into the kitchen and returned with two glasses of wine and a beer. "You were saying?"

I reached into my pocket and tapped the thumb drive, but I wanted to see if I could get to the files on it myself before I asked for help. "Is it possible to hack into a cloud-based backup?" I asked Chad.

He nodded. "It's happening somewhere right now, probably to some unsuspecting starlet who doesn't know the sexy photos she sent her boyfriend last night are about to be all over the internet."

I smiled. "How do you feel about trying it?"

"Which one?"

"I don't exactly know."

"You want me to get into all of them looking for one account? I—I can't. I mean, I could, but it would take a year."

"What if I could find out which one it is?"

"Then I could probably do what you're asking."

"How long would it take?"

"No idea. Could be three hours, could be a week. Depends on a lot of things."

Wow. "I thought those things were supposed to be safe?"

"For the average user? Sure. But it's not unbreakable. It's just finding an in."

I nodded. "I'll find out which one and let you know."

"What am I looking for?"

"The woman who was shot at the hospital—I think she knew something someone didn't want her to know. She got ahold of an email I'd like to have a look at. Her friend said she'd backed it up to a cloud drive."

Chad nodded, and Jenna picked up her wine glass and twirled it before she took a sip. "You going to tell us the whole story?"

Not yet. "Plausible deniability." I winked. "What's for dinner?"

"Ham and cheese!" Gabby's voice came from the living room and I laughed.

"Maybe we should talk after the tiny tape recorders go to bed."

Jenna nodded. "I have plenty of wine, and I've missed you this week. We got used to you being around more this summer."

I grinned when Gabby barreled around the corner and flung her seven-year-old self into my lap. "Yeah, auntie Nicey. When are you bringing Darcy back to play?" Carson trailed his sister into the room and sat down on my foot.

I fluffed his blond curls and smiled at Gabby. "She misses you too, sweet girl. Let's help Momma with dinner and make plans for Darcy to visit this weekend, okay?" I shot Jenna a look and she nodded approval.

The kids bounced into the kitchen and we followed. Jenna pulled bread and sandwich fixings from the fridge and watched me lift Carson onto my hip. He blew a sticky raspberry on my cheek and I laughed.

"You're going to be a good mom, you know that?" Jenna smiled.

I rolled my eyes and spun the baby in a circle.

"How's it going with Captain Mystery?"

"Not in the direction of babies. Or if it is, it's crawling there."

"And how's Kyle?"

"Shut up, Jen." I put the baby down and opened the bread. "Kyle is dating. Sort of. And I want Kyle to be happy."

"I want you to be happy." She passed me a knife.

"I am. For now."

"And for later?"

I put Carson's sandwich on a plate and added a few potato chips. "For now is enough. For now."

* * *

Still pondering Jenna's words when I took Darcy out to play fetch four hours later, I wasn't closer to a long-term answer. Joey was...Joey. He was sexy and exciting and mysterious.

I leaned against the doorjamb and tossed the squirrel again, watching the dog take off after it.

Was it the mystery that made me want him?

No. It made me nervous.

Was it the danger?

No. I worried.

Was it, like Emily had said six million times, that I knew deep down it couldn't really ever work?

Definitely not—the thought of him leaving made my throat close up.

But the way he held me, the way he kissed me, the way I felt when he was there—that made me all tingly and weak-kneed and slightly ridiculous.

I grabbed the toy and turned to go inside, bending to scratch Darcy's silky ears and sighing. "What am I going to do, girl?"

She didn't answer.

Staying under the shower until the hot water ran out didn't get me any further, and my thoughts returned to the story as I toweled my hair off.

I propped up on pillows in my big cherry four-poster and flipped my computer open, popping the little drive into the port on the side.

It wasn't even password protected. I couldn't decide if that was awesome or terrible, because surely if there was anything good there it would be locked. Right?

Three folders, all labeled with numbers. I clicked the first one up and found just one file inside: a spreadsheet. Four columns of numbers, none of them labeled, though the decimals in the second set sure made them look like dates. I opened a calendar.

Three week intervals for the past three years. Huh.

I stared at the other two columns 'til the clock ticked from Monday to Tuesday and my eyes wouldn't stay open. The second set were all within ten of each other, with several numbers repeated. The third were bigger values, and all in a few hundred number gap, save for one. A 750,000 came at the end of a single line with one date (assuming I was right) that was just three months ago.

I scrolled back to the top. No heading. No file name that made any sense. Slamming the laptop shut, I turned off the light. Everything led to more questions.

The fan crept through the dimness, and I flipped over more times than a well-done steak trying to shut off my brain and sleep. Maynard. Stephanie. The Ellingers. Joey. Bob. My mother. So much hanging over my head. So many people I wanted to help.

I wished Joey was there—he made it easy to drift off to sleep and stay that way. But that just brought Jenna's questions swirling back up. How on Earth did I end up here? Me, the girl who lost her heart on the second date and nearly didn't survive losing Kyle all those years ago—I'd protected myself from being hurt again (Emily said) by shying away from relationships all together. And here I was falling for this man. But it could never last.

I turned on my side and punched the pillow into submission.

This was what happened when I let myself think about forever. I should stop.

Who was ever guaranteed forever, anyway? Sophia Kochanski had a husband with a normal job, children—and got her heart broken because he was weak and Elizabeth Herrington was ruthless.

The thought of that kind of pain was enough to send me running for the nearest convent. But Joey...

The best thing about Joey was how safe I felt with him. Kyle could wave caution flags 'til doomsday, but I never felt scared when I was with Joey. Whatever else there might be, whatever else he might have done, it was simple when you cut through all the crap: I could trust Joey with my heart.

Maybe that was more than enough.

26

By the time the first yellow-orange rays filtered through my roman shades at seven, I'd missed Body Combat for the third day in a row. But I had an idea.

I dove for the laptop before I got out of bed and clicked from Facebook to Google Plus.

Stephanie Whitmire had a profile. An active one with hundreds of people in her circles. I clicked to her info page and found what I was looking for: a gmail address. While it was unlikely that an errant work email had gone there, maybe it could help us find the backup.

I grabbed my cell phone and texted Chad.

She used gmail. Can you get into her account? Or find out if it was a Google drive backup? Her friend said the password was something to do with her birthday.

I paused and clicked back to the profile, then tapped: *September 22.*

I stared at the screen and waited.

Bing. *Email address?*

I sent it to him and scrambled out of bed, flipping on the coffee maker on my way to let Darcy out.

By the time I'd pulled on a navy wool skirt and a rose cotton tank, I was back to Maynard and the possibility of a computer or tablet that might tell us what he'd been working on.

Would Kyle know?

Maybe.

Could I get it out of him?

Questionable.

Considering my best options for that, I pointed the car toward my office.

My cell phone and my scanner started bleeping at the same time.

I glanced at the phone screen and saw a number I didn't recognize, then turned up the scanner.

Burglary. I listened for the address and slammed my foot on the brake, spinning the car through an intersection and heading back toward Willow Lawn.

The dispatcher reeled off the address again, but I heard it in Felicia Lang's voice, making my foot heavier on the gas.

Maynard's office had just been robbed.

* * *

I parked in the narrow lot and surveyed the plain façade of the concrete building. It certainly didn't look like the sort of place a genius doctor would choose if he were trying to attract patients: flat, gray walls led up to a red metal roof. There were no signs—just insignias on the doors and numbers next to them.

I climbed out of the car and walked the length of the building, looking at the doors. The fifth one had plain white letters that spelled out "David Maynard, M.D."

"I guess this is it," I said.

"This is what? It looks like a lot of nothing to me." Charlie's voice came from my left, and I turned to see her climbing out of her van, waving at the cameraman to go park.

Crap. Check surroundings before speaking, Nichelle.

"Exactly," I said, sliding in front of the door with Maynard's name on it. "This is it. As in, all of it. Nothing more than this." Every word true.

Not that she wouldn't find out where we were at the briefing. Then again, given how tight-lipped Aaron had been lately, I couldn't swear he'd say more than "open investigation, sorry folks."

She gave me a once-over and tipped her head to one side, turning back to the van. "Who would want to rob this joint?" Her tone was conversational, but forced.

"I have the exact same information you do," I said.

"Somehow I don't think that's the whole truth. You've been a leg up on me all week," she said. "Don't you ever sleep?"

I sighed. "I miss sleeping."

"There's driven, and then there's psychotic." She nodded to Dan Kessler from WRVA. "And then there's I've-been-here-too-long-to-get-fired." The words came out of the corner of her mouth and I coughed over a laugh as Dan walked into earshot, pointing his cameraman to the building exterior and the street sign.

"I don't have to ask which one I am?"

"I think you might need meds." Charlie lost interest in Dan and rounded on me. "It's always been the extra kick I need, keeping up with you. But there's a difference between being a good reporter and making the job the be all and end all of everything. It is just a job, Clarke. What's with you?"

I paused four beats, but I knew the look on Charlie's face well. She had a scent and she had me cornered. I could cough up something, or deal with being hounded until I did.

"Bob," I said. "Bob is what's with me."

Her brow furrowed and she laid a perfectly manicured hand on my arm. "He's not sick again?"

Competition or no, Bob was an institution in the Richmond news business.

I shook my head quickly. "He's fine. At least for now. He just turned sixty-five and Andrews is trying to shove him out. As long as I'm on top of my game, Andrews stays off his ass."

Her eyes widened and she gave an exaggerated nod. "No wonder." She scrunched her petite nose. "Rick Andrews is a weasel. He remind you of a politician, too?"

"I've never liked him. Though I'm minding my p's and q's this week, thanks to my temper. I may have told him off the other day when I caught him chewing Bob's ass."

"Over your PR piece for the PD." She didn't even bother with the question mark. Charlie's ambitious, ruthless, and occasionally bitchy, but she's not stupid.

I nodded.

She rolled her eyes. "At least now I know you're not losing your mind. And I can stop beating myself up on top of the ass kickings you're delivering." She glanced over her shoulder and waved a hand toward the squad car turning into the parking lot. "Showtime. Wonder what took them so long?"

I shrugged, but I knew before the car door opened that Landers and Aaron had come all the way from the river. When Kyle climbed out of the back of the cruiser, Charlie elbowed me.

"That's your old flame, right? We'll revisit how you let that get away another day—but since when does he work at the PD?" The accusatory undertone made me bristle.

"He doesn't work at the PD," I said, the words clipped. "And he has been less than no help with whatever's going on here."

"Simmer down." She pasted on a smile as Aaron pointed two patrolmen who'd just pulled up in another car to the walkway, instructing them to tape it off and waving us into the parking lot. "I wasn't suggesting anything unseemly. Just wondering what I'm missing. If he's still captain hotshot at the ATF, why is he here?"

"Your guess is as good as mine."

She threw me a sharp look and I raised my right hand. "I swear. They're not talking."

"No inside police info for you this time?"

I shook my head.

"So if I want my producers off my ass," she said, stepping into the parking lot and plopping her sunglasses over her blue eyes, "what I have to find is who will talk."

She walked back to her cameraman and motioned orders, and I pulled out my cell phone and texted Chad.

Hurry.

* * *

Thankfully, Aaron and Kyle weren't on the list of people willing to talk—to Charlie or anyone else.

"The former tenant was in the process of vacating the space," Aaron told the small circle of reporters twenty minutes later, his best poker face firmly in place. "The landlord notified the RPD of a suspected break-in when he went in to make sure the air conditioning had been turned off."

A hail of questions followed, and I held my breath until the last "no comment" had been uttered.

Charlie caught me on the way back to my car. "What's gotten into him? It'd be easier to get a dossier on the President's mistress from the White House chief of staff than it is to get a decent story out of White this week."

I nodded full agreement. "Ain't that the truth?"

Her blue eyes narrowed. "Something tells me you know why."

Sharp, that Charlie. "He's under a lot of pressure." Every word true.

"From what?"

"If you manage to find out, let me know." I smiled and spun on my heel before she could utter another question, tucking my notes back into my bag as I opened the car door.

More than eight years, and I'd never seen Aaron be so stubborn about giving up a victim's name. I liked the leg up on Charlie, but the deeper this silence went, the more unsettling it became.

Political sleight-of-hand: reveal the beloved doctor as the victim and release the killer's mugshot on the same day, and most people become so focused on hating the murderer, they forget to wonder why the victim is dead.

I wanted the who, probably nearly as bad as Landers did. But I needed the why. My mom might someday need the why. Amy Ellinger needed the why.

And my window for getting it out before whoever was pulling the PD's strings could make it vanish with PR smoke and mirrors was inching shut.

27

Speeding toward the office with Richmond's hallmark side-by-side art deco and classic architecture blurring into a mash of brightly colored concrete, I was so lost in the story I almost didn't hear my phone ringing.

I fished it out of my bag and glanced at the screen. The office.

"I'm not late yet," I said, putting it to my ear. "And wait 'til you hear what I've got."

"I'm not Bob," Shelby's high pitched twang came back at me through the speaker. To listen to the two of us, you'd think she was the one who grew up in Texas.

"Sorry, Shelby. What's up?"

"There was a woman here looking for you," she said.

"Who was it?"

"Alisha Roy-something? She was bawling so hard I didn't get the rest. She said she's a nurse over at St. Vince's."

Oh, crap hell.

"She was crying?" My throat tried to close around the words, heaviness settling in my gut.

"I told her I'd tell you. She said she's working the second shift at the hospital today."

I stopped at a red light and made a slightly illegal u-turn. Alisha might not be at St. Vincent's, but I needed to know if Amy still was.

"Thanks, Shelby."

"You're not going to tell me what's going on, are you?"

"Not until I have more of it figured out. But I haven't told Bob much, either, so it's nothing personal." There was something I never thought I'd hear myself say.

"I get it." The words had a sad tinge. "But thanks for saying that."

"Can you do me a favor and let Bob know I'm going to be late? He gets pissy when I miss meetings, but I think he'll approve of the reason."

"Will do."

"Thank you. See you in a bit."

I hung up and turned into the hospital drive, bolting for the door and tossing the valet my keys. I repeated a quick prayer for Amy's health on a loop in my head as I told the security guy where I was going and waited for the elevator.

When the doors binged open on five, it was everything I could do to avoid breaking into a run. I breathed easier when I saw the uniformed officer still posted outside the door to Amy's room.

"Miss Clarke." Never have I been so thrilled to be on the business end of a go-to-hell look.

"Everything okay?" I asked.

"Sky is blue, sun is shining, dude in there is getting away with murder. What do you think?"

"That I'm not arguing with you, Officer. Have a nice day."

I walked past him into Amy's room, and stopped cold.

Three little girls stood in a ring around the bed, two of them holding their mother's hands and a third clinging to her sisters for dear life.

Tom looked up when the door clicked shut, and I nodded to him as the children finished the last chorus of "Jesus Loves Me."

Amy smiled and raised her hands to their dark, glossy curls. "Beautiful. Just like you."

"Mommy, I don't want you to go see Jesus. Daddy says you can't come back." That was the littlest one, probably three, standing at the foot of the bed. The words were followed by a wail and a torrent of tears.

I stepped backward. Not only was it heart-wrenching to watch, but I'd never felt more like an intruder than I did in that moment.

"Nichelle." Amy settled her hands in her daughters' and smiled at me. "Please come in. You haven't gotten to meet my girls."

"I don't really feel like this is the best time to pop in on y'all." I smiled apologetically. "I wanted to make sure you were..." I searched for words. "Okay."

Amy nodded. "I'm always better when I have my babies here."

"Mommy's not okay." The words strangled out of the tallest little girl, who looked maybe eight or nine. Except for the eyes, which were about a hundred and forty and sizing me up. "Who are you?"

"I'm a reporter at the *Telegraph*."

"Why are you here?"

I paused. I didn't want to worry this child any more than she already was.

"Nichelle is my new friend," Amy Ellinger said, and one glance at her eyes told me she knew exactly how much trouble Tom was in. Potentially in. She was worried about her kids.

The little girl lost interest. "She's not a doctor," she said, turning back to her mother.

Amy shook her head. "I get tired of seeing doctors all the time. You know what she is?"

"What?"

"She's nice. And she's really funny."

I smiled. "I do what I can."

She looked more animated than I'd seen her thus far, and it cracked a tiny ray of hope in my heart. Was she on a new treatment? Had they found a different doctor? I couldn't really ask with the kids in the room.

Tom half-smiled at me, hauling the littlest child into his lap and quieting her tears. "Mommy's not going anywhere today, love. All we know about is today."

Amy nodded and eased over so the other girls could get in the bed with her. "You munchkins want to watch a movie?"

The children were careful of the tubes and wires attached to their mother—the kind of careful that comes with constant coaching.

I was an adult when this happened to my mother, and I remember how down-in-your-bones, can't-eat-can't-sleep terrifying it was.

These poor babies.

Damn David Maynard, and whoever killed him, too. How could he turn her away? Leave these kids either living in constant fear of hurting their mother, or just not having her there altogether?

But if he weren't dead, maybe I could have convinced him to treat Amy.

Damn, damn, damn.

She flipped to an in-house video on demand service and found a kids' movie, and Tom turned his chair so he and the baby could see too. He laid his head on Amy's arm, and she moved her fingers to run through his hair, her eyes falling shut.

I backed toward the door, checking my watch. Alisha wouldn't be there for hours. I wondered if she'd left a number with Shelby. New day, new question: if Amy wasn't dead, why did her nurse show up in our newsroom in tears?

* * *

I barreled off the elevator looking for Shelby, but a ten-minute search of the building failed to produce my old arch rival.

I dropped my stuff at my desk and went to the break room in search of caffeine. Parker's lower half protruded from the cabinet under the sink, his top half muttering something I couldn't make out.

"Lose something, Parker?" I reached into the upper cabinet for my mug, filling it with what I hoped was fresh coffee, since the pot was pretty full. Reporters don't go through anything faster. Well, except alcohol. But that had been absent from the newsroom since the seventies.

He didn't emerge from the cabinet, making the words muffled when he replied, "I know there was a bag of chocolate under here. I saw it last week."

I glanced at the clock. "At nine in the morning? You have PMS?"

He stood up, brushing dust off his knees. "Mel does. I've done the math enough months to know what helps. But I can't find any."

I laughed. "I have some Godiva pearls in my desk. You're a pretty decent guy, you know that?"

He winked. "Shhh. Don't let that get around."

"Richmond's Casanova, domesticated to the point of hunting up hormone-quelling candy." I shook my head, unable to keep the grin off my face. "Who would've thought?"

He put one arm around me and squeezed briefly. "Certainly not I. Thanks, Clarke."

I patted his arm. "I'm sorry I didn't have a chance to get back with you last week, but you look better. Everything okay?"

He nodded, his eyes taking on a sheen. "I think so. I'm happy. Nervous as all hell. But happy."

My eyebrows floated toward my hairline. "How happy are you, Parker?"

He flashed the grin that made women in five counties feel faint—and feign interest in sports at any event where he was speaking. "That happy. Just waiting for the right time."

Well, hot damn. It had been better than a year since I'd pointed our quietly striking city hall reporter and superstar sports columnist toward happy hour at the same time, and I felt a warm flush from fingertip to toes at having a hand in something so wonderful.

That's why he'd been freaked—any guy who'd been through as many women as Grant Parker had to be terrified at the thought of forever with just one. But he was more in love than he was afraid.

I bounced, a small squeal escaping my lips, and hugged him. "That's awesome. I can't wait to hear all about it."

"Trying to do it right." His words were soft in my ear. "I only plan to do it once."

"Holler if you need a sounding board."

"I may." He turned for the door.

"I'd be honored." I told him where to find my candy stash and he disappeared with a thank-you wave.

I doctored my coffee with milk and Splenda, still grinning. My story and my own life might be tangled as hell, but my friends were happy. Go, me.

I made it to the door just as Shelby rushed around the corner.

"There you are!" I said, just as she blurted "Nichelle! I've been looking everywhere!"

I laughed. "Me too."

"I figured if all else failed, I could find you near the coffee."

"Always a safe bet." I smiled. "I'm hoping Alisha left a phone number with you this morning."

Shelby shook her head. "That's what I wanted to talk to you about. I tried, but I couldn't get one out of her. This woman was visibly distraught, and she seemed...scared. What the hell is going on at that hospital?"

I shrugged. "I can't make anything of it."

"But the dead guy from last week was a big shot doctor."

I paused before I nodded. "How'd you know that?"

"Larry. He said it was the doctor who treated Bob's wife and asked me to babysit the story."

Awesome. I loved Larry. Didn't want to have to kill him. "You're, uh, you're keeping that to yourself, right?"

Shelby rolled her eyes. "Of course. My days of trying to sabotage you have passed. Pinky swear."

She looked earnest enough, but it was still hard to buy that. "Nothing personal." Much. "In my experience, the fewer people who know about a lead, the less likely it is to show up somewhere else before I can run it down."

She nodded. "Sound advice. When I make it off the copy desk, I'll remember it."

I sighed. Shelby was a good writer, and I knew all she wanted was to be a reporter. It was the coveting other people's jobs (especially mine) I didn't love. But she really had been different lately. Benefit of the doubt isn't my strongest suit, but I gave it all I had.

"Someday, Shelby. Helping out and not causing trouble goes further toward earning Bob's trust, that's for sure."

"That's what I keep telling myself. Thanks."

I pulled a chair away from the closest table and plopped into it, sipping my coffee. "Walk me through what happened this morning."

"I came in early because I wanted to get a jump on the features budget for the day. We lost another copy clerk Monday. No notice."

"Nice. I've been too busy to pay attention."

"I seem to recall you bitching about it being slow not too long ago."

"I'm aware of the fact that karma fried up those words for me to chew on, thanks. Aaron White hasn't let me forget it."

She snorted. "I was playing catch-up and in need of caffeine since I was here until after midnight, and when I walked past the front, this woman was sitting on the bench crying."

"Before eight?"

"It might have been before seven."

What the everloving hell?

"She was asking the janitor where to find you, so I stopped and told her you weren't in yet and she said she should've figured that. The whole thing was strange. Who the hell is she? A witness?"

"She's the day nurse for the shooter's wife. She's been his biggest champion all week."

"Except for you," Shelby drawled.

"Yeah, yeah, I've heard it. I'd do it again. Something isn't right here."

"Like what?"

"I'm currently wondering if Alisha might have an idea about that."

Shelby's eyes got big. "Why wouldn't she have said before?"

That was the sticking point. She'd seemed so earnest all week, and I have a pretty decent bullshit detector. "Maybe she learned something new." I drug the words out, considering the possibility as I spoke.

"From where?" Shelby got up and made herself a cup of coffee.

"A colleague? A file? A pat—"

I paused. A patient.

I jumped to my feet. "I gotta run, Shelby," I said, gulping the rest of the coffee and rinsing my mug. "Do me a favor—if anyone else comes looking for me, keep them here and call me?"

"I'm not going anywhere anytime soon," she said.

"Thanks."

I ran for my desk, my brain on fast-forward. Shit. I'd been in and out of that hospital a dozen times, but somehow, I'd missed something.

I checked the clock. Alisha would be at work in five hours, and I had a deadline in seven and two trials that needed attention if I didn't want to be banned from the courthouse forever.

I also had about a dozen questions for Aaron. Hoping he might answer at least a couple, I texted him a coffee request. He binged right back with a yes.

So he wanted to know something too.

I sent Bob an email to hold space for the trials and made tracks for the coffee shop.

28

By the time Aaron walked into Thompson's I had three texts from DonnaJo wanting to know why I wasn't covering today's action—the last one letting me know that Charlie and two radio reporters were.

She had three defendants charged with running the biggest meth lab the PD had ever busted, and was itching to make a political statement with the trial. It would lead the metro front—three people had died in the fire someone set when the cops raided the warehouse, and her defendants had all been picked up at the scene.

I wouldn't miss much by talking to Aaron first, though, and Maynard was definitely my top priority.

I'm coming, I tapped back as Aaron took a seat across from me. *Emergency.*

Bing. *Avoiding me won't help you. You've already been served.*

Not for today, I wasn't. And I know your "evils of drugs" speech by heart. The jury's going to love it. Hope I make it in time to catch the end. I added a smiley and put the phone in my bag, focusing on Aaron.

"That gag order still in effect?" I asked.

"I've grown weary of giving a shit." He sipped his latte and sighed, lacing his fingers together on the tabletop in front of him. "Look, you know as well as I do there's something pretty messed up going on here. Not talking about it isn't helping us. I think you might know something that would. I'd rather trust you to know what to print and what will fry my ass before someone gets away with a murder or two. So let's talk."

"On the record or off?"

"Like I said—I trust you."

I pulled in a hitching breath. That sounded good on the surface, but a comment like that is an anvil worth of pressure for any scrupulous reporter. Run too much, and you've burned a good source. Run too little, and you lose the exclusive. Ugh.

I just nodded. Above all else, I didn't want him to leave.

"So how's it going?"

"Frustrating." He glanced around and leaned forward. "I know you've been poking around, and I know you know Maynard was a superbrain."

"I know a fair bit about him. But I still don't know for sure how he died."

"Strangled. The marks were faint enough to be questionable, but Miller's friend finally found a microscopic crack on the hyoid." I jotted that down.

So the killer wasn't too strong, or wasn't an amateur.

Kyle's face, in Maynard's undamaged doorway, floated through my thoughts.

"The door wasn't forced. So it was someone he knew," I mused, making notes. What if our old society climber was stronger than she looked? Was it physically possible for her to strangle a grown man? I hadn't paid attention to her hands.

"Or someone with a key," Aaron said.

I'd bet Elizabeth Eason had one. Somewhere in my gut I knew I just wanted it to be her because Bob disliked her so much. That old woman might be a lot of things, but strong enough to throttle someone in a way that would bother Aaron probably wasn't one of them.

Who else?

"The building management? Someone he worked with? A mistress no one knew about? A jealous husband no one knew about?" I tossed out possibilities as fast as they occurred to me.

"Yes." Aaron threw up his hands. "Now do you see why I'm losing my mind?"

I sat back in my chair. "You're a week in and you have no leads?"

"Not a single good one."

"Someone's got a talent for covering their tracks."

"No shit. And someone important is determined to give the impression they want us to find out who."

"Explain."

"They sent in your friend at the ATF, which is not at all normal. But he can't find anything that makes any sense, either. Everyone as far up the food chain as I can see is really hot on us not sharing—we're restricted such that a lot of our normal channels of getting help are blocked."

"Someone wants it to look like you're getting loads of help, when in fact they're tying your hands."

"That's the feeling I'm getting." He sipped his coffee. "And it's pissing me off."

I held his gaze, years of mutual admiration and respect warring with my desire to keep this story close until I had it nailed down. "I trust you, Aaron. Eight years, and you've never screwed me out of a story. This one is a big deal to me for a lot of reasons, but if I tell you what I'm working on and it ends up on TV or the internet, I swear on my favorite shoes..."

He held up one hand. "I get it. I'm kind of in the same boat, remember? I'm trusting you too."

"Have y'all found much on what Maynard was working on?"

"Not really. We tried searching the office, but there wasn't much there even before it was burglarized. They're still dusting for prints, but most everything has been flung into a giant shitpile I don't have the time or the medical training to sort through."

I nodded. "The secretary didn't happen to tell you if he had a tablet?"

Aaron's eyes widened. "I'm not sure we asked specifically, but that's a hell of a good question."

"I'm thinking it wasn't at the apartment, because if the killer was after it, wouldn't they have taken it the night of the murder? And then why break into the office? I know I'm assuming a lot, but it's what we have to go on."

Aaron nodded absently, his baby blues fixed on something behind my left shoulder. "What the hell was this guy into?"

All or nothing.

"Some folks think he was into discovering a cure for cancer."

His jaw fell onto the table. "Come again?"

"It sounds crazy, but it'd certainly be worth killing for, wouldn't it?"

He just nodded. When he found his voice, he croaked a "Where did you get that?"

"It's why Ellinger wanted me in the hospital. Why he was sending me those messages. Why he wanted Maynard. He didn't want a consultation. He thought Maynard could cure his wife."

"Nearly everything I have points to this guy, Nichelle."

"I'm telling you, Aaron, he didn't do it. You're better than I am at reading people. Go sit with that guy for five minutes and then come back and tell me you think he's a killer. He deserves about forty Oscars if he was acting when I told him Maynard was dead. He'd pinned all his hopes for the love of his life's survival on the guy. Taking hostages to get his way, absolutely. That's pure desperation. But he didn't kill the doc. I can't see how it's possible that he killed that woman, either."

"I'm waiting for ballistics, but the rounds were from the same kind of rifle. You think someone else shot her with the same model rifle your guy—who was sending you messages online that bothered you enough to call me, let's not forget—was toting in the hospital right around the same time she was murdered? Whatever you're on, don't get caught with it. I'm low on bail money and have no favors to call in."

All cards on the table.

"She worked at Evaris."

"I know this. Marketing."

"Did you also know she stumbled across an in-house email that had her scared shitless?"

He shot me a Look. The kind that said he was pissed about just now hearing this. I returned it, just as annoyed with his secrecy. He held the stern face for a moment before he drummed his fingers on the tabletop. "I did not. What kind of email?"

"The friend I spoke with didn't really know. Thought Stephanie was paranoid. Didn't ask."

"Damn." His lips disappeared into a worried line, and he steepled his fingers together.

He wasn't saying something.

I waited, watching theories flit across his face faster than I could count them.

"Aaron." I clapped my hands in front of his nose. "You there?"

"Thinking."

"I have someone trying to find a backed-up copy. If you have her laptop in evidence, it's worth trying there, too."

"I'll see what they took from her apartment when I get back to the office."

"Speaking of evidence…" I let the sentence trail off, raising my eyebrows expectantly.

His lifted too. "Yes?"

"The rifle?"

"The—oh, shit, I forgot about that." He shook his head. "I'm sorry. I called down, but I never got an answer. I'll follow up on it today."

"There's no way that woman is dead by mistake. And Tom has no motive."

"A drug company. A dead oncologist who thought he'd found medicine's holy grail. And a sales rep who might have known something someone didn't want her to know. Who is also dead." Aaron ticked off points on his fingers.

I nodded.

"It sounds crazy." His flat stare told me he wasn't so sure.

"Don't the really good ones always sound crazy?"

"Where's all that boredom we were bitching about last week?"

"If you find it, tell it we won't complain ever again." I swallowed the last of my coffee. "My week has had enough excitement to last me forever."

"DonnaJo cornered you, huh?"

"You knew that was coming?"

"She'd have my ass if I warned you. But it's not like you shouldn't have expected it. Sorry."

"Uh-huh."

"Let me take a pass through the evidence room. I'll call you later." He sighed. "I'm so damned tired of talking to people I could cry."

I tipped my head to one side. "Someone who had a key to Maynard's place. How'd Elizabeth Eason strike you?"

"Meh. She's a bitch, but she's not a murderer."

Noted.

Goetze. Would he have a key? Aaron's goose chase radius was far wider than mine. I'd keep digging. I could always hand the well-to-do doc over in a few days if I needed to.

"Thanks for coming to talk to me." I stood.

Aaron pushed the door open. "Damn, Nichelle."

Yep.

I waved as I climbed into my car, then aimed it toward Goetze's office. There had to be a way to get the guy alone. He was my reigning biggest question mark, and I wanted an answer.

29

The posh decor in Goetze's front office had nothing on the doctor's private suite. Which I found by slipping through a back door in the hallway, staying hidden, and making a couple of educated guesses. The second largest crystal chandelier I'd ever seen hung from the center of the pressed tile ceiling, over a handsome oak coffee table and a set of silk chairs. The Persian rug under them was bigger than my living room.

A massive cherry desk filled the corner opposite the door, bookshelves lining the two walls behind it. I chose the sapphire silk armchair facing the door, crossing my legs and pulling a notebook and pen from my bag.

I didn't have to wait long.

Goetze entered the room with his head bent over a small laptop, closing the door behind him before he looked up. He almost dropped the computer when he saw me.

"How did you get in here?" he asked when he'd recovered his composure.

"Doors. None of them were locked."

"Who are you and what do you want?"

"To talk," I said. "I have some questions I'd like for you to answer."

"You can schedule an appointment with the receptionist." He stepped toward the door and moved to open it.

"I don't need medical care. I need information," I said. "About David Maynard and what he's been working on."

He flinched, but recovered nicely, his hand frozen to the doorknob. "What makes you think I know anything about that? I haven't worked with David in years."

"I'm not sure I believe that." I kept my tone light, holding his gaze across the wide room.

"You break into my office and now you're calling me a liar?" His voice rose in pitch and volume. "I'm not sure what you're playing at, lady, but I think it's time for you to go." The knob made a quarter turn.

"I wouldn't do that if you don't want your lunches at Frank's Diner all over tomorrow's front page." The same light tone, but I added a slight edge to the words. Goetze's eyes popped so wide I could see white all around the hazel.

"How do you know about that?"

"I pay close attention. And I'm guessing you'd rather not have the whole city know about it—probably especially not my friends at the PD. So have a seat, and let's chat."

He stepped away from the door, but stopped well short of a chair.

"You're a reporter?"

I nodded.

"Why do you care who I have lunch with?"

"I care about Dr. Maynard. I care even more about his research. I'm curious about how your choice of company fits into this."

Another step forward. "It doesn't."

I sat up straight, clicking the pen out. "I think I'm going to need some elaboration there."

"I have no idea what David was up to. Or how he died."

"Yet you know he's dead. And you're passing envelopes back and forth with a bigwig from Evaris over greasy food."

"Of course I know he's dead. He was my mentor for years. What I don't understand is why his death is a secret." He dropped into a chair. "And you have no proof of anything."

"I don't?" I pulled my cell phone out and called up one of the photos I'd taken at the diner. "Surely someone on the university's board will recognize your companion. Crenshaw, right?" The more agitated he appeared, the cooler I kept my tone. "Help me understand."

He grabbed for the phone and I pulled it back. "I'm not a moron. They're backed up." Only because of Chad's haranguing, which I was suddenly grateful for.

He stared at the far wall for a minute, then swung a fist down into the arm of his chair. "Look, kickbacks from the drug companies are part of the business." He slouched back in the seat, rumpling his expensive camel pinstriped suit. "I prescribe their stuff instead of someone else's, and they make a fortune. So they pay me to prescribe their meds."

I narrowed my eyes. "What if a competing drug would have a better result for your patient?" I had to fight to keep calm there.

"They're not that much different." A defensive edge crept into his voice. "I can't say for sure what will work best on who, anyway. Evaris's technology is just as good as everyone else's."

Sure. That's why they had to cheat and use bribes to get their stuff prescribed. I jotted a few notes. In balance, admitting to being a douche and taking kickbacks was better than copping to murder, so I wasn't entirely sure I bought his story. But I didn't get the feeling he was lying, either. I looked up from my notes and arched an eyebrow at him.

"I'm not up on my medical/legal technicalities, but I'll take your desire to hide what you're doing as a sign you shouldn't be doing it. Is that all you're selling them? Access to your patients?"

"What else would I possibly doing?"

"Selling them Maynard's research."

He snorted. "They don't want it. Maynard was on a quest for a cure. No one in this business is interested in that."

I closed my eyes and pulled a breath in for a ten count. When I didn't actually slam my fist through his smirk, I counted it a win.

"Is that why he went off the grid?"

"I'm not sure I'd phrase it that way. He made enough money to go do what he wanted."

"But none of the pharma companies he worked with wanted to sponsor the studies."

"He didn't want them to. David was a brilliant doctor, but lady, he was a little crazy. A massive heap of do-gooder. He wanted to find a cure—so he could give it away. He used to proselytize about how something that could benefit all of mankind belonged to the people. Like he thought he was Jonas fucking Salk. He complained all the time about how medicine had become a business."

I scribbled notes, considering the words as I wrote. So who would have been interested in Maynard's research?

"Insurance companies?" I asked.

"What about them?"

"It would save them a ton of money if someone found a cure. Would they have wanted to know what he was working on?"

"Only so they could stop him," he chuckled. "You think drug companies are bad? They got nothing on insurers. A free cure for one of the most expensive, catastrophic illnesses a person can get? Do you know how far their premium structure would plummet? And with the law requiring insurance now, the government would lean on them to practically give policies away to young, healthy people. Their bottom line would get eaten right up."

I didn't miss a word, my thoughts speeding past his assertion. "So there really was nobody who wanted to help him?"

"I can name twenty people who wanted to stop him."

I looked up. "Yourself included?"

He rolled his eyes and ran one hand through his sandy hair. "Look—"

"I know. I don't get it."

"This is the only thing I've ever wanted to do."

"Don't most people become doctors because they want to help people?"

He stood, pacing the office. "I did." A muttered refrain of something I couldn't make out followed. I couldn't tell if the tirade was directed at himself, me, Maynard, or Jesus. But he was selling his point hard.

He stopped and turned to me. "I spent years studying for this career. Several of them under one of the most brilliant oncologists of our time. I wanted to help people. But yeah—I wish Maynard had felt differently about things. We could have revolutionized treatment if he wasn't so stubborn."

Stubborn? That's what we're calling wanting to save people's lives now?

Nice. "I'm not sure you're using the right word," I said. "Humanitarian, maybe?"

"Come off it. What's wrong with making a few bucks along the way if you're going to save the world?"

I shook my head. "I'm not sure a person like yourself is going to understand the answer to that if I bother to offer it, Dr. Goetze."

Journalism in any Age where money is a concern 101: people who hunger for it seldom understand what it means to want anything else. Or how to be happy.

I made a few more notes and stood.

"I'm sure you'd like to keep these photos off our front page."

He nodded. "Something tells me I don't have much say in that."

"One last time." I stepped closer to him. "What was Maynard working on?"

"I don't know." He spread his hands. "Why wouldn't I tell you if I did?"

I studied his face and nodded. "But you know someone who does. Let me suggest that you find out. By six o'clock tomorrow evening. I'll see you then."

I didn't wait for him to answer. My temper levee had held so far, but it was failing fast. I strode for the door and slammed out before memories of my mom, connected to a million tubes and wires and writhing in a bed, let the dammed-up anger flow at Goetze.

* * *

I sped toward the courthouse, the clock on the dash telling me DonnaJo was probably good and annoyed with me. She'd get over it, though—besides, her case was a slam dunk. She just liked seeing her more memorable speeches quoted in the newspaper.

I stopped at a light, my pulse finally slowing from the furious hammering that sent me running from Goetze's office.

What did I know?

That Goetze was a greedy bastard.

That someone, somewhere, had to know something about Maynard's research.

That the murders were connected. Aaron might not be convinced, but after talking to Goetze, I sure was.

Could I print any of it?

I needed proof. Letting everyone know what trail I was on before I found the end wasn't smart.

Would Goetze actually nose around—or pretend to nose around—Maynard's research? Maybe. But my chances were even up that he'd just vanish. Hoping a sense of responsibility for his patients would prevent that had evaporated during our short conversation. That dude was in medicine for the money and the God complex. Not the good of his fellow man.

My cell phone started buzzing as the light turned green, and I glanced at the screen as I put my foot on the gas. My lips tipped up in a smile.

"Hi there!" I said brightly, putting the phone to my ear.

"Nichelle, dear, it's been too long." The warmth in the voice on the other end was genuine, and so close to my mom's it made my grin widen.

"I talked to you last Saturday, Grandmother."

"I do love the sound of that word. And that's a long time, when you have as much catching up to do as we have."

"I suppose it is. I've been a little wrapped up in work."

"Of course, of course." She got quiet. "Your mother called."

"So I heard. We're kicking around coming to California when I have enough of a break from dead people."

"She didn't tell me that!" Her voice edged up slightly, and I frowned. There was something there, but it wasn't excitement.

"Everything okay?"

Nervous laughter. "Of course it is. It's perfect. I'm just thinking. You don't want to come here—we're in the middle of this dreadful drought, and there's nothing to do but go to the beach."

"I love the beach."

"Everything here is so blasé. I require something a bit...more... for meeting my only granddaughter. Not the same old sunshine and waves I see every day." She took a breath. "I know! We should have a girls' vacation, the three of us." Words tripped out of her. "My treat, of course. Where would you like to go? New York? Paris? A spa? A cruise?"

I smiled, unable to believe I'd let resentment keep me from knowing her sooner. She was light and bubbly and enthusiastic—an older version of my mom.

"A vacation sounds amazing," I said softly. "But not necessary. I just want to meet you."

I'd ask her to share what she remembered about my father when I could hear it face to face. I wanted to know her better, I wanted her to trust me, and I also wanted to be able to watch her expressions when she spoke of him.

I'd never been terribly curious, but the possibility of unknown people walking around with similar DNA had chipped away at my resolve in the past few months. I still wasn't sure I wanted to know, but I needed to.

What I didn't want was for my mom to hear me ask. It had been hard enough for her to tell me the things she did.

"When can we go?" she asked.

"Work is crazy for me right now, but it will calm down soon. I hope."

"I had a feeling you were trying to find out more than the paper lets on about the man who was murdered last week," she said. "You take care of yourself, young lady."

I laughed. So much like mom. "Yes, ma'am."

I turned onto Ninth and had a thought. "How about right after Thanksgiving? The anniversary of Mom's remission is that week. We'll celebrate all at once."

"Remission?"

Um. "Breast cancer. This will mark seven years."

"Lila had breast cancer?" Strangled such that I barely heard it. Damn.

"I had no idea you didn't know. But she's fine."

"I'm glad to hear that, sweetie. And I know you didn't mean to upset me. But she's my only daughter. How could she shut me so far out of her life that she didn't tell me she was that sick? That's the kind of thing you call your mother about."

"I'm sorry." I didn't think it was the time to point out that they had shut my mom out, not the other way around, but the urge to jump to her defense was so strong, I felt a sudden need to hang up.

"Thank you." The words were stiff. "And late November should be perfect. Where?"

"I'll ask Mom." I said. "If that's okay."

"Of course."

Thirteen kinds of awkward silence. I didn't mean to upset her. And I shouldn't get in the middle of a conversation she needed to have with my mom, no matter whose side I could see or what I thought.

I stopped at a sign a block from the courthouse and clicked my tongue. "I'm sorry, Grandmother, but I have to go. I have a trial to cover, and I'm already late."

"Of course, dear. We'll talk soon."

"Looking forward to it."

I clicked off the call and parked the car, opening a text to my mom.

"Grandmother is upset because she didn't know you had cancer...until I told her just now. Sorry. She might call you."

I hit send and noticed the missed call icon in the corner of the screen, clicking on the number. Nope. Still didn't ring a bell. I touched the call back button and waited. A man's voice, rough and breathless, was behind the "hello?" but my bells still weren't ringing.

"This is Nichelle Clarke," I said. "Did someone try to call me from this number?"

"If you want to know what happened to Maynard, meet me in the rear parking lot at Cary Court at five-thirty."

Click.

"Hello?" I repeated it a dozen times, then pulled the phone away from my head and stared at it.

Jiminy Choos, what was I jumping into this time?

The voice still running through my head on a loop, I started toward the courthouse, spotting Kyle walking out a side door with Jonathan Corry, the local Commonwealth's Attorney and DonnaJo's boss. I raised an arm to wave, but they were so deep in conversation, they didn't notice.

It wasn't until I'd squeezed into the last seat in the last row for the meth trial that it occurred to me to be nervous about what Kyle wanted with Corry.

Surely it didn't have anything to do with Joey.

30

I ducked DonnaJo and Charlie both and sped across town to St. Vincent's as soon as the judge adjourned for the afternoon. Alisha should've been at work for an hour and a half. Hopefully that was long enough for her to be able to get a break without catching anyone's attention.

The beefy guys at the desk—still there a week later, and quite possibly a permanent fixture in the lobby—just nodded in my direction, and the sweet ladies in their candy stripes and matching red lipstick smiled and waved.

I stepped off the elevator and nearly walked into Goetze, who was talking to a tall, gray-haired doctor I remembered from the day of the shooting. I didn't catch a word of what they were saying before Goetze fell silent, his wary eyes settling on me. I skipped mine right over him and smiled at the other doctor.

I turned for the nurse's station and the two of them stepped onto the elevator. I didn't need to turn around to know Goetze was glaring a hole through the back of my tank top. Not that I cared what a man like him thought of me, but I wanted information I was fairly sure he could get. In that respect, I was glad to see him. Maybe he was looking for dirt on Maynard's work.

Alisha wasn't behind the nurse's station, nor was she in Amy's room. I peeked into two others before my eyes settled on the door I'd watched the slight, quiet man move to and from in the past few days.

Alisha wasn't in there, either, but he was kneeling next to the bed, holding an elderly woman's hand to his forehead and sobbing what sounded like a plea or a prayer. I didn't recognize the language.

His mother? She was still and silent, the beeping of the heart monitor and *whir-click* of the IV pump the only sounds in the room that weren't coming from him.

I swallowed an onslaught of painful memories and stepped backward, pulling the door to behind me.

"I've never seen anyone keep a vigil like that with a parent, and I've been here a long time." Alisha's voice came from behind me.

"I can relate," I said. "My mom is a breast cancer survivor."

She nodded. "How long?"

"Six years. Well—seven next month."

"Good odds." She tried for a smile and managed more of a grimace.

I glanced around and dropped my voice. "I heard you were looking for me this morning?"

She nodded, tipping her head toward the door, then waving me toward the little break room.

The medical supplies and bottles from the closet had taken up residence on wire shelves, crowding the tiny kitchen. Alisha squeezed between the fridge and a shelf, looking behind every piece of furniture in the tiny room before she started to speak.

"Look, I know you're writing this series on Tom and Amy and what led him to a breaking point," she said. "I also know he's probably going to prison from here, either way this works out. But it's capital murder if he killed Stephanie, right?"

I nodded. "Possibly. Murder committed during the perpetration of another felony qualifies, but it would depend on the prosecutor."

She sighed. "I want to protect them all," she began, then stopped, turning huge, tear-filled eyes up at me. "Can I trust you?"

"Of course. The people are what make this job for me, Alisha. Not the headlines. I don't want Tom to go to prison for something he didn't do."

She sniffled and nodded.

I waited. She stared at the floor.

"He didn't do it, did he?" I asked. "And you know it. I know it. I'm pretty sure my friend Detective White will buy it if we can come up with proof."

A hitching breath in, and words spilled out. "I don't want to give up Benny and his family, but maybe there's a way we don't have to?"

"I'll do my level best." My gut twinged. "Benny is the gentleman across the hall with the sick mother?"

"Their visas are out. They're refugees, but getting the INS to recognize that gets harder every year, and they've run into a problem with a judge in California. He's scheduled to be deported in six days."

"What?" I fumbled for a notebook and started scribbling.

"They'd deport her too, but she's too sick to move."

My head spun. I had exactly no experience with the Immigration service, but surely they wouldn't send this man away from his dying mother. Even bureaucrats have mothers. And souls.

"I need you to slow down a touch. Tell me what's going on. From the beginning."

"Benny came here with his mother from Serbia about six years ago. They ran from the military, where service is forced on all men over eighteen, because he'd never signed up for the draft. His father and brother were killed in an accident and there was no one left to take care of his mother."

I kept my head bent over my notes, catching every word, and nodded for her to go on.

"They had work visas, and they applied for asylum. But the application was denied. Benny married a young refugee woman and they have a child —a little girl."

"She was born here?" I glanced up.

"In this building."

"I didn't think they could deport people if they had a family member who was a U.S. citizen."

"They keep one parent with the child. Benny doesn't want his wife separated from her, so she's been naturalized."

I sighed. Ship sailed.

"Why hasn't he? Can't he take a class or something?"

"It's more difficult than the politicians would have you believe."

"Why is that?"

"I haven't exactly studied up on it, but he says the requirements are way beyond taking the class. That he tried many times and failed. And then they started with the hearings."

"What hearings?"

"They sent him a court summons to go to Los Angeles—all the way on the other side of the country—to appear before a judge and plead his case. He bought a plane ticket and went. When he got there, they told him his hearing had been held the day before and he'd missed it, and he was scheduled for deportation."

"He missed it?"

"They say he had the date wrong. He swears he didn't, but he didn't keep the letter, either."

I put one hand to my forehead. "Okay."

"So now his mother is sick, and he's supposed to report to L.A. in a week to be sent home—I did read about that. Look it up. He's facing years in a prison camp, and that's if they don't kill him. His mother is dying. I don't want anyone to know he's here. They have to find him to kick him out of the country, right?"

"There's no one else we can talk to?"

She shrugged. "I wouldn't begin to know who."

"Let me see what I can find out." In all my copious spare time. But what else was I going to do?

She smiled, gratitude oozing from every pore. "Thank you."

"Sure. Can you tell me what the heck all this has to do with the Ellingers?"

She nodded. "Benny was hiding in the medroom that day."

"The one where the woman was shot?"

Leaping. Louboutins.

She nodded. "Behind two shelves in the corner. The police were gone before he came out. No one but Dr. Lessing and I saw him."

I forgot to breathe. "Did he shoot her?"

"I'm not sure he'd know how to work a gun if you gave him one. He's the nicest man. And he didn't say anything—not to anyone—for days. I didn't tell the police he was in there because I didn't think he knew anything that would help. He said the door was open, and Stephanie was hiding behind it, peeking out around the corner. Then she got shot. And now I'm afraid they'll arrest him for keeping quiet and the INS will send him off to prison or execution." Her eyes welled with tears again.

I kept control of my voice, though I'm not sure how. "But he does know something. What did he see?"

"Another man with a rifle. In the empty room across the hall."

Jesus, was Aaron going to owe me.

"Did he recognize him?"

"No. But he took a picture with his phone. He didn't think anyone would believe him, and he says he likes the Ellingers."

I rolled my head back and shot a silent thank you to the heavens. "Did you recognize the shooter?"

"The picture is...not good."

"But there was another gun on the floor."

The impossible. Caught on camera. Thank God for cell phones. My brain whirred forward in twenty directions. From a phone, it should have a date and time stamp, and a GPS location. Aaron would have to admit Ellinger wasn't guilty and find this other gunman. Other gunman who had a clear shot at the victim.

There were seventy hows and what-ifs zinging around my head. The stickiest ones: how'd he know where to be to get a clear shot? How'd he go unnoticed getting in and out? And how in the world did he know about Tom?

I tapped a foot and turned my attention back to Alisha.

"I need the photo."

"You can't tell the police where you got it."

"Confidential source only." If I played it right, I wouldn't get tossed in a cell for obstruction. Probably.

She nodded and reached over to squeeze my hand. "Thank you."

"I haven't done anything yet."

"You're willing to try, and I appreciate that."

I squeezed back. "In that case, you're welcome."

* * *

It took fifteen minutes of back and forth with Benny's limited English, but I left the hospital with a grainy, dark photo in my text messages—and a thousand pounds on my shoulders.

I wanted to help the Ellingers. Finally, I had something that would, at least a little. Hostages were better than murder, both in court and on Tom's conscience.

And now there was this poor man who needed to stay here with his family. Alisha had dropped heavy doses of pleading into the conversation we had with him. He ran a successful restaurant, paid his taxes, took care of his family. But some spreadsheet somewhere said he had to leave, and whoever held the stay or go stamp couldn't see the person for the paper.

Government makes very little sense to me a lot of the time.

First things first, Nichelle.

Six days.

The two murders were connected. Though someone had taken huge pains to make sure it didn't look that way.

I'd stopped to ask Tom if anyone knew about his plans that day, but he was sleeping such that I wondered if he had a narcotics stash. I'd go back later.

Killer first. If I could untangle this mess, surely the INS would be little more than a bump in my morning.

I rushed to my desk and wrote up the trial day one, plus a follow on a serial flasher at a rest stop on the north side of town. I emailed both stories to Bob and dug a cable out of my desk to connect my phone to my laptop.

Pulling up the photo, I moved it to the computer, crossing my fingers under the desk as it loaded.

Dammit.

If anything, the image was grainer and harder to make out than it had been on Benny's phone.

I stared at it 'til it blurred into a big black-brown blob, not sure even Larry's wizardry could save my bacon this time.

"Worth a shot," I muttered, copying the image file to a thumb drive and hopping up.

I found my favorite photographer in front of his bank of giant computer monitors, clicking through photos of a fall festival parade.

"Sometimes I wish cute kids and animals on the front page didn't sell so damned many papers," he said without turning around. "I get tired of having to hunt people down and get releases for the kids' pictures. Used to be, people were excited to see their kid in the paper. Now they want to sue someone over every damned thing."

"The times they have a-changed," I said, stopping next to his chair. "Were you talking to me, or the universe in general?"

"I can always hear you coming from the other side of the building. It's the shoes." He looked up and grinned. "You find out any more about our old friend Elizabeth?"

"Only that she's not a murderer"

"Why is it we're not saying much about what's going on here? The headline is usually the prize in this game, but you've had like three on this case in a whole week. Hell, you're not even giving up the guy's name. Charlie Lewis is running some bullshit every morning, and we're sitting on information. Did Bob tell you to back off?"

"This whole thing is fishier than a trawler just back from a three-month salmon run," I said, pulling out the thumb drive. "I'm not losing to Charlie, because she's rehashing the same nothing over and over. I have the exclusives with the shooter and his family from inside the hospital, so Andrews is mostly staying in his office. I'm not printing a damned thing I don't have to until I have it nailed down."

"That's a luxury you don't get too often."

"And I'm taking full advantage."

"Hope you don't get burned by some jackass on Twitter."

"Girl Friday is the thing I'm worried about, but so far she has less than Charlie." And from the increasingly hostile tone of her posts, she wasn't happy about it.

"So what's on that thing? Picture of your murderer?" My eyes popped wide and Larry laughed. "Wouldn't that be nice?"

"Actually, I think it might be," I said. "But it was taken with a crappy cell phone from far away in the half-darkness."

He rolled his eyes so far I couldn't see anything but white. "I was kidding, Nichelle."

"One photo restore for all the marbles." I waved the drive in his face. "Want to be the hero? I'll interview you and everything."

"Seeing my name in the paper isn't the thrill it once was," he said dryly, snatching the memory stick out of my hand. "But I do love a challenge."

He pulled up the image. Aw, hell. It looked worse on his screen than it did on mine.

"You've gotta be kidding." He spun the chair to face me.

"Sorry."

He lifted his Generals cap and ran a hand through his thinning hair. "You're lucky it's a slow week and I like you so much."

I patted his shoulder. "Thanks, Larry."

"Don't thank me yet. If I can do anything with this, it'll be a miracle." He turned in the chair and shook his head. "I can tell you right now, I'm not getting a face out of that."

"Of course not." Why would it be easy? I smiled. "I have utter faith."

Larry chuckled. "Kinda sorry it wasn't Elizabeth. Bob might've fought you for the *Telegraph's* seat at the trial."

I grinned. "Me too, but I just don't see it. Whoever that is," I gestured to the screen, "killed Stephanie Whitmire. Whoever killed her killed Maynard. I'm sure of it."

"Why?"

"Money."

He snorted. "What else is new?"

"Money or sex. Almost every time."

With Elizabeth Herrington crossed off my suspect list, I was pretty sure this one was the former.

I was halfway to Carytown, thinking early arrival for this particular meeting could be a good thing, before I realized what I was missing.

Elizabeth planned Maynard's funeral. If she didn't kill him, she was my best in.

Way to catch up, Nichelle.

Clock check: creeping up on four.

I made an illegal u-turn on West Broad and sped toward the river.

31

I smiled and waved at Jeff, who was chatting with a tall man in an expensive suit, and ran for the elevators before he could ask where I was going, or when I wanted to get coffee.

I knew Elizabeth was Maynard's neighbor, but upstairs, I found a choice of three doors. I crossed my fingers and picked the middle one. No answer.

I tried the one on the left. Light footsteps stopped on the other side of the door. I smiled at whoever was looking out the peephole.

A minute ticked by. Three. I knocked again. Two beats later, the latch slid back and the door swung open.

"What do you want?"

It was Mrs. Eason—but the sweet old lady act she'd given Jeff was nowhere in sight, the face in front of me shrewd and suspicious.

I took an involuntary step backward. So much for surprise. Or creating a comradeship. Her expression said she'd just as soon spit on me as tell me what time it was.

Regroup. Parker. What would Captain Charisma do? Pasting on a bright smile, I stepped forward and put out a hand. "I'm Nichelle. I was hoping we could talk."

"You're Bob's golden girl. Why the hell should I want to talk to you?

That bastard made the last few years of my career miserable and then fixed it so I couldn't get work covering sand beetles in Timbuktu."

My temper bubbled. Deep breath. My job today wasn't to defend Bob. It was to make her talk.

"It looks like things have worked out pretty well." I waved a hand to the luxe surroundings, keeping the smile and the sugary tone.

"No thanks to the *Telegraph*."

"Really? The press pass into society events isn't part of what got you here? Just between us girls of course."

She narrowed her eyes. "What do you want?"

I returned the stare. She might not be the nicest person I'd ever meet, but she wasn't stupid. And she knew the business. So what was in this for her?

If Maynard was really her friend, seeing justice done might get me in.

I let my face fall, leaning forward with a conspiratorial tone and a glance in the direction of the crime scene tape still hanging from Maynard's door. "Honestly? The cops have squat, and it's been more than a week. I've been around crime and courts long enough to know every day that goes by lessens the chance they'll catch whoever did this." I left a long pause, looking around the hallway. "Which means whoever it was will still be around." A bit of fear for personal safety didn't hurt.

Her eyes widened further as she took a long look up and down the hallway. She clamped a hand around my wrist and yanked me into her apartment, shutting the door and slamming two locks home behind us before she turned to me.

Recovering my balance, I rubbed my wrist. She was strong for such a little thing. It was hard to see through the layers of designer clothes, but I had a feeling the figure I'd written off as frail was more wiry. Interesting.

She waved to the long white sofa and I took a seat. Perching on the mahogany and horsehair wing chair across from me, she twisted her legs around each other like a length of rope. I stared a bit longer than I should've, fascinated at the way they wound around. There's thin, and then there's circus-y.

"I worked crime at my first job," she said. "Three-stoplight town in Northern Maryland. The cops didn't ever seem to know much about what was going on—there was one murder while I was there, and they let the guy get away. It sounds like the big city guys aren't much smarter. I don't give one damn about helping Bob Jeffers, and I'll throw a party the day the newspaper goes under—but I can't sit by while David's killer walks free."

"My cops are generally pretty smart guys, but this has them stumped. Have you spoken to them?"

"Of course. I told them everything I could think to tell them about David. He never talked much about his work, but I gave them lists of people he knew. People who might have been jealous."

"You don't happen to still have a copy of those lists?"

"Sure. I can print it for you. Most of the names are probably searchable in the newspaper's society archives. Though I understand they did away with the section altogether when I left."

"They rolled it into Lifestyles and Features. Cutbacks are such fun. But I'll ask around. Thanks."

"So what else can I tell you?"

No forced entry.

"Who had a key to Dr. Maynard's condo?"

She didn't flinch. "I do. I think his assistant did. And the building management has a key to everyone's door."

Hmm. Didn't Kyle say the assistant had a fit about them searching the office?

"Did he have a habit of leaving the door unlocked?"

"Nope."

"Friends? Did he see other doctors socially?"

"Of course. They see each other outside work just like reporters do."

What if he'd told someone else in the field what he was working on? "Anyone he might have confided in?"

"There were four of them who went for drinks and poker every Thursday night. David, and Dr. Shoyner, Dr. Reyes, and Dr. Vine."

I jotted the names down. Worth checking into.

"You said he didn't talk about his work much?"

"I found it horrifyingly depressing." Her tone was so dismissive it set my teeth on edge.

Not that he didn't talk about it. That she didn't want to hear about it.

I nodded, tapping my pen over top of the names of his doctor friends. It was something I hadn't had when I walked in here. That plus the assistant could equal time well spent.

Hauling in a deep breath and blowing it out slowly, I stood. "Thanks so much for your time, Mrs. Eason. My condolences for your loss, again."

She nodded. "You don't want to know anything else?"

"Is there something else I should know?"

"He was paranoid about someone stealing his research. Became obsessed with computer security in the past three months."

"Why did he think someone would want to steal his research?"

"To corrupt it, he said. He was a fine man. Brilliant doctor. But a bit crazy."

"Since he ended up dead, I'm not so sure I'd rush to that particular judgement." I checked the clock on the mantle and turned for the door.

It was ten after five, and I had an appointment to keep.

* * *

I pulled into the back lot at Cary Court at five-twenty-eight, wondering if I was brilliant or stupid for showing up. On one hand, whoever my mystery caller was, they knew something because they'd used Maynard's name. On the other...parking lot meetings with mysterious sources haven't exactly gone well for me in the past.

My hand drifted to the back of my skull and I sucked in a deep breath, backing the car into a space and locking the doors, leaving the engine running. I wouldn't make the mistake of getting out this time. And it was still daylight, though fading fast, but there were plenty of people in the shopping center just a few feet away.

I scanned the lot, not finding an occupied car, and fixed my gaze on the entrance.

Nineteen minutes later, I tried the number again.

Out of service.

I double-checked it and dialed one more time.

Same recording.

Putting the car in gear and rolling out of the lot, I peered inside every vehicle I passed.

Nothing.

Curiouser and curiouser.

* * *

The last rays of sun disappeared over the western horizon as I turned onto my street, still wondering what could've gone wrong. I'd texted Aaron, who said he'd run the number but guessed it was a tracfone (and what the hell was I doing meeting strange men in parking lots anyway?), and that no, he had no new dead bodies or missing people.

Which left me shaking my head as I turned into the driveway, my headlights glinting off the shiny bumper of the black Lincoln parked by the fence.

My face split into a grin, the day's tension ebbing as I stepped out of the car and heard Darcy yipping and Joey laughing in the backyard.

"Sounds like all the fun is back here," I said, stepping through the gate.

Darcy didn't even look at me, her attention honed on the raggedy squirrel in Joey's hand. He tossed it and she took off, kicking up dirt on her way to the far corner of the yard.

He smiled and walked toward me. "Long day, baby?"

I nodded, stepping into his arms. "There's so much to sort out. Aaron is banging his head against a wall. Hell, even Kyle can't make heads or tails of this. But I'm going to talk to them first thing in the morning. I got a huge lead today, but I want to keep it quiet until I see what Larry can do with it."

I cast my eyes at my shoes, biting down on the events of the past half-hour because they were probably nothing, yet I knew he would flip. I didn't want to fight. I wanted to have fun. Hopefully my tipster was a well-intentioned intern or something who just forgot to pay his phone bill, and Aaron would turn him up when he ran the number.

"Does this mean you're going to be working all night again?" Joey dropped small kisses up the side of my neck between the words, pulling back to show me an exaggerated pout on his already full lips. I smiled.

It'd probably be easier to find Maynard's assistant and friends during business hours, anyway. And I wanted a sharpened photo to take my cops.

"Larry might be, but I'm off for a few hours." I reached behind his head and pulled his face down to mine. "Can you think of a fun way to spend them?"

He kissed me, his hands moving under my shirt and up my back.

"I think I can." He pulled back a millimeter and turned his lips up in my favorite sexy smile. Kyle picked that moment to bop through my thoughts talking about rock climbing.

I took a small step back, allowing a puff of air between our bodies, and smiled up at Joey. "Me too. And we have plenty of time. But you know, I was thinking: we don't go out. What kinds of stuff do you like to do?"

He tightened his arms around me and lowered his mouth to mine again, tracing the bow of my top lip with his tongue. "I think you have a good bead on my favorite thing to do." He murmured against my skin, moving his kisses to my earlobe.

I rustled all the self-control I'd ever thought about having and wriggled my arms between us, put both hands on his chest, and pushed gently. "I'm serious."

He stepped back, his dark eyes confused. "As am I."

I ran a light touch over the muscles in his arms and shoulders. "It's obvious to casual passersby that you're in great shape. I like running and kickboxing. What do you like to do? That doesn't involve a bed?"

"Doesn't have to involve a bed. Counter, table, rug..."

I rolled my eyes. "How far are we into...whatever we're doing? Months? And I don't know much about you." His eyes popped wide and I raised one hand. "Not what I mean. Not work. Fun. Tell me a hobby. I want to do things with you. Besides food and sex."

"We've never done food with sex."

"Joey." I drew the syllables out and added an edge.

He raised both hands in mock surrender. "Okay. Serious business. You want a date."

"A fun one."

"Are you saying the others have been less than fun?"

"No. But I want to do something. Rock climbing?"

He wrinkled his nose. "I've never understood the point of going up a plastic wall so you can drop right back down."

"The point is to have fun."

"But wouldn't it be more fun to get somewhere climbing?"

I shrugged. "I've never been, so I can't say."

"I think it would." He slung an arm around my shoulders.

"Well then, what does sound like fun?" I turned for the house.

He planted a kiss on my head and whistled for the dog, who had abandoned her game of fetch to dig in the small garden I didn't really use in the back corner of the yard.

"Anything I do with you."

"Oh, good. We're on the same page."

I kicked my shoes under the coffee table and opened my laptop, searching "fun dates in Richmond" while Joey browsed my wine rack.

He put a glass of red on the table next to me as I clicked to the website for a go kart racetrack. He loved his car, and I knew he was good at driving fast.

"How about go kart racing?"

"Like a real live Mariokart?" He sat next to me, his thigh pressing against mine as he sipped his wine and looked over my shoulder. "That could be cool."

"Done. Let's go." I slammed the laptop, shoved my feet back into my canary Nicholas Kirkwoods and jumped up, ignoring the protest from my still-sore toe.

"Right now?"

"Why not? Seize the day."

He laughed and put his glass on the table. "Your enthusiasm is contagious. Why not, indeed."

I led him to the car and waved him to the passenger seat. "I haven't checked the mail in days. I'm going to grab it and we'll go."

Opening the box, I pulled out a stack of sale flyers, three catalogs, five bills, and a large, flat manila envelope.

With no writing on it. And no stamp.

I fumbled at the tab on the back with clumsy fingers, reaching inside to find a photo and a slip of paper.

Bills and catalogs scattered around my feet.

My mom, leaving her shop. Shot with a short lens, from the wide angle that fattened the doorway.

A square of plain white paper lay across it, BACK OFF etched into it in black ink.

I studied the picture. Recent, because she'd told me Sunday she got a haircut last week.

My throat closed, my heart taking off like a greyhound with a bead on Thumper.

I heard a door slam, then running footfalls, managing to catch my breath as Joey snatched the papers from my hand.

He looked from the photo to the note to my ghost-white face, folding his arms around me and glancing up and down the street.

"Come on," he said. "Whatever this is about, the safest place for you to be right now is away from here."

Settling me in the passenger seat, he tossed the envelope and its contents in the back and squealed the tires pulling out of the driveway. I fumbled for my phone and texted my mom. A call would scare her—she'd hear the panic in my voice and freak out, and I couldn't have that.

You there?

Bing. *Hey, baby.*

Thank God. *I need you to do me a favor.*

Bing. *Anything.*

I checked the clock. Just after five in Dallas. *Call Kevin and tell him to come get you, and go away somewhere. To Austin or San Antonio. Just for a couple days.*

Pause, pause, cringe. Bing. *WHAT? Why? Nicey, are you in some kind of trouble?*

Deep breath. *I'm safe. J is here. But please—trust me. Just go. Think of it as a spontaneous mini vacation. But go.*

Pause. Tick tock. Bing. *All right. Promise you're safe?*

Promise. You swear you'll go?

Packing now. Love you.

Love you more.

Joey was silent 'til I put the phone down, turning to me when he stopped at the corner of Monument and Thompson. "Now. Let's hear about this lead you got today, huh?"

* * *

I told him the whole story as he drove, his hands tightening on the wheel every few words until his knuckles had sailed past white to in-danger-of-splitting-open.

"And that's where you come in," I said. "I hope."

"Care to explain?"

Deep breath. "I need a favor. Kinda hoping you have a friend that can get me a shot at pulling off a minor miracle."

"Anything to get you out of this, so I'd say your shot is decent."

"This guy, the one who took the picture. He's an immigrant. With an expired visa and a deportation date."

"Damn." He laced his fingers with mine.

"You know anyone who knows anyone at the INS?" Another stolen glance. The shock and anger had been replaced by concentration. He drummed the fingers of one hand on the wheel and swiped sparks across my knuckles with the other.

"I might. I'm not sure what I can do, but let me look into it."

I squeezed his hand. "Thank you."

He turned into the parking lot at the go kart track, meeting my quizzical eyes with a determined stare.

"You said you wanted to go out. We're going out. I will make some calls about your refugee family, and I can help protect your mother, too. But for right this second, my focus is to get your mind off work." He pulled me close and buried his face in my hair. "And don't think for three seconds I'm letting you out of my sight until someone goes to jail. Meeting anonymous sources with no background. How do you manage to get yourself into this shit, anyway?"

I pulled away and forced a smile that was brighter than I felt. I'd be damned if these people were going to scare me off the trail. I'd call Aaron first thing, but for tonight, I was safe with Joey. And Aaron needed a break —possibly even more than I did.

"Natural talent," I said. "C'mon. I'm going to kick your ass at driving."

He laughed as he kicked the door open. "Bring it."

32

I took two out of three, and the way Joey kissed me when we got back to my house said he didn't mind the loss—or my helmet hair. I ran my fingers up the back of his neck and pulled him closer, forgetting everything but how he made me feel for a good two minutes.

"That was fun." He kissed the tip of my nose and grinned. "Good distraction?"

"Excellent." I ignored the twist in my gut and returned the smile before I opened the car door. "You're not too shabby in that department, either."

My cell phone binged and Joey groaned. "Breaking news sucks."

I giggled as I dug through my bag. "It might be my mom."

Or not.

Chad. I crossed my fingers and clicked the message.

No dice.

Dammit.

You couldn't get in?

Please. There's nothing in it.

Nothing at all?

Zip.

Isn't that weird?

Not really. Not everyone uses cloud storage.

I glanced at Joey. "Sorry. Trying to find a clue. It's like looking for a black-soled shoe in the Louboutin factory this week."

He put a hand on my thigh. "Can I help?"

"Yes. But not with this. I don't think. Give me sixty more seconds."

He winked. "Always happy to help you with things that don't involve dead people." He squeezed my knee and went inside. I stared after him for a second before I resumed tapping my phone screen.

But her friend said she did.

Maybe she heard wrong. Or maybe it's one of the eight million other services.

Sigh. *Yeah.*

Sorry.

No worries. What about the doc? Find anything on him?

Haven't looked. I'll get on it.

I owe you.

This saving the day thing is sort of fun.

When it works.

Have a nice night.

Planning to.

* * *

My cell phone bleated long before sunrise, and I lifted my head from its spot on Joey's chest and groped for the nightstand. "What?" I muttered.

"They don't even let you sleep now?" Slumber lent a sexy scratch to Joey's voice.

I cracked one eye at the screen. "I guess not." I sighed, clicking the talk button and putting the phone to my ear. "Morning, Aaron."

"I have good news and bad news."

I sat up and looked at the clock. "You're calling me about this at four-forty-five because why?"

"I owe you one." He sounded annoyed. And exhausted.

"Good news first?"

"We do have the woman's computer in the evidence room."

Ah.

"But the bad news is you can't get in or didn't find anything." I plucked at the blanket.

"Correct."

"Damn. You had the cyber guys try?"

"They had it all night."

Double damn. "I have a friend who's pretty good with that stuff."

He sighed. "Somehow that doesn't surprise me."

"Totally legit. He gets paid for it and everything."

"This doesn't increase my confidence level."

"You know what I mean."

"Even so, I can't let it out of here. It's evidence in an open murder investigation."

Who would know? I didn't bother to ask. Aaron would know.

"Could I bring him by there? After normal people are awake?"

"It could compromise our case if I let him touch the damned thing." The last words were practically a growl, the frustration wearing on him. "We're running out of time, Nichelle."

I bit the inside of my cheek and plucked the blanket threads faster. Did I trust Aaron? With my life.

Whoever was running this show?

Not as far as I could throw a Buick.

But we'd worked together for so many years. On so much stuff.

"You sound like you could use a coffee, Detective," I said, keeping my tone light. Whatever I was going to tell him, I'd do it in person.

"That an offer?"

"An invitation. Twenty minutes?"

"Absolutely."

I clicked off the call and giggled when Joey locked his arms around my waist. "Stay here with me. It's cold out there." He still hadn't opened his eyes.

I wriggled around and kissed his scruffy cheek. "I wish. But I have to go see Aaron. One way or another, we're going to put this together."

That was worth opening his eyes. "Who 'we?' You are not a cop. Let them put it together."

"I know something they don't know."

"The photo you were telling me about?"

"Ellinger didn't do it."

"They will figure that out."

"They're getting pressure. Lots of it, from someone who ranks roughly alongside God on an org chart, from what Kyle can tell. Someone who wants Tom Ellinger to hang on this. I don't trust any of it, but I have to tell Aaron. In person. I trust him. He'll know what to do."

He pulled me close and kissed me before he let go. "Be careful."

"I always am."

* * *

Aaron looked as tired and frustrated as he sounded, sitting across a round teak table from me gulping a small vat of straight black coffee while eating a box of chocolate-covered espresso beans. "The evidence keeps mounting against this guy. Your guy. The same one who's so distraught over his wife I can't get him to talk."

"But you did go up there?" I waited.

Aaron sighed. "I really hate it when you're right. As hard as I tried, I just don't get the vibe from him. If he shot anyone, it wasn't on purpose."

I let my head drop back and sent a silent thank you to the heavens. Having Aaron on my side would be great for the Ellingers. He was stubborn. And a hell of a good detective.

"I told you."

He nodded. "I deserve that. But my gut isn't going to do that guy any good if we don't figure something definitive soon, Nichelle. Everything— and I mean everything," he lifted his eyebrows to hit the word home, "points to him. If he was set up, it was by someone who dotted every 'i.'"

"Did you check the rifle?"

He nodded. "One in the chamber."

Hot damn. "That's definitive. He said he took two with him. That means he really only fired one."

He pursed his lips. "If you take the word of the accused. But we can't prove that."

My eyes wandered the room until they came to rest on a photo of

Arthur Ashe, racquet raised over his head and face-splitting grin in place, walking off a tennis court. Courage. Taking chances. Even when you might lose something in the bargain. Hopefully the exclusive was the only thing at stake here. Surely whoever was pointing the cops to Tom Ellinger couldn't discount Benny's photo.

"There was another rifle inside the building, Aaron. On that floor."

"I appreciate your doggedness, but I can't take your gut to my bosses."

"Can you take them a photo?"

His cup hit the table with a thunk and fell over. The last of his coffee trickled across the teak and I grabbed a napkin and blotted at it.

"A what?"

I pulled out my cell phone and opened the picture, pushing it across the table.

"Larry's trying to sharpen it, because I know the quality is beyond shitty. But that's a man with a rifle. In the empty room straight across from that meds closet."

He put the screen a centimeter from the end of his nose and squinted at the picture for at least a commercial break before he looked back up at me.

"How long have you had this?" He laid the phone on the table.

"About fourteen hours."

"Fourteen hours could make a difference here, Nichelle." His voice was tight, and I heard mine get defensive when I opened my mouth.

"What if whoever wants Ellinger to hang for this gets ahold of it and it disappears? Someone made Maynard disappear off the freaking internet, Aaron." I pulled the photo and note from my bag and pushed them across the table. "And I found this in my mailbox last night. These people are smart, and they're not playing."

He picked it up and studied it, then dropped it back to the table, shaking his head. "Your mom?"

I nodded.

"You thinking what I'm thinking?" He held up the note.

"That my mystery tipster call was a decoy so I wouldn't see whoever dropped this off?" Joey and I had gotten there about eleven-thirty last night, and the look on Aaron's face said he agreed.

"I ran the number. Prepaid cell, no name registered. Watch yourself."

Aaron touched the ghost image of the second shooter on my phone screen and ran one hand over his face. "As for this…Even if you don't trust me," the words were muffled by his fingers, resting across his lips, "I would think you'd trust Miller."

"How? Why the hell is he even working on this? Has anyone told you? Because if they've told him, he's not telling me. You've all been clammed up tighter than Uncle Scrooge's checkbook for two weeks. Why should I run to bring you evidence when you won't talk to me?"

"Because you want this to go toward what's right. We're getting pointed to what's easy." He raised one hand when I opened my mouth to argue. "Let's not. Us jumping at each other won't get us what we want."

"Which is?"

"The truth." He glanced around, tapping a finger on his chin. "I might have found something interesting myself in the wee hours, but even I'm getting paranoid. Want to take a walk and talk it through? Tell me what Richmond's resident Lois Lane has to say about this?"

I stood. "You'll think I'm nuts."

"Historically, that's when you're right." His lips disappeared into a grim line. "Let's finish this."

He held the door open as I stepped out into the October sunshine.

I turned back to ask about his late-night epiphany and screamed as my favorite detective crumpled to the ground, a black-red stain spreading across his green shirtfront.

33

The air thickened, the blood pounding in my ears blocking the neighborhood bustle and traffic sounds of the morning.

I grabbed Aaron and threw myself back through the door, dragging him with me. From far away, I heard a shrill voice, saying "help us," over and over. Pretty sure it was me.

Clattering commotion as chairs overturned and people rushed forward. A million shouted variations of "What happened?"

I groped for my phone, punching 911 and trying to catch my breath and corral my thoughts enough to be useful.

"What's your emergency?"

"RPD officer down," I said, holding the panic out of my voice so she could understand me. I wriggled out from under Aaron and turned, snatching the towel the barista was offering and pressing it over his chest. It was soaked in about two and half seconds. Shit. I kept talking.

"This is Nichelle Clarke. I'm at Thompson's Coffee Shop on West Cary with Detective Aaron White, and he's been shot. He's losing a lot of blood."

Stunned silence for half a second. But dispatchers are used to processing quickly and moving on. Her tone was all business, keys already clicking in the background. "I'll have an ambulance there in a blink, Miss Clarke."

She disappeared for a few seconds and then was back, her voice soothing as she asked me about his condition. "Is he responding?"

I pinched the phone between my cheekbone and my shoulder and slapped Aaron's face. "Aaron! Answer me!" I shouted, getting up on my knees and leaning on the towel I was pressing over the wound.

His eyelids fluttered as he mumbled, but I couldn't make out what he said.

"He's about half-conscious," I said into the phone. I laid two fingers over his carotid artery. "His pulse is thready, breathing shallow, but they're there."

"Where is the wound?"

"His ribcage." I pressed harder, blocking thoughts of all the vital organs under those bones. He would be fine. He had to be.

"What happened?"

"I…" A wave of panic crashed over me and I swallowed tears, turning to scan the street outside the window. "I don't know. We walked outside. He was holding the door. And he just fell. Bleeding." I choked the last word out and hauled in a deep breath. Losing my shit was not an option. Plenty of time for that when Aaron was safely at the hospital.

"You didn't hear a shot?"

"No. But I wasn't listening for one. We were going for a walk."

"It's okay, Miss Clarke." Same soothing voice. Like you'd talk to a frightened child.

Like hell it was okay. My friend was bleeding out under my hands.

"Where is the ambulance?" I said through gritted teeth, pressing harder on Aaron's chest.

Computer keys clicked. "Two blocks."

Okay. "Hang in there, Aaron. When was the last time you took the girls fishing? Think about that."

"Good. Keep talking to him."

Sirens. My breath came easier, and I pressed harder still, my arms shaking.

The front door slammed open.

"Nichelle!"

I turned from murmuring to Aaron to see Landers and Kyle rushing forward, paramedics on their heels.

Kyle's hand closed over my shoulder as a broad-chested medic dropped to his knees next to me, putting his gloved fingers over my bloody ones and motioning with his head for me to move. I pulled away and fell into Kyle's legs. The medics went to work on Aaron, the guy holding his chest sporting arms twice the size of my thighs. They had him on a stretcher and out the door in less than a minute.

I turned my face into Kyle's khakis and sobbed. Kyle's hand went to my hair. Landers said something about going with Aaron and disappeared.

Kyle put his arms under mine and hauled me to my feet. "You in there?" His voice was gentle, his head tipped to meet my eyes.

"What the actual fuck, Kyle?" Tears followed in another wave.

His arms went around me, pulling me close. "I don't know, honey. But I will find out. And I will keep you safe."

"I was having coffee with a cop." The words hitched out between sobs. "How much safer can you get?"

He grabbed a towel for my hands, pulling me to a table and waving to the barista, who appeared with two full cups a nanosecond later. Her pale face and big eyes said she'd seen more than she wanted to this shift. Me too, sister.

Kyle pushed my cup toward me and picked up his own. "Tell me what happened."

Whoever was trying to frame Tom Ellinger wasn't screwing around, that's what happened. I knew good and well the bullet could've been meant for me, but either way...I raised my eyes to Kyle's and shook my head.

I told Aaron, and somebody shot him twelve seconds later. My eyes drifted to the shoulder of Kyle's red polo, where I knew a scar was still fading underneath.

"I don't know," I said, standing. "I have to go wash my hands."

Every word true. And I couldn't put anyone else in danger.

* * *

Thirty minutes of SuperCop interrogation should be enough to break anyone, but I was more determined to keep Kyle safe than he was to make me talk—and he liked Aaron, so that was saying something.

He asked me the same questions seventy-six thousand different ways, and I came to admire his technique. He was good. If I wasn't still half-panicked, I could've paid enough attention to learn a trick or two.

"We stepped outside. I was facing away. I turned, and he fell. I didn't see anyone, didn't hear anything," I repeated calmly.

"Dammit, Nichelle, why are you stonewalling me?" Kyle bit out.

I looked around. Nearly an hour had passed, and we were still at the same table I'd been sitting at with Aaron. The rest of the place had been cleared by the RPD, the detectives taking statements from the customers and staff and the forensics team studying the scene.

"I don't know what you're talking about," I said, bringing my gaze back to Kyle's. "I'm answering the questions you're asking me."

"You are?" He leaned forward. "Tell me why you were here. What were y'all talking about?"

"Nothing really." Okay, that was a lie. But while I knew it wasn't logical that anyone could have heard me and Aaron, what if? This whole damned thing was so crazy. Bugs. Teamwork. I could think of several scenarios, and none of them made me want to share anything more than the law required with my friendly ex.

"Bullshit. He was up all night. I know, because I was too. He didn't come meet you to shoot the breeze."

I raised cool eyes to Kyle's. "Prove it."

"Talk to me." His tone flipped from annoyed to pleading. "I can help. I can't let you get hurt."

"Back at you," I mumbled.

He tipped his head to one side. "I'm sorry?"

"Nothing."

I ran scenarios on fast forward. If whoever shot Aaron did in fact know what we'd been talking about, I was in very real danger. The kind that made my stomach feel heavy and my skin clammy. But what good would it do anyone to pull Kyle into it? The smartest thing would be to keep my head down and focus. Digging until I found the answer—and the mystery gunman.

"Can I go back to work now?" I asked, keeping my tone neutral. "I'm pretty sure I'm leading the front page tomorrow."

He shoved his chair back from the table. "You are so damned stubborn."

"I'm sorry you feel that way. I know how frustrating it is to ask people questions and not get the answers you want." I stood.

"Does this have something to do with getting even with me for shutting you out of this case?" Kyle looked like someone had slapped him. "White is your friend, for Chrissakes."

I shook my head. "Nothing of the sort." I couldn't stand that disappointed puppy look on his face. I grabbed his hand and squeezed. "Trust me, Kyle. You asked that of me last week. Your turn to give it back."

He locked eyes with me. I didn't blink.

He returned the pressure on my fingers. "I do trust you. Take it down. It might be the one and only time I ever say those words to a reporter. But you have to trust me too."

I had to give him something. "Aaron said he found something interesting last night. But he didn't get a chance to tell me what."

"Thank you. I'll go have a look around his office."

My head ducked involuntarily when he pushed open the back door of the restaurant to walk me to my car. Every other reporter in fifty miles was on the front walk, and I didn't want to be today's top story, nor was I telling Charlie one damned thing.

"I'll call you," he said as he shut the car door.

I nodded, starting the engine.

When Kyle disappeared inside, I fished my cell phone out of my bag and pulled up a text to Joey. *You still in Richmond?*

Just heading out now, came the instant reply. I smiled. He liked getting texts from me.

Can you stick around today? I need a safe place to crash tonight.

The phone started buzzing before I could say "Manolo."

"Don't go flipping out on me," I said, putting it to my ear.

"Why would I have cause to do that? Should I turn on the TV?"

"Aaron's been shot."

"Aaron who you were meeting for coffee?"

Calm, cool, and matter of fact. "We were leaving the shop. He wanted to go for a walk while we finished talking."

Didn't work.

"Someone shot a cop while you were STANDING NEXT TO HIM?" I pulled the phone away from my head as Joey roared in my ear. I put it back in time to catch a string of swearwords so impressive I didn't fully recognize a couple of them.

"Where are you?" His voice was so tight, I could see his stoic, unreadable expression though he was more than a mile away.

"Leaving Thompson's for my office."

"Like hell you are. I'll be there in five minutes. Stay put."

"Don't give me orders," I snapped. "I have a huge story to write. And a nutcase on the loose. No way anyone's going to try to pin this on poor Tom Ellinger, which means my exclusive is going to disappear if I don't figure something out fast. I'm going to work." I glanced down at my shirt, the blood drying on the front sending my eyes to my hands, which I had scrubbed raw in the coffeehouse bathroom.

Fabulous. I couldn't go to the office like that unless I wanted to give Bob another heart attack.

I couldn't go home to change—Joey's tone said he'd lock me in my own house and not think twice about it.

I couldn't exactly go into a store dressed like a slasher flick extra, either.

Gym bag. A stinky t-shirt was better than bloody silk.

One problem solved, I put the car in gear and sped out of the lot before Joey could get in his car and drive the seven blocks to the coffee shop. I knew him well enough to know that's what he was doing even before I heard the soft *thunk* of the door closing in the background. But he wouldn't dare try to drag me out of the newsroom. I just had to beat him to my office.

Which, on one hand—I'm a big girl, and my office is full of people. He was being slightly absurd. On the other, his heart was in the right place.

"Listen, Captain Overprotective, I'm not stupid, and I have less desire to end up in a body bag chasing this story than I do to wear clogs for the rest of my days. I appreciate the offer to play bodyguard, and I will take you up on it. When my story is done. Let me go to the office. I'll call you when I'm ready to leave. I promise."

Heavy, Nichelle-is-driving-me-nuts sigh, followed by silence.

I knew this game. I waited.

Crickets.

"If I wasn't being careful, I wouldn't have called you," I said softly.

Four beats, and another sigh. "Fine."

"Make yourself at home."

I turned into the garage and parked next to the elevator, checking the clock. Coming up on eight-thirty. Bob would be out of the staff meeting in a few minutes, and I had nine hours and change before drop dead on the front page.

Time for a miracle.

34

No matter what happened in the rest of my day, nobody saw me changing my shirt in the front seat of my car.

Thankful for small favors, I stuffed my Donna Karan blouse into the garbage can outside the elevator and tapped one tangerine Kate Spade mule on the sticky floor as the elevator climbed toward the newsroom.

I needed to talk to Bob. And light a candle before I went to talk to Larry. I knew the photo was a longshot for anything other than what it had already provided, but it was all I had. With Aaron on an operating table at St. Vincent's, it was only a matter of time before Charlie caught up. For all I knew she might not be that far behind to begin with.

I shook off the competitive itch and refocused. Tom Ellinger. Benny Shabani.

And now Aaron.

Beating Charlie was a distant fourth. Even Rick Andrews could take a flying leap today.

I dug my phone out and shot Landers a text begging for updates as the doors opened.

Bolting off the elevator, I waved hello to three people between it and Bob's office, but I couldn't have put faces to any one of them. The story was all I could see, because it was the only way to help anyone.

"Chief, I know I missed the meeting but I—"

I stopped when I rounded the corner into Bob's office, Andrews and two other suits just taking seats. I got blank stares from the ones I didn't know and a sneer from Andrews.

"Bob has another appointment just now."

"I have an exclusive for tomorrow's front page I need to talk to him about." I hovered in the doorway, a heaviness in the air giving me pause.

"On what? Every TV station in town has a live feed right now about the shooting of an RPD detective this morning. Our website has nothing. How are we supposed to compete for advertising money when we missed the biggest breaking story of the year?"

"I was—"

Andrews raised a hand. "I'm not interested in excuses, Miss Clarke. And we have business to discuss. I'll deal with you when I'm done here."

My eyes flew to Bob, whose lips had vanished into a thin white line, his posture ramrod straight, his hands white-knuckling the arms of his chair.

Andrews and the suits turned to face my editor, and I closed my eyes, the firing squad image on the backs of my lids popping them right back open. Bob wouldn't look at Andrews. He was looking at me. "Close the door on your way out, please."

Andrews grinning in my peripheral, I kept my eyes locked on Bob.

I will fix this. I mouthed the words, and he shut his eyes, his nod almost imperceptible. He wasn't mad at me.

I wasn't even mad at myself. I hadn't failed Bob, and we both knew it.

But his face said he knew Andrews wouldn't care. Arguing was pointless.

That was it.

He had resigned himself to whatever was coming.

Lucky for our readers, I don't do resignation well.

I backed out the door and shut it, sprinting for the photo cave.

* * *

Larry wasn't there.

"I'm sorry, Nichelle. He called early this morning and said he wasn't sure when he'd be in. Something about telling Bob to hold space for a cover shot tomorrow." Lindsay offered a half-smile and turned back to her computer monitor.

"He didn't say what he had?"

"He might have told Bob," she said, not looking away from her screen. "You could ask him."

No, I could not.

I thanked her and stomped back to my desk. A cover shot was a rare thing these days—a photo worthy of all the available editorial space above the page one fold would have to be pretty damned special.

Flopping into my chair, I drug my laptop from my bag and flipped the screen up, opening a blank file and closing my eyes.

To hell with Rick Andrews. I'd lost to Charlie plenty of times, but not today. I hoped I had time to stick around and see the egg on his smug asshat face when he figured that out.

A Richmond Police Detective was shot on the street in broad daylight Thursday morning, and officers are combing the Carytown shopping district, searching for the gunman who wounded Detective Aaron White outside Thompson's Coffee Shop just after 6 a.m.

"No one in this department will rest until an arrest has been made," Detective Chris Landers said in a statement issued by the department an hour after the shooting.

The incident marks only the third time in the past two decades an RPD officer has been shot, and detectives at the scene refused to speculate on motive or name suspects.

I paused, staring at the blinking cursor. Stay out of the story. It's Journalism 101. But today, being in the story was the only way I had more than anyone else. I clicked to Channel Four's website and scrolled through Charlie's write-up. All quotes from the press release, plus a couple of bystanders. Interestingly enough, she hadn't used my name. I wondered if that was because she didn't know the "female friend" the barista mentioned was me, or because she didn't want to send the *Telegraph* readers. No way to tell.

Clicking back to my document, I switched tenses.

This Richmond Telegraph *reporter was with the detective at the time of the shooting. Below is the exclusive firsthand account of what I saw.*

The shot wasn't audible from where we stood, nor did I see a gun. One moment, Detective White was talking to me, and the next he was bleeding. I grabbed Detective White and dragged him back into the coffee shop, calling for help and applying pressure to the wound as I dialed 911 from my cell phone.

I continued through the point where Aaron was loaded into the ambulance, pulling out my cell phone and checking for a text from Landers.

There were three.

He's in surgery.

Ten minutes later:

It nicked an artery. They're giving him blood by the bucketful. Damn damn damn.

My stomach turned inside out as I scrolled to the next one.

Stable. But they're still working on him. Miller says you're not talking. Don't know why, but you better be ready to answer me when I get out of here.

I closed my eyes. Nice, Kyle. Let's drag the detective with the young family into this manure pile.

Fingers shaking, I texted him back a thank you, ignoring the latter part of his message.

I wanted to ask what kind of bullet it was, but I knew there wasn't any way they had ballistics back yet, and I also knew it didn't matter. If the same person hadn't shot Aaron and Stephanie Whitmire both, I'd give Alexa Reading my Rolodex and go sell shoes for a living. And I'm a lousy salesperson. Same gun, different gun: wouldn't do anything to alter my gut feeling about who fired the shots, and I wasn't in a position to ignore my gut.

I added Aaron's condition to the story and popped out of my chair to check Bob's door. Still closed. Andrews had many lousy qualities, not the least of which was his utterly shitty timing.

I sent an email to our web editor, attaching the story and marking it urgent before I picked up my cell phone and texted him to make sure he saw it. Four minutes passed and I got: *Do you have art?*

Nothing live. Too busy trying to not let my friend die.

Stock?

Ten seconds.

I pulled a publicity photo of Aaron from the PD's site and emailed it to Ryan.

Up in two minutes, came the reply. *Nice work.*

Bob's door was still closed. I hoped it was nice enough. I tapped the screen for two seconds, then opened a text to him. *Give Ryan five and check the website. Hang in there, Chief. We have your back.*

I turned back to the computer. What else did I know? That might help, anyway?

Stephanie's computer.

Aaron said they couldn't get in. And he hadn't wanted to compromise their case. But what if it held the key to why he was lying on an operating table?

I texted Chad and asked if he could meet me at the PD.

Before I could call Kyle, Chad texted back that he had Maynard's cloud file loading onto a USB for me.

Jiminy. Choos.

You're my hero. I'll come get it, and we'll see if we need the PD.

The answer to this whole mess was floating around the ether. If only I could manage to snatch it out of the air before anyone else got hurt.

35

"You're going to need someone who knows a lot of medical jargon." Chad handed me a thumb drive, shaking his head. "I only opened a couple of them, but I might as well have been reading Greek, and I'm not a stupid guy."

I kissed his cheek and tucked the drive into my bag. "You are a freaking genius. Someday there will be parades in honor of your intelligence. But until then, you'll have to take my word for it—you're a hero."

He patted my shoulder. "I saw your story. I'm sorry about your friend."

"Don't be sorry. Say a prayer and believe he's going to be fine. Because he is."

I refused to consider any other possibility.

He nodded and stepped into the elevator to go back upstairs, and I pulled out my cell phone for the forty millionth time in an hour.

Aaron was still in surgery. But no news certainly wasn't bad news.

I sped back to the office and pulled the drive from my bag, closing my fist so tightly around it the plastic bit into my fingers as I waited for the elevator doors to open to the newsroom.

Plugging it into my computer, I grabbed the phone and dialed the NIH from memory.

"Miss Emma," I said. "It's Nichelle Clarke. I need your help. Do you have a computer that can screen share with me?"

"You sound serious, there, Lois Lane," she said. "I'm not sure what screen whatever-you-said is, but I'll help however I can."

"I have Dr. Maynard's files. A lot of them, anyway. But I have no idea how to read them." I clicked open the drive and pulled a couple up for confirmation as I spoke. Yeah. Chad was right—I needed a translator.

"What kind of files?"

"Medical charts, study results." I scrolled through and read her file-names. "Stuff I have no experience with, but it could mean everything to this case."

"You've come to the right place," she said. "I don't have a degree, but it's not because I haven't done the reading."

"You're a rock star," I said.

* * *

Thirty minutes later, I had Emma set up on a remote desktop app, and she was looking at Maynard's file list.

"If this isn't the damndest thing," she said. "Imagine, being able to look at someone else's computer from hundreds of miles away."

"Technology is awesome when it works," I agreed. "Do you see anything we should look at?"

"See those numbers? That's a code for an experimental treatment. It looks like several variations that are close together."

I clicked the first file open. "And this?"

"Go down."

I scrolled.

"It's a study." She moved a pointer between columns. "Patient ID numbers, codes for what type of cancer they had and the stage, and whether they were in the control group or treated with the protocol he was using. This is the result." She hovered over a column of letters.

"What does it mean?"

"Let me see the rest of it," she murmured, her wispy voice softer than usual.

I scrolled.

"Holy Mary," she whispered.

"Miss Emma?"

"Cured. Every one of them." The pointer skipped back and forth on my screen. "If they got the treatment, they got well. How? Why wouldn't he file this?"

I sighed, Goetze and his kickbacks flashing through my thoughts. "Money."

Emma's voice picked up speed and tempo. "What was he doing? Go down more. I want to see the protocol."

I obliged, stopping when she told me to and listening to her murmur to herself for half an hour. My shoulders slumped back into the chair.

Finally. Concrete evidence that Maynard had something worth killing for. This wasn't one freak recovery. With the amount of effort that had gone into this cover-up, Felicia Lang could be dismissed.

Not this.

"I'll be," Miss Emma breathed finally. "It's so simple. Such a brilliant, brilliant man."

"What is it?" I asked.

"Ions. He used negatively charged ions to attach the treatments directly to the cancer cells. Like setting a search and destroy mission inside the body. Not only did it obliterate the disease, it didn't kill the whole system. People didn't get sick like they do with chemo and radiation."

"What kind of drug is it?" I scribbled, trying to make sure I got every word exactly as she said it.

"It looks like he used existing drugs. Without reading all those files, I can't be sure, but this one is a drug that's been in wide use for five years. It's just a completely different delivery approach. And it worked, according to this. Why hide it? I mean, this is the medical discovery of the millennium. He'll be in history books for generations. There's immense pressure on doctors to discover new things and get research published."

My fingers got a cramp getting the last of that down. "Enough pressure for someone to want to steal it?" I asked, shaking my hand.

"Possibly. Though they'd have to keep Maynard quiet. Or discredit him."

Goetze? I'd dismissed him as a weasely suck-up who cared more about himself than his patients. But what if he'd slid under my radar? Maynard wouldn't have tolerated less than brilliance in an assistant, and this murderer was certainly smarter than your average criminal.

"Thank you, Miss Emma," I said. "You're an angel."

"Happy to help," she chirped. "Listen, honey—I'll do what I can to keep Dr. Maynard from getting in trouble, but you're going to have to get me those files."

I didn't like the sound of that for a number of reasons, not the least of which was Aaron lying on an operating table. "Miss Emma, I understand that, and I can't tell you how excited I am about helping people with this research, but maybe we should keep it to ourselves for right now."

"Why's that?"

"If someone does want it, and we don't know who it is yet..." I let the sentence trail off.

Silence. "Oh." Her voice was small.

"I'm sorry. Soon."

"Of course." Her tone brightened. "Go get 'em, Lois."

"Happy to."

I hung up the phone and clicked back to the file list. What was I looking for? Not the first damned clue. But there had to be something. He'd backed this stuff up and encrypted it because he wanted it protected, not because it's a fun way to spend a Saturday night.

I scrolled, the strings of numbers in the file names not making much more sense than they had before I talked to Emma.

I glanced at the top of the file window. One thousand, three hundred and seventeen files. Oy.

Three hours and four emergency Diet-Coke-and-glazed-eyeball breaks later, I was considering a second pass when I found three files that weren't spreadsheets.

I selected the first and waited for my PDF reader to load.

A letter. From Alan Shannon at Evaris.

I didn't risk breathing as I scrolled.

Pleasantries. A hello for Maynard's assistant. So they did know each other.

I kept reading.

And found the biggest pile of horse shit ever seen outside the downs on Derby day.

Double-talk 101: I'd never met a politician or a cop who had an inch on this Shannon dude. In the same paragraph, he told Maynard "the results of seven studies with such a small sample are hardly conclusive," then turned around and offered to pay him for the research records.

"Nothing to it, but sell us the results."

So they could get rid of them. Or sell the treatment to patients who could afford to pay.

I sent it to the printer and clicked the next one open.

From the same guy, but this time proposing that Maynard work with Goetze. "Get the old team back together, better than ever."

Sure, because Goetze was on his payroll. I wondered if Maynard knew that as I clicked print and moved to the next file.

From Maynard, to Shannon.

One sentence: *All of mankind has a right to access this protocol, regardless of race, gender...or income level.*

Busted.

I clicked print, checking the date on the top left.

Two days before Maynard was murdered.

Holy. Manolos.

Days before, Aaron had Shannon in for questioning and let him go. My cops were closer to the why than I thought, whether they were looking for it or not.

Did a suit from the drug company actually kill these people? Probably not. Could he pay someone else to? Absolutely.

Murder for hire adds some edge to an already sexy story.

Whatever Charlie had, she couldn't be close to this. I pulled up the research I'd done on Shannon after my after-hours visit to his office, then texted Chad. Maybe the bad guy had a cloud account, too.

I'll look, came the reply.

I shoved my chair back and stood, ready to sprint to Bob's office, when a million things happened at once.

My cell phone binged. I snatched it up.

Landers.

Fingers shaking again, I clicked the message.

He's in recovery. Doc says it looks good. His wife and the girls are here.

My knees buckled, relief pouring through me in waves as I leaned on the edge of my desk.

Thank you, God.

Thank you, I tapped back.

Bing. *No problem. You figured it out yet? (I'm kidding.)*

Getting closer. (I'm not.)

Bing. *Not getting closer? I know that feeling.*

Not kidding. Keep your phone on.

Bing. *No shit?*

I'll call you when I have something concrete. This bastard isn't getting away with this.

I grabbed the memos off the printer and squared my shoulders as I turned for Bob's office. It had been hours. Andrews and his army of suits could go straight to hell—Bob and I had work to do.

"Nichelle!"

I stopped halfway to the door, something in Larry's tone gluing my shoes to the tacky brown carpet.

I spun slowly, the hand holding the papers dropping to my side.

My favorite photographer looked like his long out of shape self had been for a run. Through the woods. Up a mountain.

I hurried to where he stood, red-faced and gasping. "Larry? You okay?"

He grabbed my wrist and turned, hauling me toward the photo cave. I hustled to keep up—maybe he wasn't as out of shape as I thought.

"Larry?" I tried to tug my hand free to no avail.

He stopped inside the door to the old darkroom, motioning for the photo staff to beat it before he slammed the door and turned to me. "Just wait 'til you see what I've got."

36

I sat in Lindsay's big black leather chair, rubbing absently at the friction burn Larry'd left on my wrist in all his hurry. His fat fingers fumbled with the cord that attached his Nikon to his MacBook.

A gorgeous portrait of Carytown's resident one-man-band popped up on the screen. The photo was striking, and perfectly executed, but it didn't scream "cover shot" to me. I furrowed my brow.

"I don't understand. Lindsay said—"

"That I had something amazing?"

Larry nodded, moving his hand to the trackpad.

I squinted at the screen.

Oh, shit.

"Larry, when did you take this?"

He looked up, his wide face spreading into a slow grin. "This morning."

"Out—" My head swam, the room wavering in front of me. "Outside Thompson's?"

"Just up the street. I heard a muffled crack and I turned in time to get this." He clicked the trackpad and my breath stopped.

The screen filled with cornflower blue October sky, the sun lighting the bakery rooftop across from the coffee shop. And in the center, behind the air condenser, was a crouching figure. Holding a rifle.

"You see it, right?" Larry asked. "There's the asshole who shot your friend."

"Jesus, Larry," I breathed, my fingers drifting toward the screen on autopilot. "Talk about the right place at the right time."

"I'm just sorry I was looking for a feature. I had the wrong damned lens. If I'd been on my way to the racetrack, we could count his nosehairs. I tried to get over there before he disappeared, and then I talked to people for hours, but I couldn't get anything better than this."

"Telephoto on this one would've been amazing, but let's not be greedy. You got him. How much can you enhance this?"

"Not enough for an ID. He's doing a pretty good job hiding his face."

"And the one I brought you last night?"

He clicked a couple of windows and Benny's photo appeared on the screen. Sharper relief around the figure in the doorway—or maybe just looking at it differently, bigger, on the other screen—made every hair on my arm stand straight up.

"Jiminy Choos. Larry, go back to the other?"

"What?"

"The photo you took. Pull it up."

He did. "What is it?"

"Can you get closer in on this?" I put one fingernail over the rifle.

"Closer, yes. Close enough? Dunno."

I paced, my brain racing, while Larry hunched over the keyboard and worked his magnifying and filter magic.

Dammit, what if it had been right under my nose since day one?

I yanked my cell phone from my pocket and scrolled back through the photos, turning to look over Larry's shoulder.

Yep.

How could I have missed it?

Because there wasn't a motive, that's how.

Not one I knew about, anyway.

Twenty-three of the longest minutes in the history of the world later, Larry looked up. "This is the best I can do. What are you looking for?"

I closed my eyes.

Please.

Crouching in front of the monitor, I let my breath out in a long, slow sigh. The sun had hit just right, and Larry's wizardry brought it up sharp enough to tell me everything I needed to know.

Right. Under. My. Nose.

Damn, Nichelle.

I jumped to my feet, pulling Larry into a hug. "You are a genius."

"I know. But what am I getting credit for today?"

"Just keep working on that. And the other one. I'll let Bob know to hold the cover open—those photos are the answer to the story of the year, my friend. I just have to get the rest of it."

I bolted for my desk before he could ask any more questions.

* * *

Mrs. Eason didn't answer on the first try, and I didn't dare leave a message.

Should I go over there?

No. There's chasing the story, and then there's just stupid. I like to think I'm not the latter.

I tapped a finger on my phone.

Aaron was the other person I'd usually call.

Kyle? He was annoyed with me.

Landers wasn't in a place to look.

I dialed Elizabeth Eason again.

"Yes?" she snapped, answering on the second ring. I breezed right past the prickly tone.

"Mrs. Eason, it's Nichelle over at the *Telegraph*," I said, fighting to keep my voice even a shade under panicked. "I need to ask you something."

"I didn't help you enough yesterday?"

"Just one more quick thing. Please?"

She offered a put-upon sigh. "What is it?"

"Was Dr. Maynard particularly close with Jeff?"

"Who?"

"The doorman."

"Oh. He used to help David with letting people in and out to clean and service things." She paused. "I never thought..."

I waited, but she stopped talking. "You never thought what?"

"I never got the idea he liked David. Nothing I could put my finger on, you understand, but just that old reporter gut feeling."

"He never said anything?" My breath came faster.

"Not an impolite word. He's a nice boy, really. Just seemed to have flashes of stress, or anger, or something."

Just like Tom Ellinger.

Felicia Lang's voice floated through my head. Someone died during her study.

The files. They flashed up on my screen when I woke my laptop.

"Mrs. Eason, do you happen to know Jeff's last name?"

"Moseley."

I blew out a breath I didn't know I'd been holding. "Thank you. Have a nice evening."

"Why—"

I clicked off the call before she could finish that question.

I had the who. The sharpened version of Benny's cell phone photo showed a relaxed at-attention stance. The same one Jeff employed at the door to Maynard's building, in the photo I'd taken of Percival's old mistress that first day.

And Larry, God love him, had honed in on the rifle barrel enough to show me the swords on Jeff's watch.

Landers and Kyle would need more. Especially with the weirdness around who was giving their orders being so desperate to make Tom Ellinger look guilty.

I clicked into the window for the USB drive and opened a search. All Files. Word or part. Moseley. Find.

The little wheel that meant the computer was thinking popped up and a dialog box told me it would take thirty-one minutes to search the entire drive. I leaned back in the chair, my head spinning. How did I miss it?

Because who cares about a random dog's welfare while they're killing people? He was so nice. There had to be something in these files that would make this make sense.

Twenty-nine minutes left. I checked the clock in the corner of the display.

"How the hell did it get to be five-twenty?" I dropped my head onto one hand, suddenly starving. Maybe Eunice had left something in the break room. That was still there with the sports guys lurking about? Not likely, but worth a shot.

I found a mostly empty pan at the back of the bottom shelf, only because I knew that's where Parker stashed stuff he didn't want the other guys to see. Why men won't look anywhere but in the front of a fridge for food baffles me.

Croissants. I popped one in the microwave and bit into it to find ham, swiss, and béchamel sauce. I snarfed the entire thing down in twelve seconds and went back for another.

"No time for lunch today?" Parker's voice came from behind me and I jumped and smacked my head on the fridge.

"Not even close." I rubbed the back of my head with one hand and held out the pan with the other. "You want the last one? Sorry. I think I ate dinner last night, but I couldn't swear to it. This story is trying to kill me."

His golden eyebrows shot skyward. "Not literally, I hope."

"Not this time." I smiled. "But it's trying to kill plenty of other people."

"You making any progress?"

"I have a helluva lead for tomorrow's front, if I can get it to come together in the next hour." I elbowed him. "You making any progress?"

His trademark grin took on a goofy, lovesick edge that made me want to squeal just from being in the same room with it. "Tomorrow night. We're going to a Halloween party."

"As?"

"Cinderella and Prince Charming."

"Naturally. Why did I ask?"

"I got a glass slipper. To put the ring in." He shoved his hands in his pockets and puffed out his chest.

"And you're not proud of yourself, or anything." I laughed.

"It's the perfect surprise. She's going to be all dressed up, she'll love the pictures, and she gets the fairy tale."

I nodded. "Well played. Can I be a fly on the wall?"

"It's a benefit for the university. Get a press pass from someone."

"On it." I glanced at the clock on the coffee maker and hurried to the door. Thrilled as I was for Parker, I had a murderer who needed my attention. "I have to run and catch a killer, but you've totally got this proposal thing. She'll love it."

I rushed back toward my little ivory cube, fingers crossed behind my back for every bit of good luck this day could muster. Less than two hours to drop deadline, and the answer to the biggest story in forever somewhere in my laptop. I looked at Bob's door for the nine millionth time that day.

Closed.

Had I missed it opening? Surely to heaven Andrews had left my boss alone by now.

I started to turn that way, then paused. Andrews was gunning for Bob under the guise of what he thought was a slip on my part. I went back to my desk and texted Bob.

Have something huge. You done in there yet?

No. Send when it's ready.

You okay?

No. But this is not your fault. He punctuated that one with a smiley. Lord save us.

Andrews is an ass. Hang in there. I tapped a wink and a heart.

I think he's hoping if he talks long enough I'll just die of boredom.

I snorted. *He's obviously never sat through a meeting with Beatman.* Our business editor was a nice guy, but the interesting gene had skipped him, two helpings of dry taking it's place.

Another smiley. Two in one day from Bob meant the universe was trying to tell me something. I touched the trackpad on my laptop.

Three results.

Holy shit.

I clicked the first one up.

A Katarina Moseley was in the part of the spreadsheet Miss Emma said was a patient list.

Maynard treated the doorman's—what? Mother? Wife? He certainly didn't seem married, from the number of times he'd hit on me.

They knew each other. But neither of them had ever mentioned it to Elizabeth.

No. Way.

I went back to the spreadsheet and looked at the other columns, pulling the notes from my reading medical documents lesson with Emma.

Katarina Moseley had lung cancer.

I read the third column three times.

Maynard put her in the control group.

Oh, shit.

I didn't even stop to think about why Jeff would try to frame Tom Ellinger, who was in the same damned boat. I had the photos, I had the woman's name. I clicked the other documents.

She was the entire list of deceased subjects at the end of the third one. I scrolled up and found Felicia Lang's name, and it all fell neatly into place. The woman who died in her study, who didn't get treatment until it was past too late. The only patient Maynard lost.

Motive.

I snatched my cell phone off my desk and texted Kyle.

The doorman did it. Jeff. At Maynard's building. Do your thing, SuperCop.

Nine seconds later: *You're sure?*

I have two photos, and Maynard let someone he loved die.

Bing. *Shit. White had the interviews with this guy and the drug company VP open on his desk, and a note that the building manager told him Shannon referred the doorman for the position when it came open last year.*

My eyes flicked back to my screen. Of course. Maynard sent Shannon the study and Katarina's name was right there. Three seconds of research brings up Jeff's service record, and Shannon has the perfect plan—get Jeff close to Maynard and greenlight the kill when the doc won't sell out.

My stomach twisted.

Their alibis? I typed.

Bing. *Each other. Dammit. On my way.*

Careful. He's a good shot.

Bing. *Thanks. White is going to be okay.*

I heard. Call me when you've got him?

Smiley face. *I believe you get the exclusive, ma'am.*

I believe I'm going home to have a glass of wine and some chocolate while I wait.

I texted Bob that a late hold on the front would be worth it, stuffed my laptop and files into my bag, and shuffled to the lobby, the adrenaline drain leaving me slightly more erect than a wet dishcloth. Texting Joey, I stepped into the elevator.

Kyle's on his way to get the bad guy. I'm on my way home. Open some wine.

Dropping the phone into my bag, I dug out my keys. His reply buzzed as I stepped into the garage.

I climbed into the car and locked the doors, letting my head fall back against the seat.

The rustle of fabric on leather came from behind me, and a cold circle about an inch in diameter dug into my temple.

"Evening, Miss Clarke." Jeff's voice was familiar, his breath hot on my ear. "I did hope I could avoid this, but you can't seem to keep your nose out of where it doesn't belong."

Crap. Hell.

37

Don't panic.

The words pounded through my head on repeat, my hands frozen to the steering wheel. I swallowed hard and licked my lips, trying to force them to form words.

I've dealt with my share of nutcases. But a gun pressed to my head, locked in a car with a guy who'd killed at least two people and shot a cop in broad daylight—this took the gold trophy for worst day ever.

Talk, Nichelle.

Getting him to ramble was the only way to buy time.

Until what? A tiny voice in the back of my head asked. Kyle was on his way to Rockett's Landing, and Joey was pouring wine and waiting for me.

Damn.

I glanced at the elevator.

A hundred people forty feet above my head, but I couldn't run for it. This guy was in better shape than I was, and I couldn't have a massacre in the newsroom.

I tried for even breathing and willed my lips to function.

"Why?"

It was all I could manage.

"Come on, Nichelle." His voice was colder than the steel of the gun boring into my head. "Haven't you written about a hundred murders? More? 'Why' is the most trite question. Is there ever a good answer? Start the car."

"What? Where are we going?"

"You drive. I'll navigate." He jiggled the gun. "Now."

Shit. Hands shaking, I turned the key.

Jeff lowered the gun when I pulled out of the garage, digging it into my side just under my ribcage. "Take a right up here."

I complied, looking around at all the normal people milling around the sidewalk. How the hell was I going to get out of this? I could honk, and he could shoot me. I could jump, and the car could kill a lot of people. I snuck a look in the rearview. Was Jeff buckled into a seat?

No.

I could hit the brakes, but I needed more speed behind that than downtown at six will allow.

"Maynard let someone you love die," I said. "But why Stephanie? Why Tom Ellinger? What's going on, Jeff? You don't seem like the crazy mass murderer type."

"You think you're so smart, don't you? Figured it out, when the cops were a mile off base. But you don't know a damned thing."

I turned at the light.

"I know we're going to Maynard's office."

"I have a plan. You're trying your best to fuck it up, but I'm not going to let you. I tried talking to you, feeding you information that would make you look elsewhere. But you didn't follow."

"I'm just trying to find the truth, Jeff. Help me understand. Tell me your story."

A glance in the rearview showed his lips clamped together, his eyes stony and staring straight ahead. He stayed that way until I pulled into the empty little lot and parked. Maynard's office door was still crisscrossed with police tape.

"What if the police come back?" I asked.

"They have better things to do. Somebody shot a cop this morning, didn't you hear?"

I tightened my grip on the steering wheel to keep from slapping the smirk off his face.

Bastard.

He shoved the muzzle of the gun into my ribs hard enough that I yelped.

"Get out. Don't try anything stupid."

The sun had disappeared entirely as we drove, the lot dimly lit by the streetlamp a football field down the block.

I opened my door and stepped out. My bag. I'd put my cell phone in the bag. My mace was in there, too.

I reached for the handles and Jeff knocked my hand away, hard. "You won't need lip gloss, princess."

"It'll be easier for them to ID me if my purse is in there," I blurted the first words that came to me, and he stepped back and tipped his head to one side.

"I suppose it will." He grabbed the bag with his free hand and pulled it over his shoulder.

Not exactly what I wanted, but I tried to keep that from showing on my face.

He fished a set of keys from his back pocket and opened the door.

No forced entry.

"You did the robbery, too," I said, stumbling over the high threshold when he shoved me through the door.

"Needed the files."

"And did you find them?"

"Nobody else has, either. I've been listening to the cops every day. Who notices the doorman? They all just talk."

"Why did you want them?"

"None of your business," he barked.

Puzzle piece: he didn't know I had them.

Gear change. "How did you know? About me?" I asked.

"Mrs. Eason was going out and she said you called and asked about me. After what happened with the cop this morning, I knew it was only a matter of time. I was just hoping to get my money and go before it happened."

He gestured with the gun, and I backed toward a hallway. He kept the gun trained on me, following slowly.

"What money?"

"There are a lot of people who don't want anyone to know what Dr. Maynard was working on, because it would kill their profit margins."

"Shannon," I breathed. I stepped backward into a small room that reeked of funky chemical smell. "Shannon wanted the files. So he could bury them."

"You did your homework."

"Enough to know that dude wasn't getting his hands dirty."

No time to be proud of myself for getting it all right on a couple of photos and a file list.

Don't die now. Be excited later.

Jeff flipped on a light and I looked around.

Oxygen cylinders. A truckload of them. Plus some nitrous canisters.

Open ones.

I closed my eyes.

"If you just breathe it in, this will be much less painful," Jeff said.

My eyes settled on the gun.

"Don't." I coughed. "Please."

"With this?" He gestured with the pistol. "I don't have any intention of dying with you. My baby Rosie is here." He nodded to the door and I caught a glimpse of a soft rifle case. A pet name for his gun. Cute. "She can take those canisters at seven hundred yards."

"You're awfully sure of yourself."

"If I can hit the temple of the driver of a moving vehicle with IEDs all around me outside Baghdad, I can hit this. I hit the cop this morning."

I clenched my jaw. Probably not the best time to let my temper loose.

"I read your record. You're a freaking hero. Explain to me how a sniper ends up on the wrong side of the law. Money isn't everything."

He shook his head, his eyes glistening in the fluorescent light. "The money will let me get away with it. But this was never about money. It's about justice. Maynard took Kat from me, and I took his life from him. Eye for an eye, like it says in the Bible."

Oh, for heaven's sake. I bit blood out of my tongue to avoid asking him if he should be stoned to death over his polyester blend chinos.

"I thought we had a legal system for that."

"They don't care that he let her die." His voice caught. "She was nineteen years old, and never smoked a single cigarette. He could have cured her. People walked out of there and went back to their lives. Why not her?" A tear slipped down his cheek and he swatted it away. "My baby sister. I promised my momma on her deathbed I'd take care of Kat. But I was deployed and couldn't argue with Dr. God Complex. And now she's gone."

I blinked. I was going to start feeling sorry for the guy if he kept talking.

My tone softened. "I don't argue the injustice of that, but it's how these things work. If there's no control group, how can they tell whether the treatment is getting results or people are just getting better? Or if the new treatment is more effective than the old one, like in the case of Kat's trial?"

His head snapped up and he waved the gun. "You don't think I know that?" Another tear fell, followed by another, the pistol drifting back to his side. "But the funny thing about that is, it's all in the name of science until the one that ends up in the ground is someone you love."

My mom, weak from chemo and smiling at the doctor who'd come to admit her to the trial, flashed through my thoughts.

Yeah. I know, dude. "My mom had breast cancer. A trial saved her life. I get it."

He swiped at the tears, shaking his head as he leveled the gun at me. "I don't think you do. Because why are you helping them?"

Helping who? The poor guy they had set up to take the fall? My temper flared. Deep breath. "For what it's worth, all I'm 'helping' is the truth. Once it's out, the chips fall where they fall. Speaking of, why Tom Ellinger? He's pretty much in the exact same boat you just described as being so shitty."

Jeff's eyes were glazing over from the gas, his voice thicker when he opened his mouth. "If I'd managed to find the damned files, his wife would be getting ready to go home to his kids. I bet he'd trade a few years in prison for that in a heartbeat."

Wait. "What?"

He braced his free hand on the wall. "I couldn't let Shannon bury Maynard's research. I wanted the bastard dead, sure, but his work—that's something the world has a right to know about. I found a guy online, a researcher at Duke. I was going to send him the files. But Shannon double-crossed me before I could double-cross him. Asshole." His eyes flicked to the rifle. "Ellinger fell into my lap, the last piece I needed to make this work. I lost Kat. I would've given him a way to keep his wife if Shannon hadn't gotten there first."

Well, hot damn. Tom would've taken the trade outright, given a sliver of a chance. And I suddenly wanted nothing more than to get out of that building and watch Alan Shannon go to prison. For a long, long time.

"How'd you figure out it was me?" Jeff asked, dumping my bag onto a table. My cell phone hit with a clatter, my makeup bag falling on top of it. The mace canister rolled off the end and under a cabinet. Dammit.

I tried to shake off the cotton-candy haze in my brain, inching toward the table and hoping Jeff'd direct his eyes back to the floor. "Pictures."

"Come again?" He turned his back, walking to the other side of the room and turning a valve on another canister. My head spun. Dammit. I tiptoed to the table and slid my hand under the makeup bag, my words tripping out, not wanting to give him reason to turn around again.

"There was a cellphone photo of you at the hospital, in the room across from the closet. Just a silhouette, but I recognized your build and sentry stance from the door at the complex. Then one of our photographers got a distant shot of you this morning on the rooftop. The watch. It's so different."

"We all had one, the guys in my unit. Jimmy's dad was a jeweler in Chicago." He flipped another valve and burst into peals of laughter.

My fingers closed around my cell phone.

I turned as a canister clattered to the floor, and found Jeff doubled over in a giggle fit.

"Something funny?"

"The way things work out. I liked you." He scrubbed a fist over his eyes. "You're hot. You're smart—I spent months planning this like we planned missions. Every detail. Who suspects a sniper of strangling a man? Enough pressure to kill him, but not enough to point to me. Ellinger is weak. It fit. Months of going over everything. And you got me from a couple of photos? You handled yourself in that hospital ward with Ellinger. I could fall in love with a woman like you. And now I have to..." He shook his head, the smile fading as he stood and turned for the back door—and the rifle. "Anyway. Just funny how things work out."

I opened a text.

Maynard's office. He has a gun.

Kyle.

Joey.

Landers.

Send.

I looked up just in time to see Jeff drop the handgun as he tried to unzip the rifle case.

It fired, and my eyes fell shut.

38

The roar of the gunshot faded, silence following behind it just as loud.

I kept my eyes closed for close to a minute, the lack of fiery death pain processing. When I opened them, Jeff was putting his rifle together, the handgun tucked in his belt and a surgical mask covering the lower half of his face.

His eyes were as flat and cold as the black metal in his hands when he looked up.

"Casualties of war. They happen every day." The mask muffled the words and I felt my brow furrow.

"Huh?"

"Ellinger was hanging around outside the building. Looking for the doc. I chatted him up. Got him talking about deer hunting. He had a rifle. I found out what kind. Picked one up at the sporting goods store. Offering suggestions is so much easier than giving orders. And almost guarantees he won't mention it to anyone."

"And Stephanie?"

He shrugged. "Part of the deal with Shannon. Bonus fifty grand. Something about a document. I didn't ask."

"Aaron?"

"The cop? I heard he was asking about me. Someone told him Shannon put in a good word for me with the building manager. I followed him this morning. Didn't know he was with you until you came outside, though."

A high giggle escaped my lips and I flinched.

My head felt two sizes too big, and everything was suddenly hilarious.

Damn, damn, damn.

I grabbed for the edge of the table.

He clicked the last piece of the gun into place and set it gently on the floor.

Stepping toward me, he reached for his belt buckle.

I stumbled to the other side of the table. Laughing gas be damned, that wasn't funny.

He stopped, his eyes rolling back. "I'm not into that. I need you to stay put."

Because he had to go outside.

He tapped a finger on the table.

"If I tie you to something, it doesn't look like an accident."

"You think people will believe this was an accident?" The words sounded slurred, coming out too slow.

"You broke in looking for information, knocked over a canister, caused an explosion. Sad cautionary tale for your colleagues."

"I'm not exactly going to sit here while you blow up the building."

He drummed his fingers on the table. "You will if the doors are locked." He crossed to the one we'd come in and threw a keyed deadbolt, and my stomach fell to my ankles.

"I'm sorry it had to be this way." Jeff gave me a sad look and grabbed the rifle and case, disappearing out the door.

Shit, double shit. I fished my phone out of my pocket. No new texts.

Nice time for everyone to be occupied.

I had however long it would take Jeff to run several hundred yards.

The windows.

I needed something heavy. That wouldn't make a spark if I missed and hit the metal window frame.

The table was steel, and heavy.

The canisters were metal.

My eyes scanned the corners.

There.

Under a pile of hospital-grade blankets and pillows sat a wooden ladder back chair. I lunged for it, the linens scattering as I raised it and swung at the window. From the corner of my eye, I saw Jeff's back retreating into the dark. He thought he had it all sewn up.

Asshole.

The glass gave with the second swing, a spiderweb crack spreading across the window as Jeff stopped and turned back.

Could he see me? Didn't care.

I turned the feet of the chair toward the glass, braced them, and shoved.

A jagged hole appeared, the cool fresh air hitting my face as I dropped the chair. I gulped it. Jeff took a step back toward the building, then raised the rifle.

Righting the chair, I stepped up onto it, my head clearing a smidgen with every breath.

I dove for the sidewalk as the gun fired.

Pain ripped through my left arm and hip as I hit the concrete, but I didn't have time to be hurt. I rolled to the right, my arm coming with me under heavy protest, and scrambled to my feet. The bullet hole in the window frame told me he was shooting at me, not the canisters. Shit.

I bolted, three steps from my car before I realized my keys were inside with the rest of my stuff.

The footsteps on the gravel behind me told me Jeff was double-timing it back, and his double-time was faster than mine.

I ran anyway, my feet slipping in the mules and my sore toe throbbing with every step.

When he was close enough for me to hear the swearwords punctuating every footfall, I panicked. The adrenaline-fueled burst of speed got me to the corner. How could this part of town be so dead? Ten minutes from the capitol building, and a guy with a rifle on his back could chase a woman down the street without an audience. Something I normally found charming about Richmond. Right then, not so much.

My legs and lungs burned, and I wished desperately for the foresight to have put on my sneakers with my gym shirt that morning. It seemed like a million years ago, changing in the car. Snippets of events and people flashed through my head.

Joey's headlights rounding a corner last summer as another fruitcake with a gun chased me through an alley.

I stumbled over a curb, the street in front of me wavering.

Not Joey's headlights.

Not a memory.

Landers's unmarked police sedan squealed to a halt, his door opening before the car had stopped rolling.

"Get down," he shouted, his Sig 9 coming up over the roof of the car.

I screamed as my shoulder hit the pavement a second time, raising my good arm to cover my head as the evening exploded around me.

Everything stopped.

I couldn't look.

If Jeff was about to shoot me, so be it. Where could I go?

"Nichelle?" Landers's breath came hard, but the voice was his.

"Oh, thank God." I half-sobbed the words, tears forcing their way out against my better judgement.

I didn't want to cry in front of Landers, dammit. I had to work with him.

I rolled onto my back, something warm and sticky spreading under my side.

"Jesus, your arm." Landers grabbed my outstretched, uninjured hand, then dropped it. "Nope, stay there. We need another ambulance." He pulled out his phone, and I noticed his gun was still trained on Jeff, who was writhing on the ground several yards away, blood pouring from his lower half. I looked back to Landers.

"I thought center mass was the target for a gunman?" The words sounded far away.

"Not when you think he might be wearing a vest. I needed him down. Took hitting both knees, but he's down."

Landers stepped into the light from a street lamp and I saw a darkening spot on his brown polo.

"He shot you." I tried to sit up.

"You stay put. It's my shoulder. I'll live." He stepped closer to Jeff, kicking the rifle away from him. "This is the bastard who shot Aaron?"

I nodded, the sirens in the distance the best sound I'd heard all day.

Landers pulled a foot back and landed a solid kick to Jeff's ribs. "No vest. Oh, well."

The lights from the ambulance wavered across the pavement, my eyes fighting to stay open.

"It's okay, Nichelle. Everyone is going to be just fine."

"My story..." I forced the words out.

"Will wait. You texted me. I called for the ambulance from my phone. Nobody else has it."

The last words filtered in as I drifted off.

39

"You ready for this?" DonnaJo arched an eyebrow at me from across the polished cherry table, her blue eyes trailing to my sling.

I nodded. "I'm not even on painkillers anymore."

She shook her head, pushing her chair back and standing. "I suppose you better get used to being on the stand if you're going to keep ending up in the middle of your stories."

"Not like I do it on purpose," I said, rising slower than she had. The compound exposed fracture to my left ulna had required three hours of surgery, two plates, nine screws, and a lecture about my calcium intake. Joey'd been shoving milk and yogurt at me every seven seconds for three weeks. But it was nice, having him around.

I'd even mustered the nerve to ask a few questions.

His last name was D'Amore. Because the universe has a twisted sense of humor.

DonnaJo pushed the conference room door open and stepped into the hallway. "Your story this morning about that woman and her recovery was the best piece you've ever done, friend. I heard a rumor they have you to thank for more than the write-up."

"Only because I quasi-blackmailed a doctor into helping them." I winked. "Shhhh."

Goetze had been only too happy to read up on Maynard's protocol and test it on Amy Ellinger once the story about Shannon and Jeff and their involvement in the murders broke. Turned out Evaris had a city councilman in its back pocket. A councilman who'd leaned on the PD's brass to arrest Tom and keep the case quiet, citing a desire to avoid bad press for the department. He'd also kept Shannon apprised of the investigation, putting Aaron's life in danger. I'd taken great pleasure in helping Mel write up his resignation.

A honcho at the FDA who suspected Alan Shannon of playing dirty had Kyle assigned to the case. Though Kyle didn't know that until Shannon was in a cell.

Goetze wanted less than nothing to do with any drug company these days—pay cut be damned, if his new Honda was any indication. I promised to lose the photos of his meeting with Shannon's flunky, and he claimed no responsibility if the treatment didn't work.

Amy would be back to driving carpool in another few weeks. Best story ever, indeed.

"I'm a sucker for a happy ending."

"Where is that going?" DonnaJo asked. "I saw suspiciously little mention of Maynard's miracle in the news."

"I sent all the files to the NIH. They're reviewing them, talking about setting up large-scale trials. Bureaucracy is a bitch, especially when there're millions of dollars at stake. We'll see how it turns out, but I'm beyond thrilled to know it's there if anyone I love ever needs it."

"Thanks to you and your computer geek friend." DonnaJo winked.

"The funny thing is, when Kyle's team searched Shannon's office, they figured out that spreadsheet file I...um...borrowed...was a code for payoffs. A handful of doctors, plus a hacker collective in Finland that pulled off the search engine deletion with a virus designed to find and block Maynard's name. He paid them three-quarters of a million dollars, but the research he wanted erased was never published in the first place. Kyle said he was trying to stop it before Maynard had a chance to put it out. In case Jeff chickened out or missed."

DonnaJo whistled. "Such a tangled web. The courthouse grapevine says Maynard left his entire estate to Doctors Without Borders. Except a trust to put his assistant through medical school." She winked. "Seems Mrs. Eason wasn't his only girlfriend."

"A revelation that pissed her right off." I nodded. "That explains why the assistant was so protective of his stuff, though. She was in love with him. Hopefully she'll be able to do as much good as he did."

"I saw a file come through for your gunman yesterday." DonnaJo patted my good shoulder. "The first one, anyway."

Tom was out on bond, awaiting trial for the weapons charge.

"Something tells me the Ellingers can handle whatever y'all might throw at them." I smiled. "The lack of a murder charge is a nice bonus."

"For all concerned, believe me," she said.

Benny's mother had taken her last breath while I was breaking my arm trying to get away from Jeff, but Joey's friend had pulled some nautical-rope-sized strings and gotten him a new hearing. One not in California. Can't win 'em all, but at least Benny had a shot at staying with his wife and daughter.

A surveillance camera at the ATM next door to my mom's shop had footage of the creep who took the photos of her—an online reporter, no less—but since he claimed he didn't know what they were for, the threats were just added to Shannon's list of infractions. The teenager across the street liked his binoculars, and had seen Crenshaw leave the envelope in my mailbox.

My cell phone was the only extra casualty of Jeff's plot, because I'd crushed it along with my arm. An hour at the Apple store and a few hundred bucks wasn't a huge price to pay when I thought about the explosion that didn't happen.

Two defense lawyers waved as we turned the corner for the elevator. I smiled a hello and focused on DonnaJo's recounting of more courthouse gossip. She was chattering to put me at ease, and I loved her for it.

"Who's here for the *Telegraph* today?" she asked.

"Shelby."

She laughed. "Miss obvious question? She knows not to talk while the trial is going on?"

"She's not so bad these days." I wanted to shrug, but knew it would hurt, so I shook my head.

"What ever happened to that blogger?"

"She thinks I'm on the PD's payroll and covering up a police brutality story because Landers shot Jeff Moseley."

DonnaJo hit the call button for the elevator and turned to me. "You're not serious."

"Sure I am. She doesn't like me. And she's not going anywhere. But I have more important things to worry about." I traced the toe of one yellow Louboutin along the edge of a tile.

She grimaced. "How's Bob?"

I blew out a heavy sigh. "Rick Andrews is a bastard of the highest order."

"He can't just fire Bob Jeffers. The man is an institution."

The elevator doors opened and I stepped inside. She pushed two and shook her head.

"He can't fire Bob without the board's approval," I said. "He's still pushing for an early retirement. To the tune of nine hours trying to wear him down. With the two board members he's managed to convince there for show."

"How many votes does he need?"

"Three more. But he's making Bob miserable. This exclusive backed him down half a step, but nothing like before."

"What are you going to do?"

"Rally the troops. Stay on my game. Try not to screw up." I stepped off the elevator. "All while helping Mel plan a wedding. Word of advice: don't play Cupid—people make you their maid of honor when it works out." I grinned and DonnaJo laughed.

"Sounds like a full plate."

I nodded. "But today, I'm focused on helping you put this asshat away."

She squeezed my hand. "Just tell your story. His lawyer will do a lot of fancy talking. You stick to simple phrases and the truth. He tried to kill you. He confessed to killing a Commonwealth's Attorney and culpability in the deaths of two cops. That's what the jury needs to know."

I squeezed back, turning to the courtroom. "Let's do it." The words faltered on my lips as my eyes met Kyle's.

He closed a hand around the door pull and nodded. "Ladies."

"Agent Miller." DonnaJo looked back and forth between us and bit her lip. "I think I should step into the ladies' room before they call us back to order."

She scurried down the hall.

"Kyle." I smiled, but it felt tight.

"Nicey, I have to talk to you."

"I don't think I want to hear what you have to say."

"You couldn't know that, you won't return my calls."

"You're nosing around in my personal life. I'd like you to knock it off." I'd spotted Kyle sitting across the street from my house more times than I cared to count lately, and he'd tailed Joey twice: once to the grocery store and once to the bank.

He didn't even have the decency to look apologetic. "I'm worried about you," he said.

"I didn't ask you to be." There was more bite to the words than I intended, but he didn't seem to notice.

"Look, you're my friend."

"And I'm happy. Leave it alone, Kyle."

"Coffee?"

"Not until you back off your little solo investigation." I shook my head. I missed him, too, but I was terrified of what might happen to the happy bubble I'd spent the past few weeks in if he kept digging. I knew he couldn't have enough to prove anything. If he did, he wouldn't be bugging me, he'd be getting an arrest warrant. Kyle was very black and white when it came to his work.

He held my gaze and shrugged. "I can't do that."

"Then I'm not talking to you." I put my own hand on the door. "On the record or otherwise. Excuse me, Agent."

"Everything okay?" DonnaJo asked, her heels clicking across the marble of the floor.

"We're done here," I said brightly, pulling the door open as Kyle let go and took a step back.

I took a seat in the back of the gallery, and DonnaJo parked behind the Commonwealth's table. The bailiff announced Judge Vargas, and my new iPhone buzzed in my pocket as his honor walked to the bench.

I pulled it out to turn it off, glancing at the text alert by force of habit.

Kyle.

Closing my eyes, I swiped a finger across the screen, the little blue bubble twisting my stomach into a pretzel.

We are not. But it'll keep.

LETHAL LIFESTYLES: Nichelle Clarke #6

The groom is the prime suspect in a murder at his own rehearsal dinner. Crime reporter Nichelle Clarke doesn't believe he's the killer-but now it's up to her to find out who is.

"...kept me on edge the entire time..."

When Nichelle Clarke is invited to be the maid of honor in her friends' Virginia Vineyard wedding, she looks forward to the celebration. The storybook ceremony has been planned to the tiniest detail, and the rehearsal dinner is going off without a hitch.

Until a dead body is found in a barrel of award-winning Riesling.

But when the dust settles, the corpse is no longer Nichelle's biggest worry. There is a growing list of evidence pointing to her friend the groom as the killer. Nichelle doesn't buy it, but finds herself the lone skeptic.

Wading through skeletons of past love and loss, Nichelle sets out to prove the groom's innocence. But the journey forces her to face hard truths about how well she really knows her closest friends.

Can Nichelle track down the truth in time to save her friend from life in prison--or worse? Assuming he is innocent, who is the real killer? And more importantly, will they strike again?

**Get your copy today at
severnriverbooks.com/series/nichelle-clarke-crime-thriller**

ACKNOWLEDGMENTS

Every time I open a blank file, I wonder if I can really turn all that whitespace into another novel. But no book is a solo project, even though there's only one name on the cover.

My favorite computer experts, Elliott Cutright and Andy Hallberg, thanks for explaining complicated computer things in terms my not-very-technical brain could understand and use.

One of the best things about this gig is the writer friends I've made: Wendy Tyson, Larissa Reinhart, Susan O'Brien, Barb Goffman, Craig Lancaster, Art Taylor, Mollie Cox Bryan, Ellery Adams, Hank Phillipi Ryan, Julia Spencer Fleming, Laura Levine, Gretchen Archer, and Mary Burton—thank you for offering advice, listening, and just being your wonderful selves.

The other best thing? The amazing readers. Thank you to everyone who's come to an event or sent me an email or online message—knowing that you connect with the stories and the characters keeps me writing on the harder days.

Thanks to Andrew Watts and the team at Severn River Publishing for helping readers find Nichelle's stories. Y'all are such fun to work with.

Julie Hallberg...well. Just, thank you. For all the things. None of this would be here without you, doll.

My littles, who I love with the fire of ten thousand suns: thank you, yet again, for understanding when mommy needs to play with her imaginary friends. You are the best children any mom could ever ask for, and I am proud of you every single day.

My husband, my partner in adventure, and my very best friend: thank you for believing in me, and helping me find time and motivation to finish this one. I love having you in my corner, and I love our life together.

As always, any mistakes are mine alone.

ABOUT THE AUTHOR

LynDee Walker is the national bestselling author of two crime fiction series featuring strong heroines and "twisty, absorbing" mysteries. Her first Nichelle Clarke crime thriller, FRONT PAGE FATALITY, was nominated for the Agatha Award for best first novel and is an Amazon Charts Bestseller. In 2018, she introduced readers to Texas Ranger Faith McClellan in FEAR NO TRUTH. Reviews have praised her work as "well-crafted, compelling, and fast-paced," and "an edge-of-your-seat ride" with "a spider web of twists and turns that will keep you reading until the end."

Before she started writing fiction, LynDee was an award-winning journalist who covered everything from ribbon cuttings to high level police corruption, and worked closely with the various law enforcement agencies that she reported on. Her work has appeared in newspapers and magazines across the U.S.

Aside from books, LynDee loves her family, her readers, travel, and coffee. She lives in Richmond, Virginia, where she is working on her next novel when she's not juggling laundry and children's sports schedules.

Sign up for LynDee Walker's reader list at
severnriverbooks.com/authors/lyndee-walker
lyndee@severnriverbooks.com

Printed in the United States
by Baker & Taylor Publisher Services